TOO MANY GHOSTS was serialized in The Saturday Evening Post in 1959.

Novels by
PAUL GALLICO
published by IPL

THE ABANDONED
THOMASINA*
TOO MANY GHOSTS

*forthcoming

PAUL GALLICO
TOO MANY GHOSTS

A CRIME CLASSIC ®

INTERNATIONAL POLYGONICS, LTD.
NEW YORK CITY

TOO MANY GHOSTS

Printed and manufactured in the United States of America.
First IPL printing May 1988.
10 9 8 7 6 5 4 3 2 1

CONTENTS

TOO MANY GHOSTS

The fact that the grim and extraordinary haunting of Paradine Hall, East Walsham, Norfolk, seat of the Lords Paradine since the year 1523, did not reach the ears of the scandalous press was not only fortunate but little less than a miracle. Had it done so, it might well have destroyed the Paradine Country Club connected with the Hall, and the Paradines themselves.

As it was, one nervous couple packed up and left at the first appearance of the mischievous and noisy poltergeist that suddenly infested the apartments in the east wing, the rooms reserved for the guests of the Country Club, and that coincided with the first reappearance after a century and a half of the lengendary nun of Paradine Hall, whose figure in habit and cowl was said to have been glimpsed gliding along darkened corridors.

Luckily the departing pair were North Country people whose range of acquaintanceship did not reach into urban circles and the tale of whose experiences remained merely another ghost story.

As for those who stayed on and did not talk, they were either hardheaded skeptics and unbelievers or persons who for selfish or other reasons of their own wished to keep to themselves what appeared to be the first modern authenticated case of haunting and manifestations by supernatural spirits.

The Paradines, of course, kept silent about the happenings that took place in the west wing, occupied by themselves and their friends: the shocking damage to the room of the Hon. Isobel Paradine, the mystery of the harp that played by itself in the night in the locked and disused music room, and the terror that came to an American visitor, a friend of their daughter.

The private west wing was cut off from the guest rooms of the Country Club in the east wing by the great baronial dining hall in the center, the only common meeting ground, for it was the custom for east wing and west wing, guests and family, to dine together nightly in this main hall.

The Paradines were close-mouthed but rumor and whispers had crossed the gap swiftly, and when the poltergeist itself moved over from the west wing and began playing its tricks among the members of the Country Club the secret was out.

But it was only later, at that appalling dinner attended also by the Rev. Harry Witherspoon of St. Dunstan's Church in East Walsham and by Dr. Winters, that those present became aware that behind the manifestations was something horrid, dangerous, and quite possibly deadly.

This put quite another light upon the matter and brought about the eventual summoning of Mr. Alexander Hero, psychical researcher, private investigator, ghostbreaker, and dehaunter of houses, to the scene.

There had been great northeasterly gales for two days prior to the twenty-ninth of June, when first it all began, but by then the high, tormenting winds that had been banging shutters and doors, whistling and moaning around corners, gables, chimney stacks, and towers had died away, so that on that night there was neither sound nor portent when something or someone violently shook the great carved mahogany four-poster bed in which Isobel Paradine lay sleeping, and snatched the covers to the floor. She awakened startled in the darkness, with a feeling of presence, and that first alarm that she was being roused either by her brother or sister-in-law because of something wrong in the house.

Instinctively she reached for the covers, and again felt them slide from the bed, and she was aware now that there was no sound of another person, no breathing but her own, and, more fully awake, she sat up and switched on the lamp by her bedside. Her door was shut. There was no one in the room besides herself.

She sat up, watching and listening, in the huge bed in which her father and his father's father and grandfather had slept, and where the late Thomas, Lord Paradine had also died, for this had been his room. A year after his death she had moved into it, and no one had ever disputed her right to be there, not even her brother John, the present peer.

She reached for a light bed jacket and pulled it about her shoulders and waited. She was a calm, intelligent, and fearless woman. The room was empty, and yet it was not. Something had been at her, something unseen was there stirring and moving. She remained sitting quietly, thinking and remembering—things she had known and things she had heard about specters, apparitions, spirits, and phantoms, gentle and ungentle, that were supposed to have made their appearance from time to time in the Hall down through the ages. None of these thoughts shook either her poise or her nerves. She was ready for anything that might have to be encountered.

If there was the semblance of a ghost in the room it was she herself in her white nightdress, with her pale grayish-green eyes shining out of a long, aquiline face browned by outdoor country living, and the silver hair that hung to her shoulders. She was a tall, regal, angular, striking-looking woman of middle age—she was then forty-two. Her hair had always been so fair as almost to be white. The angularity of her person stemmed from the fact that it had never been curved or ripened by love. The prominent eyeballs and too small mouth of the Paradines were less emphasized in her features. Her lips were thin, mobile, sometimes saturnine in their twist. She was a spinster who had devoted the whole of her life to her late father, whose portrait in the uniform of a Guards colonel in World War I stared at her from the opposite wall out of the painted, protuberant Paradine eyes.

In this huge, high-ceilinged room, in itself almost a museum of perfect period furniture and objets d'art, old Lord Paradine had lived as the last of the great and untamed aristocrats.

In this room likewise, two years ago, Lord Paradine had died at the age of eighty, a year too soon—just one year before his deed of gift of the estate and fortune to his son would have become effective. Unable to reconcile himself to modern tax laws, he had waited too long. The enormous death duties all but wrecked the family financially. Only Isobel, the daughter who had stood by him throughout her life, knew how the old man would have hated the Paradine Country Club, that stopgap initiated by her brother to enable them to keep the Hall going, how he would have detested the strangers who were now able to encroach upon his home for a fee.

The one bedside lamp impinged only weakly upon the shadows that concealed the portraits of long-gone Paradines, man, woman, and child, in the costumes of their era. It reflected from the polish of exquisite chests, tallboys, tables, and mirrors of dark mahogany. By its light the woman watched one of a pair of Sèvres vases arise from the mantelpiece on which it stood, as though impelled by the hand of an unseen, malevolent vandal, and hurl itself onto the stone flagging of the fireplace, where it shattered into a hundred pieces. A moment later it was joined by the second, whose flight was farther and more violent, but instead of breaking it merely bounced upon the thick carpet pile and stayed intact.

The Hon. Isobel remained motionlessly upright in the bed, her hands crossed over her chest as she drew her garment more tightly about her shoulders. She did not stir or cry out or make a sound, not even when those same diabolic invisible hands appeared to grip the sides of a graceful Queen Anne tallboy and sent it hurtling to the floor upon its face with an appalling crash of splintering wood.

Simultaneously an Adam mirror in a gilt gesso frame shattered before the eyes of the imperturbable woman, the shards of glass falling in tinkling heaps to the floor.

But the next and final manifestation did wring a cry from her lips: the portrait of the late Lord Thomas Paradine seemed to leap forcefully from the wall and fall to the floor askew, chipping and damaging the corner of the golden frame. It remained there oddly balanced, and gazing at her crookedways. Isobel drew in her breath sharply and murmured, "Father," and then more softly repeated, "Oh, Father!" And thereafter her door flew open and members of the family appeared with robes thrown hastily over night attire, wakened and drawn thither by the noise. They burst in upon the room that was a shambles, and the woman who sat fearless and unmoved in her bed.

The Hon. Isobel watched them come tumbling in and stand there, at first silenced by dismay at the spectacle of ruin that met their eyes. There was her brother John, short and stout, his small mouth covered by a moustache, prominent eyes seeming to start from his head, and next him Enid, his red-haired wife, whom she could not abide. She was aware of her nephew and niece, Mark and Beth, the Paradines' grown son and daughter, and the fat, florid, suety figure of that other nephew of hers, known to one and all as Cousin Freddie, and next in line for the title after Mark.

Before anyone could speak there was a further scurrying of feet from the corridor and the two guests of the Paradines appeared. One was Sir Richard Lockerie, lifelong friend and neighboring baronet, who was staying at Paradine Hall over the summer while repairs and decorations were being carried out at nearby Lockerie Manor. The other was Susan Marshall, the American girl, a friend of Beth's, who was spending the summer with them likewise. It was characteristic of the control the Hon. Isobel exercised over herself that even in the face of this nerve-shattering assault by unseen forces she should notice that Sir Richard and Susan had come in practically together, and how exquisitely beautiful the dark-haired American girl was, despite the evident concern upon her countenance. The time was just before two o'clock in the morning.

Lord Paradine was the first to find his voice: "My God, Isobel— what's happened? Are you all right?" And then the room was filled with cries of astonishment at the damage, cries and queries, and yet they all appeared to be as spellbound as she, quite possibly themselves reduced to immobility by the fact that she herself remained motionless and watching them. She could read their minds and what was going on in them—surprise, fear, concern, bewilderment—but they could not look into hers.

Lord Paradine repeated, "Are you all right, Isobel?"

At last she replied, "Yes, I am."

Sir Richard then found his voice and said, "In heaven's name, Isobel, what has got in here?"

Isobel regarded them all out of her pale eyes and replied, "Nothing human—it is a warning. The nun will be seen in Paradine Hall before long."

Two days later the news reached the fascinated ear of Mr. Alfred Jellicot, a retired draper from Manchester, that there had been a poltergeist manifestation in one of the rooms of the west wing, with considerable damage resulting. Since Mr. Jellicot was the only one of the guests staying at the Paradine Country Club who was not considered a gentleman, he was able to gossip with the servants, and it was one of these, the Boots, who conveyed the information to the fat little merchant whom nature had fashioned in the shape of a modern Mr. Pickwick. Probably Boots embellished the story.

Mr. Jellicot had several hobbies: one was dabbling in spiritualism and psychical phenomena, and the other was collecting the nobility, and he already had several large scrapbooks of same who had in any way, shape, or form impinged upon his otherwise quiet and uneventful life.

The morsel about the west wing haunting, gleaned from Boots, was too good to keep, and Mr. Jellicot promptly imparted it to Mr. Horace Spendley-Carter, M.P., whose position and seat in the House of Parliament impressed him enormously. Spendley-Carter forthwith told his wife, Sylvia, a weak, timid woman with washed-out eyes and hair, who immediately succumbed to nerves and begged him to take her and their twelve-year-old daughter, Noreen, away from there. Spendley-Carter simply laughed at her —he had a particularly loud and explosive laugh—and told her not to be a fool.

To be accepted as a guest at Paradine Hall was paradise enough for Mr. Jellicot—it had been arranged by a friend in Manchester to whom Lord Paradine was under obligation—but to find himself in a haunted house as well was almost too much good luck. Mr. Jellicot invested ten shillings in Boots to keep open the lines for further intelligence and was rewarded by the story of the harp that played by itself—Lord Paradine and some others had gone bustling into the room and when they had got there there wasn't a soul to be seen.

The following morning when Dr. Everard Paulson, the atomic scientist who was staying at the Country Club while surveying the surrounding marshland for a possible safe site for a new installation, asked casually whether they now included a nun as one of their number, since he thought he had encountered one, or at least seemed to have seen one in robe and cowl gliding along the corridor during a nocturnal visit to the bathroom, Mr. Jellicot's excitement knew no bounds. He could put two and two together, particularly since there appeared to be no Sister of Charity on the premises. He knew his Norfolk legends and hauntings, and particularly those connected with Paradine Hall. The nun and the harp went together in the story and forecast disaster for the Paradines.

Three days later the poltergeist struck in the east wing.

It caused acute anger and annoyance to Major Howard Wilson, an irritable army officer with the underslung jaw of a shark, holidaying there with his wife. The Major, a no-nonsense skeptic, was of the opinion that it was that little bounder Jellicot who was playing tricks.

It interested and amused Mrs. Geraldine Taylor, the stout, horsy-type widow with the blued hair, who was a gay old girl and liked anything that was different or exciting.

It had no effect whatsoevever upon the stocky, iron-gray personage of Mr. Dean Ellison, a hydroelectric engineer with a string of letters and honors after his name. Ellison, who was recuperating from an illness acquired in Singapore, was a taciturn man with sharply observant gray eyes. He was given to minding his own business and playing golf.

On the other hand, little Noreen, the hideously ugly child of the Spendley-Carters, appeared to be wholly enchanted with the poltergeist, in spite of the fact that the manifestations seemed to keep her mother in an almost permanent state of upset, such as when a series of pots and pans somehow found their way from the kitchen to the top of the attic stairway and then apparently under their own volition had gone clattering down four flights.

The more Mrs. Spendley-Carter begged to be taken home, the more adamant her husband became in his refusal. If what Jellicot said about poltergeists and the difficulty heretofore about authenticating them was true, here was a chance for publicity to be neglected neither by a politician nor by an inordinately vain man.

With its taking up residence in the east wing, the poltergeist suddenly turned more mischievous than vengeful and damaging, as though by the havoc it had created in the room of the Hon. Isobel Paradine it had temporarily satisfied its spleen and was content now merely to harass, irritate, and annoy. It enjoyed switching the shoes outside doors between midnight and morning, after Boots had polished them; it liked to hide articles such as Mrs. Geraldine Taylor's reading glasses, which vanished for three days and were finally discovered stuffed down a crack behind the sofa, or sewing scissors, or books that people were reading, or articles of clothing.

Like all bullies, it caught on quickly to the weakest member of the group and the one most easily terrified, and seemed to concentrate its attention upon Sylvia Splendley-Carter, reducing her to tears and chattering hysteria. Curious things seemed to drop from the ceiling or fly in through closed windows—vegetables from the kitchen, an egg that was fortunately hard-boiled, nuts, and small flint pebbles. At night it went around tapping and knocking on walls, and playing odd tunes on exposed plumbing. And in the meantime several persons, including Mrs. Taylor, were certain that they had caught glimpses of the figure of the nun after dark.

Eventually the nerves of even the skeptics began to fray. The entity seemed to know how to help this along by remaining quiescent for a day or so, to make people think it had gone away. Then it would begin again. Peace was gone from Paradine Hall.

The attack that took place upon Susan Marshall in her room in the west wing between midnight and morning of the fifth of July, however, was something else again.

After the gales and violence of late June, a hot spell had set in with fine weather as the moon began to fill. The American girl, ordinarily no light sleeper, found herself awakened by a cold wind or current of air that played about her face, neck, and shoulders. At the first instant of this awakening she found herself alert, though not yet wholly aware of the presence in her room. She was uncomfortably conscious of the chill upon her skin, and that there ought not to have been such a drop in temperature. Her eyes sought the slight parting in the drawn curtains covering her wide-open windows, through which appeared a sliver of moonlit night sky. The curtains did not stir; there was no wind to account for the cold that enveloped her. An instant later she felt the icy hand at her throat.

In this dreadful moment she neither screamed nor panicked. The fingers assaulting her, chill, damp, boneless, filled her with an appalling disgust and horror rather than fear. There was no strength in them, and it was revulsion at the sliminess and obscenity of whatever it was that pervaded her, rather than dread for her life.

She was herself a healthy, nerveless, athletic girl of twenty-three, strong and fit. Furiously angry, she prepared to grapple with the horror at her throat, spun quickly and grabbed for it—but there was nothing there. Her curtains stirred momentarily, and she was aware that her door had been opened. By the sliver of light from the window she caught a glimpse of a shrouded figure in some kind of cloak and cowl, like a nun's habit, disappearing. The door closed noiselessly, the curtains by the window subsided.

Susan Marshall felt for the lamp at her bedside and switched it on, but no glow came to the bulb. The room remained in darkness. This, if anything, gave her almost more of a shock and fright than the attack upon her person. The feeling was intensified when she went to her door and tried it, and found it locked, and for a moment she wondered whether she ought to cry out for help. Then she mastered herself and her superb nerves again stood her in good stead. She remembered that there were a candlestick and matches on the mantel. She felt her way thither and lit the candle. There was no one in the room.

She took the candle over to the mirror and held it up. Dark, large eyes stared back at her from her pale face beneath deep chestnut hair. She had not been harmed. There were no bruises at her throat, and yet . . .

She held the candle higher for closer inspection, and as she did so the light by her bedside came on unexpectedly and provided further illumination. She saw that there were five damp spots on her skin in the vicinity of where she had felt the cold hand. She touched the moisture with a finger and thought that it might be perspiration brought on by shock.

She realized at this point that indeed she was wet with perspiration under the arms, on her chest, at her temples and brow and upper lip. She picked up a towel and dried herself, then went to the door and tried it. It was unlocked now. She opened it and looked out. The corridor was dark. There was no one there. She listened for any sounds of footsteps and heard none, but faintly she thought that she heard the distant strains of harp music. She listened again, but it seemed to have ceased. She closed the door and went back to bed, and sat up thinking. Had it happened? Might it not have been a dream or a nightmare? Might not the door have been temporarily stuck? Could there not have been a loose connection to the lamp?

She felt her heart. It was still pounding violently, but did it not often do so after a nightmare? She picked up a book by her bedside to calm herself, and read a chapter or two before she felt drowsy once more. She put out the light and went to sleep.

The following morning she awoke merely with the memory of having gone through something unpleasant; there was nothing abnormal about her room or in any way indicative of the presence of an intruder. She convinced herself quite easily then that she had imagined or dreamed the whole thing, and determined not even to mention the episode, if such it was, to anyone. Nor would she have done, or ever referred to it, or even hinted to Sir Richard Lockerie about the affair, had it not been for what happened at the dinner in the great hall three nights later.

It had been Lord Paradine's idea, this communal dining, when temporary members or guests of the Country Club mingled with the family. Paradine was a straightforward, uncomplicated man of no great force of character but a good deal of sense of justice; it was his opinion that if people parted, as they did, with a good stiff fee to be at Paradine Hall, they were entitled to the amenities. This mingling likewise furnished an opportunity to talk hunting, fishing, shooting, sailing, riding, and other kindred sports or agricultural activities local to the shire, which formed the compass of his life. But it was his spinster sister, Isobel, who preserved the formalities and organized the dinners in some part on the scale, and certainly in the manner, in which her father had wished dining conducted in the great hall.

Although it boasted the modernization of a great crystal electric chandelier, candles only were used for illumination at dinner, in candelabra and wall sconces, and since they had always been used, there was an enormous supply of them on hand.

The armor and clusters of swords and pikes were kept polished; faded but still colorful pennons of the Paradines hung from the blackened beams of the two-story-high chamber. At one end the great fireplace, large enough to roast a sheep or ox whole, gleamed with copper. At the far end, in the second story, was the minstrels' gallery with balustrade and heavy velvet curtains framing the opening.

The wax tapers shed a soft and glamorous light over the twenty-foot-long refectory table; those in the wall sconces were reflected from steel, copper, and polished oak. But candles illuminate merely their immediate surroundings; behind the candles' light shadows are deeper, heavier, and sometimes mobile with the flickering of the light. Half concealed in those shadows in the great hall were sideboards, settles, chests, and armchair carvers of heavy Jacobean oak ranged around the room, backed by famous tapestries displayed on the dark oak-paneled walls.

On this night, as on previous ones since the manifestations had first begun, there was no escape from ghost talk, even though the Rev. Harry Witherspoon, vicar of St. Dunstan's Church at East Walsham, and Dr. Samuel Winters, the local G.P., had joined the gathering.

Lord and Lady Paradine sat opposite one another at the far ends of the table. They would have needed a walkie-talkie set to communicate. It was Isobel, from a more strategic location at the center, who kept things moving, signaled to Huggins, the butler, and his assistant servers, and watched over the guests.

At mid-meal the subject as usual had been reduced to the hardcore skeptics, the convinced believers, and the middle-of-the-roaders, the ones who insisted they had an open mind on the subject, when a new note was suddenly introduced by Major Howard Wilson, the Regular Army officer, who was the leader of the skeptics' camp.

"I say, Lord Paradine," he rasped, "I understand there's talk of having some kind of spiritist fellow down here to hold séances or something of the kind. Is that right?"

Lord Paradine flushed crimson with annoyance and, forgetting that the moment before he had been engaged in warm and friendly conversation with Mrs. Vivyan Wilson, the Major's handsome and undeniably stimulating blonde wife seated at his left, replied with some asperity, "Certainly not. I wouldn't know where you would come by a piece of nonsense such as that."

The Major laughed silently to himself; timidity was not one of his failings. "From your nephew, sir," he said.

The exchange had taken place in the midst of one of those momentary lulls, and now the entire table engaged itself in staring at the disagreeable young man known as Cousin Freddie. He was the son of Lord Paradine's younger brother, Philip, deceased. Frederick Paradine was that somewhat unusual combination, an unpleasant and malicious fat man. At twenty-nine he was already huge, gross, puffy, and malignant. The Paradine features—the bulging eyes, small mouth, and arrogant nose—were not becoming to a fat face; they gave him the appearance of a particularly bane-ful and vindictive parrot.

When Lord Paradine was irritated he did not bother to conceal this from anyone. "Confound you, Freddie," he said. "Won't you ever learn to hold your tongue?"

"Aha," barked the Major, "so it is true?"

"No," interrupted Sir Richard Lockerie, "it is not," and brought all eyes turning toward him. He was a distinguished-looking man, widowed, who had commanded armor during the war. Taken prisoner, he had escaped and later married the French girl member of the underground who had aided his flight to England. She had died shortly after the birth of his son. "I merely suggested to Lord Paradine that if these disturbances continue it might be useful to have a chap down here I used to know at Cambridge shortly after the war, and whose profession today, I believe, is to get to the bottom of such things."

Horace Spendley-Carter, the M.P., took over at this point. He never spoke except in a bray, and he was also the possessor of a shattering laugh which began with a violent expulsion of breath. He was a large, loud man with a Guards moustache, although he had never been in the Guards, a blunt nose, and a pair of moist eyes. He was wearing an unforgivable puce-colored dinner jacket. "You ought to have a word with our friend Jellicot here. He's supposed to know all about such things."

Mr. Jellicot beamed and prepared to take the floor, but he lost it to Beth Paradine, the shy, gentle, brown-haired girl who sat next to Sir Richard. "Oh! Uncle Dick," she said, "is there really someone like that?" And Susan Marshall, sitting opposite, said, "Do tell us about him, Dick."

Sir Richard said, "It was just an idea. After the war I went back to Cambridge for a year to complete my reading—a lot of chaps my age did. There was a teacher of philosophy there of whom we were all extraordinarily fond—one of those beloved men who make a college more than a college, if you know what I mean. Some very unpleasant things began to happen; they came close to costing Dr. Bingham his life."

Susan Marshall was following the narrative, dark eyes shining with excitement. "You mean supernatural things?" she asked.

Sir Richard hesitated before replying, "Yes, in a way. This young chap, Alexander Hero, cleared the thing up, and just in time, I might add. But Hero is no spiritualist. I understand he does work occasionally for the Society for Psychical Research."

"What? What?" shouted Major Wilson. "What's the fellow's name, did you say? Hero? What an absolutely preposterous name for anyone!"

Cousin Freddie snorted. "Is it his own, or did he make it up?"

Sir Richard eyed Cousin Freddie coldly and said, "I don't doubt but that you will find it in the genealogies if you are really interested. It was originally a Huguenot family, Heureux," and he spelled it for him. "They trace back to the eleventh century, I believe."

Susan Marshall asked, "What is he then—a kind of ghost detective?" And Lady Paradine said languidly, "How fascinating," but did not mean it, for she was not interested at all; she was occupied with the manner in which her son Mark, who had inherited her red hair and handsome features, was looking at Susan Marshall.

"What's that?" Major Wilson barked. "There's no such thing as ghosts. Why, the man must be an out-and-out fake. I imagine I'd have a bit of fun with a fellow like that."

"Is he good-looking, Sir Richard?" asked Vivyan Wilson. She was blonde and avid, with eager, roving eyes, and that bony, somewhat too thin prettiness of British women past the first flush of youth.

Sir Richard caught only the tail end of the remark, but noted the absurdly stiff manner in which Major Wilson suddenly leaned backward in his chair to throw a glance at his wife behind the heads of the intervening diners.

Mr. Jellicot remarked importantly, "Once a poltergeist has arrived, there's nothing can be done. I have read a great deal on the subject and am familiar with——"

"There is something can be done, sir," interrupted Mr. Witherspoon, the vicar, reprovingly. "You forget there is a power to which all things visible and invisible must defer."

Mr. Jellicot, who had great regard for the clergy, accepted the reproof in hot-flushed silence, and again an uncomfortable hush fell over the table. It was suddenly brought to a startling end by the shrill, high-pitched, girlish giggle ending in a titter that emanated from Noreen Spendley-Carter, seated next to Cousin Freddie and opposite her mother.

At the awkward, in-between stage of twelve, Noreen was an incredibly ugly child, with irregular features, too large mouth, too large ears, freckles, and a sallow skin. In an endeavor to make her presentable for dinner, her mother had frizzed her dun-colored hair and put her in a pink party dress made stiff and voluminous by petticoats, and had even added a touch of make-up to her face and lips, which of course had succeeded only in making her look grotesque.

Everyone stared at the outbreak, since there seemed to have been no cause for it. No one had said anything funny or even faintly amusing.

Once more the penetrating giggle arose, even over her mother's command, "Noreen, do be quiet!" until all eyes turned toward her and saw that the child was gazing straight across the table and to the other side of the room. Then, with one bare arm and bony hand emerging from the pink taffeta party dress, she pointed over her mother's shoulder and cried, "Oh, look!"

Upon her ugly little face there appeared an expression of captivated and wholehearted delight, as one of the great Jacobean carver armchairs that had stood as solidly as a throne at the side of the dining hall began to move apparently of its own volition out of the deep shadows casts by the many glowing candles, toward the table across the polished flagstone floor, over which the legs scraped with a singularly unpleasant grating noise.

A thrill of horror ran audibly round the table as the hearts and stomachs of the people gathered there sank within them. Believers and unbelievers among them, the credulous, the realistic, and the cynical in that shocking moment were united in doubt and apprehension, and nerves already taut from events that had gone before were stretched still further.

Among the cynics cherished opinions and beliefs were being shattered before their eyes; to the superstitious confirmation came upon the wings of fear. The chair could not move, should not move on its own unaided by any visible human agency, and yet on that night of July the eighth, at four-hundred-year-old Paradine Hall in the Shire of Norfolk, it was moving.

Later there might be rationalizations, explanations, or even sheer disbelief in what they had seen, but for the moment all those around the table were spellbound with a kind of clammy horror by this object that had no right to wander out of the dark shadows and break every law known to nature and to man.

Matters were not helped by the almost insane giggle of delight still issuing from Noreen, or the sudden scream of her mother on the other side of the table, "It's coming for me—don't let it!" and the sharp cry of Spendley-Carter vis-à-vis, "Sylvia! Keep quiet —you're being hysterical."

It was after the main course had been served. Neither the butler, his wife, nor the second servers were in the great hall, the guests at the dinner table were alone with the phenomenon, staring white-faced and seemingly paralyzed by the spectacle as the chair inched forward. There was not only sight but sound—the scraping along the flagstones to the edge of the heavy carpet, which began to crumple from the force of its passage.

"I am not afraid. It is not real. It cannot be. I will not be afraid," Susan Marshall was saying to herself, and yet fear was squeezing her heart too, for she was remembering the cold hand that had clutched at her throat while she slept three nights before; the ghostly figure of the nun that had seemed to slip out of her bedroom door, which had then locked itself; the light that would not burn, and the terror of those moments of contact with the unknown. They had suddenly become all too real again.

Lady Paradine, the candlelight reflecting from her fox-colored hair, half arose from her place at one end of the long table, clutching her napkin and calling to her husband across the length opposite, "John, what is it? What is happening?"

The Hon. Isobel Paradine had risen likewise and was standing by the tableside, her light hair and long white evening gown giving her the aspect of a queen cast in silver. She too was staring at the moving chair with a kind of uncertain fascination and bewilderment.

To the scraping of the chair on the stone flags was now added the soft rustle as the folds of the carpet began to pile up. Beth Paradine cried out, "Uncle Dick—I'm frightened!" Sir Richard Lockerie did not reply, but placed his large hand firmly over hers and pressed it comfortingly. He was afraid of very little on earth, but as a human being he was greatly disturbed by the thing that moved by itself.

Four candles in one of the three great nine-branched Paradine silver candlesticks on the table suddenly went out for no particular reason, and the blue smoke of the extinguished wicks rose without wavering straight up into the air, for there was no draft or even so much as a breath of air moving in the great hall, but nobody took any notice. They were all by now hypnotized by the relentless forward motion of the black armchair, as though someone invisible were coming to join them all at the dinner table.

"He-he-he," giggled little Noreen, "look, it's moving."

Major Howard Wilson shouted, "This is a lot of damn nonsense. Somebody's playing monkey tricks." He got up from his seat, went and looked behind the chair, and cried in quite a different voice, "By God, there's nobody there!" and suddenly scuttled back and sat down, blowing out his cheeks in the strangest fashion. His exquisite blonde wife so far forgot her own uneasiness at the manifestation as to regard her husband with an expression of distaste about her mouth.

Lord Paradine arose at his end of the table and shouted, "What is this? What is going on here? I'll not have any of it." He started for the chair. Mrs. Geraldine Taylor, the sporty, huntin', ridin', husband-hunting widow, laid a hand upon his arm, saying, "Do be careful, Lord Paradine." Next to her Dr. Everard Paulson, the little atomic scientist with the face of a Capuchin monkey, added, "Yes, sir, for God's sake do be careful. We are standing on some kind of a threshold. You cannot tell what——"

But Lord Pardine shook off restraining arms and warnings and marched solidly to the transient chair. At fifty-six his sandy hair was beginning to thin, he had taken on middle-aged flesh, and the somewhat too prominent hazel eyes, small mouth, and moustache gave his face an expression almost of petulance. But there was nothing petulant or evasive about his actions; he was a simple man of principle and courage, not extraordinarily intelligent, but one who would always go straight to the heart of the matter. So he went directly to the chair and gripped it by the back.

"By God!" he shouted, shaken but not at all daunted. "I can't hold it—the thing's got a life of its own."

"Go it, chair! Go it, Unkie!" cried Cousin Freddie, unable to forbear one of his tasteless remarks.

Mark too was on his feet crying, "Father—wait! I'll help you." But his mother put a restraining hand upon his arm, crying, "No, Mark, no! Don't touch it!"

In the yellow light of the candle-illuminated hall Lord Paradine had gone quite red in the face from effort. Alfred Jellicot, the little draper from Manchester, cried a warning. "Do be careful, sir—for God's sake leave it be ! Can't you see it's infested?"

"Blast and damn!" gasped Lord Paradine, still struggling.

At the far end of the table, close to the seat that Lord Paradine had vacated, the square-faced man with short-cut iron-gray hair, the engineer Dean Ellison, watched the proceedings with the most curious expression on his florid face. One might almost have sworn, unless it was a trick of the light, that there was a half-smile at his mouth. At the opposite end of the table the Rev. Harry Witherspoon too had risen to his feet with a look of horror fixed upon his broad episcopal countenance, but horror mixed with courage and determination, and he raised one hand and began making the sign of the cross in the air, while his lips tried to form the phrases that he could hardly remember from the long-disused Litany of Exorcism: "Lord Almighty, be with us, vanquish this evil spirit——"

It was at this point that, without rhyme or reason, in pairs, by ones and threes, and sometimes four at a time, all the candles in the great hall began to go out. There were twenty-seven in the three nine-branched Paradine candlesticks on the table, thirty-six held in sconces distributed about the three sides of the dark paneled walls, six more on either side of the raised minstrels' gallery, the dark folds of whose curtains loomed above the heads of the diners.

The candles were not blown out or snuffed out; the flames simply sank and died. With the extinguishing of light, shadows began to leap menacingly in the dark corners of the room. The first note of panic was sounded by the scream of Mrs. Spendley-Carter, which pierced over her daughter's high titter, and the angry shout from the bull-like voice of Major Wilson, "Lights! What the devil's the matter with the lights?" And the fruity tones of Spendley-Carter seconding him: "Here! Here! Leave those lights alone, whoever is doing it." From fat little Mr. Jellicot arose a frightened wail, "Oh dear! They're all going out."

For the candles continued to die with a kind of willful regularity as though an unseen finger were tapping or pinching each wick to obliterate the light. Only a few remained still burning in the candelabrum at the far end of the table, revealing the pale, shocked faces of Lady Paradine and her daughter Beth, the thunder-dark countenance of Sir Richard Lockerie, and the glowing eyes of Susan Marshall. Then they likewise went out.

This left but two burning in one of the sconces to the left of the minstrels' gallery. At the end of the table vacated by Lord Paradine, Dr. Paulson leaped to his feet and pointed up to the minstrels' gallery. "The nun! The nun!" he shouted. Eyes were turned from the possessed chair and the man struggling with it to the high gallery. Was it the curtains, or was there indeed the lurking figure wrapped in the habit and headdress of a nun?

Major Wilson bawled, "What the devil? I don't see anything," but the stout, iron-haired widow, Mrs. Taylor, was on her feet calling, "There! There! I see her now." They all saw her then. Motionless, forbidding, she seemed to be watching them out of the shadows that half concealed her.

Out of the darkness came the bitter voice of Isobel Paradine: "Now will you believe?" and with that the last two candles went out, plunging the hall into total darkness.

Panic immediately followed this, simultaneous with a curse and a cry from Lord Paradine, after which there was a great crash as though he or the chair or both had been felled. The women were screaming now as more chairs were overturned, knives and silver clattered to the floor, glasses and dishes were broken.

Over the shrieks and groans two voices were raised, that of Isobel commanding, "Huggins! Huggins, come in here at once! Turn on the lights," and that of Sir Richard Lockerie, firm and hard above the pandemonium, "Be calm! Be quiet! I order you to be calm. There's nothing to be afraid of really. Be calm, please." Then there came a slight rush of wind and the sound of running footsteps. Someone cried, "Lights! Lights! Turn on the lights!"

A shaft pierced the gloom from the pantry as the butler burst into the dining room. He was at first blinded by the darkness and shaken by the chaos, but he kept his head and moved swiftly to the side of the room. There was the click of a switch and the great overhead chandelier burst into a stunning brilliance that at first dazzled all eyes and then enabled them to see.

Lord Paradine lay on the floor on his back with the chair on top of him. He was not hurt, only winded and very angry. In his fright fat Mr. Jellicot, his black tie around under one ear, had crawled up onto the table. Sylvia Spendley-Carter had slipped to the floor in a faint, and her big, gross husband had risen to his feet and was staring at her but making no move to go to her as the doctor arose and hurried to her side. There was a cry and a rustle from the ministrels' gallery above, to which all eyes were turned. The Hon. Isobel was there, parting the two side curtains of the gallery like an actress with wide dramatic gestures of her arms, her hair, face, and figure gleaming in the bright light. She cried, "There's nothing here—no one, or anything at all."

Sir Richard Lockerie added his calming voice, saying, "There now, you see, there's nothing to be frightened of—nothing at all. It was an accident." He was looking about the shambles of the dining hall with the same air of self-possession and command with which he had peered from the turret of his tank in the war. "Nothing to be frightened of," he repeated. Then instinctively his hand sought that of Beth, who was trembling and staring before her almost as though she were hypnotized, and hardly realizing he was doing it, he threw a protective arm about her shoulders and said, "Come on, old girl, buck up. It's all right now."

But it wasn't all right at all, for he saw then where the frightened girl was staring, and he saw too the attitude of recoil of Susan Marshall, and the unconcealed horror as she looked down upon her plate. "Oh! How horrid!" she whispered. "How disgustingly, revoltingly horrid!" Noreen was staring likewise, too fascinated now, too engaged, even to giggle. Across Susan Marshall's empty plate lay a dead rabbit, the strangling wire still visible around its throat.

There was no doubt whatsoever as to the agitation and urgency of the distinguished-looking gentleman asking to see Mr. Alexander Hero, psychical researcher and private investigator of the paranormal. Mrs. Harris, Hero's daily woman, having admitted the visitor to the library-sitting room of the neat whitewashed house at 88A Eaton Mews North, near London's fashionable Eaton Square, went scuffing and flapping off to the laboratory at the back, impressed by the stern and martial good looks of the caller, as well as pleasantly excited at the excuse to poke her nose into forbidden territory.

In the laboratory the tall young man wearing a long white linen coat was standing in the midst of a tangle of gadgetry, mostly of his own devising. He was watching an oscillating needle on a dial, a lip curled in disbelief, and at the same time trying to keep an eye on a boiling flask. He had an engaging personality, characterized by an unruly mop of light brown hair, which had a way of gathering itself like a cockscomb over the top of his brow, a mouth that was easily mobile, and an extraordinarily stubborn chin. He did not even bother to turn around when he heard the scuff of Mrs. Harris' musical-comedy shoes, but merely called out, "Hoy, there! Out of bounds! Shut the door, there's a good girl."

Mrs. Harris stood her ground. "Oh, go on with you," she said. "There's a 'andsome gentleman here to see you. He said it was wery urgent."

Alexander Hero called out, "Eh, what's that? Come in or stay out, will you, you're making a draft."

"You said I wasn't never to come in."

Hero said, "Oh, Lord—well, you may now." He removed the Bunsen burner from beneath a flask and turned around, grinning at her. His eyes were intelligent and full of humor, and he had the large family nose of the Huguenot Heureux, anglicized to

Hero, which had always kept the men of that line from being prettily handsome but had not interfered with their being usefully attractive. "Now," he said, "let's have it from the beginning again, love."

Mrs. Harris gazed upon him fondly and unabashed. "Coo," she said, "what a stink! He said his name was Sir Richard Locker-something, and 'e's come from some place sounded like Paradise 'All. 'E don't 'alf seem to have the wind up. You'd better see him, ducks."

The young man said, half to himself, "That's odd—if it is Sir Richard Lockerie, he doesn't live *at* Paradine Hall. You're sure you've got it straight?" He flipped a switch, turned out the Bunsen burner, and wiped his hands on a piece of chemical-stained toweling. He located his ancient briar and, clutching it between his teeth, trailed Mrs. Harris to the library, where he found his visitor nervously pacing. He recognized him at once. Piercing blue eyes, clipped moustache, graying temples, military air—he had not altered.

Hero said, "How do you do, Sir Richard. It has been a long time since I have had the pleasure."

A look of intense relief spread itself over Richard Lockerie's features. "By Jove, Hero," he said, "I am fortunate to find you. I should have telephoned first for an appointment, but I have come straight from Paradine Hall."

"Ow, I must of got it muddled," said Mrs. Harris, who had ensconced herself comfortably in the middle of the doorway. "I thought you said 'Paradise.'"

Mr. Hero went to her and turned her gently about. "Go away, dear," he said, "I'll tell you all about it later."

The apple-cheeked char with the naughty eyes grinned wickedly and said, "You'd better just—always keepin' the interesting things to yourself," and flapped off.

Hero turned to his visitor and said, "Sorry. She runs things here. I couldn't do without her. Please sit down. It was at Cambridge we last met, wasn't it? We were mightily impressed at you chaps coming back after six years of war to take refresher courses."

Sir Richard said, "I remember rather being impressed myself

by an extraordinary bit of work you did while I was there. You surely saved Dr. Bingham's life. As a matter of fact that is why I looked you up and came to you." Sir Richard suddenly became agitated again. He arose, lit a cigarette, went to one of the bookshelves, then to the window, before returning to face the younger man. "Look here," he said, "I feel like a damned bloody fool."

Hero said, "You needn't. Most people of sane and common sense do when they think they have seen something."

"We are haunted down at the Hall," Sir Richard suddenly blurted. "Damned nastily and visibly haunted. There has been a filthy attack on a young girl. If she weren't the pluckiest thing in the world it might have killed her. I only found out about it last night. Something's got loose there. The place is turning into a hell. I would have thought they were all mad, and telling the wildest and most fanciful tales—Isobel, Beth, Susan, and all of them. I simply should not have believed it, only I saw it with my own eyes. I am not a fool, Hero, and I don't think I am a coward—but I am a badly shaken man."

"What was it you saw?" Hero asked.

"Last night at dinner at Paradine Hall, a chair that moved by itself; candles, dozens of them that extinguished themselves suddenly, one after the other; a dead rabbit that materialized out of nowhere; and in the minstrels' gallery the figure of a nun. We all saw it, but afterward there wasn't anybody there."

"Oh yes," Hero said, "the nun, to be sure." He went to the bookshelf and took down a volume called *Ghosts and Ghostly Legends of Old Norfolk*, opened it to a chapter heading, "The Phantom Nun of Paradine Hall," and showed it to Sir Richard. "It's a well-known legend."

Sir Richard looked down at the book and for a moment seemed flustered. "But that is all a lot of nonsense, isn't it?" he said.

"Mostly," Hero explained.

The expression on Sir Richard's face altered again as he remembered. "But I saw her——"

"Ah, did you?" Hero said.

"With my own eyes. Just before the last of the lights went out and panic set in. Look here, I'll try to make some sense. You know about the Paradine Country Club, of course?"

Hero said, "Vaguely. Another stately home gone west."

"Yes, the old man died just a year before the deed of gift could take effect. The present Lord Paradine has had to turn the Hall into a kind of gentlemen's sports club to keep it going. You can imagine what will happen unless this is stopped. Some of the guests have left already. If word spreads about——"

"Yes," Hero said, "I see."

"There are two wings, you know—the east, reserved for the guests, and the west, where the family live. It began in the west wing in the room of Isobel Paradine," and then in reply to Hero's querying glance, "Lord Paradine's sister. She's unmarried. Rather runs the place. Something made a shambles of her room in the night. Furniture knocked about, chairs and tables upset, pictures flung down from the wall, bedclothes pulled from the bed."

"Was Miss Paradine present?"

"Yes! When we barged into her room, awakened by the noise, she was sitting up in her bed—great big four-poster—apparently frozen with terror. The painting of her father, the late Lord Paradine—she worshiped him, you know—was flung from the wall. She seemed absolutely in a daze."

"When did this happen?" Hero asked. "Would you have the exact date?"

"About ten days ago," Sir Richard said, and then, reaching into his pocket, produced some notes which he consulted. Hero too produced a small note pad. "The morning of the twenty-ninth of June, to be exact."

Hero wrote it down. The date meant something to him, but at the moment he could not tell or remember why. "Were you there?" Hero asked.

"Yes," Sir Richard replied. "I am staying at the Hall at Lord Paradine's invitation while my house is undergoing some renovations. I am his neighbor, you know—Lockerie Manor is the next estate."

Hero nodded and said. "Good. When things like this start, it is essential to have a few level heads about."

There was a tinge of desperation in Sir Richard's voice as he said, "I am afraid mine is not very level any more. This foul attack upon Susan Marshall——"

"Who is Susan Marshall?"

"Sorry, I thought I told you. She's the American girl visiting there. See here, you had better have the picture properly. In the west wing there are Lord and Lady Paradine, the Hon. Isobel, his sister, and Lord Paradine's son and daughter, Mark and Beth. I think Mark went up to Cambridge shortly after you came down. Susan Marshall is Beth's friend and is staying with her over the summer—they met in London—a girl of extraordinary beauty and amazing courage. Oh! I almost forgot Cousin Freddie, Lord Paradine's nephew." The expression on Sir Richard's face altered as he said this, to the point where Mr. Hero gathered that Cousin Freddie might be someone it would be pleasant to forget. "And myself, of course," concluded Sir Richard.

Mr. Hero had pulled his pad toward him and was scribbling a few notes as Sir Richard talked—names and places. He had the faculty of being able to write down one set of facts and think upon another. His cases often began far from the scene of happenings and manifestations, and were usually as intimately concerned with those who reported them as the actual phenomena. There was nothing that was unimportant, nothing that one could overlook, nothing that one should not think about and file away in the back of one's mind for future reference. As he scribbled, into his mental filing cabinet went a whole flock of questions: What was Sir Richard Lockerie's interest in this affair? Why had Susan Marshall's name already come up twice, and what was the connection between "extraordinary beauty" and "amazing courage"? Why did Sir Richard dislike the person referred to as "Cousin Freddie"? If guests had already departed the Hall in panic, endangering the successful operation of the Country Club, why had Sir Richard come to see him and not Lord Paradine? It was Paradine's business. Or was it? Hero had noted the intensity of expression and fervor that had come into Sir Richard's eyes and voice when he spoke of the girl's courage.

Hero apparently finished his notes, poised his pencil, and asked, "What happened to Miss Marshall?"

"Something got into her room one night, something shocking and nasty, and had her by the throat—some kind of icy hand. She thought she saw the nun, but when she was able to put on the light there was nothing and no one there. I can assure you that she is neither an imaginative nor a hysterical type—she hadn't even intended mentioning the episode to anyone until the affair at dinner last night. It was after this that I insisted something be done about the situation and persuaded Lord Paradine to let me try to engage your services. I—ah—had been telling them a little about you earlier, during dinner."

Hero said, "I see." And then filed away, *"Widower, aged around forty-two, with son who ought to be about nine; romantically interested and concerned about American girl. That's for a beginning. I wonder where the son is?"* Aloud he asked. "Are the manifestations confined only to one portion of the Hall—the family side?"

"No—it's got into the east wing as well, where the guests are lodged—objects flying through the air, things falling off shelves and mantelpieces, footsteps and noises and knockings, and nobody there."

"Oh!" said Hero in geniune surprise. "That too—stones and things?"

"And odd bits like occasional potatoes, or walnuts, or people's slippers. I suppose it all sounds like a terrible lot of twaddle to you."

"No, it doesn't," Hero said seriously, "to the contrary."

Sir Richard said, "A harp played—I'm trying, sort of, to give you a picture, to tell you everything as briefly as I can—or was played by no visible means or person. It stands in the music room and belonged to Lord Paradine's mother. I mean, there was no one in the room or even near when we went there."

Mr. Hero looked up from his note taking. "Eh? What's that?" he said sharply. "Are you sure?"

Sir Richard, slightly taken aback by the rasp in Hero's query, blinked and after reflecting a moment said, "I don't know how one can be sure of anything any more, after what we have been through. I can only tell you what we heard and saw. It took place on the night of the attack made upon Susan, except that at the time we were not aware there had been an attack."

Mr. Hero suddenly looked grave. He said, "Did it, now? Were you aware that in the legend as it exists there is a connection between a harp and the nun?"

Sir Richard nodded. "I had heard something to that effect."

"From whom?"

Again the question was sharp, and Sir Richard looked astonished. "Well, I suppose from anyone. One hears or knows such things, doesn't one?"

"Cannot you remember?"

Sir Richard thought hard. "I believe Isobel mentioned it, and a fellow named Jellicot—one of the guests there."

Mr. Hero noted this. "Thank you. And now as to this dinner last night, and what happened . . ."

"I suppose you'd want it from the beginning?"

"Yes, please."

Sir Richard lit a cigarette to help him compose his thoughts and said, "I'll try to leave nothing out—but you know how it is."

Mr. Hero smiled encouragingly and said, "You are making a very excellent witness. I wish there were more like you in my business. Supposing you try."

Slowly at first, and then increasing in tempo as memory of every incident seemed to come flowing back to him, Sir Richard launched into his narration, which Mr. Hero did not interrupt. Nor did he even take notes, which might have distracted. The ex-soldier was a vivid narrator and, concluding, he showed Hero Isobel standing dramatically in the minstrels' gallery, arms outstretched, flinging the curtains aside and crying, "There's nothing here—no one, or anything at all."

"She was right," Sir Richard concluded. "There wasn't anything either, that we could see. But elsewhere there was something far worse."

"What was that?" Hero asked.

"When the lights came on Susan Marshall was staring horrified at her plate, at something which was there which hadn't been there before. It was a dead rabbit. There was a strangling wire about its throat."

"Ah," said Mr. Hero, "I don't like that at all."

"Then I am not mad," Sir Richard said. "You don't think we have all gone out of our minds?"

"No, you have not."

"And you think you may be able to help us?"

"Perhaps," Hero said. "Who were the other guests present at the dinner?"

"I have brought a list," Sir Richard said.

Hero scanned the meticulously written paper which Sir Richard had handed him, and read:

Members of Country Club

Major and Mrs. Howard Wilson; Middlesex Regt.
Mr. Horace Spendley-Carter, M.P., Mrs. Spendley-Carter, and daughter Noreen Spendley-Carter (aged twelve).
Mr. Alfred Jellicot; retired draper from Manchester.
Mr. Dean Ellison; engineer.
Mrs. Geraldine Taylor; widow.
Dr. Everard Paulson; scientist.

Extra guests at dinner

Rev. Harry Witherspoon; Vicar, East Walsham.
Dr. Samuel Winters; General Practitioner, ditto.

Only two of the names meant anything to Hero. He recalled Spendley-Carter, the Member of Parliament, as a windbaggy politician, and Dr. Paulson as a well-known atomic researcher. He said to Sir Richard, "In what capacity would you wish me to come to the Hall? For the Society for Psychical Research, or as a private investigator?"

"Oh, private by all means, Hero. We are desperately anxious that there be no publicity, as you can well imagine."

Hero tapped Lockerie's list. "Are any of these likely to get in contact with the press?" he inquired.

Sir Richard reflected. "I wouldn't put it past this fellow Spendley-Carter, if he thought he could gain any political benefit from it. As for the rest, they are ladies and gentlemen—with the exception of little Jellicot."

Hero elevated half an eyebrow. "Oh?" he said. "Who is Mr. Jellicot, and how did he get in?"

Sir Richard said at once, "He's not a bad little chap, you know. Sort of fat and bustly and frightfully eager to please. He was something in linens, from Manchester, and I gather was able to prevail upon a friend of Lord Paradine's who was obligated to him for something or other to speak up for him. He appears to be something of an expert—or at any rate is well read upon the subject of psychical phenomena. At least he is voluble upon the subject and seems highly pleased, although last night he panicked with the rest of them."

Mr. Hero said, "H'm. Is he now?" pulled at his lower lip and underlined Mr. Jellicot's name on the list, adding, "There always seems to be one about, doesn't there?"

Sir Richard almost hastened to try to dispel any bad impression he might have given of the man, saying, "I rather think the little chap is harmless——" when Hero interrupted.

"That may be, but the manifestations definitely are not." Then he asked, "Am I right in gathering that Lord Paradine is not exactly pleased with your mission or the idea of my coming to the Hall?"

Lockerie rather evaded the question and replied, "You will find Lord Paradine a straightforward man who speaks his mind. He is the type who has no truck with anything he cannot understand, but he has been badly shaken by the incidents that have taken place, particularly after he had wrestled with the chair and it knocked him down. He is sufficient of a businessman to see that if this gets out it will be ruination. In this I had some assistance from his sister Isobel. It was in her room it all began, you will remember. I pointed out to him that, when a house becomes infested with rats or other vermin so that one can no longer call it one's own, one doesn't hesitate about calling in the rat-catcher." Sir Richard became suddenly flustered and crimson, and stammered, "See here, old man, I do beg your pardon. I didn't mean——"

Hero smiled at him amiably and said, "Not at all. I think your point is very well taken. Very well then, my fee is two hundred and fifty guineas, plus expenses incurred, and there are several conditions attached to my taking this case. Have you the authority to accept them?"

"Yes, Lord Paradine has agreed to leave it to me."

Hero knocked the ashes from his pipe, reloaded it, and got it going. He said, "You realize, of course, that I have no police powers whatsoever. No crime has been committed, and even if one were, I should have none in my capacity as an investigator of psychical phenomena. Hence no one is compelled to give me any information whatsoever, to answer any questions, or even tell me the truth. In matters of this kind people are often incapable of telling the truth even though they wish to do so. They claim to have seen things they have not seen, and more often than not have not seen things they ought to have noticed. I therefore have to conduct the investigation upon my own lines. I gather since Lord Paradine, through you, is agreeing to a stiffish fee, I will be able to count upon some co-operation from him and the members of his household."

"Oh yes, yes," Sir Richard assured him a little too quickly. "I am quite sure that you can. There will be no difficulty about that. We will all do our best."

Hero said, "Thank you," and filed away the mental note that there would be in all probability precious little co-operation. "I should have preferred to be able to work for a little with my identity concealed, but since you have already discussed the possibility of my coming I should say that was out the window. Very well then, I am to be given the free run of Paradine Hall at all hours; my instructions, when I give them, are to be obeyed without question, and once this investigation has begun, it must be carried through to the finish—no matter how unpleasant it may turn out and for whom. . . ."

Lockerie repeated, "Unpleasant? I don't quite understand, Hero. When the safety of innocent young girls is being threatened

in a revolting and disgusting manner, what further unpleasant-
ness . . . ?"

Hero dropped another card into his mental filing cabinet:
"Girl" had now become "girls." Who was the other? "Quite so,"
Hero remarked, and after a moment's reflection said, "The whole
trend of psychical research and investigation into phenomena has
shifted within the last twenty-five years. It is as though we have
emerged from the Dark Ages. Ramifications are endless. Sometimes in these investigations people get hurt. The point to which
I must ask you to agree is that, if I am engaged, I cannot be dismissed from this case for any reason unless I should decide myself
to pursue it no further. In other words, I can resign but you cannot
sack me. However, if I do not succeed in putting an end to the
manifestations at the Hall there will be no fee."

Sir Richard said, "Your conditions are unusual, but I do think
I see your point. I will accept your terms on my own responsibility
and try to make the necessity clear to Lord Paradine."

Hero nodded. "Very well, then. I shall be finished with some
work I am doing today; tomorrow is Sunday—I will arrive at the
Hall by car sometime tomorrow evening before dinner. In the
meantime, may I enlist your intelligence and level head in the
cause of observation? Oh, and one thing more—before you return
I suggest you pay a visit to an ironmonger and secure a number of
strong, old-fashioned bolts. Fasten one to the inside of the door of
Miss Marshall's room, and the room of anyone else you consider
threatened or about whom you are anxious. It might not be a bad
idea to put bolts inside all the rooms."

"A bolt!" cried Sir Richard. "Would a bolt be of any use against
a ghost or poltergeist or whatever it is that is loose at the Hall?"

"No," replied Mr. Hero, "but it would confine things strictly to
that element, and at least halves the possibilities for further un-
pleasantness."

When Hero opened the door to permit Sir Richard to leave,
Mrs. Harris practically fell into the room, but was not a bit put
out and merely said, "Oh, is the gentleman going? I was just
coming to see if you mightn't be wanting a spot of tea. I'll just
get on with me dustin', then."

When he returned from the front door she was still flicking imaginary specks from already gleaming furniture. She said, "Coo, that was a long one, wasn't it?"

Hero said, "Yes," almost absent-mindedly, and then, "Be a good girl—pack a bag for me for tomorrow, for a week in the country. You do it so beautifully." And then, smiling to himself, he asked, "What do you think?"

Mrs. Harris said, "I couldn't rightly 'ear everything through the door, but 'e seemed to 'ave the wind up proper, didn't 'e, for a gentleman?" Then suddenly fixing him with her beady eyes, she said sternly, "And don't *you* go getting yourself into trouble now, do you hear? What with all the lights going out, and nuns, and rabbits and things—we don't want you going and getting *yourself* 'urt."

Hero said gravely, "I'll try not to for your sake, love. Run along and pack the bag—and don't forget to put in black tie and enough evening shirts."

Mrs. Harris had the last word. "Coo," she said, "not enough to 'ave to be where spooks are, you've got to dress up for 'em."

Mr. Hero went over to the wall and got down his copy of Burke's Peerage.

Burke had a good deal to say—four columns' worth—about the Barons Paradine of Paradine Hall, whose lineage and title went back to 1462, and Hero made himself a précis of the living, noting that the late Thomas, Lord Paradine had died in 1956 at the age of eighty, his wife predeceasing him by nine years, and that he had three children: John, the present Lord Paradine, born in 1902; the Hon. Philip, born in 1904, and deceased; and the Hon. Isobel, born 1916, still living and unmarried.

He raised a slightly surprised eyebrow at the marriage that John had contracted in 1928 to someone apparently of no lineage whatsoever, by the name of Enid Clay. He observed further that John and Enid had issue—a boy, Mark, born in 1932, and a daughter, Elizabeth, who saw the light of day four years later. The eyebrow went up again. The Paradines of Paradine Hall apparently had of late almost made a habit of marrying out of their class, for here was the Hon. Philip espousing in 1929 a lady by the name of Viola Snape. Both the Hon. Philip and his wife were deceased, sole issue of this marriage being a boy called Frederick. This would be the one referred to as Cousin Freddie.

Hero closed the thick volume, reached for the telephone, dialed, and when the receptionist at the other end said, "Barbizon, Court Photographer—good afternoon," Hero asked absentmindedly, "Is Meg there?" and then corrected himself. "Oh! I beg your pardon. May I have a word with my stepsister, please— Lady Margaret Callandar. This is Alexander Hero speaking."

When she came on he said, "Hello, Meg—Sandro. Busy?"

His stepsister replied, "I have a sitter, but if I leave him alone for a moment he may be able to get his jaw muscles relaxed and relax the fixed stare. How are you, my pet?"

"Flourishing. Look here, I've just been called in on a case. I may be needing your help."

Meg sounded enchanted. "Lovely," she said. "Do I drop everything?"

"Not yet. But I need a little gossip. You wouldn't by any chance be free for dinner tonight, would you?"

"Yes, I would."

"The Antelope, at eight?"

"I'd adore it."

"See you," concluded Hero, and hung up, and did not seem to find it at all strange or unusual that a girl as attractive and popular as the Earl of Heth's daughter should invariably be free when he needed to talk to her.

There was a pleasant fug going on the second floor of the Antelope, created by smoke, ale fumes, and people, by the time Mr. Hero and his stepsister tested the light, flaky crust of their steak and kidney pie. The Lady Margaret Callandar—the family name of the Earls of Heth—was a tall girl with a wry sense of humor and a light manner which concealed her enormous competence not only as a photographer but in everything else she did. Only daughter of the once widowed Earl of Heth, whom Hero's mother, likewise widowed, had married in 1934, when Alexander was eight and Margaret five, she was at the age of twenty-nine already in partnership with Barbizon, the court photographer, and her portraits had taken prizes at a number of exhibitions.

However, in addition to her studio work there was very little she did not know about photography. She had had a year on the street for the *Express* with a news camera, had worked and studied in the Eimar Teknikon factories and laboratories in Germany, and included in her knowledge of camera work were a number of things that would have shocked and scandalized some of her royal patrons. It was because of her little bag of tricks as well as her intelligence and understanding that Hero sometimes called her in to assist him.

However, at the moment it was another facet of his many-sided stepsister that was engaging him, but he waited until some of the gusto with which she tackled her pie and beer had subsided. She finished a glass of the light lager, set it down, and said, "Now, my pet, you may satisfy my curiosity: who is haunting whom, and where?"

"Paradine Hall," replied her stepbrother, "and as for the 'who' and 'whom' . . ." He did not finish the sentence but permitted himself a slight shudder, while Meg regarded him with grave, interested eyes.

"Oh," she said, "is it that bad?"

"It just isn't very nice, and that's a fact," Hero said. "Let's have another beer, and I'll give you the details."

He began with Sir Richard's visit and everything that Lockerie had told him, and when he had concluded Meg sat silently for a moment in deep thought before she said, "Yes, I see. It might not be very nice at all." Then she looked keenly into her stepbrother's face and asked, "What is it that is worrying you most?"

Hero said, "The harp."

"Oh?" said Meg in surprise.

"Harps don't play in locked and empty rooms."

"Nor chairs move, nor lights go out for no good and sufficient reason . . ." Meg mused.

"Look here, there are some things you may be able to tell me. Who was Enid Clay—that is, the present Lady Paradine?"

Meg threw her head back and eyed the ceiling for a moment, and Hero was momentarily aware of how handsome she was. She had golden tawny skin, unlike the usual English pink and white, and her russet-colored hair was turned under at the neck in a soft and weighty roll. Her eyes were hazel, and beautifully shaped, her mouth generous and full and highly expressive of the sudden inner amusements that illuminated her.

"Clay—Clay?" she repeated. "Wasn't there something just recently? Oh, I remember—her father, Harvey Clay, who manufactures all the beer bottles, just married a little bit from Chelsea with straw-colored hair and a nose like a pig, and he's going to leave all his money to her when he dies. Of course the Paradines are perfectly furious. They were counting on it, you see, so that they wouldn't have to operate Paradine Hall as a country club any more, though I really think Lord Paradine likes it, in a way." She brought her eyes down from her look back into memory, and with an expression of virtue and satisfaction poured another draught of beer into her glass, remarking, "A Clay bottle, no doubt."

Hero looked across the table at her with amusement and affection. "You couldn't sort that out a bit for me, could you?"

"Little Enid's claim to fame was that she was the first British debutante whose daddy bought her a press agent for her very own. Thirty years ago she was called 'The Flaming Debutante.' From her pictures, she was a raving beauty—red hair, you know. When she bagged John Paradine her father gave her five thousand pounds for a wedding present and settled another ten thousand on her. But of course it was the expectations which were really important to the Paradines. Now, of course, with Papa Clay prancing and arching his neck with his new wife, that's all out of the window. I was once at the Hall for a shoot with Daddy, while old Lord Paradine was still alive, but that was so long ago I hardly remember anyone but Isobel."

"Oh yes—Isobel," Hero echoed.

"Astonishing creature. Should have been a queen. Snow Queen. Some Vikings must have intruded into the family somewhere. Her hair was so light it was almost silver, and I remember she had the most wonderful eyes and presence."

"Unmarried, according to the indispensable Burke," commented Hero.

Meg said, "Disappointed in love, I think, and devoted herself to her father. Ran the Hall for him. When he died and the new Lord Paradine took over, she stayed on at the job—little Enid just couldn't cope. I've forgotten the story, but I'll dig it up for you if you like."

Hero asked, "What kind of a chap is Paradine?"

Meg leveled her knife at the far corner of the room like a sporting piece, and gave it both barrels with two clucks of her tongue. "Right and left, old man," she said. "Frightfully sporting, I understand, and very little else in his head. Supposed to be an all-right sort when you get to know him. Incidentally, one hears that his wife is rather under Isobel's thumb. She runs the place."

"Oh," Hero said, and made another mental note. "Ever hear of an American girl named Susan Marshall?"

"Her father was First Secretary at the American Embassy in London for five years. I think he's been assigned to Switzerland now."

Hero said, "Encyclopedia, I love you."

"I know," Meg remarked, "if I were a woman you'd marry me." Then suddenly she queried, "What's Sir Richard doing in all this, by the way? I know he's a neighbor of theirs, but——"

Hero told her, and Meg said, "Oh yes, of course. His boy must be of school age. I knew there was something I had forgotten— I remember now. Isobel was once supposed to be in love with him, or he with her, but he went off to war and married a girl from the French underground, and that ended that. They had a child, and then she died—the French wife, I mean. If Sir Richard wanted to resume with Isobel, this might be an opportunity, might it not?"

Hero said, "My impression was that Isobel is a resigned spinster and that Sir Richard's interests are otherwise engaged."

Meg said, "M-m-m, yummy! Gossip!"

"The American—Susan Marshall," Hero declared. "It was all sort of fun and games and musical chairs until something nasty got into her room one night and had her by the throat. That put the wind up Sir Richard for fair. I gather he practically dragooned Lord Paradine into engaging me, with some assistance from Isobel, since the rumpus seems to have begun in her rooms. Apparently sister Isobel didn't like whoever or whatever throwing Father's picture down from the wall."

Meg asked, "Is it all true?"

Hero replied, "Half of it, perhaps—a quarter, even, if I'm lucky."

"When will you go there?"

"Tomorrow."

Meg looked at her stepbrother with a curious expression on her face. "You're pleased, aren't you?" she said.

"Yes, enormously," he said. "The harp, you know—for the first time it looks as though there might be a breakthrough. If I could hear it with my own ears, see it with my own eyes—just once——"

His lean face had become fired with excitement and enthusiasm, and his stepsister watched him with a wistful smile as she concluded for him, "Just once—something genuine. And what if it isn't?"

The light went out of Mr. Hero's face and his mouth set in the hard lines that made his stepsister sometimes a little afraid of him. "Then they'll wish they had never been born," he said.

There was a silence between them then for a moment, after which Hero said, "Look here, Meg, with a nun dead some four hundred years supposed to be gliding about the place, and people ready to swear that they have seen her——"

"You may be wanting me," Meg said.

"Yes."

Meg toyed with a piece of bread, molding it between her long fingers. She said, "Call me if you think you need me, Sandro—I would come immediately, you know that. Don't wait too long." She laid one of her graceful hands upon his arm and said, "I don't like any of this. Please take care of yourself."

Hero nodded rather absent-mindedly, for he was occupied with reflections upon what she had told him, and therefore was quite unaware of the urgency and concern in her voice, or the tenderness of her eyes as they rested upon him.

Alexander Hero, private investigator of the supernatural, member of the Society for Psychical Research, dehaunter of houses, and unrelenting enemy of the fakers and swindlers of the occult world, driving his cream and black Bentley Countryman across the Suffolk border into Norfolk, gave himself up for the moment to the enjoyment of the countryside. He would be there before lunch now, instead of the late afternoon, as he had promised Sir Richard. He had acted upon impulse and departed in the morning. He had not even bothered to try to analyze the impulse. He believed that hunches had a sound psychological basis and usually a sensible purpose behind them. A more superstitious person, or one less versed in the intricacies of the human mind, might have taken this sudden urge that Hero had felt that morning to get on down to the Hall without further delay as a kind of answer to a clairvoyant cry for help. Had Mr. Hero stopped to work it out, he would have realized he did not need clairvoyance—the cry for help had been inherent all through Sir Richard Lockerie's visit.

He had not been back to Norfolk since his Cambridge days, and with a thrill of satisfaction he recognized that special pale blue of the sky, that essentially Dutch blue that went with the flat landscape so like that of the Netherlands across the North Sea. And there was more of it the farther north he drove. Nowhere in England did there seem to be so much sky as in Norfolk, for there was nothing to relieve it but the occasional arms of a windmill or the square Norman tower of a flint church in some distant village rising from the marshes.

He smiled to himself happily, almost like a schoolboy, at his first sight of the triangular sail of a yacht afloat apparently on a plowed field—a sight to be encountered nowhere else in the world, for here in Norfolk the dikes of the canals were built up so that often there was no water visible, and the boats appeared to sail magically over dry land. Here too, as the heavy car rolled along the flat road between Norwich and Yarmouth toward East Walsham, Hero experienced that well-remembered sensation of a land that was almost afloat—earth, one felt, that ought to rise and fall with the North Sea tides, as a breast moves gently breathing in sleep. A rich and pleasant land—he had driven past a vast estate and the fields were full of golden pheasant. And he thought of Meg's graphic description of Lord Paradine and the shooting there would be in the autumn. He forged farther eastward, gulls circled overhead, and the reeds and marshes close to the sea, Hero knew, would be full of waterfowl nesting and feeding.

Hero checked the mileage and the time on the dashboard of his vehicle; fifteen miles, another half hour, would see him comfortably there. He was not a fast driver—he liked to enjoy the road and to see all there was to be seen. Hero's taste in cars was rather characteristic of him: expensive—the best there was—but practical. His was no low-slung sports model but a special body constructed to his own specifications and embodying, as he liked to point out to anyone who was interested, all the features of a ten-room house. The interior of the saloon body could be converted into a shooting brake and luggage carrier. With a few moves it could be turned into two beds. There were further compartments which enabled him to point out his bar, library, office, kitchen, and washroom.

The day was clear, bright, warm, and sunny. Five miles from his destination Hero could already see, rising above the tops of the trees in the park in which it was set, the square Tudor east, west, and central towers of Paradine Hall, and two miles to the east the church and village of East Walsham. He looked at his watch—it was a quarter to twelve.

Mr. Hero wondered what reception would be accorded an investigator, apparently already not too popular with the lord of the manor, who turned up unannounced for lunch, when he was scheduled to arrive before dinner.

He was not at all prepared for what he found upon his arrival there, and the welcome, if such it could be called, that was bestowed upon him.

Hero drove his car up the broad avenue of approach, with its splendid opening up of park, moated garden and the stately Tudor manor hall. He turned left around a gravel drive and parked the car alongside several others drawn up in what seemed to be a parking space opposite the east wing of the Hall, which consisted of two such great wings and towers, and surmounted by a central tower that was almost a belfry in size and shape, and reigned over a scattering of dormers and tall thin red brick chimneys. He noted, but at the time did not register, the fact that there was some construction going on on the grounds in front of the house, apparently something to do with the drains, for there was a deep ditch with a barrier and several lanterns hung from it to be lit as warnings at night, and also what appeared to be a large conservatory window boarded up.

As always when approaching a house reputed to be haunted, Hero felt his mind and pulses quickening. Though by profession he was the dispeller of ghosts, called in when manifestations of the supernatural threatened the value of properties or the health or lives of inhabitants, by nature he was a pioneer and a seeker after truth. In spite of many disillusionments, there was always the chance that the next time might see the barriers broken through and the genuine establishment of communication with the other side of the hitherto impenetrable veil.

Hero glanced at his calendar watch; it was shortly before twelve o'clock of a Sunday morning, the tenth of July. He proceeded to the doors beneath the central tower and sounded the bell. There was a long wait and no one came, so he rang again.

This time the carved oaken doors were swung open by exactly the venerable type of butler he expected to see. Hero said, "Would you be so good as to announce my arrival to Lord Paradine. The name is Hero—Alexander Hero. I am expected."

The butler looked worried. "I am afraid I cannot disturb his lordship at this moment," he said. "They are about to begin the —ah—the ceremony."

Hero looked up in surprise. "Eh?" he said. "What's that? What ceremony?"

The butler replied somewhat stiffly, "That is not for me to say, sir." He indicated a small anteroom. "Would you care to wait in here, sir, until it is over?"

Hero decided upon intransigence. "No," he said succinctly, "I would not." He extracted a card from his case and handed it to the butler. "Would you please hand this at once to Lord Paradine, or if he is not about, see that it reaches Sir Richard Lockerie."

The butler returned in a few moments and said, "Will you come this way, sir?"

For an instant as he was led through the high double doors into the oak-paneled and bannered great hall, Mr. Hero was under the weird impression that he had somehow managed to blunder into a moving picture or television studio just before the shooting of a scene, that static moment when the actors stand about in little groups, frozen like statues, or on spots designated on the floor by chalk marks, until the action-shout of the director and the whir of camera motors galvanize them into motion.

At the center of the vast hall, by the twenty-foot-long oak refectory table, stood a gray-haired clergyman in his white and black Church of England vestments, pink-faced, wavy hair nicely parted, and wearing steel-rimmed spectacles. In one hand he held an open book, in the other an asperge for the sprinkling of holy water from an earthen patera resting on the table. There were some thirty people standing about in various groups and odd little clusters in the hall, and the effect was all the more curious because the women seemed to be dressed up as though for church, and were wearing their hats, while the men were clad in country suits or tweed jackets and stood, ill at ease, with their hands crossed before them.

The full complement of the staff at Paradine Hall seemed to be there, and could be identified by the discomfort of grooms, gardeners, and chauffeurs in their white Sunday collars and the uniforms of those who were still on duty. As Mr. Hero entered the hall all of the static figures stirred suddenly and, as though animated by one impulse, turned their heads to look at him. The clergyman too somewhat testily closed his book, put down his asperge, and turned to glare over the steel-rimmed spectacles upon the intruder.

"Oh, Lord!" thought Mr. Hero. "There's going to be an exorcism. I should have come earlier." It was his experience that the one thing that ghosts, real or fancied, did not react to in a kindly manner was the service of exorcism. Well, it was obviously too late to stop it now, but he was glad he had come when he had. He had not the slightest doubt that trouble would result.

s he followed the butler into the hall Hero looked for and found the figure of Sir Richard Lockerie standing next a going-on-elderly man of medium height, with thinning sandy hair and rather protruding eyes. This, then, would be Lord Paradine.

Hero, who was something of a physiognomist, tried to win some information from his features as he approached him. The slightly too small mouth, partially concealed by a nondescript moustache, had some of the petulance of the autocrat, but the expression about the eyes was that of a basically innocent man. At that particular moment Paradine was looking uneasy and uncomfortably embarrassed, and Hero guessed that it was the average male's repugnance at being involved in any kind of religious ceremony.

Sir Richard came forward and greeted him warmly: "Hero—delighted to see you. This is a surprise, isn't it? We hadn't expected you until this evening. Lord Paradine, may I present Mr. Alexander Hero?"

Paradine's welcome was markedly less enthusiastic. He extended his hand almost absent-mindedly and said, "How do you do. So glad you could come."

The clergyman in his vestments came over, causing Lord Paradine apparently more embarrassment. Sir Richard too seemed suddenly somewhat ill at ease. The ex-soldier said, "Mr. Witherspoon, may I present Mr. Alexander Hero, who has come here—ah—to assist us."

The vicar extended a likewise limp hand and said, "How do you do. I understand you have been called in because of the—ah—rather unhappy manifestations here. However, your presence may not be necessary. I have persuaded Lord and Lady Paradine to permit me to conduct the service of Exorcism of Evil Spirits, which I am about to begin now, and which I hope will rid the premises of these spirits forever."

An extraordinarily large, fat, and gross young man of some twenty-nine years, with lank hair, polyp mouth, and insolent eyes said to Hero, though he had not been introduced, "The Rev's going to get his licks in first. You'll have to get in line, old boy, what?"

Lord Paradine and Sir Richard simply ignored the young man and his remark, and Hero did likewise, replying noncommittally to Mr. Witherspoon, "Yes, I see."

"You have no objections, have you?" asked the vicar with more aggressiveness than seemed to be called for.

If there was such a thing as a spot, Mr. Hero was well aware that he had been put on it, and that his answer was awaited with more than casual interest. He was aware of hostilities. He had no time even to look about him, but within range of his observant glance in one group Hero noted a stunningly handsome dark-haired girl and a young man with red hair, and nearby an exquisitely slender and well-groomed woman with pale skin, pale, intense eyes, and moist red mouth. She was standing next to a man who had army written all over him, and a squat, tweedy woman with a broad seat and blue-tinted hair, who was obviously the horsewoman type.

"I should have preferred the opportunity of looking about a bit first, but since you are prepared to begin I have no objection."

Mr. Witherspoon said, "Now that is very wise of you, young man," in a voice that was slightly patronizing. "I shall use an Anglican reformed version of an old service from the seventeenth century. Do you know it?"

Hero replied, "I know some dozen services of exorcism, but it doesn't very much matter which one you use, as long as the heart is pure and the purpose sincere—otherwise it is likely to prove dangerous."

The vicar looked at Hero sharply but could find nothing in the young man's expression at which to be offended.

Lord Paradine said, "Yes, yes, of course. Could you hold off just a sec, Padre? Enid, this is Mr. Alexander Hero."

Hero bowed to the bored-looking woman with the red hair and remains of what once must have been extraordinary beauty, whose limp hand rested in his for a moment, and who was Lady Paradine.

"My sister Isobel."

"Ha!" Hero thought. *"The one under whose thumb Lady Paradine is supposed to be. And I can well imagine it."* Hers was apparently a genuinely cordial greeting. The hand she gave him was firm, and the smile open and gracious. She said, "You are most welcome here." With her fair, silvery ash hair, long face, and greenish eyes, she was easily the most striking figure there. She was elegantly clad, but he had the feeling that the hat she wore belonged to another decade, as though she had not worn hats for a long time.

"My daughter Beth and my son Mark," Lord Paradine said, "and this is Susan Marshall, who is staying with them."

Hero liked the three instantly. The two girls were of an age, the son, Mark Paradine, was older. He had inherited some of his mother's looks but there was an air of authority and vitality about him that Hero found attractive.

Hero recognized the type of the Hon. Elizabeth Paradine immediately—the too sheltered British girl of too overpowering parents, the pallor, the shyness, the tremulousness accentuated no doubt by the recent happenings at the Hall. Yet even in that moment of introduction he was aware of yet another element to the confusion and unhappiness she seemed to mirror, but he could not gauge what it was. Beneath the surface of her pink and white prettiness and shyness lay some acute kind of misery.

The contrast between her and her American friend, Susan Marshall, was so marked as to cause Hero to smile inwardly and paraphrase, *"Extrovert and introvert make the best of friends."*

Susan Marshall was an American beauty but not the ordinary kind. For while she had all of the physical attributes demanded of its women by that nation—the perfectly proportioned athletic figure, clean, handsome features, with clear brown eyes and fine white teeth, dark, glossy hair, and red gypsy mouth—there was also an unusual self-awareness, self-possession, and what seemed to be a persistent enjoyment of living, coupled with frankness and intelligence. There was no denying, Hero thought to himself, that Susan Marshall was a person, and a highly attractive one.

His admiration must have showed in his own face and eyes for it brought forth an equally warm smile from the girl and a sturdy handclasp. She said, "I'm glad you've come—very glad." Her voice, he noted, was as pleasant as she, and held no trace of locality. He judged that she had been educated abroad.

"Dick," Paradine commanded Sir Richard, "you do the rest of the honors."

From Sir Richard, Hero had already had a fair description of the guests of the Country Club, besides which he had memorized the list of names given him. Now he was meeting and estimating them in the flesh, and finding that Lockerie's observations and judgments had not been far wrong. Mr. Jellicot was indeed a rotund little Mr. Pickwick, popping with importance and suppressed excitement. He was familiar from photographs with the monkeylike features of Dr. Paulson, in which he was surprised to observe a faint hostility as he was introduced. The iron-gray engineer, Ellison, acknowledged the introduction with no show of interest whatsoever. Horace Spendley-Carter was fulsome, expansive, and effusive, his wife wan and plaintive. Hero was not quite prepared for the almost pathetic ugliness of the child, Noreen, who was attached to them. He remembered that Lockerie had said that Major Wilson, the army type, had a blonde wife, but had not expected the exquisite intensity and hunger of the pale, slender woman who held his hand at introduction several seconds longer than the others and challenged him with her gaze. The Major with the underslung chin and cold eyes was definitely hostile. He did not even bother to shake hands but merely nodded his head and grunted. The stout, horsy widow with the slightly blued hair, Mrs. Geraldine Taylor, was exactly as described. And finally, the gross, rude young man was, of course, Cousin Freddie, Lord Paradine's nephew, who gave him a flabby hand and said, "Welcome to Madame Tussaud's Waxworks—Chamber of Horrors below, sixpence extra."

When the introductions had been finished and there was a momentary buzz of conversation, Sir Richard's embarrassment revealed its source as he murmured sotto voce, "Sorry about this, Hero—it was rather sprung on me. When the vicar heard you were engaged he insisted upon an immediate——"

Hero asked, "Who told him I had been engaged?"

Sir Richard dropped his voice still lower and replied, "Cousin Freddie. He can always be counted upon to muddle matters." And then added, "I don't suppose you hold with this sort of thing?"

Hero said, "I don't mind personally. When there's black magic about it doesn't hurt sometimes to have a bit of white on hand. But it has been known occasionally to bring matters to a head, and often with unpleasant consequences. Well . . ." The unfinished sentence, and his glance toward the vicar, who was now preparing to proceed, implied that they would not be long in finding out.

The Rev. Harry Witherspoon, the ancient leatherbound volume open in one hand, the asperge dipped into the chalice of holy water in the other, now moved to the center of the hall, knelt, and began, "O Holy Lord, Almighty Father, Eternal God and Father of Our Lord Jesus Christ, Who didst one time consign that fugitive and fallen tyrant into everlasting hellfire, Who didst send Thy Sole-begotten into the world to crush that spirit of evil . . ."

Mr. Hero felt a sudden pang of sympathy for him, for his simplicity and evident sincerity. Where a moment before he had been the pushing and even aggressive busybody human intent upon his own will and ideas, an aura of dignity had descended upon him. He believed and, because of this, for that moment was in command.

Hero, standing beside Sir Richard, took rapid note of those who like himself and Lockerie remained standing, and who did not. Lord Paradine remained upon his feet, an expression of flushed exasperation upon his face, but Lady Paradine was kneeling, as was her sister-in-law Isobel. The latter suddenly appeared to Hero as exquisitely and strikingly medieval. There was nobility in the poise of the silvery head and a quiet tenderness of expression about the mouth. She was giving herself to the moment. Hero

thought that perhaps Isobel was one who was not likely ever to
hold anything back.

Mrs. Wilson had assumed the devout attitude next to Beth,
but her eyes were roving. He was not surprised to see Susan Marshall remaining erect with a kind of fierce and unbending pride
that was yet not antagonistic. Whatever her beliefs, it seemed
apparent from her bearing that she was prepared to yield the
spirit but not the body. Her physical person belonged to herself.
She was well in control of Susan Marshall and would be difficult
to capture, Mr. Hero thought. Mark Paradine's red hair flamed
at her side, close to her own dark chestnut mane. His gaze, as rapt
as that of a young knight watching over his armor, was bent not
upon the praying cleric but upon Susan. *"Well! Scion of the
Paradines head over heels in love with American girl. So, with
slightly more reserve, is handsome neighboring baronet."*

The twelve-year-old child was kneeling beside her mother, Mrs.
Spendley-Carter, but Hero caught her stealing a look up at him
out of the corners of her eyes, and had to control an impulse to
wink at her. He was sure had he done so she would have burst
into a shrill giggle. All of the men rebelliously kept to their feet,
with the exception of Mr. Jellicot.

The vicar arose from his knees, sternly made the sign of the
cross, and intoned, "I command thee, unclean spirit, whosoever
thou art, along with all thine associates who have taken possession
of this house, that by the mysteries of the Incarnation, Passion,
Resurrection and Ascension of Our Lord Jesus Christ, by the
descent of the Holy Spirit and by the Coming of Our Lord in
Judgment, thou shalt tell me by some sign or other thy name
and the day and the hour of thy departure."

Paradine was looking fierce and Hero felt almost that he could
read his thoughts, adding to the clergyman's banishment his own
version, *"—and if I catch any more of you playing your tricks in
my house——"* The investigator turned his head, to be caught
fully by the gaze of Major Wilson's wife; she had been staring
at him frankly and unabashedly. Their eyes met and she sent him
a message that was unmistakable. He disentangled himself from
the avid look and found himself watching Susan Marshall again.

What was the mystery about her? Was it the seemingly impregnable citadel of her person? He said to himself, "*Careful, Hero, that way lies trouble.*"

Lady Paradine's eyes were cast down but Isobel's were not; they roved about the great hall, resting upon the cold, polished steel of suits of armor, the warmth of the tapestries, the pennons once carried by now long dead Paradines, and the dark mysteries of the galleries above. Then they fixed themselves upon the exorcist. Hero decided here indeed was the real chatelaine of Paradine Hall.

The Rev. Harry Witherspoon thundered, "I adjure thee, therefore, thou ancient serpent, thou profligate dragon, in the Name of the Spotless Lamb who walked upon the asp and the basilisk, depart from this house, quake and fly afar as we call upon the name of the Lord before Whom hell trembles." He sprinkled holy water in the four cardinal directions.

From somewhere abovestairs there sounded the most appalling crash, followed by a series of piercing screams, each one louder than the next; they seemed to be approaching—flying footsteps were heard. All of those present stood frozen with horror except Mr. Hero, who had been rather expecting it, and who murmured to himself, "Nicely on schedule—but what?"

His question was answered by the figure of an upstairs maid, in uniform, apron, and cap, who came hurtling through the doors of the great hall in a state of shock and terror. But the sight of the assemblage seemed to restore her somewhat, and the next scream died upon her lips. She ran forward, ignoring Lady Paradine, straight to Isobel, clutching at her and crying, "Miss Isobel! Miss Isobel! Oh, my God, I'm so frightened—it's in the young lady's room—Miss Susan's."

Isobel rose to her feet, calm, controlled, unmoved. She said, "Come now, Lucy, pull yourself together. What is it? Surely there's nothing for a grown woman to be frightened of."

The girl made an effort, but her eyes were still panic-stricken and she had difficulty speaking. She gasped, "I went into the young lady's room, and——" The memory of what she had seen apparently overcame her and she suddenly sank to her knees with her face in her hands.

Hero snapped, "Come on!" to Sir Richard Lockerie, picked up Mark Paradine with a nod of his head, and cried to Susan Marshall, "Miss Marshall, will you lead us please to your room—at once, quickly!"

Susan stared at him uncomprehending. "My room?" she said. "But why? I don't understand."

Hero said peremptorily, "Never mind understanding, do as I say. Immediately, please."

She had caught the urgency in his voice now and hesitated no longer but ran with him, Sir Richard, and Mark. Close in their wake was Mr. Witherspoon, still clutching his asperge. Lithely Susan took the stairs three at a time, her dark hair streaming out behind her. At the top she raced down the corridor to the left until she came before a closed door, the one which had been slammed shut by the maid in her fright. She paused before it uncertainly, not from fear or nerves, but from uncertainty as to what it was Hero wished her to do. For the moment he had captured her completely, though she was hardly aware of it.

"All of you stand back," ordered Hero. He turned the knob of the door, pushed it open, and went in. From behind him rang a high-pitched cry, a mixture of hysteria and revulsion. "Satanas! Satanas!" It was wrung from the throat of the vicar, who was looking through the door, the color drained from his face, his mouth open. He was making the sign of the cross convulsively.

Inside the door the room was a shambles. At first sight it looked as though a tornado had struck it and whirled the contents about almost beyond recognition. Covers and bedclothes had been ripped from the four-poster bed, pillows removed from pillowcases and piled helter-skelter on the bare mattress. The floor was a mass of feminine belongings, disorderly heaps of frocks, dresses, tennis clothes, evening gowns, mixed up with nightgowns, negligees, underthings, and tangles of nylon stockings. Coats, shoes, and hats were jumbled in another pile, and there were open suitcases, vanity bags, and a hand trunk littering the floor.

Chests of drawers, dressers, and dressing tables were in an equal state of chaos, the drawers open, make-up and powder spilled out on the glass top, bottles upset, clothes brushes and other toilet articles littered about. Mirrors had been turned to the wall, so likewise had pictures, which hung askew, their backs showing. Things such as glasses, lamps, vases, water jugs, which should have been right side up, had been turned upside down; all the bulbs that ought to have been in the electric light sockets had been taken out and likewise lay on the floor.

Susan Marshall stood in the doorway for a moment next the distressed and frightened clergyman, tears of anger glistening in her eyes and her fine color heightened. She was filled with a kind of irate shame that her intimate garments and possessions so closely related to her personality had been touched and were now exposed to view.

"Oh," she cried, "my room has been frenched! But it isn't funny. It isn't at all funny. It's horrid!"

Mark Paradine was white with rage, his hands opening and closing into convulsive fists for which there was no earthly use. But Lord Paradine cried, "What the devil's the meaning of this? This room's been searched. Isobel, we shall have to get to the bottom of this!"

Isobel went and put her arms about the American girl and said, "My dear, what a very poor joke."

"Oh," lamented Susan miserably, "all my things!" She went to the dresser, where her jewelry collection of innocent bracelets, bangles, a few rings and brooches, and a string of pearls lay in a heap of spilled powder, and Hero said sharply, "Wait, if you please, Miss Marshall—and everyone. Do not touch anything." He stood in the center of the room looking about him, an expression of distaste at the corners of his mouth.

The Rev. Harry Witherspoon had managed to recover some of his composure. He now shouldered his way through the press of those at the doorway staring into the room with horror, saying, "Allow me. Allow me. I must go in. This is terrible—terrible. The exorcism—must be continued immediately."

"No," said Mr. Hero positively, "no more. Another time perhaps, but not now. It has failed."

A harsh, scathing voice made itself heard from the press at the door, savage and mocking: "Oh, come, you aren't going to tell us that you believe in all that mumbo-jumbo stuff!" The attack came from the sardonic elderly soldier, Major Wilson.

Hero replied, "No, I do not, but it ought to be quite apparent to you that something does, and has reacted violently."

Lord Paradine gave an irritable snort. " 'Something'—you mean 'someone,' don't you? Someone's been after something in Susan's room."

Hero answered him with only a kind of half attention, for his eyes and the rest of his mind were still intent upon what had happened to the room and what it suggested to him. " 'Someone,' " he said, "would seem to call rather for a police officer than a psychical investigator."

Mr. Jellicot managed to wedge himself into position for a peek into the room and murmured, "Dear me, the poltergeist was very angry, wasn't it? Someone must have annoyed it." And then added, flushing, "I beg your pardon, Vicar, I didn't mean——"

Paradine, thoroughly exasperated, shouted, "Rubbish, sir!" and then, "I don't need to go beyond the evidence of my eyes. Somebody's been at Miss Marshall's possessions in an effort to find or steal something."

Hero knew now what had struck him as peculiar and even orderly in the disorderly chaos of the room, and he came to a decision. He whispered something to Sir Richard, who in turn did the same to Lord Paradine. His words apparently had a calming effect, and Paradine then turned to those at the door and said, "We're all very sorry this has happened, but this is rather a private matter now, don't you know. If you don't mind, we'd prefer to be ——" He left the sentence unfinished, and then added, "We will have a talk about this later, Vicar. I am sure you'll all excuse us now."

Cousin Freddie interpreted for him. "He means scram," he said, and laughed. "Leave us to our private horrors."

There was nothing for the guests to do but go with as good grace as they could muster, and with obvious reluctance, leaving inside only the members of the Paradine family, including Cousin Freddie, Susan Marshall, Sir Richard, and Mr. Hero.

WHO WOULD HATE
SUSAN MARSHALL?

Hero turned to the confused and angry group standing in the midst of the chaotic room and said, "Sorry for being somewhat highhanded about this, but it is necessary for me to speak with you all privately about the condition of this room."

Paradine remarked testily, "Well, they've gone now. What is it?"

Hero said, "I will ask you all to look at this room again—its condition and the position of the various things in it—but with different eyes."

Paradine said, "Eh? What do you mean, 'with different eyes'? It seems to me plain enough——"

The insufferable Cousin Freddie, who had been as sallow as any of them during the interruption of the exorcism, had recovered now and to re-establish his importance said, "You're not going to try to tell us a ghost did this, are you, old boy?" Actually he was voicing what all were in one way or another feeling or wondering.

Hero replied, "I don't know—but I was asked to come here because some of you, or all of you, had reason to believe that Paradine Hall was being haunted. However, it is something else about the condition of this room I wanted to point out."

Lord Paradine, who was badly rattled, shouted, "I should think it was as plain as the nose on your face what's happened—some thief had been in here and turned everything out, and when I lay my hands on him——"

"I'll break his neck," Mark Paradine concluded for him, and looked as though he would.

Beth said, "I feel so very ashamed—in our house, Susan."

But Susan was narrowly watching Hero's face for the true explanation that she felt was about to come, and Sir Richard said, "If you have any theories, Hero——"

"It isn't a theory," Hero said, "it is a fact. Lord Paradine just used the phrase 'turned out.' The phrase is correct, only the context is wrong. There has not been a search for anything. It is not so much the belongings, it is Miss Marshall herself who is being literally turned out of her room."

Into the shocked silence that followed this statement there broke the gasp of recognition from Susan. "Oh!" she cried. "Why, of course! I can see it now—all the bedclothes removed, everything taken out of my closet and bureau drawers."

Hero's gaze traveled about the room again. "Yes," he said, "that's it, I'm afraid. You will note the suitcases have been opened, the mirrors reversed, pictures turned to the wall, articles turned upside down, wastebasket upset—even the electric light bulbs have been removed. Everything about the room is a kind of dramatization of the American phrase, which, if I remember, goes, 'Here's your hat—what's your hurry?' It is either a warning of some kind or a very strong hint from something or someone that Miss Marshall is not wanted at Paradine Hall any longer."

The force of his words, coupled with the shock of the humiliation she had suffered from the exposure of her possessions, suddenly was too much for Susan. She put her hands to her face and began to sob, and was instantly surrounded by them all with words of comfort. Beth had taken her into her arms, Sir Richard and Mark stood by with that helpless air of males in the presence of women weeping.

Hero watched the group for a moment with his intelligent and observant eyes, and suddenly felt himself filled with a conviction, as his gaze rested a moment upon Lady Paradine and he noted her expression, a conviction that he felt must be utterly ridiculous, and yet there it was. "*Why,*" he said to himself, "*she doesn't care —she doesn't care one single bit. But Isobel does—Isobel cares very much.*" At the moment she was saying, "I am so very sorry. We all feel for you Susan, as though we were your own family and this your own home."

Susan resorted to her handkerchief, blinked, and wiped her tears, and even managed to smile a little. She was again self-possessed and in control. "I'm sorry I made a spectacle of myself," she said. "It all sort of seemed to hit me at once. This—and—

the other." And then she added, "But—but it *is* true, you know."

Sir Richard turned to Hero. "Is it? Are you sure about this?"

Hero replied, "I'm sorry—yes, it is true. Does anyone here know why any one of you, or anyone, would wish Miss Marshall to leave, and who might take this means of making the point?"

"What?" Lord Paradine roared. "Are you suggesting . . . ? Why, that's utterly ridiculous!"

"Certainly not!" snapped young Paradine angrily.

"I think you can safely forget that idea, Hero," Sir Richard said, and he was angry too.

"Or among the guests?" Hero continued imperturbably.

Lady Paradine suddenly spoke up. "But of course there are some quite dreadful people among them."

"They keep Paradine Hall going." The quiet, almost toneless remark came from Isobel.

"But I don't even know any of them—really," Susan said.

"I thought your specialty was ghosts, old boy," said Cousin Freddie.

Hero said smoothly, "I was coming to that next. To the knowledge of anyone here, is there any reason why any entity or supernormal being of any kind should concentrate its malevolence upon Miss Marshall?"

"You forget," remarked the Hon. Isobel Paradine, inclining her regal head toward Hero, "that there have been occurrences in my room too."

"I have not forgotten," Hero replied.

To his surprise, there came a sudden outburst from Beth. "The harp has played," she cried, "we all heard it, and the nun was seen. It's all a part of the legend, isn't it? And there's some awful kind of rhyme—'When the harp strings quiver and you hear the ghostly air, let the Paradines beware! Let the Paradines beware!'" She burst into tears again suddenly and cried, "Oh, Susan dear, I'm so frightened—I don't want anything to happen to you!"

Mr. Hero looked at her. The third ear within him had heard a strange note, and he was asking himself, *"Now that's odd—do you or don't you?"*

Lady Paradine spoke up sharply. "Don't be ridiculous, Beth—Susan Marshall isn't a Paradine."

Mark Paradine made a curious kind of gesture, opening his mouth as though to speak, but then said nothing.

"Maybe the jolly old curse works for anybody on the premises," Cousin Freddie said. "Susan's room used to belong to my father, and he's dead."

Mark went white. "By God, Freddie," he said, "someday I'm going to poke my fist clear through you and let all the air out."

Hero asked, "Is that true about the harp and the nun?"

Isobel replied in a voice that was hardly audible, "Yes, I'm afraid so. We have all heard it. It is a bad omen—it always has been." Then, more loudly, she said, "Susan, my dear, we'll change your room at once. We'll put you in the Restoration room—there's a lovely view of the river from it."

The American girl's dark, handsome head came up in a movement of pride. "Thank you," she said, "but it won't be necessary. I shall stay here. I'm not afraid."

"Oh, good girl!" applauded Hero, filled with admiration. "I suggest that you call the maids and have this room tidied up and restored to order and that, as she suggests, Miss Marshall remain here."

"After what has happened!" cried Mark. "Are you mad, sir?"

"I don't think anything more will," Hero interrupted. "Appeasement doesn't work on any plane, you know. It doesn't do to give in to either mischievous ghosts—or people. If you do, it is always followed by a next step." Then he added with finality, "But I think I can reassure you that there will be no further manifestations of this kind in this room from now on."

"Why?" asked Sir Richard; and drew a grateful look from Mark. "There have already been two—why not a third?"

Hero said, "Because I am here."

Lord Paradine looked at him sharply. "You're very sure of yourself, young man," he said.

Hero replied, "You have to be in my business. The point is that, up to now, ghosts have been noticeably shy in my presence."

An hour later the room had been swept and tidied, the bed made up freshly, and everything therein restored to its place. Susan was in the act of stowing away her underclothing, stockings, shoes, and frocks when Mark Paradine knocked at the open door, shouted, "Hoy! May I come in?" and did so.

"Oh, Mark dear, do go away," Susan said. "I just can't bear having anyone look at my things any more. Now everybody knows what I've got on underneath."

Mark said, "What's wrong with that—particularly when it comes from Paris?"

"Mark, I think you're horrid. Do be a lamb and go away until I've finished."

He went over to her suddenly and laid his hand upon her arm. She had been about to hang away a Cheviot coat of electric blue, and the holding of it was enriching her own heightened coloring. He said, "Don't hang it away, Susan—you'll have to take it down again."

"Why, Mark—what on earth do you mean?"

"I mean that I'm not going to have you stop in this room any longer. I've told Huggins and his wife, and they'll be along to move your things."

With careful deliberation Susan hung the blue coat in the closet and said, "But, Mark, I'm not moving—I'm staying here."

The young man with the red hair said, "Look here, Susan, I won't have it. You've had two nasty experiences here already. The third time——"

"There won't be any third time," Susan said gently. "Mr. Hero said so."

Mark's face began to color to match his hair, and he set his jaw as he said, "And I said you're moving, and not into the Restoration room either, which is down at the end of the hall where no one would hear you if you screamed your head off. I'm having you put into North Wind, next to mine, where I can keep an eye on things."

Susan had gone quite deliberate again, and this time in silence, an icy silence that Mark did not recognize, but he should have been warned, for she was now folding the articles of silk underwear about which she had previously been so shy with great care and even some little ostentation, as she laid each piece away in the drawer. After a little, when the silence had become unbearably oppressive, he said, "Well?"

Susan halted in the middle of a fold. "Well what?"

"Did you hear what I said?"

Susan bent her dark head for a moment so that he could not see her eyes, and picked at a bit of embroidery on a slip. "Mark," she said, "when I was a little girl we lived in a big old dark house in Virginia. There was an attic where things thumped, and it was full of dark rooms, and I used to have a Negro nurse who frightened me with stories about ghosts. My father found out and was very angry. He was angry, too, that I was frightened. He took me in hand and taught me not to be afraid, ever, of anything on two legs or four—or no legs at all. I don't mean to go back. Is that plain?"

"But damn it all, Susan——"

She raised her eyes levelly now and looked into his, and her chin was as truculently thrust forward as his, her color as flaming. "I'm not letting anyone or anything frighten me out of this room, Mark. I'll leave here if you want me to—for good, and not come back—but as long as I'm here it will be in this room. Do you want me to go?"

The young man emitted a groan of exasperation. "For heaven's sake, Susan, be reasonable. Would I want you to leave when I'm so in love with you that I'd go out of my mind if something were to happen to you?"

"Then stop bullying me," Susan said, "and being so British. All you British bully your women, and they curtsy meekly and say, 'La, sir,' and do what you tell them. Well—I don't."

Mark's skin turned another degree closer to the red of his hair. "Oh no, you don't," he said, "not you. I noticed you jumped fast enough when Hero cracked the whip." He mimicked Hero saying, " 'Never mind understanding, do as I say. Immediately, please.' And did you run?"

A mischievous light came into Susan's eyes suddenly. She could not keep the little quirks from the corners of her mouth. "He *is* attractive, isn't he?" she said.

"Oh yes, very. And I suppose you'd jump for Sir Richard too."

Susan's eyes widened with astonishment and she said, "For Sir Richard? Why should I?"

Mark's voice rose. "Oh, Susan, for God's sake, nobody could be that innocent. Don't you know that Sir Richard's in love with you? And I suppose now that chap Hero will come along and——"

Susan then contrived to say the one thing calculated to make any man, but particularly one of young Paradine's flaming disposition, reach boiling point. "Mark," she admonished, "you're shouting."

He did then really, and loud enough to raise the roof. "Certainly I'm shouting," he shouted. "Why shouldn't I shout in my own house? You drive a man to shout. God only knows why I love you. Once and for all—are you going to leave this room?"

Susan replied, "No," but her voice was just a little smaller as she said it.

Mark Paradine turned and slammed out of the room, and the crash of the door as he flung it to behind him made the earlier bang made by the frightened upstairs maid seem like a mere whisper.

Susan stood in the middle of the room holding her slip to her and looking at the door in which the key was still shuddering. "*Why*," she said to herself, "*he really does love me. I wonder whether I could love him back*?" She stood there for another moment, feeling and listening to the pounding of her own heart, but could not tell whether it was from the excitement of the quarrel or whether the young man had really stirred it. Then she got on with her putting away of things and tidying up.

When Susan entered the library Hero was browsing in the pages of a volume that he had fingered down from a shelf. He looked up, closed it, put it back, and said, "Hello. It was very good of you to come."

It was curious, Susan thought, how she could not tell whether she liked him or not. The sensitive features, firm chin, full lips, the somewhat too large nose and broad brow, topped by an unruly crest of light brown hair, were undeniably attractive. There was a repose about his face and demeanor that was pleasing and she felt too that he was a person capable of emotion—strong feeling, passion, anger, and also great warmth and tenderness. And then there was something that she did not like and did not under- stand, and there seemed to be no way of getting at it or finding out what it was. There was no hint of superiority or mockery about him, for Susan knew that she hated that. The eyes, a greenish- gray, that contemplated her were grave and friendly—and yet, in a still undiscovered sense, not. It was there, Susan's feminine in- tuition told her, that the secret of his ability to attract or repel seemed to lie. She found the thought passing through her head: *"One could come to be attracted to him, to like him too much very quickly, and then afterward one might regret it. Perhaps that is what he wants. Be careful, Susan—he's down here on a job."*

Aloud she said, "Huggins said you wanted me to take you about the house. I'm sure that he or one of the family could have done it better."

Hero said, "I don't doubt it. What I really wanted was to talk to you. It was the best excuse I could think up on the spur of the moment. Not very clever, what?"

Susan came directly to the point. "Are you going to ask me about,"—she hesitated—"that night?"

Hero regarded her gravely for a moment and then seemed to make a decision. "No," he replied, "not now. Another time. Now I'd like to find out something about you. Who are you?"

Susan's relief was evident. Her wide mouth broke into a smile and she replied, "Susan Marshall, age twenty-three, spinster, born May 25, 1935, at Roanoke, Virginia."

Mr. Hero fell in with her mood. "Father?" he said.

"William Marshall, First Secretary, U. S. Embassy, Berne."

"Career diplomat?"

"Yes."

"Mother?"

"Helen Marshall, nee Claybourne. Mother is so beautiful she would take your breath away."

Hero said, "That is not an unimportant detail. You've been educated all over Europe then, haven't you?"

"Yes, but mostly in Paris."

Hero said, "There's nothing like it," but did not define what "it" might be. Without changing his tone he asked, "Do you know of anyone here who might hate you?"

"Anyone? In my room you talked about 'something' too."

Hero smiled. "That was in your room," he said.

"Then you think it is—was—a person?"

Hero did not reply to this question; he merely regarded her silently and began to stuff his pipe.

Finally Susan said, "I cannot think of anyone. I don't think I have ever really hated anyone in my life."

Hero nodded. "That is intelligent," he said, "since it is usually hatred that breeds hatred. Now let me ask you something else. Do you know of anyone here who might be in love with you?"

Susan recoiled sharply. "That is a cruel question, and unfair," she cried.

The young man opposite her reacted not at all. Nothing about his expression or the grave contemplation of his eyes changed, and something inside Susan cried, *"Perhaps it is that I don't like about him—his utter and complete self-possession and composure."* She felt suddenly challenged as a woman, and thought, *"I could break that composure—I'll bet I could."* And then as swift as she had been to anger and criticism, she found excuses for him arising within her and she said, "I'm sorry. I suppose it is neither your business nor your concern to be either fair or unfair." She then looked him directly and unflinchingly in the eye and said, "Several."

Hero returned her gaze with just the faintest of smiles as he said, "I can understand that. All right, I shan't ask you anything further on the subject, but it is a beginning. Would it interest you to come about the house with me a bit and see what there is to be seen?"

"Yes," said Susan definitely, "it would, if it wouldn't disturb you."

"Lead the way," said Mr. Hero.

"Where would you like to go first?" Susan asked.

"The music room, if you don't mind."

Susan said, "Oh yes, of course—the harp. I had forgotten that."

"Did you hear it play?"

"Y-yes, I think so, but I'm not sure. I woke up once one night and heard some music, but I thought it was someone playing a radio perhaps."

"M-m-m-h. Did you recognize the tune?"

"No, but I might if I heard it again."

Hero nodded. "And then?"

"Well then, in the morning I heard—Beth told me the harp had been playing during the night. Isobel said it woke her and she got up and went down to see. Lord Paradine was there too, but when they went in there was nobody there."

The music room was one of those opening off the west corridor, but on the north side, facing the river. It contained a grand piano, a metal music stand, and a number of shelves holding music. The floor had been carpeted with an unusually thick pile to deaden the effect of the high ceiling characteristic of all the ground-floor social rooms of Paradine Hall, and Hero noted that the acoustics must be fairly good.

There was a cello in a brown canvas case propped up in one corner of the room. The pictures on the walls were engravings and mezzotints of the classicists—Beethoven, Mozart, Bach, Liszt, and Brahms. The room had been built and decorated for or by someone who knew and loved music.

A golden harp stood over by the window. It had been kept polished and was the large concert model used by soloists and also in symphony orchestras. Hero said, "It belonged to Lord Paradine's mother, didn't it?"

"Yes, I think so."

"Lady Anne Paradine died some eleven years ago. Does anyone play it now?"

Susan said, "I don't know. The room doesn't seem to be used any longer. I mean, it hasn't been since I have been here."

Hero asked, "How long is that?"

Susan replied, "Four weeks. I've been asked to stay here over the summer, you know."

Hero reflected. "And this business began about ten days ago?"

"Yes, I think so."

Hero went over to the harp and stood looking at it, tugging at his lower lip. For a moment he tried to make his mind a blank and himself attuned to whatever there might be about it that was paranormal or supernatural. He had always felt that when the breakthrough came, when something really happened that could not be explained in any other way but that, unseen, beyond the veil, filling the universe above, there palpitated another life, one would feel something—some signal would be given to set nerves a-tensing. He had seen animals react to unseen stimuli—why, then, not people?

Hero was a seeker-out and destroyer of false phenomena and the revolting specimens of humanity who created them, but he felt that somewhere in the welter of all that had been experienced, believed, thought, and reported down through the ages there must somewhere lie some kernel of truth, some visual, aural, or scientific bit of evidence that would confirm man's indestructible hope for and yearning after continuation. He knew all about psychometry and those who professed to be able to read from articles or objects something about those in whose possession or contact these had been; but the harp was telling him nothing. There was only the evidence of his eyes that it was a harp, and the testimony of others that it had played without the aid of any human agency. Still, this was not of importance; the harp was no more than an instrument.

Hero ran a finger chromatically up the scale of strings and then looked at Susan Marshall swiftly. "Are you musical?" he asked.

"No," she replied, "I canot tell one note from another."

"The harp is in tune," he said.

Susan said, "Yes, it was tuned recently."

"By whom?"

"The piano tuner. He was here a few weeks ago. Lord Paradine likes to keep everything in this room exactly as it was when his mother was alive."

Mr. Hero sighed. "Yes, I see." He turned away from the instrument. "Well, that seems to be that."

"Aren't you going to examine it?" Susan asked curiously.

Hero smiled at her. "For hidden radios or music boxes, you mean? There wouldn't be any. That isn't how it played, if it did play."

"But it did," Susan insisted. "At least the others said so, and I'm sure now that I heard it."

Hero did not reply but nodded in the manner of one whose mind was already on something else, and Susan felt a sting of exasperation. Could it be that he did not believe her?

"Is there a refrigerator?" he asked suddenly.

"Yes—in the pantry, next the kitchen."

"Let's have a look at it."

She led him back to the central hall and then along the corridor that formed the T-stem of the T-shaped building where the kitchens, larders, and service pantries were. On the way they passed through one of the smaller rooms on the ground floor belonging to the guests in the Country Club wing, one used for writing and reading. There was also a green baize card table standing in the corner, with a pack of cards thereon showing curiously flamboyant backs. They had almost traversed the room when Hero caught sight of them and stopped. "Hello," he said, and went over to them. Susan saw that they were longer and narrower than those with which she was familiar. Hero turned them over and ruffled through them. They seemed to be foreign, for the pips and the court cards were of a design Susan had never seen before. They also appeared to be a larger pack than the normal fifty-two, and contained pasteboards with both queer kinds of pictures and numbers on them, but what they were Susan could not see.

Hero, however, both saw and recognized them for what they were. "Well," he said, "this is interesting, to say the least." He looked at Susan. "Do you know what these are?"

The American girl shook her head until the dark, heavy hair swung. "No. I've never seen any like them before."

Hero nodded perfunctorily and then without another word

dropped them into his pocket and went on. Susan thought, "*If he is trying to make me ask him what they are I shan't.*"

In the pantry Hero looked over the huge double-doored extra-ice-compartmented electric refrigerator and whistled. "That's a proper one, isn't it?" he said. And then seemed to take no further interest in it, but instead examined other articles in the pantry minutely: the dish towels hung up to dry, the cupboards where glasses and dishes were stored, the soap and the soap dishes, the wire and cotton dishwashers and the bristled scrubbing brushes, the pair of rubber gloves—apparently the property of some servant trying to avoid dishpan hands—the electric appliances, such as mixers and juicers, things movable and attached.

Then, more astonishingly, he began to open pantry drawers in which were ranged kitchen utensils of every kind—knives, forks, spoons, peelers, scrapers, kitchen ladles—all of the things which at any time might be needed for cooking or serving. Huggins came in, slightly shocked and indignant at this invasion.

"Were you looking for something, sir?" he asked.

Hero replied, "Yes," and continued with his inspection. In some drawers he merely glanced, in others he would extract an implement and examine it for a moment before letting it drop back. Susan and the butler watched him wordlessly, caught up in the spell of his concentration. He had the knack of disconnecting himself from anything or anyone outside himself, and seemed fully occupied by his thoughts.

In one drawer there was a nice arrangement of skewers, long, thin, pointed metal rods with a ring at the end, in various lengths used for pinning bacon to fowl, or fastening rolled roasts or the like.

Hero stood looking down at these and then, selecting one, he examined it more closely. He took an envelope from his pocket, extracted the letter therefrom, dropped the skewer into the cover, and restored it to his pocket.

Hero addressed the butler. "I don't suppose any of the candles that were used in the dining room night before last would be about, would they—the ones that went out?"

The butler replied, "No, sir."

Susan wondered how Hero knew, and thought that his next question would surely be, "Why not?" Instead he merely said, "Never mind. We can always make more when we want them." His next request was almost more of a surprise: "Would you show me the fuse box, please?" he said to the butler.

The man led the way to a small stone room where, up on the wall out of reach, was the master switch and a great panel of fuses with a small, grimy printed card under each indicating the location in the Hall that they controlled. There was also a blueprint of the electrical system of the entire house, stables, garages, et cetera.

Hero dragged over an old kitchen chair, stood on it, and first for a few moments regarded the panel keenly with that concentration of look and thought that Susan found so fascinating. If she had been asked to describe how he looked at that moment, she would have said that his was the face of a man who knew what he was doing. Then he reached up and began very gently to test the fuses. Some he loosened momentarily, others he merely touched, and Susan came to the conclusion that somehow it *was* touch that was involved. There seemed to be an extreme sensitivity to his fingers and his use of them.

She could contain herself and her curiosity no longer. "What are you looking for?" she asked. "What on earth have you been looking for all this time?"

"The stuff of ghosts," he replied curtly, and then added, "Later on I may ask you to be both patient and brave, and submit to a rather unpleasant little experiment, and we'll see if we can't stop some of this nonsense that's going on here." He climbed down from the chair and dusted his hands. "There. That's fine."

Susan said with slight indignation, "Do you enjoy being mysterious?"

Hero grinned at her and took her by the elbow. "Come into the garden, Maude," he said, and led her forth.

That night at dinner in the great hall Hero began to confirm and expand his early impressions of the outsiders and temporary residents at Paradine Hall as he watched them in action and listened to them talk to their neighbors or try to hold the table with conversation.

There were three he classified as "no-nonsense" types, and each in his or her way different: Major Wilson was belligerently and aggressively so; Dean Ellison, the stocky engineer, seemed to be completely disinterestedly that way; and Mrs. Geraldine Taylor, the stout, elderly widow, appeared to fall somewhere between the two; she exuded common sense, intelligence, shrewdness, coupled with a most youthful interest in everything that was happening.

That Member of Parliament from an apparently misguided constituency, Horace Spendley-Carter, had done nothing to improve his marks in Hero's book. His moist eyes and lips and booming voice were physical irritants which could be disregarded, but not evidences of a sleazy character which emerged as he talked. Hero concluded that he was a windbag who was a charmer to his constituents and a beast to his family. He was also an opportunist, Hero was certain. If there was political capital or personal profit to be made out of ghosts, he was their man; if not, he would be found in the Major's camp. In the meantime he was going to let nothing interfere with his holiday at Paradine Hall, not even the obvious nervousness and distress of his wife.

Hero looked across the table at Mrs. Spendley-Carter and estimated her: self-centered, weak, neurotic, a perfect foil for a bully like her husband.

Quite the contrary was the opinion he had formed of Mrs. Howard Wilson. She was seated two away from him on the same side of the table, but the powerful French perfume she wore penetrated to him, and sometimes he was aware of the gleam of her hair and caught a glimpse of her sensitive profile. She was an avid, exciting woman and would be a handful for her husband, the Major. This belligerent soldier with his shark's mouth and sly, unpleasant, silent laughter he liked not at all.

He eyed Dr. Paulson: small, spare, dry, positive, and humorless, puffed up with the boundless assurance and arrogance of the modern scientist. Under limp, pale hair his wizened monkey face expressed in every fold the superciliousness inspired by the awesome amount of knowledge compressed within his skull. He thought to himself, "*These fellows really have invented themselves a new religion—whatever can be smashed in a cyclotron. High priests of the atom, they have exchanged the Infinite for the infinitesimal.*"

And then finally there was that enthusiastic, rotund little amateur of psychical research, the lone representative of commerce at the table, Mr. Alfred Jellicot. About him Mr. Hero had not yet made up his mind. He had catalogued him temporarily as likable, possibly harmless, equally possibly at the bottom of all the disturbances at Paradine Hall.

If Jellicot were aware of any inferiority of social position, he apparently tried to make up for it by being as friendly as a puppy and as voluble as a magpie, and was full of gabble from his reading on the subjects of ghosts, poltergeists, and haunted houses. "Poltergeists have been known to infest houses for months, sometimes even years, before anyone succeeds in driving them away," he announced. "Haven't you read Harry Price's books, *Poltergeist over England,* and *Borley Rectory,* and Elliott O'Donnell's *Dangerous Ghosts?* I've read them all, but this is the first time I've ever been *this* close to a genuine poltergeist. Mr. Spendley-Carter has promised to let me have some of the apports which have fallen in his room. I shall exhibit them to a meeting of our society in Manchester. I suppose we must be prepared for a manifestation of the fire ghost soon."

"Eh—what's that?" Lord Paradine interrupted, having heard the end of the speech. "What's that you were talking about, sir?"

Mr. Jellicot was delighted to have the stage thus cleared for him. He replied, "Why, sir, in nearly all of the famous poltergeist cases the unseen, mischievous entity eventually gets around to setting fires—fires that could have no possible other origin or explanation. There was the famous Amherst case in America, the Mill on the Eden, and the incendiary ghost at the Scotch Poltergeist Manor, where seventeen fires broke out spontaneously in the course of a few days."

Hero groaned inwardly. "*Oh, you fat little fool,*" he thought, "*that's asking for it!*" He was well aware himself that incendiarism was a favorite poltergeist trick and recorded phenomenon, and one which very often followed upon earlier, more harmless manifestations, and there was no need to invoke the fire ghost or tip it as to its duties should it be itself only an amateur or a beginner at the game. "*Or,*" Hero's again aroused suspicion demanded, "*is this little fellow himself the poltergeist, and is he thus setting the stage for his next prank?*"

Spendley-Carter could not bear to see anyone else in the rostrum. In one mighty booming sentence he elbowed Jellicot off. "Fascinating fellows, these magical wallahs," he shouted. "Saw one in Cairo once. Put down a sheet of paper with some Arabic lettering on it on the ground. Set a live chicken on it. Incense going and all that sort of stuff. Muttered some kind of mumbo-jumbo. Fowl fell over dead. Explain that, eh?"

In the ensuing silence Hero said, "The bird was poisoned." Everyone at the table turned to stare at him.

Spendley-Carter said, "Eh, what's that you said?"

"I said," Hero repeated succinctly, "the bird was poisoned— either before it was brought in, or during the incense and incantation a pellet of poison, probably cyanide, was introduced into its beak. I can do the trick for you if you like."

"Aha," brayed Major Wilson with some satisfaction, "then you don't believe in all this hocus-pocus?"

"I didn't say that," Hero replied. "I said that particular chicken was poisoned. It's one of the oldest of bazaar tricks, but I've also seen one or two things in the bush that I haven't been able to explain."

Major Wilson snarled, "Poppycock—nigger magic, hysteria, and imagination."

Hero said good-naturedly, "You're very sure of yourself, sir," and Professor Paulson added, "I prefer to accept the testimony of my own eyes and ears. I will swear that this house is haunted after what I have seen."

Hero was suddenly aware that the warm, damp hand of the child, Noreen, had stolen into his and was gripping it. He let it remain there, and a moment later the other hand arrived and with it a soft cheek laid against his fist.

"Twaddle," said the Major, "seeing things."

Spendley-Carter said, "Is that so? How about the poltergeist frightening my wife half out of her wits—and Lord Paradine struggling with the chair?"

"Twaddle," brayed the Major still more loudly, adding, "Nothing but a lot of fancies."

His insistence irritated and rattled Lord Paradine, who had undergone an alarming and unsettling experience. Since the Major was a guest, Paradine therefore turned upon his employee. "What about all this, Hero? You're supposed to be able to explain these things, according to Dick Lockerie—though I must say I don't care very much for your attitude or your methods so far. I know you young fellows have a lot of newfangled theories and notions and I suppose hold meetings in the dark and wave trumpets about, but I don't hold with any such tarradiddle. I am a plain man, we are a plain family, and this is a plain house. There's never been any flimflammery or magic at Paradine Hall. Well, what have you to say?"

All eyes were turned upon Hero to see how he would take a dressing down, but at the moment he seemed to be engaged chiefly in disentangling his left hand from the child. He was saying, "May I have it back, pet? It's gone to sleep."

Sir Richard was flushed red with embarrassment. Cousin Freddie's suety face was split in a happy grin. Susan Marshall felt that if only Hero would show the slightest hurt at this aristocratically rude and unfair attack he would touch her heart. His even-tempered, unemotional, impervious detachment had something frightening in it. He examined his hand for a moment reflectively, as though he had not seen it for some time, then impulsively put his arm about the child's shoulders and gave her a cuddle, while her mother said, "Noreen," disapprovingly, and Spendley-Carter remarked, "You've made a hit with my little girl, old man."

When Hero spoke finally it was without any show of rancor. "I'm afraid I must take issue with you as to that last, Lord Paradine—Paradine Hall is riddled with magic, you know."

Paradine said, "What's that?"

"Oh yes," said Hero. "Would you seat thirteen at table?" He watched the eyes of everyone move swiftly around the table. "We're actually eighteen but you're all counting," he continued, "aren't you—just in case? Also, sir, when you spilled salt during dinner you tossed a bit over your left shoulder."

Paradine began to turn red in the face, and Cousin Freddie guffawed loudly. "I say, he's got you there, Unkie. Touch wood every time, eh?"

Hero addressed himself to the Major. He said, "Before dinner when you lit cigarettes for Sir Richard, Dr. Paulson, and yourself, you snapped out your lighter and then kindled it again before lighting yours. What unseen spirits were you propitiating?"

Mrs. Wilson laughed deliciously, and the Major loosed an arrow of a glance at his wife that fairly seemed to buzz across the table.

Hero continued: "There's a horseshoe nailed over the kitchen door, and another over the entrance to the stables, and a witch's cross on the door of every room in the Hall. Oh, and then there are these," Hero concluded and, reaching into his pocket, he produced a pack of cards which he fanned with the conjurer's smoothness and held up where all could see them. Susan Marshall recognized the cards he had picked up that afternoon.

"The Tarot," Hero said, "the gateway to the locked doors of the future. Their origin is lost in the mists of antiquity. I'd like to know what a pack of middle European gypsy fortunetelling cards is doing in a respectable, plain, non-magical English country home. I'd also be interested in knowing to whom they belong, if anyone would care to claim them."

It was Lord Paradine's turn to redden. He hated to be faced with things he did not understand. He said, "What are you driving at, sir? I thought you were supposed to do away with ghosts. Are you trying to tell us that you believe in them?"

Hero glanced briefly at the fan of cards in his hand, closed them, and dropped them into his pocket with a movement so swift that the eye could hardly follow their disappearance. "In one sense, yes," he replied. "I am compelled to believe in them— or rather, take them on faith, since I have never had the good fortune to encounter one."

There was a titter which caused Lord Paradine to flush and Cousin Freddie to say, "Getting a bit of your own back, eh, Unkie?" which irritated and rattled the baron still further.

Mrs. Wilson stepped into the breach and said, "Then you don't think there's any real danger . . . ?" She had leaned forward to look at him as she spoke, and Hero, finding himself momentarily caught up in her eyes, wondered whether the others were aware of how they betrayed her interest in him.

He replied, "I didn't say that. There is always danger at the border line."

Major Wilson asked, "What border line?"

"Where malevolent spirits tamper with people—or vice versa."

Into the momentary silence that followed while they digested the remark Cousin Freddie's unpleasant laugh cut. "I suppose the 'vice versa' means us, eh?"

Major Wilson likewise laughed, and followed the silent opening and closing of his mouth that denoted this action with an audible snort. " 'Malevolent spirits,' " he repeated, "that's a good one—from an intelligent and supposedly well-educated man. I say!"

Cousin Freddie's eyes glistened at this bit of inexcusable rudeness.

Hero replied amiably, "The trouble, you see, Major—and which we rather tend to forget—is that if there are such things as ghosts or, if you prefer, spirits, they were people first, and what would survive would be that which had animated them. I wouldn't suppose you would change very much after death, would you?" One couldn't quite be sure whether the "you" had been emphasized or not.

Susan Marshall suppressed an impulse to shout with laughter and felt a sudden warm glow for Mr. Hero. The Major, not quite sure whether Hero's ambiguous "you" was general or personal, was momentarily silenced. Not so Lord Paradine, who said, "I don't follow all this theoretical stuff. I wish you would speak plainly, sir—is it your opinion that there is or is not a ghost at Paradine Hall?"

Hero regarded his host coolly for a moment and then repeated, "'Ghost'? I should say rather ghosts—a plurality of them—and for my taste, far, far too many."

In his room the next morning Mr. Hero briefly reviewed the legend of the ghostly nun of Paradine Hall as recounted in Bruton's *Norfolk, Its Ghosts and Legends,* and no doubt source material for such as Jellicot and others at the Hall. The story, Hero noted, ran true to form and was typical of those ascribed to its era, the sixteenth century, when an incumbent Paradine supposedly had seduced a peasant girl betrothed to a local bump-kin. Afterward when the distressed maiden, abandoning a world so cruel where such could happen, entered a convent (St. Relinda's at Wytrim Priory neighboring the Hall, and now in ruins), the wicked Lord Paradine had been unable to forget her. The upshot was that he kidnaped her from the convent and detained her forcibly at the Hall. To acquaint her former lover with her wherabouts the unhappy woman played their favorite air when they had been lovers, "My Bonnie Dear," on her harp at the window of the room where she was confined. Rescue, how-ever, came too late; she and her unborn child were murdered. Nor was any trace of her remains ever found afterward. There-after when the strains of harp music resounded through the Hall at night and the ghostly figure of the nun was seen slipping through darkened corridors, it invariably presaged ill for some member of the family or foretold some coming disaster.

Mr. Hero, after studying the usual compendium of calamities that followed the appearance of the nun in various successive gen-erations—this Paradine killed in the wars, that one lost at sea, another ushered into the next world via the executioner's block—closed the book and mused upon the ways of writers of ghost legends and what they were prepared to have their readers swal-low. Irrespective of the holes already apparent to him in the tale, and the fact that such were not at all unusual ways for Paradines to die in those times, he wondered what further light some check-ing he intended to do on the legend would throw upon it and the goings on at the Hall. For a starter he felt inclined to have a look at the ruins of the nunnery located on the grounds to the west where the river Stoke widened into Stoke Broad, and asking Susan Marshall to accompany him; he wanted to hear her own narrative of the attack made upon her.

His room, which at the suggestion of Sir Richard was located in the west wing, was at the extreme end on the first floor, and the long corridor into which it opened also ran through the central part of the building and into the east wing. It was in a sense a strategic location, and Hero was pleased with it, for it gave him the opportunity of reaching the main portion of either wing quickly in case of nocturnal disturbances. In addition to the main staircase there was a smaller one in each wing. That one nearer his room and a short distance down the corridor led to the library, drawing room, music room, etcetera, below. His windows looked out upon the front of the Hall, the sunken gardens, the tree-lined long driveway, with a glimpse of the hideous white Italian pergolas. Looking out, he saw that Susan and Beth were on the lawn in deck chairs, the light brown head and the dark one close together, poring over magazines. It seemed as good a time to catch Susan as any. He secured his pipe and stick and went out.

On the way he found himself suddenly encountering the Major's wife, who gave a little startled cry and said, "Oh! Mr. Hero." He had the feeling somehow that she seemed to have been lurking somewhere, or was aware of his approach, and had stepped out to meet him at just the right moment. She was wearing a plain, no-nonsense country tweed suit of gray and yet managed somehow to convey that beneath it the underthings were by Chanel.

"I'm Mrs. Wilson," she said. "I'm sure you won't have remembered, but——"

Hero said, "I have remembered very well."

She threw him a swift glance and a half-breathless "Did you really?" and then as though to cover herself, "But of course it is your business to remember people and things, isn't it?

Hero noted how attractive she was in spite of a kind of angularity, and thought that there would not be much in Major

Wilson to warm her flesh into roundness. She was trim, fastidious, and her head was beautifully groomed.

She asked, "Were you serious at dinner when you said there might be danger? I am not a nervous woman, but I have come here with my husband for a rest, and I don't mind confessing that I have been considerably upset by some of the things that have been happening. Howard—that's my husband, Major Wilson—only scoffs at everything, but of course he sleeps through anything at night—he *never* wakes up."

Hero was conscious of the old excitement stirring in his breast again. Was the game on so soon, then? He thought to himself, "*Oh, doesn't he? And is that what you want me to know, my girl?*" He replied, "I don't think you need worry or make yourself uneasy—after all, that is what I'm here for. My job is to see that there isn't any danger. All right?"

Mrs. Wilson nodded, and then said, "If I am nervous—or think I have seen or heard anything—may I . . . ?" She did not complete the sentence but regarded him with her pale, luminous, hungry eyes and the faintest of cat smiles at the corners of her mouth.

Again excitement stirred in Hero: yes, the signals had been unmistakable. He regarded her now as steadily and replied, "Yes, of course. Please don't hesitate."

Mrs. Wilson replied, "Thank you. You have relieved my mind." They then walked on out of the main entrance without any further speech. Hero found himself wondering when it would be and what it would be like.

When they came upon Susan Marshall sitting with Beth, Hero said to Susan, "You're the one I'm looking for, young lady. Come along for a walk with me—I'm going to do a spot of archaeologing, and want to show off."

Susan sighed. "Oh dear! Beth and I were just tearing the fall styles to pieces." But she rose and prepared to join him. Mrs. Wilson gave them a bright smile as they walked off through the park in the direction of the ruins of Wytrim Priory. Mr. Hero was quite suddenly aware that in the presence of Susan the smile and its promise were no longer as attractive as they had been a moment before, and felt annoyed with himself. He was quite sensible to the fact that his weakness was women, and that with Susan Marshall at the storm center apparently of the manifestations that crowded the Hall, this was one entanglement he must avoid at all costs; yet he knew that he was heading for it in almost the same straight line that Mrs. Wilson had taken to him. Mrs. Wilson was exciting, but Susan Marshall seemed unapproachable: was that the secret?

"She's attractive, isn't she?" said Susan, apropos of nothing in particular.

Hero, whose mind had already filed Mrs. Wilson, and who had been disturbed by his own thoughts, said absent-mindedly, "Eh—who? Oh yes, I suppose so." And then found himself harboring a slight feeling of resentment; it was the kind of thing his stepsister Meg would have said. How did Susan know? How did all women seem to know at once when there was something afoot with one of their kind? At the same time his irritation dissolved in pleasure at the fact that she had called him on it. Was there, then, a chink in the armor of this most self-contained person too, and did he only imagine her inviolability because she was a healthy, strong, athletic creature?

The ruins of the priory consisted of the tumbled walls of the cloister, which included two exquisite Norman arches, the foundations where the kitchens had been, the shell of a square tower, which was probably of later construction, and the remains of a small chapel. The Paradine gardeners had not let it become overgrown, and the flint-grained walls rose out of smooth, velvety grass. When they stood inside the enclosure, with the soft, springy turf beneath their feet, Hero looked at the mass appraisingly, pulling at his lower lip. "It's a jumble," he said, "isn't it? There've been at least three additions since the original. Destroyed by fire, too."

"Oh, how clever of you to be able to know," Susan Marshall said. "How do you?"

Hero said, "I cannot tell a lie—I looked it up in a book before I came here."

"Oh," Susan said, "and I was giving you credit for being an expert."

"I am that too," Hero said modestly. "Just you watch me when I begin experting all over the place." He wandered a bit, and then said, "Not very ghostly, is it? We ought to feel depressed, oppressed, and filled with some nameless dread, and all that sort of nonsense. By the way, everything quiet in your sector last night?"

"Yes. The bolt is very comforting."

Hero looked at her curiously. "Yes, is it? Why?"

Susan replied seriously, "Because I'm not afraid of ghosts."

Hero said, "Ah," and then, "I rather wish you were a little. There are times, apparently, when there are things to be afraid of."

Susan looked up at him with some surprise and seemed about to say something, then thought better of it. After a moment she asked, "At dinner last night when they were all baiting you, you said that you thought there wasn't *a* ghost but too many of them: did you mean that?"

"Yes."

"I don't quite understand. What exactly *did* you mean?"

"That there were indeed too many, and rather wanted sorting out. That's one of the jobs I am on now." And that was all he would say on the subject. He walked over to one of the archways and examined it, then fingered some of the stonework of the walls. He said, "I wonder if the chap who wrote that story about the nun of Paradine Hall was aware of the fact that there were no religious houses of any kind in England between the year 1558 and the nineteenth century?"

"Why?" Susan asked. "What would that have to do with it?"

Hero took out a penknife and scratched some of the mortar from the interstices of the stone where it was of a darker color and dropped the powder into an envelope he took from his pocket. "That would depend," he said. "They're doing wonderful things with carbon analyses these days—tell you right to the minute, practically, when the fire laddies were called out." He put the envelope in his jacket pocket.

Susan said, "I hate you when you're being mysterious."

Hero grinned at her. "That's a strong word for a mild irritation—in keeping, I take it, however, with the mode of expression of an American spinster of twenty-three." He looked about him and said, "Lovely blue sky, green grass, crumbling gray walls—nothing very spooky here, is there?"

Susan said, "You make it sound all sort of normal and matter-of-fact and comforting."

Hero now was eying her gravely. "That's the purpose of the exercise," he said.

Susan looked wary. "Oho," she said, "I didn't think you really wanted to talk about excavations."

"Got it in one," Hero said. "Now, what about that little funny business in your room that night?"

"It wasn't very funny, I assure you."

"I shouldn't think so. One thing that seems to be standard in ghosts of all types is a total lack of a sense of humor."

Susan was looking troubled. "*Could* it have been a ghost then?"

Hero busied himself with his black briar and then said, "Let's hear about it."

Susan sighed deeply as memories of the night's nastiness returned to her. "Oh dear!" she said. "Must I?"

Hero said gently, "Yes, please. You knew that was why I wanted to talk to you."

She told him then of what had happened to her as she recalled it, step by step, calmly, intelligently, lucidly.

They had been sitting each on a piece of foundation stone, and when she had finished Susan was aware that this not handsome yet extraordinarily attractive young man was regarding her with absolute and undisguised admiration. All he said was, "My dear old aunt—but you're absolutely wonderful!"

Susan said, "Who, me? But I didn't *do* anything."

Hero suddenly looked grim and his teeth clamped about the stem of his briar. "Anybody else would have gone into shock," he said. "I would myself. How I love courage!"

Susan suddenly felt her face burning and knew that she liked him to talk this way to her. Hero said, "May I ask you some questions?"

She nodded.

"The hand at your throat—was it really cold, then?"

"Yes, freezing—dead cold, and—clammy is the word I would want to use, even though——"

"It is probably the right word," Hero commented. "Now then, can you remember about how much time elapsed from the time you felt it at your throat and you tried to catch it?"

Susan furrowed her brow and then said, "No, how can one tell the duration of a thought or a plan? I was lying on my back and had no purchase. I thought that if I could get onto my side and reach for it at the same time I might catch it."

"While I should have been having a heart attack," Hero murmured. "What ass called you the weaker sex? Right! You say you saw the figure of the nun disappearing through the door and the wind seemed to blow it shut after her: was it the figure of a nun, or did you expect to see one because others had said they had seen her?"

Susan reflected for a moment and then shrugged faintly. "How can I tell—now? It seemed to me then that it was."

"What did you think when you saw the moist spots at your throat?"

"That it might have been perspiration. I was drenched with sweat by that time. You see, I'm not so very brave after all."

Hero said, "I could love a mind like that. And Paulson thinks *he* is a scientist. So then you found the door unlocked and looked into the hall and there was no one there, and went back to bed. What were you thinking?"

"Trying to remember how it all happened, step by step. I didn't like it, got a book, and read awhile. Then I went back to sleep. Could it have been a dream after all?"

Hero said, "I don't think so." He went to her and took her two hands and held them tightly, saying, "Lord, Susan, but you're a girl of wonderful courage!" For an instant as they looked into one another's eyes something trembled between them and could have been born, would have been born that instant in his arms perhaps, but for her odd feeling that there was something else behind his sudden show of emotion, and the next thing he said seemed almost a substantiation. If nothing else, it did serve to destroy the dangerous mood that seemed to have gripped them both.

"If you had to," he asked, "would you be able to go through the whole thing again—I mean, for it to happen to you once more, but without the danger?"

She asked, "Would that be necessary?"

He said, "If I said so it would be," and once more she felt his unemotional single-mindedness and one-track inflexibility. He was on the trail of something more important than herself.

"I suppose so," she said, suddenly listless.

"Good girl!" he applauded, but almost perfunctorily, and she saw that his mind had raced off a million miles away from her. Silently they walked back to the Hall together, where Mark Paradine was waiting on the terrace.

The red-haired young man watched warily as Susan and Hero approached, for they had not really spoken a great deal since their quarrel. He wondered where they had been, what Hero had been saying to her, and at the curious silence of both of them as they drew near. He suddenly felt horribly aware of that awful country-house cliché: "Anyone for tennis?" and yet at the moment could think of nothing better. As they reached him he thus said carelessly and tentatively, "Care for a game of tennis, Susan?" and was astonished at the almost overwhelming enthusiasm of her reply.

"Why, how nice! I'd love to, Mark." Susan was surprised herself. Was it a reaction from that strange moment that had quivered between her and the man beside her and had come to naught; or was it because she too had been a little saddened by the quarrel with Mark and was glad now that it was to be dispelled? She then became curiously aware that she genuinely wanted to be with Mark, to hit tennis strokes at him with all the strength of her young body, to run, to fight hard, to laugh again. "I'll go and change." She was off like a streak, running like the clean-limbed athlete she was.

The two men stood watching her go. Hero said unenthusiastically to Mark, "Quid she beats you—she's in the mood," and then drifted toward the house himself.

As Hero approached the massive front door of the Hall he became aware of some slight change in scene where the excavation was going on: the boards had been removed from the shattered window of the conservatory. The new pane of glass had arrived. Hero had since learned that the original glass had been broken by a pick head that had flown off the handle of one of the implements being used by the men in the ditch. Now, although the large new sheet of plate glass had arrived, it had not yet been installed, but in preparation for this it had been set up inside the conservatory, where the job would eventually be completed by the glaziers. The top edge touched the inside of the frame of the window; the bottom edge leaned inward toward the room so that the glass was safely aslant and in no danger of slipping or falling.

For a moment Hero stood on the temporary wooden-plank footbridge that had been laid across the open ditch, pulling at his lip and trying to think what this reminded him of, but could not catch it. One of the workmen straightened his back and stuck his head up out of the ditch, leaning on his shovel for a moment. "Good afternoon," he said. "Fine day, sir."

"Fine day, indeed," said Hero, breathing in the fresh air with a hint of salt brought in by a northeast wind. "I see they've got the new window."

The workman nodded. "Ay, that they have. Bad luck for Bill his pick head flew off, but Miss Isobel never so much as spoke a harsh word to him. Fine lady, Miss Isobel."

"Yes, indeed," Hero agreed. "Well, I don't doubt they'll have it put right soon." He followed his thoughts into the house, and as he marched determinedly through the writing room of the Country Club east wing he came upon Mrs. Geraldine Taylor laying out a patience with a pack of red-backed cards. He could not resist the temptation to pause to see whether there was any chance of its going out.

Come over, if you want to, but don't stand there in the middle of the room, young man," Mrs. Taylor ordered. "I don't mind being watched. I think I'm going to win. I shall be pleased if I do—I've made a wish."

Hero went over, stood by, and watched her as she manipulated the cards with stubby but nimble fingers, shifted whole rows of black upon red from one side to another, acquired spaces, then steadily accumulated the piled-up cards onto the four aces at the top.

He had a chance to study her too. She was a short, broad woman with the wide hips and seat of the lifelong horseback rider. Her iron-gray hair was cut short, nicely curled, and some of the locks in front were slightly blued. Hero was certain that when she went riding she wore a white stock and a tricorn hat, and that they would look well on her. She was dressed now in a suit of Donegal tweeds in dark green speckled with mustard color, a white shirt with collar attached, and a green tie; in the green tie was a gold and diamond pin of a horse's head and whip. She had a diamond watch pinned to her lapel, and on one pudgy hand was a diamond of no less than ten carats, and on the other a sizable, well-cut emerald. Mr. Hero catalogued in his mind: "*Widow—wealthy—fiftyish—horses, cards, and——*" Before he could make up his mind to her third interest she broke into his thoughts with "It's now or never." She had three cards left, face down. She said, "I want the three of spades, but if it is under the king of hearts I'm sunk."

Hero asked, "What do you think it will be?"

She turned to look at him out of half-amused eyes. Her face, like the rest of her, was broad and strong, the nose inclined to flatness, and the eyes greenish hazel, but the general effect was pleasant, due to the over-all aspect of strength and common sense about her appearance.

"Is this a Rhine test, young man?" she asked, and then said, "The three of spades, of course." She turned up the card; it was the three of spades. "Ha!" she cried. "I'm out—am I? Yes, I am." The three of spades went up, the next card was the wanted nine of clubs, the dangerous king of hearts being obligingly last, and the patience was completed.

Mrs. Taylor did not bother to pile up the rest of the cards onto the aces but looked at the layout of cards with a smile of satisfaction. "That's usually the way," she said. "it couldn't have looked worse at the beginning."

Hero said, "Might one ask what the wish was, or does it break it to tell?"

"Not at all," replied Mrs. Taylor cheerfully. "A husband. Haven't you been told yet that I'm down here husband hunting? My goodness, I don't know what's become of the old-fashioned art of gossip any more."

Her good-natured frankness surprised Hero, or rather her willingness to admit what, indeed, everyone was saying, and the surprise showed on his face, where the stocky woman misread it. "Oh, come, young man—what's your name—Mr. Hero, isn't it? Do you think that just because a woman is fat and fifty she is no longer a woman?"

Hero noticed with just the mildest sense of alarm that the eyes bent upon him now were full of appraisal.

"You may well worry, young man," Mrs. Taylor said, "and I'll let you in on a secret—once you're past fifty it gets worse. You know, if I were an attractive man I'd feel alarmed about having to live in a world filled with middle-aged women. It's downright dangerous for you to be about."

Hero grinned at her and whispered, "Help!" and she threw back her head and laughed loudly, and then said, "You're safe enough from me. There's too much competition."

Mr. Hero sat down on the edge of a chair opposite her and asked, "Have you—ah—seen anything you particularly fancied?"

"Oh! My little list," the widow replied and, gathering up the cards, she began to make them automatically, and quite unconsciously, using the corner shuffle expertly. "Dr. Paulson's just that much too pompous for me—I can't bear a man who's so set in his opinions and can always refer to his cyclotron to back them.

Besides which, he looks like a monkey. My late husband was handsome, even if a little retarded. You're much too good-looking yourself, my boy, to be allowed about loose."

Mr. Hero murmured deprecatingly, "So sorry," and Mrs. Taylor sniggered.

He gathered that she was a frank and naughty old girl and liked her for it.

Mrs. Taylor continued, "Now our engineer friend, what's his name? Mr. Ellison—he hasn't any sex appeal. Nice old boy, but wrapped up in his golf. I like horses, so we never meet except at dinner. Besides, what is he hiding?"

"Eh?" asked Mr. Hero, startled. "I didn't know he was hiding anything."

"Oh, I didn't mean hiding, perhaps. It's just that he hasn't always been that kind of an engineer—bridges and dams, I mean. At one time I'm sure he did something quite different."

"How do you know?" Hero asked.

Mrs. Taylor eyed him. "I just feel it," she said. "Don't you ever feel things like that?"

"I suppose so," Hero assented, "except that then it's usually something I know but don't know I know, if you understand what I mean." Then he added, "What about Mr. Jellicot?"

"Oh, I've had a good look at that little mannie, don't think I haven't," said Mrs. Taylor spiritedly. "He's sweet, but a little vulgar. Not that I'm not too, but his is a different kind of vulgarity from mine. I think people's commonnesses ought to blend, don't you?"

"It's a lovely idea," said Mr. Hero thoughtfully.

"Still, you know," she continued, "he's a widower with a gay eye, and has a certain innocence that's attractive. It would be easy to catch and eat him."

Mr. Hero leaned forward, his hands folded together. "Do you find him so wholly innocent?" he asked.

Mrs. Taylor looked shocked. "Oh, come, Mr. Hero," she said, "you don't mean to say that you suspect the little man of tricks?"

Hero reflected for a moment whether to go on or not, and then decided to do so. His was a lone hand to play in this game, he could genuinely trust no one, but he found that sometimes a kind of semi-alliance was useful. "Just a shade too interested in and conversant with poltergeists and their little ways to suit me," he said. "I shall be intrigued to see whether a fire ghost turns up here at the Hall. It is the next step, you know."

"You're thinking of the Amherst affair, I suppose."

Hero cocked an eyebrow. "What, you too?" he asked.

Mrs. Taylor shrugged. "One reads all sorts of things in a lifetime, doesn't one?"

Mr. Hero did not reply to this but instead produced his pipe, held it up toward Mrs. Taylor, and asked, "May I?" and when she nodded assent went through the familiar act of loading. She had given him considerable to think about and digest, and the manipulation of his pipe was always an aid to the process.

But there was a further surprise in store for him, for Mrs. Taylor had been thinking too, and she said, "When you have finished filling that disgusting object, which I am sure is very bad for your health, I'll thank you to return that pack of Tarot cards to me—or, if you haven't them on you, any time at your convenience."

Mr. Hero did not even bother to disguise his astonishment. "Good heavens!" he cried. "They're yours?" He drew the strange-looking pack of cards from his pocket and said, "You are the last person I would have thought they belonged to."

Mrs. Taylor nodded. "Yes. I know. I've been wavering between keeping my mouth closed and letting them go, or having to submit to a lot of questioning from you. I decided I wanted the cards back."

Mr. Hero fanned them once with that extraordinarily graceful movement of his hands, returned them to stack, and handed them to the widow. "Here you are," he said, and then asked ingenuously, "What do you use them for?"

"Telling fortunes! Reading the past and looking into the future," Mrs. Taylor replied evenly. "Would you like me to tell yours sometime?"

For all her even tone and quiet glance there was a challenge in what she said, and in the same manner Hero replied, "Yes, thank you, I should—very much. But not now. There may come a time when I will ask you to. Now I do want to ask you a few questions, if you don't mind."

Mrs. Taylor sighed. "I knew it," she said gloomily.

Hero said, "Oh no, not about those," gesturing with his pipe toward the Tarot cards, "those can wait, or at least I can sit on my curiosity. It's about that dinner on Friday night. I have the seating plan in my head. You were at the end of the table at Lord Paradine's right. You are an intelligent and observant woman. I'd like you to tell me what you saw and what happened."

Mrs. Taylor was pleased at the flattery and did not protest. She said, "The chair did move."

"You saw it?"

"I heard it first, and wondered who was getting up and leaving the table—the scraping sound, you know—and when I looked it was moving across the floor. Nobody was touching it or even close to it. I can swear that."

"And then?"

"I heard and saw Lord Paradine get up and go over to it. I forget exactly what he said, but he swore and wrestled with it. He didn't seem to be able to hold it."

"Wasn't able, or didn't seem to be able?"

Mrs. Taylor gave him a penetrating look. "Oh, I see what you mean," she said. "You think Lord Paradine might have been flummoxing the chair himself after he got there. I suppose a man could wrestle with a chair and quite easily appear not to be able to hold it."

Hero said, "I don't think anything. I am asking what you saw."

Mrs. Taylor, now doubtful of her own memories, replied, "Well, he said he couldn't hold it, and besides, I saw it move when there was nobody even close to it, and then afterward it did fall over onto him."

"Was that before or after the candles went out?"

"During—or, no—after. One does get muddled, doesn't one, trying to remember things exactly as they were?"

"Yes," said Hero. "But I imagine that you don't muddle very easily. How did the candles go out—one after the other or all at once?"

"One after the other, I think. Yes—but I seem to remember too that there were times when they were going out in twos and threes."

"Did they waver, flicker, or sputter—the flames, I mean? Was there a draft of any kind?"

"No, they just kind of died, or guttered out. There was one just in front of me. The flame simply shrank in upon itself and disappeared."

Hero nodded with satisfaction. He said, "Yes, yes. That's the way they ought to have gone."

Mrs. Taylor threw her sharp gaze at the investigator again. "Oho," she said. "I take it you know something, young man?"

Hero looked innocent. "I?" he said. "Not at all. It is just that if I were a ghost that's how I would go about putting out candles for maximum effect. Come to think of it, I could probably be a better ghost than many."

Mrs. Taylor was still watching him. "And if you weren't a ghost, young man?"

He grinned at her suddenly. "I suppose one ought to be able to hit upon some way of diddling a taper." Then he added, "And when exactly did you see the nun?"

Mrs. Taylor frowned with the effort of concentration. "It's so hard to say," she declared. "There was such a hullabaloo—the chair had fallen over onto Lord Paradine, apparently, or he had pulled it over, and that dreadful Mrs. Spendley-Carter was screaming at the top of her lungs, and I believe Sir Richard was shouting at us to be calm—when I *was* perfectly calm." She looked at Mr. Hero shrewdly. "You know, I didn't actually *see* a nun. It was just the shape of a nun, or something in the minstrels' gallery which looked like a nun's cowl—in the darkness, you know. There were only one or two candles burning at the time, so how could one be sure?"

Mr. Hero leaned forward again. "Look here," he said, "did you by any chance happen to look up into the minstrels' gallery before nearly all of the lights went out, or at any time shortly after the beginning of the phenomenon?"

"Yes," Mrs. Taylor said, "I did. It was when the candles first began to go out. There were two six-branched candelabra on either side of the gallery, and when those on the table started to go out I looked up to see whether those on the wall were going too."

"And did you see anything in the gallery at that time?"

"No, I did not."

Mr. Hero sighed. The problem now facing him seemed a hundredfold more difficult. He then asked of Mrs. Taylor, "Do you believe in ghosts?"

After a moment's reflection she replied, "I suppose so. One hardly dares disbelieve, does one?"

Hero nodded. "A hundred years ago," he said, "I should have been a most shrill antagonist. The vulgarity of it, you know, and the kind of people involved. But today . . ." He shrugged. "Perhaps we're only just approaching a threshold."

Mrs. Taylor's intelligent eyes gleamed. "Of course," she said. "If pictures can pass through the air without being seen until they come out of a machine, why not whatever it is that animates people?"

"Or their thoughts," said Mr. Hero. "Thinking expends energy and burns up calories."

The stout woman threw him another swift glance. "But there *was* something at that dinner," she insisted. "Something that worked unseen—a ghost or a disembodied wickedness—or call it what you want."

Mr. Hero sighed again and said, "Plural—ghosts. Not one, I am afraid, but several. It always seems to come down to there being at least one too many. Whatever was going on at that dinner was not one but two distinct operations. I wish I could understand it." He rose, picked up the Tarot cards from the table, spread them, and glanced through them once automatically. He said, "Thank you, Mrs. Taylor, you've been very kind and helpful— and someday I shall want to see you work with those." He put them down and went out of the room, filled with a determination: he very much wanted his stepsister on the scene as quickly as she might be summoned.

He went off in search of Lady Paradine and on his way was captured and pinioned by Horace Spendley-Carter. Since Hero had taken an immediate dislike to this big, windy man with the too loud voice and moist eyes he permitted himself to be way-laid, leaning over backward rather in an attempt to be fair, even though he was well aware that there was usually a reason for his prejudices and that they ought to be cherished rather than ig-nored.

"Aha," shouted Spendley-Carter, "our spook sleuth on the trail, eh? I've been wanting to have a little chat with you. Hear you're a Cambridge man."

"Yes," admitted Hero briefly.

"Spent a lot of time there myself," said Spendley-Carter jovially, but did not reveal when, where, or what he had been doing there. "I suppose the Volunteer and the Little Rose are still going, what? Used to favor the Mitre myself."

Mr. Hero wondered whether Spendley-Carter's acquaintance with Cambridge extended any further than the pubs he had mentioned, and would have laid himself a wager that the fellow had never set foot inside any of the colleges. He said, "Yes." Then he asked, "How is Mrs. Spendley-Carter?"

Spendley-Carter shouted, "Oh, Sylvia—she'll be all right. Suppose you're wondering why I don't take her away. Only get one holiday a year, old man. No point in having it spoiled by a lot of hysterical women, what? Sylvia knows I don't stand for any non-sense. She'll settle down. Besides which, it's a great opportunity. Doesn't happen often in a man's life that he finds himself on the spot with a thing like this going on. The newspapers will be want-ing interviews and articles from me when they find out. I was wondering whether I could ask you to lend me a hand, since you're supposed to know all about such things. I said to myself, 'He's an all-right chap. He'll probably be glad to.' My little girl has taken a great fancy to you, you know. Anyone my little girl fancies is bound to be an all-right chap. I'd see that the papers had your name as well as mine."

Hero regarded the M.P. coldly. "How would the papers find out?" he asked.

Spendley-Carter threw back his head and roared as though he'd heard the funniest joke in the world. "Ah-ha-ha! That's a good one—how'll they find out? I'll tell 'em, of course. The press is always on the *qui vive* for a story from me. I've thrown many a good one their way."

Hero asked, "Are you aware that Lord Paradine has requested that everyone maintain the strictest silence with regard to the phenomena observed here recently—at least until I've had a chance to investigate them and make a report?"

"What? I don't see what right old Paradine has to tell me——"

"Do you realize," Hero interrupted, "that if word of these unpleasant happenings and hauntings reaches the newspapers, or even becomes common gossip, the Paradine Country Club will be ruined and lose its membership? From then on there would be nothing more than a horde of sight-seers pushing and trampling all over the place. He'd lose the Hall."

Spendley-Carter was regarding Hero with considerable disfavor now. Gone was the pseudo affability and good fellowship. "Bad luck is what I say, old man. Chances one takes when one runs a place like this, aren't they? When you operate a hotel it's just your damn business to see that things like this don't happen—stones and vegetables flying about in one's rooms, things creeping about in the corridors knocking and thumping and frightening the life out of the good wife. Why, Jellicot tells me that, with my name on them testifying, the articles will have world-wide circulation."

"I shouldn't put too much weight on what Jellicot says," Hero remarked, "or for that matter the phenomena either, until they have been properly tested."

"What's that?" trumpeted Spendley-Carter, working up considerable indignation. "Are you trying to tell me what to do and what not to do, young fellow? And who's going to apply these tests?"

"I shall," Mr. Hero announced flatly. "And until such time, if I were you, I would not be getting in touch with any newspapers."

"And why not, sir, if I may ask?"

"You might not be too pleased with the results."

"*I* might not like it! Well, of all the damn——"

Hero turned his intense gaze upon the big man, and his expression might almost have been said to be friendly. "I was really only thinking of you, sir," he said. "You asked if I would be of assistance to you. I should be glad to, since in the occult world most of the time things are not at all what they seem. There have even been cases recorded where ghosts have taken a violent dislike to publicity in any form. In the meantime, the next time you find yourself the center, or in the presence of manifestations of any kind, I should be obliged if you would send for me immediately. I have enjoyed the little chat."

He walked away down the corridor, leaving Spendley-Carter confused and no longer sure of himself, standing there muttering. Hero thought he heard the words "Damned impudence!" but felt reasonably sure he had put the wind up the man and that he would not be communicating with any newspapers, at least for a little; but Hero was now all the more certain of the need for Meg.

The butler announced Mr. Hero to Lady Paradine, who was in her writing room on the ground floor of the west wing, answering correspondence in longhand. She did not look up when he entered but finished her sentence first, then she turned to him, removing her reading glasses as she did so, and saying, "Oh dear, it's such a bore not having a secretary, particularly when one is used to one."

Hero scrutinized briefly the faded, handsome face and the still beautiful fox-colored hair, and wondered what was concealed behind the façade of weariness and boredom—something—anything —or nothing? One could never wholly rely on there being nothing. Was it possible for anyone to reach the age of fiftyish without acquiring at least reaction to stimuli and experience? By Jove, she *had* been beautiful! When one was with her for a few moments one somehow forgot the age and the fading, and saw more of the original. He said, "I'm very sorry—I hope I haven't disturbed you," and looked upon her now with the frank admiration that he could never quite manage to conceal in the presence of an attractive woman.

Lady Paradine saw it too and bloomed under it, her stiffness and reserve melting into graciousness as, suddenly warmed, she turned to him and said, "I suppose you'll be wanting to ask me a great many questions. I'm afraid I really don't know anything at all. I simply can't imagine what made all those candles go out, or that wretched chair move, and of course I'm terribly upset for poor Susan—I'm surprised she hasn't left. I know I should have been perfectly terrified if any of it had happened to me—I mean, nobody could make me stay for another second in a house where dead rabbits appeared upon my plate. Would you?"

Hero reflected upon this somewhat breathless and inconsequent speech and then said gravely, "It all depends, of course, what kind of person one is and how much one wants to stay. Perhaps Miss Marshall has reasons for wishing to remain here—particularly in the face of something that doesn't seem to wish her to do so. She is a courageous girl and when her mind is made up it is not easily to be bluffed, I should say."

Lady Paradine seemed to stiffen slightly and some of the warmth and leaning toward him went out of her attitude. "Yes, I'm sure," she said. "It's perfectly dreadful to have such a thing happen to a guest, isn't it?" She glanced down at the letter she had been writing and then back to Hero as she said, "Of course, Mark's so young, you know—hardly more than a boy—and Susan is quite good-looking, and I suppose so different from our girls. Americans seem so self-sufficient and able to cope. Almost frightening in a woman, isn't it? I hate efficiency." And then she added as an afterthought, "I suppose it's because I am so inefficient."

Hero thought to himself, "*Oho, thus blows the wind, eh?*" Aloud he said, "Yes, I suppose it can be upsetting. However, I don't really wish to disturb you with questions. What I came to ask was whether I could impose upon you to invite my sister Meg here for a visit."

Lady Paradine chilled perceptibly. "Your sister, Mr. Hero? I don't think I quite understand. Perhaps my husband would . . ."

With an inward sigh Hero wheeled the artillery of snobbism into position and let fly. "The Lady Margaret Callandar," he said, "the Earl of Heth's daughter. She is really my stepsister. She sometimes assists me in my work."

"Oh!" said Lady Paradine in a manner which showed Hero he was on target. "Lady Margaret! But she's famous, isn't she? And your mother, then, is the Countess of Heth—I hadn't realized . . . Certainly, I'll ask her at once." She gestured toward a fresh sheet of stationery and suddenly hesitated with a queer kind of pout that abated memories of her beauty and turned her into a petulant, aging woman. "Oh dear," she said, "I shall have to ask Isobel, because she's the only one who really knows everything about the Hall and which rooms are ready—I mean, she's one of those efficient persons, and I don't know what we'd do without her. Whenever anybody wants anything they go to Isobel. I simply couldn't cope with everything the way she does. Poor thing, I suppose she ought to, with no husband and nothing else to do, and she's been doing it for donkey's years now—or am I being catty?"

Isobel came into the room at that moment without the ceremony of knocking. Her silver-white hair was pulled back tightly and fastened in a great bush at the back with a piece of broad black ribbon, but several untidy strands had escaped and blew about her brow, on which there was also a smudge. Her hands too were stained. She was wearing an old pair of hack-about-the-estate jodhpurs, a blue linen blouse open at the throat, and flat-heeled shoes. From a hook at her belt dangled an enormous bunch of keys of all sizes and shapes. "Oh dear," said Isobel, "I didn't know there was anyone here. I'm such a mess. I've been working in my shop."

Hero could not contain his curiosity or surprise. "Shop?" he said.

Isobel smiled engagingly, and Hero thought how of the two,

the one in dirty working clothes, and Lady Paradine in a pale green chiffon morning gown, it was Isobel who was the lady. "Spinster hobby," she said. "Some collect budgereegahs, but I like carpentry—and besides, it gets things done about the house."

"Darling," said Lady Paradine, "I'm being a bitch. I've been telling Mr. Hero how wonderful you are, and how helpless I am, hoping it will make him like me more."

Isobel said, "Dear, aren't we all? Wait until I get Mr. Hero to myself. I'm sorry to interrupt, but I've had such a time about the conservatory window. The wretched men have brought the new sheet of glass, but now they say it can't be installed until next week—something to do with a fitting. They have just leaned the new one there temporarily, but I think we ought to mark the conservatory out of bounds until then, don't you?"

Lady Paradine said listlessly, "Yes, I suppose so," and then suddenly and unaccountably flared. "Oh, why do you try to pretend, Isobel, that it isn't you who has everything to say about the running of this house, just because someone happens to be here? You do what you like, anyway—and I don't care if you do. You know I stopped caring ages ago, so why pretend?"

Isobel said quietly, "Don't you think, Enid . . . ?"

"That we oughtn't to air family rows in front of strangers," Lady Paradine completed with a bitterness that surprised Hero, and again made him revert to his stepsister's deft analysis of the Paradine household. "Of course I ought not to," Lady Paradine continued, "but I get so sick of pretending. Do as you wish."

Isobel said, with more amiability than Hero would have thought anyone could muster under provocation, "Very well, Enid—I don't suppose it really matters."

Lady Paradine let herself appear mollified and more quietly she pursued, "I am inviting Mr. Hero's stepsister, Lady Margaret Callandar, to stay, but I've told him you know more about what rooms are in order than I do."

Isobel, who seemed not in the least disturbed by Lady Paradine's outburst, said almost with pleasure, "Oh, Meg Callandar— I didn't know she was your sister. She came here once with her father, when my father was still alive. I should be so pleased to see her again. I remember her. She was all legs and eyes and mouth. Of course she's grown up into a great beauty."

Hero looked his surprise. Meg was simply Meg or, in their more affectionate moments, "the Hag."

Isobel went on, "How very delightful. The Charles suite can be made ready almost at once."

Lady Paradine made a gesture which included "There-you-see-didn't-I-tell-you?" and also dismissal, and returned to her correspondence. Hero found himself outside the room with Iosbel.

"Would you like to see the rooms for your sister?" Isobel began.

Hero said, "No, thank you. But I should like to see yours, if I might, and perhaps the music room where the harp plays."

They went together into the pleasant, sunny room, where the golden concert harp gleamed in its accustomed place over by the window that looked out onto the placid surface of the river Stoke.

Hero said, "I've been here before, with Miss Marshall, but there were some things I wanted to ask you."

The room appeared unchanged since he had visited it with Susan. His statement seemed to call for no reply from Isobel, and she made none. She remained quietly standing, leaning an elbow on the polished ebony case of the grand piano, while Hero went over to the harp and this time made a thorough examination of it. She watched him silently as he rocked the instrument on its base, sat in the musician's chair and pulled it to him in the manner of a harpist, tested the tuning keys, the strings, the pedals, thumped the frame, and then stood looking at it puzzled, pulling away at his lower lip and shaking his head slightly. There was nothing at all either unusual or wrong about the harp.

Isobel said, "I can see that we have two different points of view, Mr. Hero—yours that the harp was somehow played by human hands, and mine that—it wasn't."

"You are wrong there, Miss Paradine," Hero said. "When I am engaged on an investigation I have no point of view whatsoever beyond what is suggested by the evidence. The evidence in this case is that,"—he nodded toward the harp—"this is a first-class harp, kept in tune, and in excellent condition. I see no indication that it has been tampered with in any way. Unless someone managed to enter this room, sit at it, and pluck the strings, it ought not to have played."

Isobel sighed, nodded, and then said gravely, "And yet it did."

"Will you tell me about it, please?" Hero asked.

Isobel said, "I think my brother would be better able to do so, since it was he who was first upon the scene the night it happened."

"Lord Paradine has already been kind enough to give me his version. I should now like to have yours."

Isobel's smile contained some of that patient gentleness of the sheltered and wellborn when they encounter cynicism and suspicion. She said, "It was during the night—I heard the harp play —I could not imagine——"

"Where were you when you heard it?" Hero asked.

"In my room."

"Were you awake or asleep? That is to say, did the music awaken you?"

"I was awake—I have not slept very well since that night when——"

"Yes." Hero nodded sympathetically. "I see. Was your door open or shut?"

A faint frown momentarily passed over the smooth front of Isobel's brow, and Hero could not tell whether it was the effort of trying to remember or the beginning of an irritation with his stabbing questions. Isobel said, "Shut—no, open—no, I'm sorry, I just don't remember."

"But you heard it clearly?"

"Yes."

"Did you recognize the melody?"

"Yes. It was Gréves' 'My Bonnie Dear.' "

"Ah! You were familiar with it."

"My mother used to play it."

"Did you think perhaps it might have been—your mother—returned?"

"No. I only lay there quite cold with horror, thinking of the nun, the harp, and the doom that lies upon the Paradines when the two come together."

Hero was surprised: a dramatic and Nornlike quality had suddenly displaced the matter-of-fact housekeeper of Paradine Hall. Her face had altered, as had the whole expression of her slender body.

"Misfortune pursues those to whom the nun appears," Isobel continued. "There is misfortune upon this house."

Hero thought to himself, "*Including, apparently, its house guests.*" Was she sincere or was it an act? Aloud he said, "You believe this, don't you?"

Isobel's gaze was direct and without guile. "Yes," she said with a kind of dignity and simplicity, "I am a Paradine."

Hero returned to the thread of her narrative. "You lay there and listened. What happened then?"

"I heard my brother shout, 'Enid! Enid! This damned door is locked—fetch me your keys.'"

"Was the room ordinarily kept locked?"

"Sometimes—particularly if there were children in the house. We don't like them coming in. But my recollection is that this time it was not. The tuner had just been. When I heard John calling for the keys I arose and went to the door and listened. The harp was still playing. I then went down into the pantry to fetch my keys in case Enid should not be able to find hers—she has a duplicate set, you know."

"But why the pantry?"

"I remembered I had left them there the night before."

Hero nodded. "But she arrived first?"

"Yes. When I got here the door was open. Enid and my brother were in the room with the lights on. John was standing over by the harp staring at it. He was very much upset. When I came in he said, 'Isobel, did you hear it too? There was nobody here—I swear it! When I came in the room was empty—but the harp strings were still vibrating. I saw them! But it's impossible, isn't it?'—or words to that effect. I may not be quoting him exactly."

Hero asked, "What did Lady Paradine say?"

Isobel replied, "Enid said, 'Mightn't you both have been imagining it all? Couldn't it have been the wind or something?'"

When she had finished her narration Hero remained silent for a moment, lost in thought, and then said, "Thank you."

Isobel was now looking at him levelly. She said, "I know that my brother has engaged you to look into this, and I approved his decision, but I think that you ought to know it will do no good—you will not find anything. Paradine Hall has been haunted since the time of the third Lord Paradine. The nun has appeared since then in every century."

"I would give my right arm to hear the harp play, or if I could see her."

Isobel said darkly, "It were better not."

Hero merely nodded and said, "Might I see your room now? I believe it was there the first manifestations took place."

Isobel said, "Of course. Come, I'll take you there." She was herself again; the Nornlike quality had vanished.

They went out, and Isobel did not lock the door. Hero wondered to himself how long it would remain unlocked.

As he crossed the threshold into Isobel's apartment Hero had the impression that few, if any, strangers ever entered her sanctuary, and he wondered why she was permitting it to him, particularly in view of her stated disbelief in the success of his mission. He then thought to himself, *"Probably simply because I asked for it, and she is trying to be co-operative—which is more than I can say of others hereabouts."* In return he did her the courtesy of not prying about her room with either his hands or his eyes but was satisfied to take in as much as he could casually, noting that the portrait of the late Thomas, Lord Paradine, in his uniform as a Guards colonel in World War I, still rested on the oak floor beneath the spot where it had hung, and wondered why it had not been restored to its place on the wall. His summing up was that it was unquestionably the room of a personage, but not that of a woman, somehow.

As if she had read his thoughts, Isobel said, "This was once my father's room." And then asked, "Was there anything you wished to ask me about it?"

"About the night of the manifestations."

Isobel said with a kind of resentment, "I was invaded."

"By what?"

"I don't know. The nun perhaps. I saw nothing."

"This was the night of . . . ?"

"June the twenty-ninth."

Hero remembered making a note of the date and quite suddenly knew why. "What happened?" he asked.

Isobel replied, "It seemed as though all the furies had been let loose. I was awakened by my bed being violently shaken, and someone or something pulling at the bedclothes. When I turned on the light the bedclothes were in a heap upon the floor. Then a chair moved by itself and one after the other a pair of Sèvres vases was flung from the mantel—one was broken. I had an Adam mirror. It is no longer here—it was shattered—and at the same time that tallboy was overturned. Before my eyes my father's picture fell from the wall to the floor."

"Were you frightened?" Hero asked.

"Yes, I was terrified," Isobel replied in a low voice. "I knew it was the nun. Sometimes she is invisible, but she was there. She threw my father's picture down. It was an omen!" The Norn had suddenly returned. Isobel was again an ancient prophetess. "There is nothing you or anyone can do!" she cried. "There will be a death in this house. Someone will die!"

"Who do you think?" said Mr. Hero with such matter-of-fact simplicity that it startled Isobel out of her drama.

She said, "I—I don't know, I'm sure—one doesn't."

Hero nodded perfunctorily. "Let's hope perhaps this time it may be avoided." He then went swiftly about the room examining and sounding the walls, looking along them up to the beams of the ceiling, and noting the size and position of the bed. He went and looked out the window, which opened onto the park and river, and, returning, made a mental note of the configuration of the land as well as the shape of the room and every piece of furniture in it. Isobel had watched him wordlessly during this time. Hero said, "Thank you. You have been more than kind and generous with your time," and went out. But halfway through the door he turned and said, "Oh, I'm sorry, I've been meaning to ask—is there a tide table in the house?"

"Yes," Isobel said, "there's one in the telephone closet by the entrance hall—where the telephone is. We keep it for those who go sailing."

Mr. Hero said, "Thank you," again and went out wondering how much of all he had heard was fantasy or imaginings, or out-and-out lies, and how much truth there was in any of it, and whether Meg would be able to help him sort it out before all hell broke loose in that house again and someone got hurt.

WHAT IT'S LIKE
TO BE NOREEN

That same afternoon on the way to his car to drive to East Walsham, Hero encountered Mr. Jellicot and Dr. Paulson in the lounge in a state of considerable agitation. The dried-up little scientist was pale and his fingers were working nervously, while the rotund retired draper was trembling with excitement. Perspiration stood on his brow and his lips were quivering as, sighting Hero, he called, "Sir! Sir! We have just been witness to a geniune psychical phenomenon!"

"Amazing," said Dr. Paulson.

"The poltergeist—I have an apport—a real apport! It came flying in through the window." He reached into the pocket of his sack coat and produced a smooth, egg-shaped flint such as abounded in the neighborhood. "I have witnessed a poltergeist! Oh, I have never been so happy! Spendley-Carter is going to write a report on it for our publication, *The Spiritist.*" Mr. Jellicot's eyes were shining as he concluded, "Just imagine—a poltergeist happening to a Member of Parliament, and myself there to attest it!"

Hero looked to Dr. Paulson, who nodded and said, "Yes, it is true—I saw it all myself."

"What happened?"

Mr. Jellicot eagerly took up the narrative. "Dr. Paulson and I were coming from my room where I had been showing him a copy of our little magazine. We were passing the door of the Spendley-Carters when we heard a great crash and a scream. We rushed inside, to come upon a scene of the greatest confusion—a table at one side of the room containing books and ash trays and things had been overturned, though no one was near it; a jug of water had been spilled on the floor; shoes and articles of clothing were flying about the room; stones were coming in the window——" Here Mr. Jellicot held up his apport again. "Mrs. Spendley-

Carter was over by the mantel screaming, while Spendley-Carter was trying to calm her."

"Why didn't you summon me?" Hero asked, and caught the look that Jellicot and Paulson exchanged. "All right," he said, "so you wanted it for yourselves. But I'd like to remind you that I've been asked down here to rid this house of that sort of thing. Just exactly what was it you saw?"

Dr. Paulson began, "If you will accept the testimony of one who, you must admit, is a trained observer . . ." Mr. Hero nodded. "When we entered the room conditions seemed indeed chaotic, with Mrs. Spendley-Carter in a state of terror and articles strewn in confusion about the floor. A woman's shoe was flying through the air just as we entered——"

Hero interrupted. "Whose shoe was it—Mrs. Spendley-Carters, or the child's, or a strange shoe?"

Paulson suddenly looked somewhat nonplused.

"I thought you were a trained observer," said Hero. "Go on—where was everyone at this time?"

"Mrs. Spendley-Carter was over by the mantel with her face in her hands moaning, Spendley-Carter was standing next to her."

"And where was the child?"

"I know what you are thinking," said Mr. Jellicot, "but it was impossible for her to have been involved in any way. She was sitting in an alcove at the other side of the room with her back to us."

Mr. Hero thought: *but not impossible for you to have been involved, my busybody friend.* Aloud he said, "What was she doing?"

"She was painting in her water-color book."

"With all that row going on?"

Paulson said, "I had her under observation all the time, as well as everyone else in the room. The apport—that is, the stone Mr. Jellicot has—came flying in through the window—the one nearest the alcove."

Hero asked, "Was the window open or shut?"

Dr. Paulson said, "The window was shut. I went particularly

to look after the object had passed over my shoulder and landed upon the floor."

"How long ago was this?" Hero asked.

"About half an hour."

Hero was angry and frustrated. He picked up the stone and weighed it in his hand. It appeared to be an ordinary Norfolk flint, but the trail would be cold now, and so was this piece of rock; it could tell the little instrument he had in his pocket nothing. Had he only been there when it landed, or immediately after! Hero weighed it in his hand again and said to Dr. Paulson, "Do you believe that an inanimate object such as this can fly through the air of its own volition?"

"I saw it do so," the scientist replied stiffly.

"Not of its own volition," Mr. Jellicot tried to explain helpfully, "it is the invisible poltergeist who carries it."

"And passes through a closed windowpane without shattering it?"

"The mischievous entity can do anything," Mr. Jellicot contributed. "That's why it is called a poltergeist."

Dr. Paulson was growing angrier. "As a psychical researcher, sir, you ought to know how to evaluate evidence from competent sources and eyewitness accounts. I am telling you what I saw with my own eyes. Do you doubt my word?"

Mr. Hero contemplated the flint for another moment and then dropped it onto the table where it fell with a resounding thud before he replied morosely, "No, not your word but your common sense." He went out, got into his car, and drove off toward East Walsham.

Already regretting his loss of temper as he nosed the cream and black Bentley through the huge wrought-iron gates of the estate, Hero thought of the qualifications necessary for the perfect psychical investigator as listed in his book by Hereward Carrington, the American psychical researcher. The paragraph had fired his imagination and he had tried to model himself upon its contents. He saw the page now before his eyes: "A specialized training is necessary for this work; our ideal investigator must have a thorough knowledge of the literature on the subject; he must have a good grounding in normal and abnormal psychology; in physics, chemistry, biology, photography, and some laboratory experience; he must be a keen observer, a good judge of human nature and its motives; he must be well trained in magic and sleight-of-hand; he must be shrewd, quick of thought and action, ever on the alert, patient, resourceful, open-minded, tolerant, rapid in his observations and deductions, tactful, sympathetic, and have a sense of humor! He must be free from superstition, and at the same time unswayed by bigotry, theological or scientific. In short, our ideal investigator is hard to find, and it is probable that such a man is born rather than made. . . ."

He considered his shortcomings in this list and was not pleased. He was long enough on science, psychology, sleight-of-hand, and other physical attributes, with the exception of photography, but open-minded tolerance, tact, and sympathy did not appear to be his strong points. Just because Paulson was a fool was no excuse for calling him one. Among the first duties of a psychical researcher was that of not making enemies. The images of the attractive and available Mrs. Wilson and the cool and aloof Susan Marshall flashed through his mind—"*And not friends either,*" Hero told himself.

He entered the village, drew up at the post office, and went into the telephone box. At least his deficiency in photography was to be remedied, but he knew that in addition to his stepsister's knowledge and skill he rather desperately wanted to be able to talk to her.

He called her at Barbizon's studio and when he got through to her said, "Hoy, Meg—Sandro."

"Are you all right?" was the first thing she asked.

"Yes. Look here, Sis, you'll be getting an invitation shortly from our red-haired friend down here—vetted, stamped, authorized, and okayed by our white-haired one. When it arrives, take off on the double, old girl."

There was a moment's silence on the other end of the telephone, and then, "Oh, that's how it is. Anything particular in equipment?"

"We'll want the lot, that's for certain. Your subject has a preference for dark corridors."

Meg asked, "What about the poltergeist?"

"Yes, yes! By all means! We'll have Little Snooper," and then he suddenly added, "Damn!"

"What is it, Sandro?"

"Nothing—I just thought of something."

After a moment's silence Meg's voice came through again. "You sound disturbed, my pet. Are you in trouble?"

Hero said, "This place is positively crawling with ghosts, if you happen to like them in crowds—which I don't. And there's been the usual prophecy of doom and death, with always the unpleasant possibility that someone might be encouraged to help the prophecy along."

"I asked if *you* were in trouble," Meg said with unmistakable emphasis. "Are you surrounded by beautiful women?"

Hero replied, "Inundated. There's an old girl of fifty-odd who's got her eye on me." Even as he said it he felt irritated with himself; he didn't need television to see the expression on Meg's face, or clairvoyance to know that she was reading his mind and penetrating his purpose in mentioning Mrs. Taylor's age. Her next sentence confirmed this.

"You just stick to 'er, my love," and then, "When may I expect my invitation?"

"Probably tomorrow sometime. Hurry down when you get it, Sis."

Meg said, "You bet I will," with rather more emphasis than Hero liked. His mind *would* leap to Mrs. Wilson—to Susan—to Mrs. Wilson, and he had the most horrible feeling that as long as he was connected to Meg with a telephone wire she could read his thoughts.

He said, "Good. Good," and hung up. But the truly disturbing thought which had come to him during the conversation was that, while the manifestations in Isobel's room as well as those in the Spendley-Carter apartment were typical poltergeist phenomena, they were not the same poltergeist. In all the recorded history of poltergeistism he had never yet encountered any record of two under the same roof. From the extensive literature on the manifestations and nature of poltergeists, he doubted very much whether they would get along.

He came out into the sunshine and sized up the village, charmingly located on the shimmering Walsham Broads with numbers of elegant motor cruisers, houseboats, and sailing yachts tied up at their slips. He went to St. Dunstan's Church with its square Norman tower built of stone blocks faced with half flints, the same kind of flint pebbles, he mused, as had materialized through a closed window at the Hall.

The Rev. Harry Witherspoon was not there. It had been in Hero's mind, among other things, to apologize for his abruptness the previous morning. Instead he found a verger, a venerable gentleman by the name of Butterworth, of some seventy-five years. The old fellow was refreshingly uncomplicated; he believed in God, the Rev. Harry Witherspoon, St. Dunstan's Church, and in East Walsham as the center of the universe. He was also a first-class antiquarian and historian, and had filled some six minutely written notebooks on Paradine Hall, the Paradines, and other great families of the surrounding district, including some highly interesting observations on the legendary nun, in which local archives had been used as source material.

He was as happy as a child to let Mr. Hero delve into this material to his heart's content. Later on Hero visited the public library and the county hall, where there were further rewarding records, and finally he drove over to Great Yarmouth, where he paid a visit to the hydographic officer of the district. It was late afternoon by the time he had finished and returned full of information and disturbing thoughts.

Almost without realizing it he let the Bentley drift to a stop on the broad main drive leading to Paradine Hall while he sat eying the stately mass of the great Tudor building, the beautiful regularity of its towers, dormers, and turrets, and the equally beautiful irregularity of the tall chimneys sprouting from the dark tile rooftops.

Here was a mass of bricks welded together in beauty emerged from the brain of man. From its earliest days it had been filled with human beings good and bad, with love, with hate, and with lies. The stone had solid permanency; only the people and the lies changed with each succeeding generation. He reflected upon the magnificent effrontery that one man and his family should require so great a pile to house them, and also on egos so frail and pitiful that they needed to be bolstered by that much masonry.

He was reflecting also upon the incongruity that this manor, which for so many centuries had curtained the privacy of the Paradines, should perforce have been turned—call it what you would —into a public hotel, and what, if anything, the members of the family thought or felt about this, or whether they felt anything at all. He was wondering also what this metamorphosis might have to do with the strange superfluity of ghosts that had suddenly come to infest it, when he became aware that he was being watched. Some part of somebody was showing from behind the gray-green skin of a two-century-old elm.

"Come out, come out, wherever you are," sang Mr. Hero. Twelve-year-old Noreen Spendley-Carter appeared then diffidently from behind the tree, clad in tan corduroy slacks and sweater. Her dun-colored hair fell lankly to her shoulders in a half-tangled snarl, framing the sallow skin and freckles of her face. She looked as though she had been made of mud, and then not painted. She came forward, eying the car admiringly, then put forth a somewhat grubby hand and with astonishing gentleness touched its glossy side and stroked the small silver figure of a cat with its tail curled around its legs, which was attached to the radiator cap and which had been modeled from Sambo, Mr. Hero's own house cat. "Could I sit in it just once for a little?" she begged.

"Certainly," Hero replied. "Come around." He leaned over and opened the offside door. Inside she stretched and sighed as luxuriously as a young kitten.

"Oh, isn't it *wonderful*?" she breathed. "It's just like a dream."

"Shhhh," Hero whispered, "you must try not to wake up, then."

She sat up and looked at him now with more interest. "Oh," she said, "you know that too? Sometimes when I'm having the best dream I know that I am and try ever so hard not to wake up."

"What kind of dreams?" Hero asked.

She became slightly wary. "Oh—things," she said. And then added half to herself, "Like being a nurse in a hospital and wearing a white cap and starched uniform and holding a thermometer."

"That's a nice dream," Mr. Hero said.

The girl turned her dark eyes upon him. They were irregularly placed and the wrong color for her hair, but Hero was aware of something pleading and touching in their depths. She said, "But I always wake up." Then she asked, "What are you really doing here?"

Hero answered her frankly. "I am trying to find out about ghosts."

Noreen asked, "But what is there to find out about them? A ghost is or isn't, isn't it?"

Mr. Hero smiled and said, "It depends a good deal upon how you look at them. Do you believe in ghosts?"

"Of course I do. My ghosts are all 'is' ones—I love them. They make me feel squiggly and shuddery inside."

Hero asked, "Are you afraid of them?"

"Of course not. What is there to be afraid of—they aren't *solid*."

Hero took a long, comfortable draw on his briar. "Even those who knock vases off mantelpieces, tip over pots and pans, and throw stones?" he suggested.

"Pooh," said Noreen with fine scorn, "they never *hit* anybody."

"No, but they do seem to frighten people," Hero suggested. "I think, for instance, that your mother is greatly frightened of them."

A curious expression that Hero could not fathom came into the child's face. There was a quickening of interest. She said, "Oh, Mother's afraid of everything, including Daddy. She hates Daddy. They're not my real, *real* daddy and mummy, you know —I'm adopted."

Hero had not known, and yet now that he had been told it seemed as though it must have been at the back of his mind ever since he had laid eyes upon that ill-assorted trio. He turned to look at the girl and said, "I see. When did you find that out?"

"Not long ago," Noreen replied complacently, and got into a

comfortable narrative attitude. "They were having a row. I listened at the door. Daddy was browbeating Mummy—it always makes me furious when she lets him—and saying that she was so rotten lazy and self-centered that she wouldn't even have a child, and Mummy said that she always wanted a child but didn't want *his* child because he was mean, vain, shallow, a liar, and a big windbag, and that was why she adopted one. And Daddy said, 'Well, I hope you're satisfied with what you've got now. Look at her—me a Member of Parliament having to go about meeting people, and she's a disgrace to have to take along as our daughter'—that's me," Noreen concluded without rancor.

Hero kept his countenance expressionless during her recital and merely said, "Are you sorry that you've found out that they're not your real parents?"

Noreen gave some thought to this before she replied, "No, I'm glad, because I'm not them at all, am I—not the littlest bit? I'm just me, me, *me!*"

Mr. Hero felt overwhelmed with grief at the bleakness and gallantry of this declaration. "Yes, you are you," he said, "and never forget it, Noreen."

The child looked at him longingly. "I wish *you* were my daddy," she said. The intensity of her emotion and her wish brought a curious kind of beauty into the ugly little face. She asked, "May I put my arm around you?" And when Hero nodded she put both of them about his waist, pressed her face against his shoulder, and clung tightly to him.

They sat there thus for a while in silence, while Hero, again permeated with sadness, thought: *"This child is so full of love—what is to be done with it? How is it to be released? Who will want her?"* He was conscious that Noreen was saying something, and aloud asked, "What, pet?"

Noreen said, "Lean down, I want to whisper something." He leaned his head close to her lips and heard her sibilate faintly, "I want to be a nurse when I grow up."

Hero was startled. It seemed almost as though she had answered his unspoken thoughts. "Then that you shall," he declared. But he saw there was sudden anguish and tears in the eyes regarding him, and thereafter came the outburst.

"But they won't let me," she wailed. "They said they wouldn't let me. Daddy says I'm to be a lady. He's put his foot down—and for once Mummy agrees. I hate them, I hate them, I hate them!" Then with a quick movement she turned, released the catch on the door, jumped out, and ran off through the great trees of the park, leaving Hero sitting in his car by himself, silently smoking and thinking and looking after her until she was out of sight.

When Hero arrived back at the Hall and parked his car, tea outdoors was almost over, and there were only Cousin Freddie, Beth, and Mark left on the lawn. Simultaneously Sir Richard and Susan, clad in shorts and sweaters, approached from the direction of the boathouse.

The little eyes in Freddie's fat face shone with happy malice as he noted fresh arrivals to bait. "Ah there," he cried, "how's the super spooker snooper today? Spot of tea to keep up the courage?"

"Thanks," Hero said.

Susan and Sir Richard arrived, roaring with laughter at some joke that had been between them. Cousin Freddie said, "Well, here's our little American friend. How's that unpopular fellow, Uncle Sam, getting on these days?"

"Fine," replied Susan without rancor. "Have you been checking up on the Trendex rating of John Bull lately?"

Freddie laughed, but not pleasantly, and said, "Oh, you rich Americans can find it easy to criticize. You've got all the money in the world."

"Yes," Susan said, "we hardly know what to do with it all. In our house we eat off platinum plates and use diamond-studded spoons, and all the bathroom fixtures are eighteen-carat gold."

Hero said, "Hi there—what have you two been up to?"

"Dinghy racing," Sir Richard replied. "Susan beat me again."

Beth said, "Oh, Susan always wins." She smiled as she spoke, but Hero thought that a slightly jarring note struck his ear and that he saw no smile in her eyes. Was it simply the speech of a girl pleased and proud of her friend, or was there something else? If there was, the keen, malicious ear of Cousin Freddie likewise seemed to have tuned in.

He said, "Ah-ah there, Beth. What's this? Jelly of your girl friend—and your uncle Dick? Age having its last fling with youth."

A teacup and saucer clattered to the turf as Beth arose, her face drained of all color, her eyes brimming, and her young mouth twisted. "Oh!" she cried. "You beast—you unspeakable beast!" Then she turned and ran off to the house weeping, her hands before her face.

Mark Paradine said icily, "You're a dirty swine, Freddie. Can't you see the kid's been under a strain with all this business happening to Susan? Why do you have to pick on her?"

Sir Richard advanced, his handsome face crimson with fury. "I ought to smash that fat head of yours."

"That's it," said Freddie cheerfully, "show the girl your muscles."

It was so ridiculous that Susan broke the tension with a roar of laughter. "Oh, Freddie," she said, "you're priceless." Then, "No tea for me—I'm going to change."

"I'll walk you," Hero said, and fell into step beside her. When they were out of earshot he said, "Sweet character."

"Yes," agreed Susan, "isn't he hateful? But you know, he's so impossible I almost like him. I feel sorry for him."

"Why?" asked Hero.

Thinking lined Susan's lovely brow for a moment. "I suppose because I understand him. You see, it couldn't happen in our country. But over here, the way you do things with your families, he's in a trap, isn't he? Old Lord Paradine's will took particular pains to make him a nobody by giving him just enough money so that he doesn't have to work. And all because he's the son of a second son. He's been made a kind of pinch hitter who knows he'll never get a time at bat. That might curdle even your disposition, you know, or mine. I don't really mind him."

"Do you get much of that?" Hero asked. "I mean like the cracks about Uncle Sam, say, from the other?"

"Oh yes," Susan said coolly. "One gets quite used to it. We're not the most popular people in the world right now, you know."

"Anyone here besides Freddie baiting you?"

"Are you asking me seriously?"

"Yes, I am. Looking for cause, so to speak."

"Oh well, it wouldn't be that, surely," Susan said. "I mean, it might range from something outright, like Major Wilson wanting to know why we quit the Korean war when we had it won, to just sort of half-subtle and pitying remarks Lady Paradine might make, such as, 'My dear, do you find it just frightfully difficult to get on with what must seem to you our very strange ways of doing things?' Of course, what she is saying is that mine are barbarous. Or Beth——"

Mr. Hero raised his eyebrows. "Beth?" he said.

"Oh, she doesn't really mean it—none of them really do, except Cousin Freddie—it's just the line today to take the rise out of Uncle Sam, the way we used to enjoy twisting the lion's tail."

"What was Beth's line?" Hero insisted.

"Nothing, really," Susan replied. "It was stupid of me to have mentioned her. Well, you heard just now. It's just another variation of 'You Americans always play to win, don't you?' that we get from time to time."

"And the Hon. Isobel?"

"Oh no, not Isobel," Susan said. "Isn't it strange," she reflected, "how someone like Isobel is only 'Honorable' and Lady Paradine——" She stopped and faced Hero and said with a sincerity that was almost touching, "I don't mean that nastily, really I don't. It's only that when I think of the word 'lady' I think of Isobel."

They had arrived at the door of Susan's room and lingered there for a moment. "I think," Hero said, "it is about time for that little experiment."

Susan said, "You mean the one you said was not very pleasant. I don't like things that are unpleasant."

Hero said, "No one does. Yet it's not very pleasant either to be attacked by something in the dark and not know what it is, is it? Or to have to consider that it might happen again—perhaps in even less pleasant form—unless I can stop it. And I might not be able to unless I am sure."

Susan said, "I see. What will it consist of?"

Hero thought carefully before he spoke, and then replied, "Your going to bed tonight, leaving your door unbolted, and going to sleep. At some time during the night the exact same thing will happen to you—or at least I hope it will be the exact same thing—but with one important difference—this time it will be me."

Susan turned her cool, frank, open gaze full upon Hero and said succinctly, "I don't like men in my room at night." But the trouble was, she realized, that the thought of Hero being there disturbed and excited her in a manner that she was not at all sure that she wished to be, and she had an odd feeling that everything would depend on how Hero reacted to her flat statement.

The investigator simply nodded and said, "Don't undress—just lie on top of the bed with your clothes on."

Susan asked him, "And should your experiment succeed—will you be any further forward?"

Hero suddenly grinned at her, "Oh, lots," he said. "We can stop worrying about that phenomenon."

"I don't see why."

"Anything I can reproduce," Hero replied cheerfully, "we don't worry about any more. Then it becomes no longer a question of what, but who and why."

Susan tried to digest the logic of this and failed. "I don't see that that proves anything," she said, "just because you are able to do what a ghost can do—if it is a ghost."

"Exactly," Hero said, "if it is a ghost. The point is, if it is, it ought to be able to do things that I am not able to do. Otherwise, what would be the use of being a ghost, don't you see? All my professional life I have been trying to find a ghost that *can* do something that I can't. So far I have found them singularly restricted."

"Oh," said Susan suddenly, "and you're hoping it might be mine! I am to be the guinea pig."

Hero regarded her coolly and silently for a moment and then said simply, "Going to play?"

Susan struggled within herself. *"He's heartless—he's using me. Why don't I say no? Oh, why is he so attractive? Why don't I tell him to go and perform his nasty tricks with someone else?"* Aloud she said, "All right, if you really think it is important."

He gave her shoulders a light pressure with both hands and

said, "Good girl! Try to sleep. Don't worry, and don't be frightened." He turned and walked off.

"Do you know that Mark is head over heels in love with Susan Marshall?" Lady Paradine was speaking to her husband across the no man's land of adjoining bath and dressing rooms. Like so many couples who slept apart, they still practiced a kind of communal disrobing, the only time, really, they saw one another privately and could discuss those matters of intimate concern between a husband and wife of long standing.

"Eh, what—he is? Is he really? Well, I suppose if it were true one couldn't blame him."

"Of course it's true," said Lady Paradine. Her long red hair, down to her waist, gleamed magnificently beneath her rhythmic brush strokes. She wore a lilac-colored negligee and her figure was still good, but as far as Lord Paradine was concerned she might have been wearing a boiler suit and a derby hat. He had simply got out of the habit of noticing her. At some time past in their married life he had moved spiritually and physically from the boudoir to the tack and gun rooms. "Would you care to see the next Lady Paradine an American?"

Lord Paradine paused, one leg in his pajama trousers and balancing to insert the other. "Eh, what's that, Enid? What has being an American got to do with it? Susan's a damn fine girl. Look how she's faced up to these damned outrages."

Lady Paradine went after a gray hair and had it out by the roots. "She hasn't a penny," she said evenly.

Lord Paradine got his other leg into the pajamas and tied up the string above his bulging front. "Oho," he said, "to be a good American you have to be a rich American."

"Something like that," Enid replied. "Without money they're quite impossible, aren't they? With things the way they are, it is almost Mark's duty to the family to marry for money—and do a better job of it than you did, my dear."

Paradine paused halfway into his pajama jacket and looked at his wife sharply. "What's that?" he said. "I married you for love, and you know it."

His wife had turned back to the mirror and was studying her reflection—the sagging skin at the throat and the lines at the eyes. "Did you?" she murmured. "I wonder whatever became of it?"

Paradine panicked. "What, what? What do you mean, what became of it? It's here—I mean there. What I mean to say is, I've always loved you. I do right now, don't I?"

Lady Paradine gave up and turned a serene smile upon her husband. "Of course you do, darling," she said. "Don't let it worry you."

A look of exquisite relief came over Paradine's face at being let off what was threatening to become an unpleasant hook. He said, "Well, about the boy. Has he said anything yet?"

"Of course not. And then there's still the question, which one will she take?"

"Eh?" Paradine paused in the middle of squeezing toothpaste onto a brush and tried to cope with the new idea. "What do you mean, which one will she take?"

"Mark or Dick—they're both in love with her."

"What? You mean Lockerie?" Paradine was genuinely shocked. "Why, Richard's old enough to be her father!"

"Provided he had married at sixteen," said Lady Paradine. "How old can he be?" and then supplied the answer. "Forty-two, I think. Just because the war put some gray into his hair and he was in your division doesn't make him as old as you, you know. You're fourteen years older, John."

"But it's ridiculous, Enid," Paradine said, and made for the mouthwash bottle. "He's got a son—what's Julian now, getting on for nine, isn't he? No young girl would want——"

"Don't be silly, John—it's fashionable these days for young girls to marry older men. Some of them even like children—there's Beth, for instance."

"Beth? What's she got to do with it?"

"Hadn't you noticed? When Julian's here she spends nearly all of her time with him. They seem to adore one another. By the way, he'll be coming here tomorrow."

Lord Paradine said, "Good for a kid who hasn't got a mother," and inserted his toothbrush into his mouth.

After a moment's quiet brushing of her hair Lady Paradine said, "John, was Isobel ever in love with Richard?"

Paradine gave a strangled gargle and freed his mouth. "How would I know? You're always asking that, and what's that got to do with anything?"

"You ought to know, as the head of the family."

"Well, I wasn't then," Paradine said with some slight irritation. "Besides, I was away a good deal of the time. I suppose they liked one another as children, but there couldn't have been anything between them because the upshot was that old Dick married that French girl he'd met during the war and had the bad luck to lose her after Julian was born."

Lady Paradine brushed six more strokes and then asked, "Why did Isobel never marry?"

Lord Paradine sighed and tried to hurry his ablutions; this was turning into a regular inquisition and he hated being questioned. "Looking after Father and the Hall, I suppose. Damned shame too—she's a fine woman, Isobel. Ought to be married."

Lady Paradine continued brushing, and this time she did not speak. Lord Paradine found the hiatus even more uncomfortable than if she had continued the interrogation, for it forced him to think and wonder.

"I suppose it mightn't be bad for Dick," he said, "a fine young girl like Susan. Keep him up to scratch. Damn good match, eh?"

Lady Paradine did not reply specifically to this but said obliquely, "Whether or not she is really in love with Mark, the thought of becoming Lady Paradine must be a great temptation —particularly to an American."

Lord Paradine stared at his wife in bewilderment. "But I thought you said——"

Lady Paradine said pityingly, "Oh, John, really! With a choice of titles, naturally one takes the better one." She dipped three fingers of each hand into a jar of beauty cream and began to dab the peach-colored stuff onto both cheeks with firm, positive strokes, and in time to them she said, "I wouldn't like—my Mark—to be married—to Susan Marshall."

Lord Paradine put down toothbrush and mug in genuine surprise this time at the curiously flat, hard, and almost menacing tone that had come into his wife's voice. He stared at her but she did not say anything more, nor was there any change in her expression as, contemplating her face in the mirror, she worked the cream firmly into her cheeks. Paradine turned his attention once more to his teeth.

Susan had followed Hero's counsel and lain down on the bed fully clothed, even to her shoes. And to further the proper working of the experiment she had tried to remember and organize her room as it had been the night it happened.

Thoughts and turmoils whirled through her mind: who or what hated her? What or who wished her away from Paradine Hall, and why? Who and what was Alexander Hero that she should be disturbed by him? Did she like him? Did she not? Was Beth really her friend? Was Isobel? Was Lady Paradine? Did she love Mark? Could she love him enough to give up all her ways, her customs, and her life, to be something and someone she had never been before? Did she want to be Lady Paradine?

And what about Sir Richard—Beth's pseudo "Uncle Dick"— widower with a boy of nine, the one supposed to be coming home from school? Dick was still young and vigorous in body and mind; he had paid her marked attention. She had enjoyed his companionship, the games, the riding, the sailing, and yet there was something about him and his attentions too that disturbed her, something she felt was not wholly sincere. She was fond of him but did not think of him with that sudden warmth that came sometimes when she thought of Mark. And now there was Alexander Hero, who of all of them seemed to attract her most disturbingly. What of him, she kept asking herself—that too poised, too intelligent, too fascinating young man?

And that was the last thought she had, at which she must have dozed off. And now she was starkly wide awake. There was the cold wind again, and something or someone was in the room. The thought flashed through her mind, what if it were not Hero? Supposing . . . ? Then the icy fingers were at her throat again—

a hand, horrid, dead cold, moist and clammy, as though straight from the tomb.

It was unbearable, even though she had been expecting it, and brave as she was, she felt her nerves go. It was more than flesh and blood could take. She screamed, or thought she screamed, or would have screamed, but the sound would not come from her, the touch of the icy fingers paralyzed her, and no more than a moan, a kind of whimper, came from her lips.

And then the hand was gone and someone was whispering, "Sorry, old girl. It's all right. It's all over," and a warm, comforting palm was laid upon her brow. In her relief in reaction from the panic that had gripped her, she reached for him in the darkness like a child, her two arms found him, and hungrily held him, for she needed his comfort now, and he gave it, taking her to him likewise, and holding her, and then, as must needs happen, as she had always known must and would, their mouths found one another in the darkness, and they were both aware of that moment of losing themselves in one another, of that dizzying magic of contact, which if continued would bring the stars down from the heavens.

Yet they parted momentarily, he stroking her hair and murmuring her name, and she wishing not to let him go, wishing never to be let go, but knowing that she must, that somewhere something was not yet as it should be, that she had not yet heard the answer to the question in her heart.

It was Hero who recovered first and said, still whispering, "I think perhaps we'd better have the light now," and Susan answered, "Yes, we'd better." She felt and heard him move, and heard the click of the light switch of the bed lamp on the bedside table, but no light came on.

Hero felt his scalp tingling and his nerves taut; he had reproduced conditions of the experiment exactly with but one exception—he had not tampered with the lights. He said softly, close to Susan's ear, "Second thoughts—we'll have it as before. Light your candle as you did that night, but move very quietly." Susan groped her way toward the mantel, struck a match, and lit the candle.

They faced one another, with the knowledge that they had just shared a moment of love, or if not that, then something closely akin to love, but they were not embarrassed by it; they were able to look at one another with steadiness and appraisal, and to think their thoughts. Susan's were, *"I don't know. I don't know. I thought I wanted and needed him. I suppose perhaps I did then, but I don't now."*

Hero's were, *"Oh, you ass! Whatever did you do that for? Won't you ever learn? And how will you ever be able to know now whether she is telling you the truth? You're a fool, Hero."*

He slipped shut the bolt fastened to the inside of her door, while Susan watched him wide-eyed. She then said, "That was it. That was exactly what it was like. Are you satisfied?"

"Yes," Hero said. He was pale, and his eyes glittered in the candlelight.

"What was it then?" Susan asked.

But the only reply he made was to raise his finger to his lips and she saw that he was no longer looking at her but was eying the knob of the door handle, which was slowly, perceptibly, and inexorably turning. Susan watched breathlessly, her heart pounding, as the handle turned to its fullest extent; there was a faint noise as though it were being pulled on. Hero was watching it calmly, one hand raised toward Susan in a gesture that commanded both silence and yet gave comfort. They both saw it go through the same revolution once more. Someone or something from the outside was trying it.

In frozen silence Hero and Susan watched and waited. The doorknob made one more half turn; they heard a faint creak in the corridor, and then all was silent again. Outside the night was alive with country sounds, but within the house it was quiet.

Hero appeared not to be listening any longer but rather to be concentrating on something else, almost as though he were waiting for something, or counting time. The bulb of the bedside lamp suddenly began to glow bright yellow in its shade, and Susan gave vent to a startled "Oh!" for it appeared to have come on by itself, but Hero let go his breath in what appeared to be a long sigh of relief and recognition. "Alarm over," he said.

Fearless and controlled as she was, Susan's nerves were still shaken from her experience and she said somewhat unsteadily, "Are you sure?" And then, "Oh, Alexander—I'm very glad you were here with me. What was it?"

Hero was watching her now thoughtfully. "Not what," he said, "But who? 'What' would have come in without knocking. 'Who' finds an inside bolt a little more than can be managed."

"Alex," Susan asked, "why didn't you go after it—or whoever? Why didn't you open the door? You would have caught them, wouldn't you?"

Hero was regarding her quizzically. "Who would have caught whom?" he said.

Susan suddenly drew in her breath sharply. "It's because of me, then, that you didn't? You might have solved the mystery just by opening the door——"

"I didn't quite have the right to, did I?" Hero said.

Susan went to him and impulsively laid her hand upon his arm and whispered, "Oh, you are nice!"

Her closeness disturbed Hero, but no longer in the same way. He said, "No. Not really. Not very. Practical."

Suddenly it dawned upon Susan that he might not have wished

to encounter whoever had tried her door, that he did not trust her. It made her furiously angry. He had supposed it might have been Sir Richard . . . Then her anger passed, leaving only a feeling of deepest melancholy.

Hero said, "I'll have a look, but I don't expect I'll find anything. You need not worry—there will be no more doing tonight, but after I've gone, just slip that bolt back on the door and don't open it until morning. Sorry about everything, Susan." And then with a swiftness that was almost like a conjurer's trick he was gone.

He did not proceed down the corridor at once to search, a gesture he knew would be fruitless, but remained standing outside her door. He heard the rod of the bolt slide into place. His nostrils were assailed by a strange odor. He lifted his head and sniffed. It was faint but present and, because of his laboratory training, recognizable. It made the hair bristle at the nape of his neck and a sensation of nausea rise in his throat.

Like a hound following the scent, he sniffed his way down the door to the bottom of it by the floor, from where it emanated—a still slightly damp splotch. He sniffed closer, touched it with the tip of his finger, and then looked at the white patch of burn on the skin where he had come in contact with the acid. He rose to his feet pale and sweating, though inside him he felt sickeningly cold.

The morning of the day Hero hoped Meg would arrive, the investigator was nervous. He had felt the need of momentary escape from Paradine Hall and had taken stick, cap, and briar and gone for a walk. One of the setters from the stable, sensing the opportunity, had attached itself to him for a little stroll with company, and joyously led the way. Mr. Hero let him. He did not wish to go anywhere in particular, he merely wished to go. Paradine Hall, its occupants, its puzzles, and its sometimes amateur, sometimes wholly baffling phenomena would keep until he returned.

The setter, his copper-colored flag waving gaily, led the way through an open door in the wall and then south along the riverbank to Stoke Bridge, the old Roman arch, whose stones and craftmanship had weathered the centuries. While the dog snuffled along the banks Hero stood on the bridge for a moment and watched three roach fanning themselves with their fins on the stony bottom of the river. When the dog appeared interested in following the river bank farther, Hero, lighting his briar, followed him contentedly, breathing in the fresh salt breeze blown in from the sea and mingling with the earthy odors of the Paradine farms to the east.

One of the things which were gnawing at his mind was that there was no "atmosphere" at Paradine Hall. There had been manifestations galore, they had taken place quite properly at night, but no one as yet had complained of any sense of evil or oppression, nor had he experienced any such himself. Hero had once spent a night in a room reputed to be haunted, where the sense of "presence" and an accumulating evil had been unmistakable, and at one point had left him sick and sweating. He had never solved it to his complete satisfaction. At that time there had been no other manifestations of any kind, it had been merely a sensation of being in a horrid place that gave him horrid thoughts and feelings. So far he had encountered none of this at the Hall, and wondered why—no terrified animals, and none of the uneasy human reactions to the onset of the supernatural. People were alarmed, frightened, astonished, or angry, according to their natures, during or after a happening, but never before. He wondered whether he would solve the Paradine mystery.

Hero tried to dissociate his mind—earth and water smelled so good. In the distance a windmill lazily turned its arms. The sky was Dutch blue, one would almost expect to come upon a tulip field or one of those exquisitely scrubbed little villages with houses of red brick and slate roofs to be encountered across the Channel. How akin Norfolk and Holland were, except in their customs and people.

The dog suddenly went into a hysteria of yappings, friskings, and shriekings, and Hero saw that he was leaping upon and kissing a small boy who was fishing in the river with a split cane river rod and reel and float. The boy pushed him away, crying, "No, no, King! Go away. Go home. *Tais-toi, méchant!*"

He was a handsome little boy of nine, with light, curly hair and a pair of the most brilliantly blue and beautiful eyes Hero had ever seen. His nose was of course the button belonging to any boy of that age, but he had a grave mouth and firm chin.

"Hello, friend," Hero said. "Who are you?" There was a slight bend in the bank at that point, and a large tree just around the corner, and King had transferred his hysterics to that quarter.

"I'm Julian Lockerie. Who are you? Are you from the Hall? You must be, or you wouldn't be out walking with King. I've just come back from school. I'm on holiday. Daddy gave me this new rod."

"Alexander Hero, at your service," Hero replied. He motioned with his briar to the spot on the river where the float had suddenly disappeared. "I think you're about to do some business, young man."

The tip of the rod had begun to quiver and dance. "Auntie Beth, Auntie Beth," the boy shouted. "Come at once! Oh, do come at once, please. I have one. *Venez, venez, je vous en prie!*"

Beth appeared from around the bank and the tree, where she had been sitting with her book, which she now carried in one hand, but she stopped quite suddenly when she saw Mr. Hero, for she had not expected to see him, or anyone, and would not have come out had she known, for she had been crying; her eyes were still red and her face swollen. A tear-sodden handkerchief was in the other hand. The dog galloped frantically back and forth between the child and the girl. The fishing rod shivered and shook. Hero saw, wondered, and decided that the thing to do was simply to ignore and not to have seen. For Beth it was too late to draw back.

"I seem to have stolen your dog," Hero said, "or, if I may put it the other way round, he has stolen me. You're just in time to witness the climax of the angler's drama."

Beth smiled and came forward. "Ah, *bien fait*, Julian," she said.

The boy was dancing with excitement, "I've got him—but what shall I do? What shall I do?" It was apparently the first such success he had had, and it had taken him completely by surprise.

"Lift him gently from his element and deposit him on the

bank," Hero advised. "That is supposed to be the general purpose of the exercise."

The boy elevated the rod and a fair-sized tench came aviating out of the river, to land flapping on the bank in their midst, until Hero put his foot on it, disengaged the hook, and dispatched it with a sharp blow from his stick. "Well done!" he said. "Your father will be very proud of you."

The boy stared at his prize rapturously. "I'll give it to Daddy for his supper when he comes home, Auntie Beth," he said, and then to Hero, "Daddy's gone out sailing with his new girl, but he'll be back for tea, won't he, Auntie Beth?"

Beth said, "Of course."

"Daddy's new friend is called Susan. I like her." Julian informed Hero again. "But I love Auntie Beth best—oh, I do!" He suddenly ran to her in a curiously emotional and touching show of affection, which Hero felt had its inspiration in quite something else, and he threw his arms about her, and she about him. He said, "I'm not going to give the fish to Daddy, I'm going to give it to you. It's for you."

Beth said, "Darling, it's such a big one—we'll all have some of it. How clever of you to have caught him."

Like his father, Julian was essentially a fair man, and he said, "*Mais c' était ce monsieur-là qui m'a aidé.*"

"It was nothing," Hero said modestly. "It's all your fish. I repeat—your father has reason to be proud of you."

"Do you know my father?" the boy asked.

"Yes."

"Is he going to marry Susan?"

Beth chided, "*Mais, Julian, on ne dit pas des choses comme ça.*" "I don't know," Hero replied with some slight formality. "He hasn't said."

Julian said to Beth, "Why can't you be my mother?" Then, distracted by the fish, added, "Isn't he a beauty?"

Beth murmured, "I'm sorry. We——"

Hero said, "Never mind. It is one of the few privileges children have, to be able to come to the point. It will be taken away from him soon enough. May I continue to borrow your dog?"

"Yes, do," said Beth, and seemed relieved that he was going.

"But don't you go, Auntie Beth," Julian said. "I'm going to catch another fish." He molded a bread pellet onto the hook and returned line and float to the water.

Hero turned his footsteps back along the path he had come so as not to have to repass the pair, and the last he saw of them they were sitting on the bank together, their arms around one another's waists. This put a whole new light on matters: Beth Paradine in love with Sir Richard; "Uncle Dick," oblivious of this, in love with her best friend—*that* would want sorting out too, and he was more than ever eager for Meg's coming, and in anticipation hurried back to the Hall.

It was approaching noon by then and she had not yet arrived. As a vantage point from which to observe matters when she did, Hero ensconced himself in a deep chair at the back of the conservatory. This room, with its large pane of glass still unset in the picture window and tilted at an angle, coupled with the bright sun, made it easy for Mr. Hero to see out but rather difficult for anyone on the outside to look in. Just beyond the window, and parallel to it, was the deep ditch where the drains were being worked on, and an occasional pick or a workman's head would emerge momentarily therefrom.

He saw Noreen lying on her stomach on the bank at the top of the sunken garden, and Mr. Jellicot engaging her in conversation. Major Wilson came from the direction of the stables, apparently had his attention caught by a movement Hero had made, and stopped and peered in through the canted window. His mouth was open, the corners drawn down, and he looked sour. Hero thought to himself, "*This is what people must look like to animals in the zoo when they peer into their cages.*" He was not certain whether Major Wilson had seen him or not, and did not particularly care. He saw Wilson give his silent, self-satisfied laugh, pause for a moment to have a word with one of the men in the ditch, and go on. A few minutes later he returned, accompanied by his wife, and again Mr. Hero felt a stirring at the sight of her— slender, well groomed, appetizing, and willing.

At that moment there was the noise of a motorcar; a crested, uniformed-chauffeur-driven Rolls-Royce Silver Cloud drew up. Hero's heart leaped. He clamped his pipe more firmly between his teeth, set it going again, and leaned back in his chair grinning happily to himself. Meg's arrival was a production.

The Lady Margaret Callandar was a simple, practical girl who traveled on trains, took the bus in London, and who could live out of one suitcase if necessary, but upon this occasion she had chosen to arrive in state and emerged from the shining vehicle encased in a Balmain frock, a hat by Yves, and nine pieces of mauve-colored, cream-banded luggage.

Noreen sat up and gawked with her mouth open, various gardeners stopped work, and Mrs. Wilson frankly lost herself in Lady Margaret's ensemble. Mr. Hero had no doubt but what there would also be faces at upstairs windows taking in the performance. He was highly satisfied with his stepsister.

Lord and Lady Paradine and Isobel came forth to greet her. Because the picture window was not sealed, murmurs and sounds of voices, as well as the impressive sight, came through to Mr. Hero, concealed in the depths of his chair.

"So nice of you to come," said Lord Paradine.

"So good of you to have me," said Meg.

"Of course you and Isobel are old friends," said Lady Paradine.

"My dear," murmured Isobel, "it seems hard to credit. The last time——"

"Ugh," finished Meg, "don't even mention it. I'm sure I was all legs and plaits, and probably popping bubble gum imported from America—and you haven't changed, except to look lovelier."

Huggins appeared to take charge of the luggage. The Wilsons had drawn out their stay as long as was humanly possible, and now reluctantly moved on. Noreen had come over and was staring unabashedly, her hands clasped over her stomach. Mr. Jellicot also gaped. Hero felt Meg knew he was watching her from somewhere, and was enjoying herself thoroughly. She pulled at her gloves, dangled her fashionable handbag from one arm, and carrying a small and delicately colored rolled-up umbrella, passed with the Paradines and Isobel in the inimitable slow conversational saunter of the haut monde out of sight through the portals of Paradine Hall. They were followed by butler and chauffeur, carrying the mauve and cream matched luggage.

Mr. Hero smiled happily to himself and thought, *"If you only knew what naughty things my dear sister has in those cases!"*

With the cavalcade out of sight, Hero wandered out through the small door which led from the conservatory to the driveway, crossing over the small wood plank footbridge erected over the trench. He walked over to the gleaming vehicle, where Mr. Jellicot was bent over in a somewhat undignified posture, which enabled him to study the crest on the door, while Noreen had her long nose flattened against the car window on the other side and was taking in the exquisite interior fittings and appointments.

"Look," Noreen said to Hero as he approached, "it's even more beautiful than yours."

"In a feminine way," Hero admitted.

"Wasn't she beautiful?" Noreen said, shifting from the car to its former occupant. "Is she a princess?"

"Not quite," Hero replied.

Mr. Jellicot straightened up and spoke importantly. "Near enough! An earl's daughter." He pointed to the crest on the door. "I wonder whether I shall be permitted to meet her?"

"Little mannie," Hero said to himself, *"you wot not what you would. You shall meet her and may be the sorrier for it before too long—and so may several others hereabouts."*

Hero thought he would give Meg time to settle down a bit before he paid her a visit, so he busied himself with certain matters that were on his mind. He remembered that he had wished to consult the tide table he had asked about, and he went to the large cupboard in the hall in which there was a telephone extension.

When he got there he was aware that Noreen had attached herself to him and had come pattering after. She said, "Are you going to telephone someone?"

Hero replied, "No."

"Then what are you doing in the closet?"

Hero said, "I've told you—looking for ghosts."

Noreen said firmly, "There aren't any in there."

"Really? How do you know?"

"Because I know. I know where they are and I know where they aren't."

Hero regarded the child quizzically for a moment and remarked, "Well, that's useful. I may call upon you sometime to show me where they are. Now run along, there's a good girl."

The tide table was there attached to a bit of string, available to anyone. He examined it; his eyebrows went up, and he started with surprise as he did some rapid calculations and murmured, "Oh, my giddy aunt!" and then, "What the devil date is it today?"

"It's Wednesday, July the thirteenth," Noreen said. It seemed she hadn't "run along."

Hero said, "I know, love. That's just what I was afraid of," and to himself he added, *"Tonight's the night, then. Old Meg just did get here on time. The sooner I have a word with her the better."* But first he intended to have another look at the music room. Noreen came tagging along after him.

The child said, "Mr. Hero——"

"Yes, pet."

"Would you go for a walk with me sometime?"

Hero, who had been thinking of other things, said, "What's that? Yes. Yes, of course, if you like."

"I mean, just us two alone together—no grownups or anyone else along."

Hero felt himself suddenly touched at the exclusion of grownups. "Very well then—just we two alone."

"Promise? Cross your heart?"

"Very well."

"Do it," said Noreen.

They had reached the threshold of the music room and Mr. Hero solemnly performed the ancient ceremony which to a child is the only trustworthy seal of a bargain. They went into the music room.

Hero said to Noreen, "Are there any ghosts in here?"

The child reflected with a doubtful look on her ugly little face. "I'm not sure. Would you like one?"

Mr. Hero replied, "Yes, please—very much," and then stood in the middle of the room looking about him. Nothing was changed; everything seemed to be as it was before. Apparently the maids came in, for the room was clean and dusted, and the curtains half drawn. The great golden harp stood in its place in the corner by the window, the chair and music stand next it; the lid of the grand piano was closed; the music was still in the orderly piles undisturbed; none of the pictures or statuary had been moved.

And yet as Hero stood there taking it all in he had the curiously uncomfortable feeling that something *was* slightly different— something missing, altered, or moved, or perhaps even added— and for the life of him he could not discover what it was. He walked about the room racking his mind, searching with eyes and instinct, while the child, Noreen, watched him gravely and lovingly, doting on his every movement. He ran a tentative fingernail up the chromatic scale of the harp strings and stood puzzled, pulling as usual at his lower lip. Was there any point in sealing the room, in setting one of those complicated traps that psychical investigators of a decade or so ago had been so fond of contriving— seals, sifted flour, electronic eyes, bells, trip wires? For a moment he even harbored the notion of removing the harp from the room altogether, and then decided against any of this; it was here the harp had been heard and practically seen to play, and it was here under these same conditions that he wished to observe it, with perhaps one slight exception which he would discuss with Meg, and this would be merely a perfunctory precaution. He had an idea that none of the traps would work anyway. What the devil was it that was different about the room? His irritation showed on his face.

"Why don't you come and see our ghost, then?" Noreen said.

She brought Hero back from his thoughts. "Eh—what's that? Your ghost—which one?"

"The one that makes Mummy good and sick—but I'm not frightened of it. The other two gentlemen have seen it."

"Mr. Jellicot and Dr. Paulson?"

"Yes. They *loved* it."

Hero regarded Noreen but there was neither skepticism nor

amusement in his eyes when he asked, "What time? Does it keep a schedule?"

"In the afternoons sometime, when Mummy's there," Noreen said. "It hates Mummy but it loves me."

"Will you be there?" Hero asked.

Noreen reflected for a moment and then replied, "I might— if I knew you were coming. I love you." Then she cried, "Don't forget your promise," and went skipping off out of the room and down the corridor.

When shortly afterward Hero strolled into Meg's room she looked up from her unpacking with just the slightest air of guilt and anxiety. "Oh, Sandro," she said, "was I just too awful? I thought perhaps with so many odd bods about you might like something a little impressive——"

"My dear Lady Margaret," Hero said, and kissed her cheek, "you were absolutely superb. It was better than the entrance of the Good Fairy in the pantomime. It could only have been improved upon if they had let you down on wires."

He eyed appreciatively an expensive-looking brown leather lady's handbag that stood upon her dressing table. "Ah," he said, "Little Snooper." It contained their own adaptation of a Japanese-German Icaflex mini-camera loading the most sensitive of films and operated by a small, delicate, and practically noiseless clockwork motor. The lens peered out invisibly from the fold of the handbag.

"We'll be wanting him," Hero continued. "I think I've been invited to see a poltergeist this afternoon."

"Oh," said Meg, "by whom?"

"Personal friend of the ghost," Hero said. "A child. Her parents are real nasty bits of work. The poltergeist doesn't like them."

"Oho!" said Meg.

"Exactly," Hero echoed. "Oho!" and then told her about the Spendley-Carters and the manifestations taking place about them, concluding, "I'd prefer to get that one settled first."

"That one?" Meg raised an eyebrow.

Hero said somewhat bitterly, "Huh—you don't know yet. This place is riddled with ghosts. I can't break them until I sort them out." He brought her up to date on the further attempts to drive Susan Marshall from the Hall, and the horror of the acid splotch outside her door.

When he had finished, with wonderful irrelevancy Meg asked,

"Who was that terribly attractive woman who was watching me when I got out of my car?"

"That was a Mrs. Wilson, one of the guests at the Country Club. Her husband's an army Major.

"She looked dangerous to me."

Hero snorted. "She—I'm sure she had nothing to do with any of it."

"Oh no," Meg said, "I meant to you. Has she made eyes at you yet? She looks the type."

"Lord," Hero said, "I'm in enough trouble without that!"

"Is Susan Marshall very attractive?"

Hero said irritably, "Certainly—but what's that got to do with it?" He felt that exasperation that comes to all men when women appear to stab in the dark and hit the bull's-eye.

Meg was suddenly contrite. "I *am* a beast to tease you, Sandro. But you know, you did ask me once to keep an eye on you."

Hero did remember that at one time he had invoked Meg's aid, and had regretted it ever since. From that day on she had constituted herself a kind of amatory nanny. He said, "Oh, I suppose it's called for, and if it's love affairs you're interested in, requited, I gather, as well as un-, you've come to the right place. This house is a prison of torments. I am surprised that anything from the beyond could have gained a foothold here. But something has, and it is both wicked and dangerous. We must try to stop it before someone gets hurt."

Meg was serious at once. "I'm sorry I was naughty," and then she said as though it summed up the miseries of the world, "Love!"

"And hate. As for the love part, do you remember Schnitzler's *Reigen?*"

His stepsister grimaced, and he continued, "Sir Richard Lockerie is in love with Susan Marshall, the American girl. Beth Paradine, her best friend, is eating her heart out for Sir Richard, whom she calls 'Uncle Dick.' "

"And who else?"

"Mark Paradine has fallen head over heels for Susan too."

"And Susan?"

"The great uncommitted."

"Whom does Isobel love?"

Hero blinked for a moment at his sister's question and then replied, "Paradine Hall, apparently. In the meantime, young Beth consoles herself looking after Sir Richard's boy, Julian, who has just come home from school. Lady Paradine is not at all pleased with the possibility of Susan as a daughter-in-law; I suspect Susan's crime is having no money, as well as engaging the affections of her son. Lady P. also hates Isobel. Cousin Freddie hates everyone—an attitude, as far as I can gather, which is mutual. And someone or something hates Susan Marshall enough to entertain the notion of spoiling her looks with acid."

Meg shuddered slightly and said, "Who?"

Hero replied, "I don't know, and it may be no more than an accident that all of this coincides with the reappearance of the nun."

"Ah well," said Meg practically, "maybe we can get our teeth into something there. Ghosts that wander about in a nun's habit, fiddling with doorknobs and bearing acid ought to register on film."

Hero said, "Mmmh—but what won't is a harp that plays by itself in a locked room in which there is nobody."

Meg said, "Still . . ."

Hero concluded, "I know, we'll set one up just to make sure there is nobody—but you won't get anything."

Meg was watching her stepbrother narrowly. "Sandro," she said, "you're really worried, aren't you?"

He replied, "Yes. What if this were the breakthrough? What if 'something' instead of 'someone'—not necessarily the nun—were really playing that harp? What if it were true, and amidst a welter of what I consider hanky-panky and general nastiness, something had got through and were trying to signal? And if this were the case, then perhaps other things going on here might be true as well. How the devil am I to get them all sorted out? And as for the truth—it isn't in anyone. Everybody has told me at least one lie since I have been here, so far."

Meg asked, "Have you seen and heard the harp yourself?"

"Not yet. I'm hoping—tonight. In the meantime, from Lord Paradine's account——" In reply to a look that Meg threw him he amended, "Oh, Paradine's as honest as a man can be—he isn't exactly lovable, but he's honest and fair-minded enough. Paradine woke up sometime toward three o'clock in the morning and heard the harp in the music room playing Gréves' 'My Bonnie Dear.' He ran downstairs, found the door locked, and shouted to his wife for the keys. Lady Paradine had a duplicate bunch that confirmed her nominally as head of the house—but of course it is Isobel who runs everything. She brought them as the last strains of the song were heard coming from the instrument inside. When he rushed in and switched on the light there was no one in the room, and he swears nothing could have passed him. He ran over to the harp—the strings were still vibrating."

"Could he have imagined it?"

"Lord Paradine is not an imaginative man. A few moments later Isobel came in. She had heard it too. Together they searched the room and the surrounding apartments. There was no one there. Lady Paradine thought it might have been the wind."

"Could it have been?"

"Susan Marshall heard it too. It was the night she was attacked by the nun. That makes three witnesses."

"Oh dear!" said Meg.

Hero struck his head with the heel of his hand. "I can't find anything wrong with the harp, and I can't seem to work out any way of doing it myself either. And yet when I just went into the music room there was something there that I couldn't get at, and which is driving me up the pole." He looked fiercely at Meg and said, "Even if I find out how, there's still the why to know before this house can be dehaunted."

As always, practical, Meg said, "Let's see if we can settle the 'how' first." She opened ore of her bags, removed a layer of lingerie, and revealed a nest of equipment.

There were a half dozen of the small X-100 wide-angle-lensed cameras, each no bigger than a bar of soap and fitted with a suction cup which held it to ceiling or wall, and which, using infra-red film, when coupled with an infra-red flash jolted by tiny but powerful mercury batteries, took pictures in the dark. Flash and camera were set off by an invisible black silk thread fastened at ankle height. Whoever sprang the trap might be conscious of a momentary slight red glow and nothing more, but probably not even that, since the flash equipment, about the size of a matchbox, was likewise fastened above eye level. There was also Meg's and Hero's adaptation of an 8-mm. cine camera for infra-red, and another still camera for daylight work, whose shutter was operated by a photoelectric cell. Meg had indeed brought the lot.

"Beautiful," Hero murmured, looking down at them. "We'll try out the X-100s tonight. I should say about five of them would do for a starter. If you'll come along with me I'll show you where I want them. There's more confounded creeping goes on in this house after dark. . . ."

Meg looked at her stepbrother and murmured, "I wouldn't doubt it," in a manner which should have warned him had his thoughts not been already racing ahead.

After lunch Hero managed to isolate Sir Richard Lockerie and maneuver him into the library where he talked to him earnestly for ten minutes, told him something of his fears, and enlisted his aid. "I probably shan't have another opportunity to talk to you alone. I'm not certain what kind of a performance is scheduled for tonight—only that there will be one. What I need is one more of our side alert, so to speak."

Sir Richard said, "Yes, yes, you may count on me," but he was not exactly sure now that he completely trusted the young man he had been instrumental in bringing there to solve the hauntings at Paradine Hall.

"Good," Hero said. "Whatever you see or hear, or think you may see, don't pursue and don't try to touch—leave that to me. One important rule of spirit hunting is 'don't grab.'"

"Ah," Sir Richard said, "then you'll be setting a trap for the ghost?"

Hero looked at him curiously and repeated, "'For the ghost'? Not at all—for people. What on earth would be the use of setting a trap for a ghost? I should say that one of the conveniences of being a ghost is that you no longer have to worry about such things as traps—or locked doors, eh?"

Sir Richard asked, "But what if I were to see the nun?"

Hero repeated, "Don't grab. Whatever it is, let it be, or you may regret it all your life. I prefer her on the loose. Simply use your eyes and your head and observe."

Sir Richard looked disturbed and shocked. "By God, Hero, then you mean that someone here in the house—one of us—is playing a series of very nasty and dangerous jokes?"

"I couldn't tell you," Hero replied. "Investigation of occult phenomena and paranormal manifestations about a premises has changed a great deal in the past ten years. Formerly, one used to study the ghost, its history, nature, and character. Today one tends to concentrate more upon those who saw it, or thought they saw it."

Lockerie said, "You mean, we're all under suspicion?"

"Yes."

Lockerie laughed somewhat grimly. "That's a good one! Who will be watching me?"

Hero said calmly, "I will."

Sir Richard snorted. "Oh, come now, aren't you taking rather a strong line, Hero? What about the testimony of such reliable and authoritative witnesses as Lord Paradine, the Rev. Harry Witherspoon, Dr. Paulson, and, I might add, myself, who am not to be taken in too easily? After all, if the word of a clergyman and a scientist . . ."

It was Hero's turn to laugh. "Nonsense! And if I am taking a strong line, it is because you are the only one in this house with whom I can trust myself to do so. Your doctors, clergymen, and scientists are the greatest gulls in the world, and are invariably found at the head of every easy-mark and sucker list. You only have to go back to the beginning of the twentieth century to read of the revolting performances endorsed by eminent scientists and doctors. Let the worst spiritualist charlatan and faker produce a nauseous bit of cheesecloth from some body orifice in a darkened room, and lo! a lifetime of painstaking method and scientific search for facts by trial and error go out the window; they believe like little children."

"And clergymen," said Sir Richard with some asperity, "you include them too? If one can't trust——"

Hero said, "If you'll forgive me, when you consider the level at which any honest clergyman operates, it is entirely in the realm of faith. It seems to me that nothing would console and satisfy a priest more than to be witness to some kind of a miracle—even a black one. The vicar was happy as a child when he thought he had actually caught Satan under this roof."

"But damn it all, Hero," Sir Richard protested, "what about what all of us saw that night at the dinner—nineteen of us right there in one room? You yourself would have had to believe."

Hero said, "Sir Richard, I am a younger man than you and ought not to be taking issue with you, except that I have devoted the past ten years and more to the study of just such phenomena as were reported to have taken place that night in the great hall. There is a difference between seeing and knowing what it is at which you are looking. You did me the honor to pay a small compliment in the matter concerning Dr. Bingham: if you will remember, in that case all of us, including myself, saw only what someone wanted us to see. Fortunately—before it was too late . . ."

Sir Richard suddenly thawed. He came over and laid a hand on Hero's arm and said, "Forgive me, Hero. I had forgotten. You are right. This is a field I know nothing about, and I am afraid my nerves have been somewhat shaken. You are in command here, and I'll do my best, and I think you may count on me not to do anything foolish. When do you think one might expect . . . ?"

Hero replied, "At about three o'clock in the morning there will be one hellish rumpus. It will come from the neighborhood of Isobel's room, where the manifestations first began. It is my theory that the disturbances will spread to other parts of the house, including the east wing. The nun may be seen again, the lights go out—the harp may play; I am hoping that it will."

Sir Richard said, "By Jove! You are anticipating quite a program. Exactly what is it you wish me to do?"

Hero said, "Put out your light, open your door. You may stand in the doorway, but do not come out into the corridor or prowl unless . . ."

"Yes," said Lockerie, following intently, "unless?"

For a moment Hero felt himself at at loss for words. Finally he said, "There is someone here—I need not mention names—who means a great deal to you. I want her watched—and protected. Should she appear, you may follow her and see that she comes to no harm."

Sir Richard looked up sharply and his face had become suddenly flushed. "Ah," he said, "then you know?"

"Yes," Hero replied, "I know." It was his first and only serious mistake of the entire investigation.

Hero returned to Meg's room later in the afternoon. He found her changed into a brown ensemble. She was walking about the room with her brown handbag clutched under one arm. Ever and anon she would pause, stand still, turn around, move off again. Not even Hero's keen ear was able to detect the whir of the small motor inside the bag or observe the lens of the camera concealed in the fold of the leather. Meg said, "Rehearsing. One's hand gets out after a while. Stand there for a moment, like a good boy." She walked a few steps away from him, turned her back. After a few moments she said, "Poifick."

Hero said, "How can you tell?"

Meg replied, "Practice. It just wouldn't do to have it rigged up with the finder, and go peering at it, would it?"

"What have you accomplished, my love?" Hero asked.

Meg said, "I've wangled an invitation from Spendley-Carter to come and see their ghost. Your Mr. Jellicot is coming too. I thought he was rather a pet."

Hero said, "Did you now? I'm not quite so sure. What do you think of the rest of our cast of characters?"

"Shockers, some of them, aren't they?" Meg replied. "Your Major Wilson gives me the creeps. I know that type of soldier. Professional killers. They enjoy it. I like that old girl of yours, Mrs.

Taylor. You may flirt with her if you like. She could probably teach you a lot of things you don't know."

"And Aunt Isobel?"

"Hasn't changed, as I remember."

"What about the girls—Susan and Beth?"

"Judgment reserved."

Hero did not press the point. He looked at his watch. "It's about time for the party," he said.

Meg nodded. "Right. I'll feed Little Snooper first. He wants his din'." She opened the bag and extracted a small, beautifully compact camera of Japanese make, a precision job as carefully tooled and put together as a watch, and not much larger than an old-fashioned Hunter. The lens, however, was German, and the film in the tiny steel cassette with which Meg loaded it the fastest superpanchromatic on the market, which would record a clear image in the light of a single electric bulb. Hero and his stepsister had labored long, arduously, and happily over this prying piece of machinery. Coupled with the clockwork motor, which was started by a small spring which Meg depressed with her thumb on the catch of the bag, Little Snooper photographed everything going on behind Meg's back at the rate of a picture every three seconds, with some hundred frames available in the cassette.

Hero watched the glossy head and serious mien of his stepsister as she bent over her meticulous task, noting the practice and agility of her fingers, and experienced a great feeling of relief and relaxation in her presence: good old Meg, she did stand by when she was wanted. If anything of substance moved across the lenses of her cameras she would capture it. He would have been surprised had he been able to penetrate the busy person of his stepsister to hear how her heart was singing with the happiness of helping him. She looked up at the final click as the bag snapped shut. "There," she announced, "all set."

"Let's go," Hero said. They went down the corridor toward the Spendley-Carters' room arm in arm.

NEVER HUNT A GHOST
WITH A GUN

The visit to the room of the Spendley-Carters was not exactly a social success. Sylvia Spendley-Carter was nervous, worried, and ill at ease. Her husband was not at all glad to see Mr. Hero, and little Mr. Jellicot was as anxious as a parent awaiting his child's appearance at the annual theatricals. He was desperately eager that his poltergeist should perform for Mr. Hero and the daughter of an earl.

Spendley-Carter said, "I wasn't expecting you, Hero. Still, I suppose you're entitled to come and have a look-see. Don't expect anything will happen now."

Hero murmured, "I know. It's like the dentist's waiting room and the vanishing toothache. It has been my experience, unfortunately, that spirits are notoriously shy in my presence. Enter Hero, exit ghosts."

Meg managed to suppress a giggle, and got on with her part of the amenities. She gushed, "So good of you to let me come, dear Mr. and Mrs. Spendley-Carter. You know, we are supposed to have a ghost at Heth Castle. My father claims to have seen it when he was a boy. I think you are extraordinarily brave, Mrs. Spendley-Carter."

Sylvia Spendley-Carter had risen reluctantly from the couch on which she had been lying, and now she limply took the hand that Lady Margaret held out to her. "I am not brave," she said in a voice that trembled. "I am absolutely terrified. I wish Horace would take me away from this horrid place."

"What's that?" Spendley-Carter brayed, impressed to death with Lady Margaret. "Oh, come now, Sylvia, my dear, it hasn't done anyone any harm. You've just heard Lady Margaret say they have a ghost of their own."

"Poltergeists aren't often dangerous," ventured Mr. Jellicot. "They are really only mischievous. Your husband will be famous throughout the scientific world when he writes this up."

Spendley-Carter glared at his wife as though she were pinching his dessert off his plate. "There now, you see?" he said. "If Noreen and I can stand it, I guess you can."

The room was at the corner of the building in the east wing and consisted of a large bed-sitting room, pleasantly furnished and decorated, including flower stands and ornamental vases. From it there opened out a kind of small alcove, which was a part of the east tower, and an offshoot from the main room. This could be cut off by a curtain which was now drawn back. This enclosure, which was occupied by Noreen, contained her bed and a dresser with a mirror, as well as a small table. The window looked out onto the park and the east pergola. In the manner of children lost in their own work and disinterested in the chatter of the world of grownups, Noreen sat at the table and painted with water colors.

Hero wandered across the room and looked over her shoulder. She had made a passable enough sketch of the ugly white pergola, the trees, the river, and the priory ruins in the distance, and was engaged in filling in the water colors with such concentration that she scarcely so much as looked up from her task.

Hero said, "That's not bad, young'un. Wants a bit of black mixed in with that green, and then you'll have those shadows just under the trees."

Noreen looked up and whispered, "Oh, I'm so glad *you* came."

Hero inspected her drawing a moment longer and then sauntered back to the group, being most careful not to stand too close to his stepsister. "It wouldn't be your imagination, would it, perhaps, Mrs. Spendley-Carter?" he asked. "Forgive me for seeming incredulous, but often in cases like this——"

Spendley-Carter blustered, "Damn it, sir, I guess I've got eyes in my head. You'd believe it soon enough if it happened to you. I only wish it might."

"Goodness knows," Hero replied equably, "so do I."

Sylvia Spendley-Carter emitted a sudden gasp and then a wail of fright as an object came sailing through the air and fell with a crash of breaking porcelain at her feet.

"Ha!" cried Spendley-Carter. "There you are! Now are you convinced?"

The object was a small vase, one of a pair from the mantel, for the other, a not very expensive affair in blue china, was still standing at the opposite end. Apparently this one had risen of its own volition and shattered at their feet.

There was a swish and two thuds as an apple and an orange fell from the ceiling and rolled into a corner, and a moment later several smooth, rounded, dark flint pebbles likewise sailed through the air to clatter onto the floor.

Mrs. Spendley-Carter began to shake, hid her face in her hands, and squealed agonizedly, like a muffled pig. Spendley-Carter was too triumphant even to notice her. In her corner, painting imperturbably, Noreen giggled shrilly and carefully mixed black with the green, as instructed.

"There, you see?" cried Mr. Jellicot. "A genuine apport!" and he made to pick up one of the pebbles on the floor but Hero cut him off sharply.

"Don't touch it!" he exclaimed, and, kneeling suddenly, drew from his pocket a small dark instrument with a glass panel and indicator with oscillating needle on one side and a small grid on the other. Swiftly he held the little box close to the so-called apport on the floor—the flint. The indicator needle quivered and jumped halfway up the dial, then fell back.

"What the devil's that?" Spendley-Carter asked.

Hero replied, "A little notion of mine—supersensitive to heat."

Mr. Jellicot's eyes bulged. "Ah-ah!" he cried excitedly. "Is it too hot to handle? Is it the fire ghost, then?"

Hero replied with just a tinge of irritation in his voice, "Not 'too hot to handle,' just too hot—and I wish you would stop babbling your damned nonsense about your fire ghost. I rather fancy this instrument would have reacted in the same manner to the rabbit at the dinner table that night, if I'd had a chance at it."

In the corner of the room there was a tall, slender mahogany flower stand, and upon it a brass bowl containing roses. The flower stand now for no reason apparent, since no one was standing within a yard of it, suddenly teetered and fell over on its side, and the brass bowl with a clangor and splashing of water scattered its contents over the floor. Mrs. Spendley-Carter rocked and moaned. While the others gazed at the scattered flowers a trussed chicken ready for the pan sailed into the room, from which quarter no one could tell, and was followed by another shower of stones.

Hero picked up the overturned stand and set it on its feet, gathered up the flowers and the bowl, and replaced them.

Spendley-Carter, his moist eyes filled with triumph, bawled, "Well—are you satisfied now?"

"The chicken came in through the window," asserted Mr. Jellicot. "I saw it." He went over to it and looked down, adding, "There isn't anyone down there—there isn't anyone in sight at all," which, considering that the window was shut, seemed rather superfluous.

Meg murmured, "I shouldn't have believed it if I hadn't seen it."

Noreen came over to Hero with her painting. "Is that where the black should go?" she asked.

Hero inspected the drawing. "Yes—but straight lines are better than wavy ones."

The child nodded and then suddenly went on tiptoe to reach his ear. "How do you like our ghost?" she asked. "Isn't it fun?"

"No," Mr. Hero replied, "not very."

She went back to her table clutching her drawing and picked up her brush again. Hero watched her and caught her looking at him in the mirror, and when she saw his reflection she smiled a funny, friendly, doubtful little smile at him.

Mr. Jellicot had picked up the chicken and was regarding it with wonder and affection. "I'll wager the mischievous entity stole this from the kitchen," he said, and then, lifting his head, he addressed himself in the direction of the ceiling. "Did you steal this from the kitchen?" he asked loudly. In reply were heard two distinct, sharp raps. Mr. Jellicot turned triumphantly to Hero. "In the spirit world, two raps mean yes," he explained.

"In that case," Hero remarked dryly, "I gather Cook would be glad to have it back again. Why don't you take it to her?" Then he added, "Don't any of you care what is happening to Mrs. Spendley-Carter?"

She was prostrate on the couch now, close to a state of shock from terror. He went over to her, knelt beside her, placing a hand on her brow and another on her shoulder with great gentleness, and for the moment his touch seemed to calm her. He said, "You must try to pull yourself together. I assure you there is nothing to be afraid of. If you can bring yourself to ignore this there will soon be an end to it. Poltergeists are very much like children; they like to attract attention. If you don't give in to them, very often they get bored and go away." He rose and said to Spendley-Carter, "If I might suggest, I'd have Dr. Winters to look at her. I rather think she could use a sedative."

Spendley-Carter said, "Damn it, man, I know how to look after my own wife."

"Well then, do so," Hero said abruptly, "before it's too late. She is ill."

Mr. Jellicot was standing over by the door holding the trussed chicken in his hands and looking a little foolish. Hero said to him, "I think you can get on with it, sir. End of performance. No more today, I think." He picked up Meg with his eyes, and added, "Thank you. Thank you very much for letting us witness this extraordinary business."

Lady Margaret added, "Oh yes, thank you very much indeed. It was so kind of you. I do hope Mrs. Spendley-Carter will be all right," and she and Hero went out together.

Back in Meg's room Hero said, "Well? Do you think . . . ?"

"Loverly," said Meg, and, opening her bag, disconnected Little Snooper from its motor, took it out, and examined the film indicator. "We ought to have about forty shots from which to choose. The light was just fine."

Dinner that evening was a somewhat nervous affair, even though at Hero's suggestion the Paradine candle lighting was omitted and the meal served under the blaze of the electric chandelier and lamps, but it went off without incident. After the men had drunk their port and later joined the ladies in the library, the parties broke up for bridge and billiards. Sir Richard sat in at the young table with Beth, Susan, and Mark, and another four was put together which included Mrs. Taylor, Spendley-Carter, Dr. Paulson, and Dean Ellison. Mrs. Spendley-Carter had not appeared for dinner at all, having been put under sedation after a visit from Dr. Winters. Major Wilson, Lord Paradine, and Mr. Jellicot went off to play billiards, leaving Isobel, Lady Paradine, Mrs. Wilson, Cousin Freddie, Meg, and Hero to desultory conversation in the library.

Hero wondered who had been maneuvering and to what extent. Had Mrs. Wilson arranged it deliberately to be a member of his group and to manage that he sat next to her, or she next to him? He saw the little pig eyes of Cousin Freddie watching him, and thought once that he caught a sharp glance from his stepsister as Mrs. Wilson in a conversational gambit planted a flag on him. In the presence of the more than attractive Lady Margaret Callandar, the secret of whose relationship to Hero apparently not even Cousin Freddie had as yet penetrated, Mrs. Wilson was losing no time in staking out her claim.

At half past ten, as had been agreed between her and Hero, Meg pleaded change of air and sleepiness, and asked if anyone would mind if she went to bed. Mrs. Wilson brightened perceptibly, and Isobel said, "Of course, Margaret—you must be tired after your journey. I'll just come with you to see that everything is in order."

They left together and when Isobel did not return Lady Paradine stifled a yawn and said, "I suppose what they will do is sit up there and talk endlessly. Isobel always captures anyone who knew her father. I'm afraid I can hardly keep my eyes open." She arose and retired.

Hero hoped that Isobel would not remain too long with Meg but counted on Meg's ability to find an excuse to be alone. She had her job cut out for her—the setting of the cameras before the others came upstairs, with the trip threads ready but not yet attached. This final triggering of the traps could be done at the very last moment after everyone had retired.

Cousin Freddie turned his unpleasant gaze to Hero and Mrs.

Wilson and said, "Two down and one to go. That leaves just me."

Mrs. Wilson said to Mr. Hero, "Perhaps if you gave him sixpence he'd go away. Isn't that the usual fee for nasty little boys?"

"It's a shilling now—everything's gone up," Freddie said. "I thought you two had been angling to be alone all evening. All right, I'll go and annoy the bridge players. Don't forget to be grateful to Cousin Freddie, you two." He wandered off.

Mrs. Wilson said, "I'm terribly nervous, Alex. I feel frightened."

Hero said, "Do you? Why, Vivyan? I've told you that there's nothing to be frightened of."

"I don't know. I feel as though something were about to happen."

Hero wondered if she knew. Could she know what was gathering and building up for that night and the early morning to come? Was she too in some way involved in these most intricate and dangerous relationships that seemed to swirl like dark storm clouds about so many of those in the Hall? He asked her, "Something pleasant or unpleasant?"

She looked at him quickly then, as though to be sure of his meaning, but his face was so impassive that she could not tell. She knew only that she yearned to hold him to her, to feel his cheek next to hers, to lose herself in him. She repeated, "I don't know—I'm all nerves on end. I feel like a child that wants to be comforted."

Hero went over to her, sat on the arm of her chair, and took her hand in his. She leaned her head against his arm. The hair was so clean, fragrant, and exquisitely soft. The pressure of her head against his arm was starting him on the road to trouble. He knew and did not care. He was in tune with her needs—they were his own. Her sleek, catlike femininity was delicious and exciting. "Better?" he asked.

"Yes, much better," she said, but she did not move to search for him or win closer contact, and this Hero thought odd, but he did not press the matter either.

"Alexander?"

"Yes, Vivyan."

"Who was that woman who arrived here?"

"The Lady Margaret Callandar? She is the Earl of Heth's daughter. She's a photographer, I believe, in partnership with Mark Barbizon."

"Oh yes, of course. I don't like the way she looks at you."

Hero said, "I hadn't noticed."

"No," Mrs. Wilson murmured, "I suppose men don't." And then suddenly with a kind of fierce possessiveness, "But you have noticed the way I've looked at you!"

"Yes, I have."

"What manner of man are you, Alex? Why am I in love with you? Why have you got everyone here eating out of your hand? You're young—you're frightfully young to be so assured of yourself—and yet they're all a little afraid of you."

Hero reflected, and then replied soberly, "They're afraid because they know I'm looking to find the truth, and today more than ever before, I suppose, there is nothing more terrifying than the truth."

"I am a little afraid of you too, Alex. Will you make me see the truth too—that I am close to middle age, too bony, too unloved, too hungry, too absurd?"

Hero bent over and placed his cheek atop the soft hair and let his lips touch and taste the strands. He said, "Shhh—don't talk." From far off deep down inside him he heard the voice of the man he really was saying, "*You blithering, blethering, dundering fool!*" but he resolutely closed his ears to it.

There was the sound of a footstep. Hero managed to put six feet between Mrs. Wilson and himself before Isobel poked her head in through the door. "Oh," she said, "everyone gone off to bed? I think the bridge party is about to break up."

It had. Susan, Beth, Mark, and Sir Richard came in from the drawing room. The other four had already gone off. The billiardists arrived too.

Major Wilson said to his wife, "Coming, my dear?"

"Yes, darling." She arose obediently. Hero did not look at her. Cousin Freddie said loudly, "Somebody owes me a shilling."

They looked at him blankly, and for a moment everyone stood around and said nothing, until Hero fished in his pocket, pulled out a half crown, and flipped it to Freddie. "Here's two and six," he said. "You've been a darling boy."

Lord Paradine said, "Well, good night, all. Let's hope there won't be any trouble. Hero, I'll expect you to see to it if there is."

Hero wondered for a moment whether he should warn them, and decided against it. To do so would be to bring about a change in the conditions. He wished matters to take their course.

Major Wilson opened his underslung shark's mouth in his silent laugh and then said, "Hah! There'd better not be any—I have my service pistol with me."

Hero, who was at the door, turned around and said, "I should lock it away if I were you, Major. Never hunt a ghost with a gun."

"What's that, young fellow? Why not, I'd like to know?"

Hero paused and then in the voice one uses to try to explain something difficult to a child said, "Well, there's this, Major: if it should be one it just doesn't do any good—the bullet simply goes right through and smacks the opposite wall, damaging the plaster."

The Major opened and closed his mouth again and then asked nastily, "Yes, and what if it isn't?"

"Ah well, in that case," Hero replied mildly, "you never can tell which one of us you might kill." He thought that rather a splendid line on which to leave them, and went upstairs hoping to God that Meg had had time to plant her little boxes, and wondering how long it would be before the house quieted down and people would cease wandering about so that she might set the trip threads.

$\mathbf{M}$r. Hero did not undress but, hooding his reading lamp so that its light would not be revealed beneath the door, sat in his easy chair and gave himself up to meditation. He reflected that if but one paranormal manifestation or ghostly appearance could be proven true or untangled from the skein of human wickedness and sometimes sheer perversion with which invariably such manifestations seemed to be enmeshed, what a different world people would arise to the morning after such a discovery had been confirmed—confirmed scientifically and beyond any shadow of doubt.

His speculations drifted back to the tensions and crosscurrents at dinner that night: the curious and almost ill-mannered behavior of the otherwise sweet-tempered Beth Paradine toward her "Uncle Dick." Could she then love Lockerie, or had he imagined it? And why the febrile gaiety of Susan Marshall and the sullenness of Mark Paradine? He recalled the interminable blethering of Mr. Jellicot and Dr. Paulson on matters occult, contrasted with the quiet of the crop-haired engineer, Dean Ellison, who never said anything.

He thought of Lord Paradine's increasing irritability, his wife's roving eyes which always came to rest so possessively upon her son; the beaming joviality of Mrs. Geraldine Taylor, the ugly acidity of Cousin Freddie, and the curious glances that overdressed little Noreen threw at him from time to time. It was the people rather than the house who were haunted.

He thought too of the role that Isobel played. If there was powder beneath the surface she was the one who kept it from exploding; she was the catalyst among them—now listening with apparently fascinated attention to the fatuous Spendley-Carter, soothing her brother, who was in a mood to complain about everything, listening to army tales from Major Wilson, joining in conversations, keeping things somehow in control. There had been nothing Nornlike about Isobel.

His mind returned to the phenomena at the Hall, and it struck him that occult manifestations seemed strangely to follow ancient and applied patterns, as though ghosts were bound strictly to the literature written about them. If there was an unseen world, if there were hidden creatures and beings who operated upon another plane, they had to stand the criticism of a shocking lack of originality. Nothing actually had turned up in the twentieth century that had not been tried or reported from two to four thousand years ago.

If there was one exception, it was the concert harp that had been played apparently by no human hands, and here he was left with the usual dilemma of the psychical investigator who arrives upon the scene after the event. He must either accept the fact that a genuinely occult phenomenon has taken place or, lacking the testimony of his own trained senses, he must disbelieve the evidence of the witnesses and ascribe it to error, hallucination, neurotic imagination, deliberate prevarication intended to mislead, or a mechanical trick. His examination of the harp had shown him at least no obvious tampering, no music box cleverly adapted, and no mechanical or electronic means of introducing a recording. Besides which there was the matter of the vibrating strings, testified to by Lord Paradine. There then remained Paradine himself. Could he be believed? Had he been deceived or had he lied? Were they all lying? And if so, why—what was the purpose?

But Susan Marshall too had heard the music of the harp, and Susan did not strike him as the type of young girl given over to hallucination; and yet why was he so certain that Susan was telling the truth—simply because she was the victim of a series of apparently motiveless and senseless attacks upon her? Unlike any other field, in psychical research the victim was among the first to be considered in the line of suspects. In murder, or where a serious injury resulted from assault, the victim was usually exonerated. Not so in the case of haunting. What had Susan Marshall to gain by making so obvious a point that she was not wanted at Paradine Hall? It was in these questions of motive that Hero felt himself lost in this investigation. The possibility that Susan Marshall had frenched her own room, invented the story of the attack of the nun, and spirited the rabbit onto her own plate could not be excluded. He knew from experience that underneath an exquisite calm and poise she was far from frigid. She was loved by at least two men. Were these manifestations an indication of her own unsettled mind and heart, or a signal to one or the other?

It was the inconsistency too of the whole business that found him most at sea, since he knew that there is a kind of logic to occult manifestations. Even if there appeared to be no *raison d'être* on the surface, human beings were usually able to find or invent something to fit the facts. It was this logic that was missing from the hauntings at Paradine Hall, for they seemed to be without rhyme or reason and nothing would fit. It certainly made no sense that members of the family would evoke a ghost and give the Hall a reputation to drive away guests and destroy their own livelihood. If there was even a modicum of truth to the legend of the nun, the uneasy spirit who appeared as a warning to the Paradine family, why had her attentions been centered upon a stranger, an American girl who was not a Paradine?

Hero looked at his watch; it was ten minutes to three. The house had gone quite silent. He snapped out the light, for he wished his eyes to become accustomed to the dark. The moon, now on the wane, was late risen and showed a half disk in the sky reflected from the thin ribbon of the river that flowed behind the Hall.

When his eyes had become thoroughly accustomed to the night and he was able to recognize objects in the room, he went to the door and stood there listening. At last his straining ears heard a sound, but unghostly—creeping footsteps that appeared to pause every so often as they approached, as though the person was stopping to listen. The footsteps were light. From his position behind the door it was impossible for Hero to gauge from which direction they were coming, but of one thing he was certain—they were a woman's tread.

They came to a halt and, from the creak of a board without, he knew they were close by. He waited for an instant and then softly opened his door, letting a slice of moonlight into the pitch-dark corridor. Toward this came a rush and scurry of light footsteps, an envelopment of perfume, and a soft cry—and then there was a woman in his arms.

She was in nightdress and negligee, as cool, scented, soft, and appetizing as he had always known she would be, and before she spoke a word her lips were on his and, responding to the passionate instant, he held her close and thought that it was thus in medieval dreams that the victim sank into ecstatic oblivion with the witch woman. Was this yet another of the hauntings of Paradine Hall? But it was not. This was firm flesh; these were living, hungry, and seeking lips; this was a body trembling with passion. This was Mrs. Wilson, whose promise of assignation he had quite forgotten in the bedevilment of his thoughts.

Yet somehow he managed to maintain control, to force his brain into command over his senses, and momentarily to part his mouth from hers, for he had no wish to do so.

"Alexander—Alexander dearest," she whispered. She rested her head upon his breast and clung to him trembling.

Hero said, "Vivyan—what is it?"

She lifted her head to regard him, and the moonlight briefly showed the pallor of her face and the passionate dilation of her eyes, but there was now an expression for an instant of uncertainty as to why he had not drawn her into his room and closed the door of the world upon the two of them. She said softly, "Alexander, I came because I was frightened. I've seen the nun."

Instantly he knew that she was lying. He said, "Where?"

"Outside my room, I think."

"How did you know?"

"I heard a noise. I went to the door and looked out and saw the figure. Then she disappeared. I was terrified."

"And your husband?"

"He's asleep. Nothing ever wakes him once he's taken his pill and gone to sleep." Then she was searching for his mouth again, whispering, "Alexander—what does it all matter? Quickly, quickly!"

He could feel her tugging at him and was suddenly aware of a distaste and disturbing resistance growing within himself. Why? Was it because of Meg's presence in the house that he suddenly no longer welcomed the gift of this woman's person? But that was absurd. Meg was Meg, his stepsister, who knew his weakness for attractive women and was inclined to laugh at it. Then why was it that she had come into his mind at this juncture? What was the reason he was suddenly seeing her amused eyes and wry smile? He resolutely forced her from his thoughts, but Mrs. Wilson's moment had passed. He was aware too, now, that it had all been too pat, too smoothly executed, and searching for another word, "practiced" came into his mind. The most absurd phrase rattled through his head: *"Mr. Alexander Hero regrets he cannot accept the kind invitation extended by Mrs. Vivyan Wilson . . ."*

From somewhere in the house there came suddenly an appalling crash, as though some heavy piece of furniture had been overturned, followed by a kind of subterranean thumping and groaning. Genuine fear now dilated Mrs. Wilson's eyes as she breathed, "Alexander, what was that?"

He said, "Quiet!" and looked at his watch, and then murmured, "Right on schedule." Now was the time for the nun to be abroad. Now was the time for Meg's little boxes to do their work. From the vicinity of the east wing there issued a clatter as though someone had tipped a set of andirons down the stairs, followed by a woman's piercing scream. Mr. Hero mastered an impulse to laugh, for the thought had struck him, *"If the Major sleeps through that one he's good!"*

But the Major had not. He appeared suddenly in the corridor in dressing gown and shuffle slippers, red-eyed, hair tousled. In one hand there was an electric torch, in the other his Webley service pistol. He was fuzzy, ruffled, and angry. Hero and Mrs. Wilson had sprung apart at the first crash, and in all probability before he appeared, but the Major's mouth twisted beneath his bushy gray moustache. He was not laughing now. He said, "Vivyan, what are you up to?" Then, "What the devil are you doing with my wife, Hero?"

Hero sent up a small prayer of gratitude and added to himself,

"*You can let* that *be a lesson to you, old boy.*" Aloud he said, "Mrs. Wilson heard a noise at her door, investigated, and saw the apparition of the nun. She came here to warn me."

The Major said, "That's a likely story. You've been making eyes at my wife ever since you came here. Do you think I'm blind and a fool?"

Mrs. Wilson interrupted sharply, "Howard, you're being ridiculous. I saw her and came to see whether Mr. Hero was still up."

The Major blinked at them. He was not sure whether he had caught them in an attitude or not. It was obvious that Hero was dressed, but not at all so whether his wife had been arriving or leaving. He did not know how long he had been asleep or how long she had been gone. Furthermore, there was no way of telling and in his befuddled state he was afraid of making a fool of himself. He was angry, jealous, and dangerous. He said, "Go back to your room, Vivyan. I'll attend to you later. As for you, sir——"

Hero cut in with, "Go back to your room yourself, sir, and put up that gun. There's something loose in this house. I've told you not to hunt ghosts with a gun. If there is a tragedy it will be on your own head. I want this corridor cleared. I have enough on my hands as it is. Go to your room."

The authority in Hero's voice cut through the muddled wits of the Major. He reversed the gun in his hand and, holding it by the barrel, looked at it and then at Hero. "If I thought——" he said, then turned and shuffled off after his wife.

A door slammed, and Hero heard a man's voice—Lord Paradine's—bawling, "What the devil's the matter with the lights?"

Hero shook himself slightly and wiped his brow. Mrs. Wilson's perfume still enveloped him, but now it only made him feel a little sick. The narrow escape resulted in jangled nerves and a sudden doubt as to his own arrangements. He had been expecting the disturbance but had had no intention of prowling. One thing that Hero wanted was not to interfere with the work of Meg's little black boxes. He was sure that Susan, with her door firmly bolted, was in no danger, and besides, he had Sir Richard as an ally, alerted to keep vigil should anything go wrong. But now he was upset and unsure and further shaken by the sound of running footsteps to the left of the corridor in the direction of the rooms of the family and their guests; a woman's sharp cry—if something were to happen to Susan . . .

He scrapped his own plan, produced a torch, and went gliding along the corridor. The first room he passed was Beth's. The door stood open. He flashed his light inside. There was no one in the rumpled bed—there was no one in the room. Unease quickened his steps. On the same corridor was Sir Richard's room; it too was empty.

He ran on swiftly, turning the corner, and then stopped with relief, for Susan's door was closed. Through it he whispered to her, "Susan—Susan, are you all right?" There was no reply. Gently Hero tried the knob. To his horror it opened, where the bolt shot from within should have kept it firm. Sick and cold at the pit of his stomach, he went inside, dreading what he might find. His torch showed that the bed had been slept in, but she was not there now. He was half relieved to find the room empty. He turned his torch to the place on the door where the bolt should have been, and relief was at an end. There was no bolt there now—only the empty holes where the screws that held it had been.

Sir Richard Lockerie groped his way through the corridors of the darkened Hall in search of that one who, in Alexander Hero's words, "meant a great deal to him," in an agony of apprehension. He had kept himself under control and obeyed Hero's instructions following the first thunderous reminder that the poltergeist had returned to Paradine Hall and the subsequent failure of the lights. He had equipped himself with an electric torch and placed himself in the doorway but remembered Hero's instructions not to use it if it could be avoided, and not to grab.

Thus he held himself in check when, preceded by what seemed to be an icy wind, something rushed past him in the corridor, and again when there appeared to be light flying footsteps in pursuit, and a soft sob he thought he recognized, and which sent a chill of fear to his heart. But when he heard a scream from the east wing and Lord Paradine shouting about the lights, he could contain himself no longer and rushed to find her. He saw that her door stood wide open. He beamed his flashlight inside. The bed was no longer occupied. She was not in her room. And at this moment his torch failed and he could not get it going again.

Lockerie was ordinarily as cool and brave a man as any, but now the thickness of the night within, the noises, and the alarm and dismay engendered by the love so long held in check, rattled him badly. He had promised Hero—he had promised himself—to watch over her, and in the first few moments of the reinfestation of Paradine Hall he had fallen down. He blundered about blindly in the dark seeking her.

He almost fell down the narrow stairway leading to the floor below but caught himself at the bottom and stood there panting, not knowing which way to turn.

In the pitch black beyond and to his left, his eyes became aware of an edge of light proceeding from a door that was partly open somewhere along the wide corridor that flanked the ground floor.

Impelled by he knew not what, he ran to it and burst through, to find himself in the library, where silvery moonlight filtered in through the high windows where the curtains were only partly drawn. Standing beside them he saw then the slender figure and pale, terrified countenance of the girl he sought, and with a great lift of his heart and an opening of his arms he called to her, "Beth—Beth! Don't be frightened—it's I, Richard."

She seemed to sway where she stood, and he feared that she might collapse before he could reach her. But her arms were out too, and it was only her movement of yearning toward him as he to her, and the next instant she was folded to him, clinging desperately.

"Beth! Beth, my darling!"

"Richard! Dearest Dick!"

"Beth—I have loved you for so very long."

"I have too, Dick—ever since I can remember."

And thereafter there were no longer any years between them, or strangeness, or shyness. The pseudo uncle and the little-girl niece had been replaced by a man and a woman who had found one another.

There were deep shadows on the far side of the library where the light from the night sky did not penetrate. Within those shadows something lurked—a dark shape, faceless through the shrouding of the nun's cowl. The lovers did not notice; they were at those tendernesses of caresses and murmurings of endearments springing from their discovery of each other, and the immediate necessity of clearing up the blindnesses and misunderstandings that had kept them apart. They laughed at the ridiculousness of the barrier that had stood between them—"Uncle Dick."

Safe in his arms, shy Beth could even whisper, "I thought it was Susan you loved, Richard. I was sure it was Susan, and I loved you and Julian so much I thought I would die. I'll be a good mother to him, Richard."

"I came straight to find you when it started," Lockerie said. "I was nearly driven out of my mind when you weren't in your room."

"I thought I saw the nun," Beth said. "I wanted to put an

end to this hateful thing that has been haunting us—I followed her."

Sir Richard said, "You were very brave," and held her more closely.

Beth said, "No. I suddenly found myself alone in the dark and was terrified, the way I used to be when I was a little girl. I ran in here, but there was nobody."

Lockerie put his cheek to her hair and murmured, "Beth, dear Beth. Julian and I need you. You'll never be alone again." And thereafter there came from them no more than those little cries and murmurs of love-hunger to touch, to hold, to cling, sounds that were then hushed by the stilling of that hunger.

Silently the figure in the shape of a nun slipped unseen toward the door and paused there for a moment as though listening for the last time to the love-drunk whispers of the two by the window, and then vanished.

Alexander Hero pulled himself together and tried to think swiftly what to do. Matters were not going at all as he had planned them. His first concern was for Susan Marshall. He had no doubt but that this time, if whoever or whatever it was that hated her had been enabled to get at her, the consequences might be tragic. This would no longer be a warning.

Then in the darkness he heard a cry: "No! No! Let me go!" It was Susan's voice. He ran thither, switching on his torch, whose spot of beam for a moment only showed her struggling with someone, then with the same suddenness with which they had been extinguished all the lights that had been left switched on came alive again; shafts penetrated the corridor from the open doors of the rooms. The person in whose grip Susan was clutched was Mark Paradine.

"Hold still, you little fool!" he was saying. "You unutterable, headstrong idiot—didn't you hear Alexander say to keep to your room and keep it locked? Are you trying to get yourself killed?"

"Oh, stop being so male and let me go! I'm sick of what Alexander says—and all of you. I'm not going to be pushed around any longer."

Mr. Hero felt such relief as he had never experienced in his life before. "Sorry to have to interrupt. Not exactly the ideal time or place for a row," he said. "Susan, why didn't you come and tell me when you found the bolt had been removed from your door?"

She turned upon him angrily and said, "Because I'm tired of all this secrecy and slinking around the house and trying of my door and being told what to do! I didn't notice until just before going to bed, when I went to slip it and saw that it was gone. It made me so angry that when all this bedlam started I decided I'd go after whoever or whatever it was and have it out."

Mark Paradine was morosely examining a scratch upon his wrist. He said, "I thought she might do something like that and came to see. I ran into her in the dark. My word, she didn't half claw!"

"Oh!" said Susan, still in a rage. "I hate men—stupid, stupid men!"

At that precise moment the harp began to play.

The sound of the music came as a shock to them all, but Alexander Hero was the most shocked—at the fact that it *was* happening, for he simply had not believed it possible in those circumstances.

He stood rigid there in the corridor, listening to the ancient strains drifting to them from the music room below, and in his mind fitting the words to them:

My bonnie dear, thy face so dear to me—
So fair art thou that none shall dearer be. . . .

Anger and temper subsided in Susan Marshall as swiftly as they had risen. "Why, Alex," she said in surprise, noting his attitude, his pallor, and the expression on his face, "you're frightened."

Hero replied, "You're damn right I am—and I'd like it better if you were a bit more too. Do you think that just because I know a few tricks I am less than human? I'm scared stiff, if you want to know."

He ran for the small back staircase leading to the rooms below, with Susan and Mark at his heels. Over their footfalls and rapid breathing the strains of the harp were still to be heard. Below they encountered Lord Paradine. He shouted, "Come on, Hero—we'll get at it this time and no mistake!"

Hero saw that Lady Paradine was likewise there—that there seemed to be a kind of convention gathering. He noted Beth and Sir Richard together in dressing gowns, and that there was something strange in their attitudes. Also stout Mr. Jellicot was there in somewhat odd attire, for he was wearing his daytime trousers over his pajama bottoms, and slippers, and Hero wondered how he had managed to get there so quickly from his room in the east wing on the other side of the house, and also how he had heard the harp at all with the noises that appeared to be going on in that quarter.

The music, tinny and tinkling, still filled the corridor. Lord Paradine with a glare of savage satisfaction made for the door of the music room. Hero said, "Sir, if you don't mind—let me. One never knows——"

Susan Marshall breathed, "Oh, Alex, be careful."

Hero turned the knob of the door; it did not yield. "Why, it's locked!" he cried. "I thought I gave orders it was to be left open."

"What? Locked?" yelled Lord Paradine.

"Where's Isobel?" demanded Lady Paradine.

"She's probably gone to get the keys," Paradine replied. "Go fetch yours."

Hero had been counting noses. Dr. Paulson, Dean Ellison, and Mrs. Geraldine Taylor had appeared upon the scene; still missing were Cousin Freddie, the Spendley-Carters, and the Wilsons.

My bonnie dear, bright are the summer days,
Sweet are the nights;
And thou, my——

The music broke off abruptly. "We won't wait," Hero said, and put his shoulder to the door. The angry power of his thrust smashed the lock and he burst through, yet caught himself in time to flick on the wall switch and illuminate the room, which was empty. There was no one there, and no place where anyone could hide. Hero ran across to the harp, closely followed by Paradine and, oddly enough, that quiet and insignificant person, the engineer Dean Ellison.

The harp stood where it had always been, but the strings were still vibrating.

Breakfast and luncheon as well usually took place in the small dining room of the Country Club, the Paradines and their guests dining privately in the west wing. But that next morning Hero had requested that they all meet together in the great hall for breakfast, and he now looked about him at a group of nervous, frightened, and thoroughly exhausted people.

With the possible exception of Mr. Ellison and Mrs. Taylor, they were all suffering from the strain of the night before, when there had been very little sleep for any of them. For the first time even Isobel was showing signs of nervousness and irritability, and there were dark circles under her eyes. Missing was Sylvia Spendley-Carter, who was in bed and had again been visited by Dr. Winters and dosed with a sedative. The Lady Margaret Callandar had likewise not appeared.

With all the exaggerated gestures of a stage magician Mr. Hero pushed back his sleeves and cuffs, picked up, and vanished a boiled egg that was in the egg cup before him.

Noreen caught the act first and her eyes threatened to pop from her ugly little face. "Oooh," she cried, "goody! Do that again," and she clapped her hands and screamed. It was as good as a trumpet fanfare to call attention to what he was doing, and all eyes were turned upon Hero.

The egg reappeared between his long, thin fingers, was apparently flung into the air, and disappeared. In the hand where it had been there was now a lighted cigarette which had come from nowhere, in the other a fan of playing cards; cigarette and cards were suddenly crumpled together and turned into a string of many-colored handkerchiefs, which in turn metamorphosed into a bunch of paper flowers, which Mr. Hero presented elaborately to Noreen, who was beside herself with delight. The others, however, were not amused.

Major Wilson snorted loudly. "Mountebank's tricks."

Lord Paradine, genuinely angry, cried, "May I ask, sir, the meaning of this untimely piece of nonsense to which you have subjected us after all of us have suffered a damn bad night?"

Hero was not at all put out. "An object lesson," he retorted, "for all of us, including myself." He held out his hand; the hand was empty. A movement so swift they could not follow it, and the egg was in it again; another, and it was gone. "Friend Wilson," he said, looking across the table at the irritable Major, "you don't believe that the egg has really vanished—dematerialized, that is, do you?"

"Certainly not!" the Major snapped. "I told you what I thought —mountebank's tricks."

Hero smiled cheerfully. "Good man! Got it in one." Mrs. Wilson laughed, and Major Wilson threw first her and then Mr. Hero a poisonous look.

Hero turned to the others. "None of you believe what you saw, and quite rightly. You have watched the same things done on the stage for your entertainment, but you do not endow the magician with supernatural powers. This little performance was simply to call your attention to the fact that this can be done—that things can be made to appear not what they are but what they seem."

Paradine said, "I don't see what you are driving at, man."

"Just showing off, if you ask me," grated the Major.

Hero threw him a brief glance and said, "If you like. The point is that, whereas none of you believe the magician has really produced a rabbit out of an empty hat, you will believe in a rabbit appearing upon an empty plate—or in a modern concert harp in a locked and empty room rendering an old Elizabethan air with no one human there to animate it."

Something like a sigh of relief came from half a dozen throats. Beth and Sir Richard exchanged glances, and Susan was regarding Hero with unalloyed admiration, an emotion which for the first time Mark seemed to share. Not so Lord Paradine. "Hah!" he exploded. "It was a trick, then! Why the devil didn't you say so immediately, Hero, instead of all this hocus-pocus?"

"Great detective must have drama," sniggered Cousin Freddie.

Hero replied, "It seemed to me that this was a more graphic

method of suggesting that all of us, myself included, approach the subject with a little more of the skepticism that you accord this performance of mine."

Dr. Paulson's dry voice was heard. "Then you don't consider last night's performance paranormal?"

"Oh yes," Hero replied softly, "it was paranormal all right."

Mark asked, "Just what do you mean by paranormal, sir?"

Mr. Hero grinned cheerfully at him. "Paranormal is anything I don't understand. As soon as I can explain, understand, or reproduce it myself, then it isn't paranormal any more. The playing of the harp may have been a genuinely occult manifestation, since there seems to be no other explanation for it, and I am always hoping to encounter one. On the other hand, if we are to approach the matter in the same manner that we have this little show of mine, there is at least one point of the phenomenon which will bear examination."

Dr. Paulson asked, "And what might that be, sir? I might add at this point that I am wholly convinced that we have had a demonstration from the spirit world."

Mr. Jellicot said, "Hear, hear!"

"Why, then," Hero asked quietly, "the locked door?" They all stared at him. "Why, I repeat, is the door to the music room always locked when the harp plays?"

Lord Paradine flushed. "What are you trying to say?" he rasped. "Do I understand, sir, that you are accusing—— My wife has a set of keys, and so has my sister. If——"

"Not at all," Hero replied gently. "Anyone can secure a key to a door. A door can be locked without a key. And anything that can be locked can be unlocked."

"A ghost can lock a door," Mr. Jellicot asserted. "A ghost can do *anything*."

Mr. Hero regarded the little man coldly. "Can it?" he queried. "Is a ghost then God? Are you saying that when we slip our envelopes we become all-powerful? *That* would be a world!" Mrs. Wilson laughed again and drew a glare from her husband. Hero then continued more mildly, "I am not asking 'who' but only 'why.' Why do it the hard way? Why bother to lock the door before, during, or after the concert? I like my spirits to achieve their ends with a little more directness and simplicity."

Cousin Freddie sneered, "All right, then, I'll ask the sixty-four-dollar question: why?"

Hero regarded him amiably. "If the harp was animated by ghost, shade, phantom, specter, apparition, or departed spirit I would not know," he replied. And then added almost as an after-thought, "Of course, if it were a person or persons it might be that they did not want anyone to get into the room too quickly after the harp had played."

There was a silence after this, and Mr. Hero was suddenly aware that Dean Ellison was watching him closely with a most curious expression upon his broad features. And then the Norns returned to Isobel again. Tall, straight, stately, her eyes suddenly unseeing, or seeming to see into the beyond, she intoned, "The playing of the harp and the appearance of the nun are forewarnings of disaster. There is a curse upon Paradine Hall."

Hero turned to her and said seriously, "Yes, perhaps you are right. But if so, it must be lifted, else there will be an end to the Paradine Country Club, will there not? People don't like curses." His voice suddenly took on a note of affability and he said, "But why must apparitions always be connected with doom, Miss Paradine?" The chatelaine of Paradine Hall looked startled at this but did not reply. He continued, "Why must ghosts invariably be connected with catastrophe and disaster? Why shouldn't there be a jolly apparition to sit at the foot of one's bed and foretell the winning of fifty thousand pounds in the Irish Hospital Sweep? Or an impending promotion to vice-presidency of the firm? Or a legacy? Why always bad news?"

"You tell us, master," said Freddie.

"The not incomprehensible pessimism of the human race, for one thing," Hero replied. "But it doesn't make entire sense, does it—any more than the belief in haunts being created as the result of death suffered by violence? For if that were the case one wouldn't be able to move about much for the ghosts of the tens of millions who had died in centuries of war, eh?"

Major Wilson snorted and said, "Poppycock."

Horace Spendley-Carter huffed, "What about the rappings and tappings in our room last night—like the driving of nails into a coffin?"

Hero turned his gaze upon the politician and tried to control the irritation this man always aroused in him. "A case in point," he replied. "But why 'like the driving of nails into a coffin'? Again the old ghost-story lingo of the groans and moans and clanking chains. Why not like the sound of someone's aunt driving a nail into the wall to hang a picture? Or Cook beating out a wiener schnitzel with a wooden mallet? Have you ever heard the sound of nails being driven into a coffin, sir? I have; it is indistinguishable from a carpenter fixing a window frame."

Susan Marshall giggled and Spendley-Carter turned red. Mr. Jellicot was pouting and started to Spendley-Carter's defense: "But, sir——"

Mr. Hero, suddenly grave, interrupted him, saying, "We are beset with sufficient mysteries in this life without creating further ones for ourselves. There is one set of phenomena I will clear up here and now, and another I expect to shortly: the poltergeists. What took place in the room of Miss Isobel Paradine was natural and the result of two unusual and extraordinarily high tides which you may have read of in the newspapers. I have visited the Hydrographic and Geodetic Offices in Yarmouth. There is a subterranean stream that runs through this vicinity. A branch of it passes close to the foundations beneath Miss Paradine's bedroom—or what was once the bedroom of the late Lord Paradine. The pressures of the tide on the coast flood the watercourse, affecting the foundations and certain walls of the Hall." He took out a small booklet from his pocket, consulted it, and said, "the highest tide in eighteen years, coupled with a gale, occurred on June the twenty-ninth, the night the first manifestation took place in Miss Paradine's bedroom. Last night's tide was only a few inches lower. The next time the furniture in that room will be shifted and the portrait of Lord Paradine knocked to the floor may not be until 1976."

"What about the nun?" cried Mr. Jellicot.

"What about the harp?" asked Dr. Paulson.

"What about the other poltergeist?" queried Spendley-Carter.

"Ah," replied Mr. Hero, "yes indeed. We should be seeing the end of the other poltergeist shortly. As for the nun, the harp and, I might add, the rabbit and the upset room—one ghost at a time, if you don't mind, gentlemen." He arose and left the dining hall to seek out his stepsister Meg.

Meg shouted, "Come in, Sandro, I'm a mess." She emerged from the bathroom, where she had set up her portable developing tank and wet printing equipment. She was dressed in slacks and T-shirt; her hair was down about her eyes; she wore no makeup, and looked as though she had not slept much that night.

Hero asked, "Get anything, Sis?"

Meg brushed hair out of her eyes with her wrist and replied, "Plenty," with an emphasis that for the moment was lost on Hero. He followed her into the bathroom, where three of the tiled walls were stuck up with drying prints, enlargements made from the mini-negatives. She had a large magnifying glass and took him on a tour of the walls like a guide in an art gallery.

"On your right," she said, "Little Snooper's bag. You get full marks for sniffing out Noreen, my beloved stepbrother—and here she is. Three of them are first-class. The other subjects—'Not Guilty.' You thought it might have been Mrs. Spendley-Carter herself, didn't you?"

"The child is the normal suspect," Hero said, "but so was the neurotic woman getting on in years—and goodness knows, Mum filled the bill. However, when I found out that Noreen was only adopted . . ." He took the magnifying glass and inspected with considerable satisfaction probably the only photographs ever taken of a poltergeist child in action. There were pictures of Mr. Jellicot, Mrs. Spendley-Carter, her husband, and even himself. None of them indicated anything abnormal afoot on the part of the subjects. Noreen, on the other hand, was being a very busy little girl.

"Oh, lovely!" he said. "Another few months and she would have become too cute to catch even with a camera. I think these will help to put a stop to it before it is too late. Darling—you're wonderful. What would I do without you?"

Meg replied, "Not too badly, I should say," and again he failed to perceive the odd note in her voice or the mischievous expression at the corners of her mouth. They moved on to another section of the tiling. "There's your nun," Meg said. "Not good. Not bad. Sorry."

"Ah yes, well . . ." Hero said. "It's something, though, isn't it?" He examined the photograph. The infra-red lamp had been attached close to the ceiling so as to flash its light downward, and the camera had caught the figure from the side. The picture was clear and unblurred, yet it told Mr. Hero very little, since the apparition was sideways to the camera and the face was not visible inside the hood. The hands appeared to be hidden in the folds of the garment.

More difficult still, only the figure showed up in the print. There were no points of reference such as background, wall, ceiling, or picture molding to give any basis of comparison as to its height. In the voluminous habit, it was not possible to tell whether it was fat or thin, stocky or broad, tall or short. It was simply a nun, and that was that. However, as Meg pointed out, there was nothing transparent or spirit photo-y about it—the figure was solid and real.

"Where was this camera located?" Hero asked.

Meg held up the magnifying glass and studied a mark in one corner of the print. "That's number 4," she said. "That was set up at the foot of the stairs leading from the Paradines' apartments, on our side of the house."

"But she could have come from any direction," Hero said.

"She could have," Meg admitted, "but in this particular instance she wasn't. She was going. That is to say, the trip thread of the camera caught her as she was heading east—in the direction of the library."

"Or the music room," Hero added.

"Or the music room," repeated Meg.

He inspected the photograph even more meticulously and then shook his head and said, "Damn!" He looked up at Meg. "What about the one in the library?" he asked. "That was set up to catch anything head on, wasn't it?"

Meg nodded and replied, "Yes, but I rather fancy someone else got there first. Have a look," and pointed to another enlargement on the wall.

Hero gave a gasp of amazement. "Oh-oh!" he inspected with fascination the most astonishing photograph of Mr. Alfred Jellicot clad in a pair of dark trousers from which the braces hung down, and what appeared to be a pajama jacket. He was bent over the big writing desk and seemed to be removing a paper therefrom.

"What on earth is he up to?" Hero asked.

"Looks to me as though he were pinching something," Meg replied, "—something he couldn't get at in the daytime."

Hero whistled and then said, "Got you, my little man. I thought you knew just a shade too much. I'll be having a word with you before too long." But then he turned to Meg, shaking his head and saying, "But why? Why? That doesn't make any sense either.

They came to a photograph which looked like rush hour in the underground. "Good Lord," Hero asked, "what's this?" And then, looking again, said, "Oh!"

Meg said, "Yes, I know. You all apparently hit the trip thread simultaneously. That's the one I had planted in the music room."

Hero mused, "Then nobody went into the music room from the time you set up your little boxes, and of course the door was unlocked then or you wouldn't have got in."

Meg nodded. "That's true. But someone might have got in before me, and then locked the door after I had finished."

"Any of the Hon. Isobel or the unspeakable Freddie?" Hero asked.

Meg indicated. "Here's one of Isobel." Hero looked at it. In it she was as he had seen her in the music room in her white silk dressing gown, girdled with the white silk rope, and her bunch of keys. In the picture she had her hands on the keys. In none of the pictures were the expressions on the faces those of people being "photographed."

Hero said, "That's all right. Lord Paradine said that she'd gone after her keys." He studied the picture again and tapped it with a fingernail. "Why would a strikingly handsome, charming, and capable great lady such as this remain a spinster?" he asked.

Meg said, "One wonders."

"That's the lot, is it?" Hero said.

Meg replied, "Oh no. There's one more over here," and she pointed to the opposite wall of the bathroom where a single print was stuck. "I've been saving this one for the last. This one wins the *Daily Express* candid photo prize for the year, don't you think?"

There was no necessity for Mr. Hero to apply the magnifying glass. Camera number 5 had registered what might be called a speaking likeness of himself before the door of his room. In his arms was the willowy and willing Mrs. Wilson. Their lips had not yet met, but it was as near as nothing. Her charming ankle had struck the thread only a moment before. Meg said, "Good, what? I thought we'd call it 'The Anti-nun of Paradine Hall.'"

Hero said, "Meg, you monster! What the devil did you mean, setting up one of your filthy boxes outside my door?"

She said innocently, "If there was any ghaistie coming after my Sandro I was jolly well going to have a photograph of it—her."

They looked at one another and suddenly burst into roars of laughter. But Meg was through laughing before Hero. She said, "Sandro, Sandro!" and then, "She *is* attractive—was she . . . ?"

Hero said, "I wouldn't know. I was just about to get rid of her when her husband turned up with a gun."

Meg was suddenly grave. "Sandro, was there any trouble?"

"Not really—it wasn't me he was hunting with a gun, it was the ghost. All hell had broken loose in the east wing at that time— little Noreen. But I think he was somewhat irritated, nevertheless. That is to say, we had managed to break out of the clinch by the time he got there. Still, she was outside my door. She claimed that she had heard and seen the nun and was frightened and came to tell me."

Meg said, "Not ruddy likely."

Hero said, "Well!" in a tone of voice.

"I know," said Meg. "Can you help it that you are fascinating and attractive and women creep to your door in their nighties to tell you ghost stories?"

Hero said, "We'll post that picture up on the Club Notice Board. That'll put a stop to it."

Meg said, "Fool!" but she was looking slightly more pleased.

"Besides which, the damn harp began to play."

Meg was immediately interested. "What about the harp? I heard it."

"The door was locked, there was nobody in the room when I put my shoulder to it and went through, but the strings were still vibrating. I saw them and felt them with my fingertips. Someone *had* been playing the confounded thing." He shook his head. "But they couldn't have, unless——"

"It seems to me the locked door . . ." Meg suggested.

"Of course," said Hero, "you're right, and I've already suggested it. Why bother? Something unseen that could play a harp should also be able to go through doors locked or unlocked. None of them seem to have thought of that."

Meg asked, "But how does someone or something get out of a locked room with people standing on the other side of the door?"

"That's just it," Hero said. "It can't be done."

Meg said, "Mmmm. Then that leaves——"

Hero concluded, "Lord Paradine's mother. The harp belonged to her originally. She was supposed to have been better than an amateur performer. Supposing——" He stopped.

Meg was regarding her brother earnestly. "Do you really believe, Sandro?"

He looked worried. "I don't know what to believe, Hag," he replied.

"Could you reproduce the phenomenon yourself—if you tried?" Meg asked.

Hero shook his head gloomily. "Not under those conditions, and under everybody's nose in a locked and empty room, with people bursting in and finding the strings still vibrating. I suppose it could be done, but you'd want a combination of musician, a genius of an artificer, acoustical engineer, plus probably a stage magician's mechanic, and possibly a lot of trick lighting and wiring. I'm telling you, that harp hasn't been tampered with. I've been over it from stem to stern."

Meg tried another tack. She asked, "Do any of them here play musical instruments, Sandro?"

Hero snorted. "Oh, Lord! Just about everybody. I've been looking into it. Her ladyship plays the piano, which is nothing but a harp in a box. Cousin Freddie plunks a guitar. Isobel in her youth once practiced the cello. Mr. Jellicot plays the organ in his church."

"And I don't doubt that Mrs. Wilson is proficient upon the syrinx."

Hero decided to ignore this sally. He said, "And then there's Beth."

"Beth!" cried Meg.

"When she was a little girl her grandmother taught her to pick out one tune on the harp."

"Crikey!" Meg exclaimed as she guessed.

"Yes," Hero said, "the tune was 'My Bonnie Dear.'"

"Sandro——"

"Yes, Meg."

"I don't care for our Major Wilson. I think he is dangerous. Do be careful."

Hero did not reply but, consulting his conscience, thought that his stepsister was probably right.

FAREWELL TO
A POLTERGEIST

There was a note for him on the table when Hero returned to his room, on Country Club stationery, and sealed. He broke it open and read its brief contents: "Please meet me by the priory ruins. I'll be there at noon. Please come, Alexander, it is important." It was signed "Vivyan Wilson." He said to himself, "Oh, Lord! Shall I? Shall I not? Of all places, why the priory, where a dozen people can conceal themselves? Why do women like that write notes like these? What does she mean by 'important'—important to whom? Damnation, and damnation again! I suppose I'd better go. I did flirt with her, I did lead her on. I'll have to see what it is." He glanced at his watch. It was a quarter past twelve. Luncheon would be served at one. He supposed she would be waiting there, attired in a colored frock that would stick out a mile. How amused Meg would be! Why did he get himself into such tangles?

He went out, got into his car, and drove it through the entrance gates to the Hall, and a mile to the left down the main road where he parked it; then he climbed and walked swiftly back along the river to the ruins of Wytrim Priory.

He was right, she was seated on the stone beneath the pointed archway of the ruins of the old chapel, clad in a scarlet skirt, white blouse, and had a matching bandeau about her head. Her shoes were scarlet too, and her stockings were of that fashionable colored nylon that was in vogue—they too were red. Hero thought to himself somewhat bitterly, "Just the outfit for an assignation in a churchyard." And then to his horror he found that he was glad to see her, that she looked lovely, charming, striking, dainty, appetizing, and that in another moment she would be in his arms. She had not yet observed him. If he turned and ran as fast as he could . . .

He continued on, and it happpened rather as he thought it would, except that she burst into tears and said, "I thought you mightn't come. I had to see you to warn you—I'm frightened, Alexander."

The curiously repetitive nature of the phrase helped him to recover his balance somewhat. He smiled at her and said, "Not another ghost, Viv?"

She did not smile in return. She said, "My husband."

"What about him?"

"He's dangerous, Alexander. I'm afraid. I'm afraid for you— I'm afraid for myself. I don't know what he's going to do."

Hero said, "Isn't it rather late in the day for you to be worrying? If he had been going to do something he would have done it by now—or shot me last night."

She shook her head and said, "You don't know Howard. He isn't like that. He broods. He keeps things to himself and he never forgives. People take him for a fool but he isn't." Then she added, "He doesn't believe that I had come to your room because of having seen the nun."

Hero thought that that would seem to confirm Vivyan's opinion that her husband was no fool. He said, "What does he believe?"

"He believes that when he caught—that when he saw us I was coming out of your room, that—that I had been there." She clung to him suddenly, her head pressed against his breast beneath his chin, and cried fiercely, "Oh, I wish I had! I wish it had happened." She clung to him for another instant and then released him and looked up into his face curiously. She said, "But you don't, Alexander. You never really did. You thought it might be pleasant or amusing, but you never really cared the way I do. Never mind, it doesn't matter." She reached up and kissed him and said, "There now, see, it really doesn't matter. But promise me one thing."

"Yes," Hero said. He felt ashamed, and wondered if his relief was showing on his face. He found himself liking Mrs. Wilson.

"Promise me that you'll be careful," she said, "very careful. Watch out."

"For what?"

She shook her head and said, "I don't know. For Howard, I suppose. Will you promise me?"

Hero's thoughts went back to what Meg had said. He replied, "Yes, I will. Thank you. I'll watch out. Will you be all right?"

"Yes," she said in a kind of half whisper, "we're always all right aren't we?" There was something curiously touching and human in the way she said it, an acknowledgment of all the faults and weaknesses of women like her. He kissed the top of her head and gave her shoulders a little squeeze, whereupon she drew her breath in sharply and Hero wondered if she had been beaten, and thought that she probably had.

"We'd best go back separately," he said. She nodded and without a word turned and went. He stood and watched her go until he had lost sight of the scarlet skirt through the trees. Then he turned and walked thoughtfully back to his car. When he reached it he saw that the Major was sitting in the front seat waiting for him.

"Ah, there you are," said the Major, and his tone was affable enough. "Thought you'd be along soon when I saw your car here. Been looking for ghosts?"

"Yes," said Hero shortly. He was conscious that his nerves were tingling and that he was watching the Major closely. Seen from the side with the jaw somewhat undershot to the Guards moustache, he looked more than ever like a shark.

"Find any?" the Major asked.

"No," Hero replied. He wondered where the Major had been, how much he had seen and heard, whether he had followed his wife and had been concealed behind some piece of the ruins, or whether he had been out walking and had simply come upon the car.

"Ought to be a good place for ghosts, that," the Major said, "if there were any such things."

"Yes, it ought to." Obviously the Major was not going to get out of the car, so Hero climbed in.

"Almost lunchtime," said the Major. "Mind giving me a lift back?"

"Not at all," Hero replied, and pressed the starter switch, and as he did so rather expected a bomb beneath the hood to explode in American style and send both him and the Major to their respective rewards. The Bentley purred sweetly into action.

"Splendid cars, these," said the Major.

"*Sandro, my boy,*" Hero said to himself, "*you are getting nervy. You're letting a hysterical woman put the wind up you. What about showing a little guts?*" Nevertheless the feeling of oppression and a kind of spiritual uneasiness persisted.

"I suppose you wonder what I really want," Wilson said.

Hero replied, "I hadn't thought . . . A lift, I suppose, as you suggested."

The Major smiled his disagreeable smile again and looked even more like a dogfish. "Well now, Hero," he said, "what it boils down to is that I feel I owe you an apology."

Hero was genuinely startled. "Oh," he said, "not at all."

"Yes, I do," the Major insisted. "Lost my head last night. Damn silly of me to go wandering about with a gun. Ought to know better. But you know how it is coming out of a sound sleep, eh?"

"One is likely to be confused," Hero said.

"Exactly. Matter of fact, I had woken up a few minutes earlier. I heard something out in the hall, then heard Mrs. Wilson go out. Don't believe in that stuff myself, you know. The next thing you know there was that unholy row, and I thought I'd better get up and have a dekko. Sorry I slanged you. All right?"

Hero said, "Yes, quite all right."

They were in the driveway and headed for the Hall. "You're a queer chap, Hero," the Major said. "One doesn't know what to make of you. Queer profession for a man. What would you do if you came face to face with a ghost?"

Hero replied, "Interview it, if possible."

The Major went through the motions of his silent laugh. "I say, that's a good one! Would you know a ghost if you saw one?"

Hero said, "Yes, I'd know."

The Major stared at him. "How?" he asked.

"By the pit of my stomach, I suspect," Hero said. The Major

laughed again and Hero found the absence of sound singularly attractive. "Haven't you ever been frightened?" he asked.

The Major laughed again. "Not by anything I couldn't see," he said. "I'm a soldier. It takes more than something in a sheet going 'Boo!' to make me sweat."

Hero said, "Yes, I see. It's only things I don't understand that frighten me."

The Major started to speak and then checked himself, and Hero thought that he detected a curious gleam in the man's eye, and told himself he was imagining things. He drew the car up before the entrance to the Country Club wing and got out. The Major said, "See here, old chap, what about a drink before lunch? Got a bottle of damn good *fino* in my room. Come up and have one with me. Show there are no hard feelings." And then he added, "Vivyan will be glad to see you. She thinks a lot of you. Of course, women are always impressed by hocus-pocus. Well?"

"All right," Hero said. "Thank you, I will. It's very kind of you." He was filled with curiosity. The apology seemed sincere enough, but he wanted Vivyan Wilson's reaction.

The Major puttered about and produced a bottle, unopened and with the tinfoil seal still about it. Hero thought, *"Probably not tincture of cyanide, but don't forget, my boy, the hand is quicker than the eye."* It took some time for the Major to find the corkscrew. By the time he had tumblers assembled and the cork out Mrs. Wilson came in. Hero threw her a hasty look, but she had carefully repaired whatever ravages their meeting had inflicted.

"Ah, there you are, my dear. Been having a little chat with Hero. Brought him up for a drink. We'll all have one." Hero watched him pour the three portions and decided that the proceeding was innocent of trickery and cursed himself again for being a fool. He returned to his initial judgment: the Major was a fatheaded ass, no more and no less than he appeared to be.

"Well, here goes," said the Major. "Nice of you to join us." He lifted his glass and looked over the edge of it, first to his wife, "To you, my dear," and then to Hero, "Cheers."

"Cheers," said Hero. They all drank. It was a good sherry. He risked a glance at Mrs. Wilson. Her face was composed and her lips smiling, but her glance caught his once and her eyes were filled with fear and warning.

"Oh, come! Come! Please hurry. Do hurry, please," Noreen was begging Mr. Hero as she tugged at his hand. Now that it was actually true that she had him to herself, that he was really keeping his promise to go for a walk with her all alone, she could not bear for him to be slow, because of all the things that might happen, or were always happening, to interfere with the promises of grownups. She wanted to hurry him out of sight before something intervened to take his attention away from her or her parents come.

She was dressed in a plaid skirt, blue jumper, and cardigan, and her legs were encased in a pair of those shiny boots reaching halfway up the leg which children wear for country walks.

Smiling, Mr. Hero let himself be tugged into a half run, until they were out of sight of the manor and through one of the exits in the unending brick wall that surrounded it, and wandering safely by the reedy banks of the Stoke River.

Now that she had scrubbed all the make-up off and flattened her hair out so that ends of it stuck out from either side of the small blue beret she wore, Hero could see what an ugly child she really was. And yet, as Mr. Hero examined what seemed to be ill-assorted features—the dark eyes, large enough but not exactly on a level, the too long nose and too large mouth—he thought they might with the coming of adulthood coalesce into features which would be in the end sincere, strong, and pleasant to look upon. The brow was good and the chin firm, the freckles would disappear and the sallow skin give way to a better complexion, the too prominent ears could be half concealed by a hair-do; even the hair would probably take on length and luster. She lacked the breeding, did this adopted child of unknown parents, to give her the looks that the world demanded, but somewhere within her there was some great strain of good, some firm determination, some quiet striving.

Through the exit from the wall she pulled him until they were safely out of sight, then, satisfied, let go his hand and was content to walk at his side, seemingly lost in her own thoughts. When they arrived down by the banks of the river and the path where they were compelled to choose whether they would go right or left, she faced him suddenly and declared breathlessly, "I love you."

"Thank you, Noreen," Hero replied gravely. "I love you too."

The ugly little face was illuminated beyond belief. "Oh," she cried, "do you really? Would you kiss me?"

Hero replied briefly, "Yes," and bending down with an arm about the shoulders of the slim figure, he kissed her gently on the cheek, whereupon she flung herself upon his breast, clutching him frantically with both hands, and began to sob bitterly. Hero let her cry, held her, and when her beret fell off, stroked her hair.

At last the fit of tears came to an end. Hero supplied the handkerchief and after she had mopped and blown she then asked him, "Will you wait for me to grow up and then marry me?"

"Perhaps," Hero said, "but I thought that you wanted to be a nurse."

He noticed the immediate change in her—her childish crush on him was surface, but this went deep. Tears, but of a different kind, came back into her eyes. "They won't let me," she whispered. "Oh, how I hate them! Daddy says I'm not to be a nurse, I'm to be a lady, and Mummy just drips."

Hero asked, "What if I were to help you, Noreen?"

The child stared at him unbelievingly and suddenly sat down upon the riverbank. "Could you?" she cried. "Would you?"

Hero produced his old briar and sat down beside her. "I might try," he said.

She was on her knees now, with her hands folded in her lap, in a touching attitude of pleading. "Would you make it a different kind of a promise—not the grown-up kind but one that can't be broken ever?"

"If I were to make such a promise," Hero said, "I should keep it—but I would want one from you too. It would be a fair exchange, Noreen. You know, nothing is ever really for nothing in this world."

She seemed to understand that and asked, "What would be the promise?"

Mr. Hero turned and looked her full in the face and then said quietly, "The rabbit wasn't very nice, you know."

For a moment an expression of cunning came into her face, but an instant later, as she looked into the countenance of the investigator, it was replaced by one of mingled worship and surrender. "Oh," she said, "that was meant for Mummy. It got all mixed up in the dark when the candles went out. Why did they go out?"

Hero replied, "The candles went out because somebody wished them to do so." In spite of himself, a chuckle crept into his voice. "I shan't show you the trick because you might be tempted to use it."

Noreen's voice took on the confidence of one exchanging shop talk with a fellow professional. She said, "But I did make the chair move. I hoped it would give Mummy hysterics and make her sick, because she's so drippy. I hate her. Instead, it fell over on Lord Paradine."

Hero sucked at his pipe and nodded. "Yes, I know that. I must tell you that you didn't invent that, though you probably think you did. You pull on the chair with two ends of a piece of string around the bottom rung held in one hand under the table; then you let one end go, roll up the string, and hide it."

The child looked at him with a new kind of respect and awe.

"I know a lot more too," Mr. Hero went on, "about stones that appear to come in through the windows or drop from the ceilings, vases that seem to fly off the mantel but are really produced from behind a curtain by a too clever little girl, flower stands that topple over for no reason at all, except they have been kicked by a little foot with a long ruler attached to it with an elastic band."

"How do you know?" Noreen asked.

"One does," Hero replied cryptically.

"But your back was turned all the time," Noreen said. "I was watching you in the mirror." And then, realizing she had given herself away, she clapped both hands over her mouth but immediately burst into a giggle and asked, "Are you magic?"

"Very," said Hero. Then he added, "Noreen, do you know what a poltergeist is?"

"No," she replied, and almost immediately drew a long breath of contrition. "Oh, I'm sorry—I lied. Yes, I do. I heard Mr. Jellicot speaking about them. He said that one had got into Miss Isobel's room and frightened her, so I thought I'd make one in Mummy's room. It's easy, isn't it? It's fun to see how easily people can be made to jump."

"I know," Hero said. "It gets to be. One can't stop. Tell me, Noreen, did you ever topsy-turvy Susan's room—turn all her clothes and things out?"

"Oh no! I love Susan. I was ever so sorry about the rabbit. Cross my heart!"

Hero nodded. "I believe you. Going back to this other business —do you think anyone ever caught you at it?"

The child reflected. "I think maybe at the beginning Cousin Freddie might have. He winked at me once."

"Mmmm," Hero mused. "He *would* let you go on. Anyone else?"

"Miss Paradine."

"Which?"

"Both—but I'm not 'xactly sure."

"You don't think our friend Mr. Jellicot ever saw you?"

Noreen made a noise of scorn and replied, "Huh, not he. He's the easiest one of all—and Dr. Paulson too. Aren't they mugs? I did it for you because you seemed to want to see a ghost so badly. And then you were only angry."

Hero let that pass and said, "There's to be no more of that then, is there, Noreen?"

"Can't I ever again?"

Hero stretched out his legs and rolled over onto his stomach beside the child and leaned on his elbows. "Look here, Noreen, it's fun and games in a way, we know that, and people, particularly grownups, are very silly to be taken in by it. A child wouldn't be, but grownups often aren't that clever. Children are afraid of the dark, but grownups are scared of so many things by day and by night that it's easy to frighten them with one more, and sometimes such a fright can result in tragedy and even death."

"Sometimes," Noreen whispered, "I want to kill Mummy for letting Daddy bully her. And Daddy too."

Hero ignored this and continued. "Grownups who believe in and are afraid of silly things are in a sense ill. They need to be made well, not more sick. You want to become a nurse, don't you, Noreen? Do you know to what the heart and soul of a nurse is dedicated?"

The child suddenly turned her head away and would not look at him.

"Yes," Hero said, "it is to make sick people well."

From afar, and very small, came Noreen's voice: "All right, I promise."

"I promise too," said Hero.

"Cross your heart and hope to die—and seal it with a kiss—real, I mean, not just on the cheek?"

"Very well then, real." He rose to his feet and she did likewise. He held out his hand and she gave him hers firmly, and they shook solemnly. Then she raised her face to his and he kissed her gently on the lips. The young and innocent mouth clung for an instant—an unforgettable moment of a kind of growing up for Noreen. Then, as two white herons arose flapping from the reeds and sailed down the river, they went off for the rest of their walk together, down the bank in the direction of the old bridge.

At three that same afternoon Mr. Hero participated in two not entirely pleasant interviews: one with Horace Spendley-Carter and the other with Mr. Jellicot, though the former did afford him a certain amount of satisfaction.

Spendley-Carter practically asked for it, for he sought Hero out in his room, saying, "A word with you, if you don't mind," and then launched into his reasons for seeking an interview. He said, "I just thought I would let you know that after last night's occurrences I have decided to notify the press. It is my duty to do so. As a person who has considerable standing in the public eye, I feel that an accurate account of what is taking place here, and in particular my own experiences, written by myself, would have the greatest value. However, as you know, I am a reasonable fellow, I appreciate Lord Paradine's position, and yours as well, and did not wish to proceed without notifying you of my intentions. Well there it is. I have friends on both the *Daily Mail* and the *Express*. I assume you can have no further objections."

Mr. Hero, who had been seated at his writing table studying the large sheaf of notes he had made upon the case up to that point, turned around in his chair and looked up at the huge, rather overwhelming man with interest but no friendliness. He did not ask him to sit down. He said, "Yes, I see. Well, I suppose then there's nothing to be done. As a matter of fact, I was just collating the facts and considering the preparation of an article of my own."

"What?" boomed Spendley-Carter. "So that's your game, is it? Try to shut me up and then go behind my back, to sell an article and get publicity for yourself. And after I'd offered to mention your name in mine! Well, we'll soon see about that." He was shaking with righteous indignation. His wits addled by anger, he was headed for the trap.

Hero said mildly, "Well, actually, no. Mine was to be rather a scientific essay on an example of the psychological factors encountered in poltergeist investigations, to be published in the monthly bulletin of the Society for Psychical Research. I have also a standing offer from the *Sunday Times* for an article at any time on the results of any of my investigations. Mine are very dignified and usually rather dull—though this one, I must say, since it will be connected with and based upon you and your family, may have certain aspects which will appeal to the more popular——"

Spendley-Carter trumpeted like a wounded bull elephant. "What?" he roared. "By God, sir, and damn your infernal impudence! You dare to write up me or my family and I'll sue you for everything you've got!"

Hero said, "Yes, I know—but when it can be proven that someone is engaged in perpetrating a dangerous hoax affecting the health and peace of mind of others, the laws of libel no longer render immunity." Hero's voice suddenly turned soothing and sympathetic, and he added, "Too bad, sir, but as you said of Lord Paradine's situation, those are the chances one takes."

Spendley-Carter had now become uneasy. "What the devil are you driving at?" he boomed. "Stop beating about the bush. If you have anything to say, out with it."

"It is a classical case of its kind," Hero said, unruffled. "In all poltergeist infestations one immediately looks for the adolescent child, usually a girl either despised or on the threshold of menses; or the vindictive servant girl; or the neurotic, hysterical woman." He paused and regarded Spendley-Carter gravely. "You know, you had two chances for it, sir," he said. "I had not excluded Mrs. Spendley-Carter as a possibility. Next to the pubic child, the neurotic and frustrated woman is often found at the bottom of such hauntings. Compensates them for neglect, somehow."

Spendley-Carter seemed to swell up like a balloon. He turned crimson and his voice rose almost to a falsetto pitch. "My God, man!" he said. "Do you realize that you are discussing my family? I ought to break every bone——"

"Yes," Hero replied, "I am compelled to do so. You are aware, of course, of the part that modern psychiatry has played in the latest poltergeist investigations. We are thoroughly familiar with how the instigators do their little tricks—what interests us now is why. Now, take the case of Noreen—I have had several long talks with her——"

"*You've* had talks!" Spendley-Carter screeched. "You'll take a damn good hiding, young man, if I hear another——"

"You, of course, are chiefly responsible, and I shall bring this out in my article," Hero continued imperturbably, "but of course the fact that she is an adopted child also has a good deal to do with it. There are some nice little psychological factors involved: father a windbag and a bully, browbeats wife and denigrates adopted child who has turned into an ugly duckling. Daughter, with typical girl's ambivalence of love-hate for father, turns on mother for succumbing to father's bullying. With the first appearance of the pseudo poltergeist in the west wing, and when she sees how the news of it affected her mother, how terrified she is, she thinks to help it along by providing a little terror of her own. Once she had begun, she learned quickly. Noreen is a smart, shrewd child. All of these poltergeist children are."

"By the Lord Harry!" squealed Spendley-Carter. "I'll——" But he paused in mid-threat, for it had penetrated to him that Hero was talking of something as though it were an acknowledged fact. He lowered his voice, but his moist eyes were now filled with hostility, rage, and suspicion. "What have you got?" he said. "Nothing but the word of a vicious child! Do you think anyone would believe that? Children will say anything. You haven't an iota of proof."

"That's just what I was getting to," Hero said. "I have. These." He opened a drawer, took three photographs therefrom, and tossed them onto the desk. "You see, it's to be an illustrated article. Most extraordinary good luck, what?"

Spendley-Carter stared at them unrecognizing at first, and then as he began to make out what they were he turned as white as he had been red before. "What the devil are these?" he spluttered.

"Poltergeist child at work," Hero replied. "Probably the first pictures of same ever made. Devilish hard to get, you know, because once these youngsters start on a poltergeist career they get cute as monkeys. They know just *when* to let fly. You will note how Noreen is sitting facing the mirror where she can watch us and wait till she is certain no one is observing her, and then—whizz, the chicken comes sailing through the air!"

Spendley-Carter continued to stare with horrid fascination at the damning photographs. Beads of sweat stood out on his brow.

Hero said, "She had all the stuff behind the curtain, of course. In this one you can see she is just fetching the vase and is about to flip it over her shoulder. Everybody thought that, because it was one of a pair and the other was still on the mantel, it had flown from there. I did happen to notice when I came in, though, that there was only one vase on the mantel at the time. The flower stand was rather more clever. Noreen had a ruler with her drawing materials; she fastened an elastic band about her shoe and slipped the ruler into it, stuck her foot out behind when no one was looking, as you see in the picture, and over went the flower stand with a satisfying crash. Back went the foot behind the curtain."

Spendley-Carter, staring at the prints with mounting horror, said, "How the devil did you get these?"

"Little Snooper," explained Mr. Hero. "It is what we call the camera Lady Margaret sometimes carries in her handbag. It takes pictures while my sister's back is turned. The thing is, you can suspect all you like in a poltergeist case—you can even *know*—but you just can't do anything about it until you prove it, can you, sir?"

Spendley-Carter's rage had completely evaporated. He looked at Hero miserably as he said, "My God, man, if you print those I shall be ruined—utterly ruined."

"Yes," Hero said, spreading the three prints out on the table and looking down upon them: the one that showed her kicking the flower stand over, the one with the vase in her hand just at the curtain, and the one with her hand over her shoulder and the released chicken no more than a foot from it flying through the air. "Yes," he repeated, "I rather thought so. That will make my blackmailing you with them just that much easier."

Something like hope came into Spendley-Carter's face, and he said, "Eh, what? Yes, yes—how much do you want for them?"

Hero arose and regarded Spendley-Carter with the utmost distaste. He said, "I ought to put you over my knee for that. I could too, you know, for all of your bluster and bullying. You're soft, man, soft and pudgy. My price is the happiness of that child. Is that clear?"

Spendley-Carter stared at him. Hero continued, "The alternative is that I report fully on this case and publish these photographs. You are ruining a life, sir. I cannot stop it wholly, for I am unable to change you or your wife, but one thing I can change —the girl's ambition and happiness is bound up with becoming a nursing sister. She is to be permitted and encouraged to do so from now on. I want her to have books on the subject, a first-aid kit or anything else she desires, and she is to have the backing of yourself and your wife in this project immediately. And under those circumstances, and as long as Noreen's ambition is not interfered with, there will be no publication and no article on my part, and the poltergeist manifestations will cease. Well, what do you say?"

Relief flooded Spendley-Carter's countenance. "What can I say?"

"Then it's agreed?"

"Yes."

Hero gathered up the snapshots and returned them to the drawer. He said, "Very well. Of course, you will likewise refrain from any communications with the press. You keep your end of it and I will keep mine, you need have no fears."

Spendley-Carter mopped his damp brow with his pocket handkerchief and suddenly contrived a sickish kind of grin and affability. "You know, Hero," he said, "I guess you're not really such a bad chap after all."

"Ah," said Hero, "that's where you're quite wrong. I am a bad chap—a very bad one—and make no mistake about it. Good day, sir."

But the interview with little Mr. Jellicot was even more painful. It took place in Meg's room, where he had been asked to meet them.

"What a sordid business," Meg thought to herself as Mr. Jellicot came bustling in full of energy and importance in reply to the summons. His sack suit fitted tightly over his protruding

stomach, but he was such a cheerful, enthusiastic old fellow that
Meg felt in anticipation the pang she would feel at his deflation,
and her eyes wandered willy-nilly to the middle button of his
waistcoat, as though that would be the place where Hero would
insert the sharp pin and let the air out of him. She did not share
her stepbrother's opinion that the retired draper had a hand in
the things that had happened at the Hall, and yet she was well
aware of the necessity for interrogation. There was that damning
photograph.

She tried to comfort herself with the thought that there was
something still more sordid in the attempts that went on from
time to time to produce fraudulent evidence on the subject of the
spirit world, and if Mr. Jellicot was one of these he deserved to
be unmasked. Nevertheless she felt sorry for him.

He said eagerly, "I hear you wished to have a word with me?
Delighted, of course. Any assistance I can render you, or ad-
vice . . ."

Hero nodded. "Yes. I may require both. You have met my stepsister, of course—Lady Margaret Callandar?"

"Oh," Jellicot said, "of course. Lady Margaret—but I didn't
know she was your stepsister. I should have—one should, you
know, if one is up on such things. I try to be."

Meg tried to help him out. "Of course, it's bound to be con-
fusing. Sandro didn't wish anyone to know."

Hero explained, "Lady Margaret often is kind enough to act
as my assistant on a case."

Mr. Jellicot looked brightly from one to the other. "Oh yes,"
he said. "I see. How interesting. And how fortunate you are.
Might one inquire in what capacity?"

"My sister," Hero said, "is a photographer—an extraordinarily
good one."

Jellicot again nodded with bright understanding and repeated,
"To be sure. So stupid of me. It must be fascinating. The advance
in spirit photography since the days of Eusapia Palladino and
Conan Doyle is, I understand, quite stupendous. Negatives have
been obtained which show——"

"Almost anything the photographer is of a mind to show," Hero concluded smoothly. "I was wondering whether you would oblige my sister and me by answering a few questions."

Jellicot might have felt alarm at this, but he was reassured by the presence of Meg, and she, feeling this, was even more ill at ease.

"Questions?" replied the little fat man, blinking. "Of course, if you——" And then added suddenly, "What kind of questions?"

Hero said, "You understand my position here, don't you? I am a private investigator engaged by Lord Paradine to clear up some rather unpleasant and apparently occult manifestations that have threatened not only the person of a guest of his daughter but also the existence of the Paradine Country Club as well. However, I have no police powers whatsoever." (At the word "police," Mr. Jellicot looked slightly startled.) "I have no right to question you, and you, sir, are under no obligation to reply."

Mr. Jellicot said, "No, no, my dear sir, I quite understand. I will be only too happy to oblige if I can shed any light upon——"

"Very well then, Mr. Jellicot, would you be so good as to give us an account of your movements last night after you retired."

The sudden dissolution of Mr. Jellicot was pathetic to behold; he appeared to shrink within his clothes, his face went quite pale, and his cheeks seemed to go flabby simultaneously; his small mouth trembled and beads of perspiration appeared immediately on his lip and brow.

"My m-movements?" he quavered. "W-why, there weren't any. That is, I went to b-bed, and when I heard the h-harp I—ah—quite naturally arose and j-joined you."

Meg had a sudden feeling that she wished her brother would stop, that he would let the little man go, otherwise something rather horrible was going to result.

Hero said, "You are sure that at no time during the night you were present in the library—the private one of the Paradine in the west wing, which is used as a writing room?"

Mr. Jellicot came further undone. "The l-l-library . . . In the west wing . . . N-no, of course not."

Hero's hand dropped to the side pocket of his jacket, and Meg suddenly cried, "No, no, Sandro, don't—don't, I beg of you!" She felt she could not bear to see him thus confronted with his lie, and besides, what would be the purpose of it now? His attitude already branded him.

Hero said, "I'm sorry, Meg, but I'm afraid we must get to the bottom of this." He withdrew his hand from his pocket and dropped the photograph onto the table in front of Mr. Jellicot.

The little man's eyes started from his head, his lips pursed, and a drop of sweat fell onto the print with a little splash. He said, "Oh dear! Oh dear, oh dear," and then looked at them both in anguish. "It's me, isn't it?"

"Yes," said Hero gently enough, "I'm afraid it is. It was taken in the dark by infra-red light with a camera previously planted by my sister."

Mr. Jellicot stabbed Meg with a look that reached to her heart —that of a child who has been betrayed.

"Would you care to tell us what you were doing there?" Hero asked.

Jellicot looked up at him miserably and said again, "Oh dear, oh dear! It's so terrible—it's so *very* humiliating." His head was shaking from side to side. "*So* humiliating."

Meg burst out, "Then don't—please don't."

But the little man had brought himself to the point now. "You see," he said, "I am leaving here in a few days. . . . I collect— that is, I am fond of *some* innocent little souvenir that does no one any harm. I keep them in a book at home to show where I have been. . . . I wanted just a sheet of their own note paper. It has the Paradine crest on it, you know. I told a lie—I wasn't awakened by the noise, I heard it later. I got up earlier and went downstairs. I thought I would get it and be back in my room——" He paused abruptly, and then said, "Oh dear! I feel so very ridiculous," and began to cry.

It was too much for Meg. She went to him and put her arms about him and whispered, "Dear Mr. Jellicot, don't cry. It's quite all right. We do understand—lots of people enjoy souvenirs. Come, you mustn't." But she could not stem the silent flow of tears that dripped from the unhappy eyes of Mr. Jellicot, and she turned fiercely upon her stepbrother. "Well, are you satisfied now?"

Hero felt miserable enough himself. These were some of the real horrors often turned up by his unique profession. He said, "I'm sorry, Meg. Look after the little man," and turned and went out.

MRS. TAYLOR PARTS
THE CURTAINS

Alexander Hero felt abject and distressed. He was young enough to hate to be made to look a fool, and in particular he disliked having been made to look one in the eyes of his stepsister, especially after she had warned him and begged him to desist. Why had he been so anxious to have her there if he did not avail himself of her intelligence and talents? Also, he was genuinely sorry for Mr. Jellicot and angry with himself for not having realized that the little man, except for his wagging tongue, was harmless.

He walked out of the Hall and strolled toward the stables to let the fresh air blow through his brains a little. He was on thoroughly bad terms with himself. What had he accomplished? Turned up a couple of poltergeist tricks and phenomena that any half-baked amateur could as easily have exploded. As for the rest, he had not succeeded in reducing the danger to Susan Marshall or come any closer to solving the real haunting of Paradine Hall. He sat on a mounting stone, fired his pipe, and gave himself up to the gloomiest of self-criticism.

There was a clatter of horse's hoofs and Mrs. Geraldine Taylor cantered briskly into the enclosure. Her seat on her mount was firm; the broad head upon which the tricorn hat perched jauntily was gray, but she rode as straight, erect, and fit as a girl. As she passed Hero she saluted him with her crop and then threw the whip to the groom who came forward to catch it and take the reins. She disdained the hand he held up to assist her to dismount and, springing from the horse like a youngster, stopped to feed it a lump of sugar, pat its sweating neck, and exchange a few words with the attendant.

Hero watched them and thought to himself, "*And you, my spry old girl, what about you? Where do you fit into this puzzle, for you are not exactly who or what you seem either? Nobody is here.*"

Mrs. Taylor came striding, slapping her polished leather boot with her crop. When she reached him she said, "Hello, young man. You're in trouble, aren't you?"

Hero said, "Yes, I am. How did you know?"

"Not any trick," Mrs. Taylor said. "I saw your face as I rode by."

Hero laughed. "Am I that apparent, then?"

Mrs. Taylor said, "Come along and talk to me, if you like. I've had a damn good ride, my head is clear, and I'm going to have a drink. The only thing the matter with this place is that it hasn't got a license. But I have a bottle in my room. You look as though a drink would do you good too."

Mrs. Taylor's room was one of the larger ones of the east wing, on the first floor overlooking the park and the main drive. Spacious and sunny, she kept it comfortably untidy. She said, "Sit down, young man," and motioned him to a chair by the window. From behind a small screen she produced a bottle of scotch whisky, poured two sizable dollops into ordinary drinking tumblers, ran some water into the whisky until the color suited her fancy, and brought one over to Hero. "There," she said, "your very good health," clinked his glass with hers, and took half hers on the first swallow. "Hard-drinkin', -ridin', -swearin' Geraldine, that's me," she said.

Hero raised his glass and took a swallow himself. "Addled Alexander," he said, "that's me."

"Well," said Mrs. Taylor, "so you've found out a few of the tricks that were being played here, but you still don't know who or why." She seated herself on the couch across from him.

"That's about the crux of it," Hero said. "There's something naughty—or I suppose by now it would be safe to say 'someone'—loose here."

Mrs. Taylor was looking at him shrewdly. "Wouldn't it be possible for someone to become possessed by something?" she asked. "Do you believe in possession?"

Hero replied, "I had thought of it. Is there such a thing as invisible and abstract wickedness—in the medieval sense—which can become incarnate and thus occupy space? Quite frankly, at the moment I don't know where I'm at."

Mrs. Taylor took another satisfying drink of whisky and said, "Have you consulted that clever sister of yours?"

"Oh," said Hero, "so you know?"

"My dear man," Mrs. Taylor declared, "you forget that I am a tottering pillar of society myself. I get around."

"Yet you kept quiet about it?" he said.

She favored him again with her acute glance. "Well, you weren't exactly advertising it, and neither was she," she said, "though I must say I caught her looking at you several times in a not exactly sisterly manner. She's your stepsister, isn't she?"

Hero said, "Yes," and wondered what she could be driving at.

But Mrs. Taylor did not elaborate her theme, and her next sentence came as a surprising switch. "Would you like me to try the Tarot?" she asked.

Mr. Hero reflected. "Yes please," he said. "I think I would."

Mrs. Taylor arose, went to the desk, and extracted the Tarot cards therefrom. Hero watched her deft shuffling of the cards and noted the hands with the short, broad fingers. They were the hands of a strong-willed and unimaginative woman. A small tea table stood close by. Mrs. Taylor removed newspapers, periodicals, and a few other articles therefrom and seated herself, prepared to begin.

He asked, "Who taught you the Tarot?"

Mrs. Taylor ruffled the cards again and replied, "When I was at school in Switzerland I had a girl friend who was a Rumanian. Her father was king of the gypsies, or something like that. He was enormously wealthy—it was an expensive finishing school—but underneath she remained a gypsy, I suppose. She believed in it implicitly. It is predestination, isn't it? I read up on it later. In nature there are no accidents—every happening in the universe is caused by a pre-established law."

Mr. Hero screwed up his brow and then quoted from an old book: " 'Cards mixed at random do not yield haphazard results but a suit of figures bound magically to the diviner and the inquirer.' "

Mrs. Taylor looked at him sharply. "Seems you know a good deal on the subject yourself, young man."

Hero replied, "Modesty forbids . . ." And then, "Do you believe in it?"

Mrs. Taylor appeared slightly nettled and said, "I have already told you about my beliefs. They wobble all over."

"Do you believe in clairvoyance—or what the scientists call hyperesthesia?"

Mrs. Taylor mocked him: "Pul-leese, Mr. Hero, I'm just a simple country girl. You and your big words."

Hero asked, "Have you ever tried crystal gazing?"

Mrs. Taylor snorted. "Don't be ridiculous!" Then, the cards held in one hand, "Well—shall we . . . ?"

"Yes, please."

She began to lay out the cards in a square open at the lower end, with a circle in the center, in the shape of what Mr. Hero recognized as "The Great Game." Sixty-six were on the board, with one—his leading card—in the middle, and eleven cards unused in a pack face down.

As Mrs. Taylor appeared lost in concentration for a moment, Hero noted that, of the twenty-one picture trumps in the pack, some eighteen were scattered about in the design: Death was there, Judgment and the Devil, the Lovers, Temperance and the Shattered House, and that supposed bearer of man's fate, the Juggler.

"You were not always fortunate as a child," Mrs. Taylor began. "I see difficulties from your seventh to your eleventh years. They appear to be connected with a man—not a relative—a dark man and an elderly woman. I see a serious illness in your youth, and that you at one time intended to train for the medical profession but changed your mind under the influence of the same elderly woman. A friendship you formed with a boy of your own age at school has had a great influence in your life. I see a fair-haired girl too . . ." Mrs. Taylor gabbled on; there were travels, false friends, paths crossed by an assortment of fair and dark strangers. At last Mrs. Taylor paused for breath.

"Dear lady," Hero murmured, "I am sorry to have to advise you, you're talking the most unsupported rubbish. So far there has been hardly a word of truth in anything you have said. My childhood was a most happy one. You'll have to do better than that, you know."

He was disappointed, for he knew that sometimes readers of the Tarot had been responsible, for, to say the least, some astonishing coincidences. Up to this point Mrs. Taylor's revelations had been no more than the usual fortuneteller's hit-or-miss gabble. The only item that had come at all close to truth was that of the boy with whom he had formed a friendship while at Eton. But that was not a difficult hazard—most boys formed firm friendships during that period, and he thought for a moment of Alan Hunter, that tall, dark, brilliantly saturnine boy who had been responsible for the turn his career had taken. He saw him now as he had seen him the last time, dead. He had lost his life while trying to rescue a friend from drowning. The scene on the bank of the river was as vivid as ever to him, and as painful.

" 'Greater love hath no man,' " said Mrs. Taylor.

"What?" said Hero sharply.

The solid woman looked up, startled. "Did I say something?" she asked. "I was thinking. Your court cards are badly scrambled. You will suffer a financial loss but gain an association . . ."

Mrs. Taylor was back at her gabble again, and yet Mr. Hero was aware of a curious sensation as of the ground trembling beneath his feet. He was sitting in a modern room in the twentieth century, with a somewhat vulgar and horsy old woman, playing at children's games with cards—and yet something had happened. Without realizing it she had read his thoughts. A vista of another dimension had opened up. He felt shaken and nervous. Would it happen again?

Mrs. Taylor nattered on: good and evil, sickness and health were nicely balanced, in happy contrast, Hero thought, to the ancient Tarot prognostications, which were invariably filled with gloom and doom and death on the gallows or by an assassin's dagger—when suddenly Mrs. Taylor's voice slowed, then ran down and stopped.

She passed a hand over her forehead and said in a voice not at all like the one in which she had been speaking previously, "I feel ill. I feel very ill." And then, her voice sinking almost to a whisper, "There is danger! There is great danger!"

There was presence then, presence enough to do him for a lifetime. For the first time since he had come to Paradine Hall the room seemed filled with it, and Hero felt ill himself—in the sick, helpless way, when the stomach turns over and the mind reels, suddenly and out of the blue, and for no apparent discernible reason.

"That's wicked," said Mrs. Taylor, and then repeated the word "wicked" as though someone had spoken to her and she was replying.

Mr. Hero fought off the nausea which was assailing him and asked, "What is wicked? Who is in danger?"

"Why, she is," said Mrs. Taylor. And then almost with an expression of surprise, "And so are you. Oh dear! I didn't know this. But why would anyone . . . ?" The expression of surprise then turned slowly to one of horror. "Oh," she exclaimed, "but the other is far worse! It's her soul that is to be taken as well. Nothing is to be left to her. How dreadfully cruel!"

Hero asked, "Who is it? Can you tell who is threatened?"

"It is a young girl here in this house." Even Mrs. Taylor's voice had changed to that of someone who was aghast at what she either saw or heard, and all the time she was gazing down upon the array of colored pasteboards, with their kings, queens, knaves, and cavaliers, and pips of red and black, and the silly and slightly ridiculous woodcut representations of angels, devils, skeletons, and jesters, mythical animals, symbolic flame, moon and stars, and all the childish hodgepodge of the magic-makers. And yet some strange and unsettling kind of shift *had* taken place, as though the universe somewhere had slipped a cog, or the curtains of time had been parted, or—as she had made her way into his a moment before—Mrs. Taylor had tuned into the thoughts or mind of another.

"What is the nature of the danger?" Hero whispered, hardly daring to speak.

"Jealousy and hatred," replied that other voice of Mrs.

Geraldine Taylor. "Demoniacal hatred and death—and the holocaust of fire—flames at every window lighting the end of Paradine Hall." Then as though there were someone else present to whom she was speaking, she shook her head and said, "But that's wicked—too horribly wicked! You *mustn't*—you'll forfeit your own soul—you'll be damned into eternity forever after. Can't you see that you mustn't?"

It was, Hero felt, like witnessing the fury of a storm at sea, where the mountainous waves were yet but a minor reflection of the abysmal power of the storm above in the air that lashed them. What were the unseen furies that Mrs. Taylor reflected? "Mustn't what? Who?" Hero felt compelled to ask.

"What's that?" she said. And then with a kind of automatism her fingers began to pick up cards from the table. She paused for an instant, seemed to realize what she was doing, and continued to collect and stack the pasteboards. Whatever contact there had been was broken.

"I don't think I care to go on, if you don't mind," she said in a voice that was now once more her own. "You don't really believe in it very much anyway, do you? I'm afraid it hasn't been very successful. Perhaps some other time . . . Would you care for another drink?"

With a wrench he could almost feel, the universe settled back into place again, the parted curtains closed. Hero heard himself murmuring the platitudes: "No, no—it was most interesting. No, thank you, I won't have another. I've taken up enough of your time. Thank you so much."

He got up and went to the door. He paused there for a moment. Mrs. Taylor was still at the table, the stacked cards in her hands, watching him heavily as though she were trying hard to remember something. Then she said, "Be careful, young man."

He went out and walked down the corridor toward his room, where he could be alone and think. Nothing seemed the same any more—the boards he trod, the carpets, the pictures adorning the wall, he himself; he knew that he was filled with a genuine fear. Something had changed, something had happened beyond his knowledge, forces had been loosed, a crisis was at hand. A warning had been received, if he could but read it. He suddenly felt bitterly inadequate to cope with this new and more deadly danger that threatened Susan Marshall and them all.

"MY DEAR, IT'S
A FAMILY MATTER"

Tea with the Paradines that afternoon seemed a monstrous mockery of banal politeness overlaying fearful and secret tensions. "*Or do I feel this,*" Hero thought to himself, "*because of the warning conveyed by Mrs. Taylor? Am I the only one who sees death and destruction beneath this placid English ceremony?*"

"You do take sugar, don't you?" Isobel Paradine said to Meg. The Hon. Isobel wore a tea gown of black and silver which enhanced her platina hair and striking features.

Lady Paradine was attired in a mauve garden frock which ought to have clashed violently with her copper-colored hair but somehow did not. She set small teeth into a piece of buttered toast with a concentration that excluded the presence of all the others. Hero found himself wondering what lay behind that mask of indolence and boredom. Was it remotely possible that this faded but still beautiful exterior concealed an internal volcano which had been responsible for all that had happened at Paradine Hall and all that might yet happen? Would a woman who had found that she was not mistress of her house go so far as to pull it down about her ears? And what about the attacks on Susan Marshall? Hero had racked his brains for further ways to protect her. He did not want her to lose her soul.

Hero looked across the room where Susan and Mark were chatting. There was no question but that young Paradine was in love and his mother knew it. It was Susan Marshall who was the great uncommitted in the household—Susan the undecided; Susan the cool, controlled one; Susan the flirt; Susan the unpopular American. Most American girls were thought to be title hunters. Was this reason enough perhaps for Lady Paradine first to try to frighten her and then literally as well as symbolically turn her out of her room and Paradine Hall? But what about the death and immolation that Mrs. Taylor had seen and he had seen her see as clearly as though she had read it in a book? Was this bored, handsome woman a murderess as well?

And what had gone wrong with Sir Richard Lockerie? He was no longer in command of himself, but nervous, uneasy and, Hero would have said, almost with a sense of guilt about him. He was by the window talking with Meg, but from the quality of his voice alone Hero was aware that his mind was not on what he was either doing or saying. What had happened? Had Susan Marshall turned him down? And if so, did this in any way affect the problem?

Beth was sitting with Cousin Freddie, sipping her tea, and she too was in a state of tension. Hero saw how pale she was, and then a moment later flushed. He caught her stealing a glance at Sir Richard with his stepsister. "*Oh, Lord,*" he said to himself, "*is she pining away for her uncle Dick?*"

He tried to remember something Meg had told him that night at the Antelope. What was it she had said? "Isobel was once supposed to be in love with Sir Richard, or he with her, but he went off to the war and married some French girl, and that put an end to that."

Hero looked with new eyes upon these three. Could it be possible? A half generation, as it were—two women of the Paradine clan, aunt and niece—each at one time in love with the same man, that same man there by the window, still handsome and virile, in love with another? Was this why the terror, the danger, and the still untrapped ghosts swirled about the head of Susan Marshall? Was this splendid creature the key to the riddle? Would her departure from Paradine Hall lay these ghosts once and for all—and with that departure, whose heart would be broken?

Sir Richard was saying to Meg, "Clever of your brother to have hit upon that tidal explanation." He then turned to Hero and said, "I suppose that is the answer to most ghost stuff, what?"

Hero replied, "A good deal of it, Sir Richard—half the disturbances in houses are hydraulic in source—underground watercourses. A fault in the substrata of rock will turn the trick as well. A too heavy lorry passing four or five miles away can crack a mirror or knock a picture from a wall."

Lord Paradine, who had been brooding over his teacup, looked up and said, "Naturally. Always an explanation. Never believed in this ghost stuff myself."

"Not much you don't, Unkie," Freddie sneered. "You've had the wind up like everybody else." The unpleasant young man turned to Hero suddenly and said, "I say, Hero, your nosing about here isn't doing me a good turn, you know. If the curse does its biz I'm the next Paradine heir, what?" He laughed loudly. "Susan, old girl," he said, "if that happens you'll have to marry me if you want to be Lady Paradine."

For a moment the brick lay where it fell, until Susan broke the shocked silence by saying mockingly, "Oh, Freddie, would you? I never knew you cared."

Isobel said in her soft and sweetly modulated voice, "Freddie dear, I wonder if I ought not to pour this tea down your neck instead of into your cup?"

"Dear Auntie," Freddie said, "one can see why all the eligibles declined and you never married."

Paradine said, "Well, dammit, it did make one just a little uncomfortable. But that's all over now, thanks to Hero here——"

"Haw," mocked Cousin Freddie, "what's all over—what about the nun and the harp and all the rest?"

"Perhaps you could tell us something about it, Freddie." Lady Paradine spoke so little and took so small a part in what was going on about her that when she suddenly did it came as a shock to them all.

"What do you mean—I could tell you something?" For the first time Hero thought he saw signs of fluster on the fat, disagreeable face as Cousin Freddie protested.

Lady Paradine turned her still beautiful eyes on her husband's nephew. "Why, you said yourself that if something happened to us you are the next Paradine heir. You wouldn't be gliding about the house inside a nun's robe and playing a harp, trying to frighten us all to death, would you, Freddie? It would be so like you."

"Well," Hero said to himself, "good for little Enid! But who would have thought it?"

Cousin Freddie seemed almost apoplectic for a moment, but

his defense came from a wholly unexpected quarter and took even Hero by surprise.

"Oh, but, Lady Paradine," Susan Marshall said, "I'm sure that Freddie wouldn't——"

Whatever else she had been about to say was cut short by Lady Paradine's gesture of turning to her, a kind of masterpiece of a gesture, it appeared to Meg, watching it—so gentle, so firm, so kindly.

"My dear," said Lady Paradine ever so softly, "it's a family matter."

For the first time since he had known her Mr. Hero saw the American girl truly disconcerted. A crimson flush mounted to the dark hair as she bit her lip and averted her face quickly. Then quietly and without saying a word she arose and left the room. Mark got up and went after her.

"Mark," his mother called softly, "do sit down." But he did not heed her.

Hero moved into the breach, saying, "Freddie is quite right, of course, I am not yet prepared to call my work finished. There are still many things we do not know."

He was feeling oppressed again. There was no doubt about it, there was an atmosphere now. It was affecting them all, making them do and say strange things. It brought a kind of half-sobbing cry from Beth: "Must we really know everything?"

Isobel said, "It's possible to know too much sometimes, isn't it?"

Freddie laughed unpleasantly. "Not for me, Auntie—not as long as I am Public Suspect No. 1."

Lord Paradine took the floor. "It seems to me you've explained it all, Hero—underground watercourses, what? I can't see what's to be gained any further. If we're satisfied——"

Lady Paradine looked approvingly at her husband and said, "I think John is right."

Hero could feel the ranks of the Paradine clan closing. Whatever they knew, whatever they suspected, whatever they felt, they had had enough; they were standing together suddenly and easing out the outsider, as Susan Marshall had just been eased from the room. His glance caught his stepsister's eye and he saw her head move almost imperceptibly from side to side. He smiled inwardly to himself. *"Good old Meg!"* The Hero-Callandar family could also close ranks. She was signaling him to stand firm.

"I think not," Hero said, "if you will forgive me. The haunting of Paradine Hall by its too numerous spirits is far from settled. I will remind all of you of the condition under which I accepted this case: that I could not be dismissed from it until such time as I decided it was closed. That time is not yet."

"Susan," Mark called after her, hurrying along the path shaded with thornbushes that led to the brightly colored patterns of the sunken garden. She stopped on the path to face him, crying, "Let it be, Mark! I've been told off properly and well."

He said, "Blast Mother! I suppose it was a family affair as well that you have been frightened, threatened, and bedeviled ever since you've been here."

"Then why didn't you say so?" Susan exclaimed, and was immediately sorry, for she laid a hand on his arm and said, "Oh, I'm sorry, Mark—that was unfair."

There was a marble bench set in the border of small, closely bunched together red and blue flowers laid out in a lovely old-fashioned design. They sat on it side by side and Susan stirred the gravel moodily with her toe. She said, "I'm sorry, Mark, but something went wrong somewhere—dreadfully wrong. Not even Alexander—Mr. Hero has been able to find out what it is. I don't think I want to stay here any longer. I don't believe in ghosts and spirits and that kind of thing, but I do think I believe in wickedness, Mark—and I don't like it."

Mark Paradine groaned. "If you'd only let me look after you, Susan . . ."

Susan asked, "Can anyone protect anyone from hatred? Can't you see how your mother dislikes me?"

Mark became suddenly changed and grim. He said, "I'm not asking you to marry my mother, I'm asking you to marry me."

Susan looked up at him in surprise. These strange British

with their weaknesses and their great strengths! And she understood suddenly the tradition of the dower house into which the mother was moved when the son became the head of the family. The Englishman wore the trousers in his home. After a little she said with a note of melancholy in her voice which made it almost childlike, "It was going to be such a lovely summer. Why do you suppose it went wrong?"

Mark asked, "Susan, are you in love with Sir Richard Lockerie?"

"Dick? Oh no!" Her reply had come so swiftly and naturally that it surprised even Susan, who had not known that she was quite so sure. She was certain of it now.

"Is it Alexander Hero?" Mark asked.

"N-no, I don't think so. He's terribly attractive though, isn't he?"

"Yes, I'm afraid so."

"I don't think I could ever really learn to love a man like that," Susan said half to herself, almost as though she were reviewing her thoughts out loud. "He doesn't really believe in anything— at least I'm sure he's never believed in me. I made him angry because his liking me interfered with his practice of logic and deduction—you see, he suspected me of making up my ghost. And besides, he wasn't quite sure of my virtue, either."

Mark cried, "What?"

Susan said, "The night Alex re-created the haunting in my room, someone tried the door—someone was trying to get in. If he had rushed out into the corridor he might have caught whoever or whatever it was."

Mark asked, "Why on earth didn't he?"

A half-smile turned the corners of Susan's mouth as she looked back upon that night. She replied, "He let on that it was chivalry, that he didn't wish me to be compromised—but really he was afraid of who it might be if he opened the door."

The young man looked bewildered. "But why?" he asked. "I don't see . . ."

Susan suddenly felt her heart flooded with tenderness at this innocence. All unknowing, Mark Paradine had answered the question as to what the man she could love would be like.

He then said, "I'm in love with you, Susan. I've asked you to marry me before—when it was too soon, perhaps, or the time wasn't right, or we didn't know one another, but time has run out, Susan—suddenly there isn't any left. I feel as though something dreadful might happen to you that somehow, if we were one—if you would say that you cared for me and would marry me, I could stop it."

The girl looked at him out of troubled eyes, for she knew now that she loved him, and wished that it could be as he wanted, but she was human and all the bitterness and hatred that had been directed at her ever since her coming to Paradine Hall stood between them, and the gulf between them was widened by the manner in which Lady Paradine had only a few moments before thrust her aside and let her know in so many words that she was no more than an outsider. She etched another design in the gravel with her toe and said, "Oh! Mark, Mark—I wish you weren't a Paradine."

"Why?" he said sharply and suddenly. "What's wrong with being a Paradine?"

"Oh!" Susan replied, startled. "I didn't mean—— It's just that in our country we don't believe in hereditary titles, or . . ."

Mark asked, "Do you believe in families?"

"Of course I do," Susan said. "I love my family."

"I meant in the importance of families. In your country families are not important—in mine they are."

Susan looked at the young man in astonishment. "Why, Mark," she said, "I do believe you're angry."

"Yes," he replied, "I am."

She drew in a quick breath to say contritely, "Oh, Mark, I'm so sorry."

He said, "You needn't be. I didn't ask you to be sorry. I am not saying that I am either proud or ashamed of my family—there have been times when I have been both—but we *are* the Paradines. We live in and own a little corner of England, and the Paradines have been a part of English history for a long time.

They go on, you know, they do—the good and the bad—but we try."

Susan was looking at him with dismay. She said, "Mark. Oh dear . . ."

The young man went on, "Let's have this clear, Susan. I have loved you ever since I first laid eyes on you, but I like being a Paradine. I hope to be a good one. It's almost like being in a relay race, where one passes along the torch to the other—except that you can't go it alone—you run in pairs. I was asking you to become a part of me and with me to hand on the flame again when it came our turn to let it go. I wanted it to be you. That's about all I have to say." And with that he arose and walked down the path, leaving Susan sitting there looking after him, feeling as though someone had closed the door in her face, and through that closing she had lost her world.

He was not yet out of sight when she was on her feet and calling after him, "Mark—oh, Mark!"

He stopped and turned around to see her standing forlornly in the center of the path, and there was no longer about her any of the self-confidence or cool assurance that had been the shell of Susan Marshall, but only a lonely and somewhat frightened girl.

He took slow, hesitating steps in her direction. It was hard for him to make his way back to her; it was harder for her to ask him to come, and yet they were human, young, and in love.

"Mark," she said again, with a wistfulness that was quite new to her, "I've been told off again." And then she added in a lower voice, "But this time I liked it."

He came closer still, until only a few yards separated them, and they stood thus looking at one another across the gulf that a few moments before had appeared to be so unbridgeable.

"Mark," Susan whispered, "I'm glad you're a Paradine. Please—might I be one too?"

And after that the gulf vanished as did the yards, and there was no longer distance of any kind between them, their hearts, and their young bodies.

Alexander Hero took Mrs. Taylor's warning seriously. Over and beyond the change in the atmosphere of the Hall, the sense of approaching climax which he had been experiencing since the interview with the widow, if there was any logic whatsoever in the course of events there an adventure in pyromania might be expected. Mr. Jellicot had discussed it openly at the dinner table as the usual last step in poltergeist manifestations. There would be no fires set by Noreen; the poltergeist in the west wing had been equally exploded—but what about the third ghost that still infested Paradine Hall?

Hero asked for and secured Lady Paradine's duplicate set of keys and embarked upon a minute and thorough exploration of the ancient manor from attics to cellars, with particular attention to the latter.

He inspected the storerooms below floors, the laundry, the heating plant, wood and coal bins that opened off what seemed to be a mass of underground corridors. As he went he tried to familiarize himself with their direction and plan with reference to the rooms overhead and to remember where he was—now beneath the great hall, now under the drawing room, the library, the music room. One of the underground chambers was a well-stocked carpenter's shop with lathe and drills, and it was here, Hero reflected, that Isobel practiced her hobby and effected small repairs. He saw nothing unusual about the place; it was neat and tidy, there were pieces of unused pine and cherrywood of various sizes, planks, and some long fir rods, boxes of nails, screws, staples, and a set of tools that advertised competency. In one room nearby there seemed to be nothing but oil paintings stored, portraits and other discarded subjects. He found his way to the wine cellars and the vegetable storage bins.

When he estimated that he was beneath the music room he was confronted with a locked door, but he located the key quickly and let himself in. This was a large enclosure illuminated by a single drop light working off a switch by the door. It was half empty in spite of a considerable amount of furniture piled up around three sides—chests, tables upended, several tallboys and a number of chairs in the style known as Country Chippendale —not good enough to grace the rooms above. A careful examination of the room yielded nothing either alarming or interesting. Hero went on.

When he had finished he was satisfied that nowhere had he come upon any evidence whatsoever of intended arson. The Hon. Isobel ran her house not only efficiently but with intelligence, and apparently was well up on potential fire hazards. There were no piles of old newspapers or periodicals anywhere about, no heaps of waste or rags or other dangerous and inflammable material. Had Mrs. Taylor been merely a garrulous woman with an overheated imagination who had been trying to impress him? He remembered then the scene, her voice, the look of horror upon her face, and the nausea it had inspired within him.

He knew a great deal by this time, did Mr. Hero, about the ghosts that had been disturbing this old family house—apparitions and cold winds and candles that went out of their own accord— but try as he would, the pieces refused to fall into place or to make sense. And then there was still that damnable harp which had not been explained, and which he could not explain. Was it indeed credible that amid all the jiggery-pokery something had slipped in that was genuine, as with Mrs. Taylor's reading? Was it possible that that wickedness in whoever was tampering with and producing manifestations of the occult to terrorize human beings had evoked something from the beyond? He wished it were so, yet his intelligence still refused to accept it. He went off to Meg's room to talk things out with her.

He found her with the print of the figure of the nun, examining it through a magnifying glass. He went and stood beside her, looking, and then asked, "Anything?"

Meg put down the magnifying glass with a gesture of exasperation and said, "I thought if I could only find *something*—some trifle we'd overlooked—perhaps it might give us a lead. But there's nothing. It's just damn bad luck."

Hero studied the photograph for a moment; it *was* bad luck that the one camera affected by the nun had had to be affixed at such an angle that it revealed nothing except the fact that threads are not tripped by disembodied shapes. He said, "You've got an idea who's inside that thing, haven't you?"

She replied, "Yes."

"Who?"

"I'd rather not say."

Hero respected his stepsister's reticence. She fell silent thereafter for so long that Hero asked finally, "What are you thinking, Meg?"

"That this house is filled with jealousies, tensions, vindictivenesses, secret and not so secret loves, frustrations and desires, and some quite horrible people."

Hero nodded gloomily. "Yes," he said, "it's hell sorting them out, isn't it? This ring-around-a-rosy business—poor Beth hopelessly in love with Sir Richard, Sir Richard in love with Susan——"

"Oh no," said Meg decidedly, "Sir Richard in love with Beth."

Hero looked at his stepsister, startled. "With Beth!" he cried. "But it's Susan to whom he's been paying attention ever since she's been here."

Meg said, "Oh, my Sandro, you are undoubtedly the world's greatest detector of bogus occult phenomena—but when it comes to men and women in love . . ."

"I don't see what that has to do with it."

She reached out her hand, cupped his chin in her palm, and said wryly and lovingly, "My dear innocent, if you at forty-two were in love with some fluffy young thing, and she had been taught to call you 'Uncle Alexander' and fetch rugs to put over your knees, and help you on with your overcoat, and there happened to be another attractive girl about, what would you do to demonstrate that there was some life in the old boy yet?"

Hero grinned and kissed the nearest finger. "Clunk," he said, "penny's dropped. But does it get us any for'arder?"

Meg looked disturbed. "What if it had worked too well and Beth were jealous and wanted to get rid of Susan?"

Hero whistled and then said, "Good Lord! Beth, that gentle child?"

Meg said flatly, "No woman in love is gentle."

An echo of something in her voice made Hero look up at her sharply, but she was gazing down at the picture again. Hero then said somewhat irritably, "But would she destroy her home as well? Take what suspect you will—Freddie, Isobel, Lady Paradine, Beth —every case falls to pieces on that rock. There have been two separate and distinct motives in these hauntings—one has been to eliminate Susan Marshall and the other to destroy the Paradine Country Club from which all of them live." He then added, "What do you think of our American friend?"

"That she is beautiful to look at, warmhearted, kind, intelligent, but with that American overlay of self-assurance that borders upon arrogance, almost—and that you've been sampling."

Hero groaned. "Oh, Lord, what an unsettling person you are, Meg. You're lucky you're living in the twentieth century—five hundred years ago you'd have been burned as a witch."

Meg was regarding him quizzically. "Oh, really, Sandro—two healthy, normal, beautiful people in the same house—one nibbles, doesn't one?"

Hero looked at Meg curiously for a moment and then asked, "Do you nibble too, Meg?"

"Occasionally."

He did not reply to this but seemed lost in thought for a moment, and Meg watched the outward reflection of his thoughts with interest; he did not look particularly pleased, which in turn pleased her enormously.

Hero exclaimed, "That perishing harp—it always comes back to that! It is the only thing I can't solve logically."

Meg was watching him anxiously. She said, "I have a feeling that you will, Sandro."

He looked at her. "Then you don't believe it might be genuine?" he asked almost hopefully.

Meg wished she could give him the encouragement he sought,

but realized she must be honest. She said, "I don't know. I only know that, whether it is genuine or not, you will find out before too long." A frown suddenly creased her brow and she said, "Sandro . . ."

"Yes, pet."

"Sandro, I'm worried." She ran her fingers through her hair, twisting the strands in a characteristic gesture, and then commenced striding up and down the room trying to grasp and give expression to something she was feeling. She said, "I wasn't before, but I am now. What is going to happen, Sandro? Something, don't you feel? Something horrid! This house has suddenly become filled with it."

Hero looked at her. "Ah—you too?" he said. "I wondered whether it was only myself. You see, I've been warned."

"Oh! By whom?"

"Mrs. Taylor."

Meg showed her surprise. "What? Mrs. Taylor—that dear old broad-beamed, husband-hunting girl? I thought all she had on her mind was men. I'd never even considered her."

"She laid out the Tarot for me," Hero said, and then went on and recounted to her his experience with Mrs. Taylor.

When he had finished Meg was looking at him with bewilderment. "Fortunetelling cards, Sandro? You?"

"Not exactly fortunetelling. It is probably a kind of autohypnosis—the cards provide a key to the unlocking of the vaults of the subconscious. She was rattling off the most inaccurate and appalling chowder about my past, present, and future, and then suddenly she was in communication—I'd swear to it."

Meg said, "Oh dear—in communication with what?"

"How is one to know?" Hero said vehemently. "With herself, perhaps. We all are chockablock with repressions, observations, ideas, fears, hopes, terrors and memories of terrors collected from everything we have ever seen, heard, or done. The difference is that sometimes the Mrs. Taylors can dredge them up by staring at their silly cards, or . . ."

"Yes," Meg said with a curious tension, "or?"

"Or," concluded Hero, "those childishly ridiculous pasteboards have yet another effect—they tune Mrs. Taylor out and let something or someone else tune in."

Meg was looking at her stepbrother now, her eyes widely distended. "Sandro," she said, "I'm frightened for the first time—for you—she said you were in some kind of danger——"

Hero said, "Never mind me, I can look after myself—but something *is* going to happen unless I can prevent it. Something or someone is going to try to destroy Susan Marshall, and I don't know who or where or how. I feel so damn helpless."

Meg went to him and put her arm in his. She said, "Don't be discouraged, Sandro. Don't give up. Try. Keep on trying. There's only you who can do it. I don't even seem to be able to help you any more."

Hero gave her shoulders a little squeeze and said, "Thanks, Hag." He bent over and brushed the top of her head with his lips and turned to leave.

She asked, "Where are you going?"

"Back to that confounded music room," he replied, and went out.

The music room was becoming a kind of Chamber of Frustration to Alexander Hero. Each time he visited it he came away empty-handed—or rather, empty-minded, so to speak—and yet he was certain that somewhere in it lay the key to the puzzle and the secret of what was troubling him. One way or another, either as a genuine manifestation or a cruel hoax, the answer must lie within these four walls, for here the harp was kept and here the impossible had been made possible.

He concentrated upon the layout and contents of the room to try to remember what it was that had troubled him once about it—some slight change, something he had forgotten. But whatever it had been, it would not float up into his consciousness, nor was it disturbing him now as he moved about from piano to the shelves and music racks and the golden harp in its accustomed place by the window. This time he laid it carefully on its side and went over it with magnifying glass and small steel rod to tap for hollow places where hollow places should not be. He found none. On the underside of the sounding board he noticed a slight discoloration and a few scratches contained in about the area of a shilling piece, but these did not appear to be indicative of anything. He examined particularly the pedals, and that portion of them which would come into contact with the player, for marks and scratches, which certainly should have appeared upon the pedals. There were none. Apparently after the death of Lord Paradine's mother the instrument had been groomed and polished to its pristine form. He next dusted it for fingerprints, and found some, but they were in the wrong places. Obviously the maids moved the harp when they swept and cleaned.

He was beginning to feel the old sense of frustration again, something within him saying, *"Give up, Hero. Whoever or whatever plays this harp does it without touching it."* And then before him rose the picture of that night when he had crashed into the room to see the strings still vibrating, and he felt a black rage of exasperation come over him and a desire to pick up the instrument and smash it, and then shout to the empty room, "Now, damn it, let's see you play that!" He realized he was being stupid, almost childish.

To calm his nerves he went over to the piano, opened and braced the lid, and sat down to play and wait for the therapy of music to do its work. He struck the opening chords of the piano transcription of the Bach Toccata and Fugue in D Minor. He played well and soon was losing himself in the music, and for the moment he forgot Paradine Hall, the dangers and the problems that beset him. The fugue swelled and rolled, modulated, and then rose again in the climactic crescendo leading to the firm, thundering, satisfying chords with which Bach closed.

Hero sat at the piano with his eyes closed, and the last of the sound died away. Then something caught his attention that caused him to open them very quickly. He swung around on the piano stool and gazed at the harp hard and long. He arose and went over to it and stood there looking as though he could not get enough of looking and thinking about what had so suddenly struck him. He did not touch the instrument, but very softly he began to apostrophize himself: "You fool!" he said. "You blithering, blethering half-wit! You feeble-minded simpleton! You absolute, unmitigated clot!" He turned and ran from the room, down the corridor, through the great hall into the pantry and down the cellar steps, until he had regained the storeroom beneath the music room.

This time he gave it another thorough going over, but looked elsewhere than he had before, and in odd places. When he had finished he thought he knew how the trick *might* be done.

"*But where is it?*" he asked himself. "*Where would it be? Where would someone keep it—and who? It must be somewhere.*"

Then began for him the most meticulous search he had ever bestowed on any premises. Once again he went over every bin, room, and enclosure in the cellars, and the storerooms in the attics as well. He was aided in his hunt by the fact that the object for which he was looking was large and unwieldy—so large that it would not be easy to conceal—and therefore he expected to find it if it was there.

By the time he had completed his work in cellars, attics, and public rooms the dinner bell had gone, which meant that shortly family and guests would forgather. Hero waited a good half hour to give them a chance and make sure they had all left their rooms, and then began a thorough and shameless examination of the apartments of the Paradines, rooms both occupied and unoccupied, to which Lady Paradine's great cluster of keys gave him access. Had anyone come upon him they would have thought surely that he had lost his mind, as flat on his face he looked under every bed, into clothes presses and cupboards, and delved into broom closets, and bathrooms large enough to hold the object he was seeking.

Not satisfied with this, though he knew by now his chances were diminishing and he must hurry, he ranged through all of the guest rooms in the east wing and, to the astonishment and indignation of cook, butler, and waitresses, pried into kitchen and pantry cupboards and recesses. Hero had no doubt that Huggins would report his actions to the Hon. Isobel or Lord Paradine himself, but he did not care.

He was not satisfied with going over the house alone; at that time of year it stayed light enough, and he sallied forth from the back of the manor and investigated stables, outhouses, and nearby barns. And when in the end he had completed his search he was exhausted, discouraged, and utterly defeated. There was no doubt in his mind—there was no possibility for that which he sought to be there, and if it was not, the theory that for a moment had given him such hope and excitement was of no avail. He was right back where he had started from, and no nearer any solution.

He went back to his room and flung himself on his bed, too tired even to think. He has a flask of brandy in his suitcase, poured himself a double, and felt better after he had drunk it but no less chagrined and despondent. It struck him that it was growing late, and that whatever danger threatened usually struck at night, and he had best be joining the others.

By the time he had dressed it had grown dark. He went downstairs, passed through the conservatory, where one small lamp was switched on at the back and the window of which still had not been set in its frame, and so out onto the lawn where on that mild night, by the light of the lanterns which the workmen had hung upon the rails guarding their excavated ditch, family and guests, as was usual when the weather was fine, were having coffee. He joined the table at which Meg and Mrs. Taylor were sitting.

It was shortly after this that the second apparition appeared to the stunned onlookers on the lawn and Mr. Alexander Hero came close to losing his life.

Seated at the table trying to placate his empty stomach with a cup of coffee, Hero noticed again the single lamp burning in the conservatory, throwing dim light and illuminating the room somewhat like a dark theatrical set. He wondered briefly why it was burning and then forgot about it.

The moon had not yet risen, but the Milky Way gleamed overhead in the starry sky, and with the lanterns and lights from the upper windows the darkness was pierced sufficiently. Scents from the sunken garden nearby were carried by a warm, gentle night breeze and mingled with the tang of salt from the nearby tidal marshes. It had all the aspects of a simple and innocent kind of country evening outdoors; there were flashes of jewelry, bare arms, white shirt fronts, the firefly glow of cigars, and subdued talk—and yet there was murder in the air.

Lord and Lady Paradine sat with Sir Richard and Isobel. The young people, Beth, Susan, Mark, and Freddie, were together. The Wilsons were by themselves at the far edge of the group. Dr. Paulson, Mr. Jellicot, and Dean Ellison made up a men's table. Hero, now sitting with his stepsister and Mrs. Geraldine Taylor, noted that only the Spendley-Carters were absent.

To Hero the oppression that had settled itself within Paradine Hall seemed to have moved outside with all of the inhabitants. All seemed to feel relief at being outside the Hall for the coffee ritual rather than within.

Mrs. Taylor suddenly shuddered and said, "I know it's hot, but I'm chilled."

Hero said, "Let me get you a scarf."

Mrs. Taylor said, "Would you? You're a pet. You know where my room is—there's one over the chair, a white one. I meant to bring it with me."

"Have it for you in a jiffy," Hero said, and got up quietly and left. At that moment the butler, with the coffee tray, and his wife with accessories of cream and sugar, emerged from the doorway, followed by Spendley-Carter, and crossed on the nearest board bridge that had been laid across the ditch. Hero decided to go the other way, and went around behind the group seated in the darkness, and into the east wing by its own entrance, out of sight and earshot of those on the lawn.

At the table Mrs. Taylor suddenly turned to Meg and said, "Why has he gone? He oughtn't to have gone."

Meg said, not quite understanding, "He went to fetch your scarf."

Mrs. Taylor said, "But we oughtn't to have allowed him to go, don't you see?" She half rose from the table, as though meaning to call Hero back, but he had vanished. She sat down again.

Meg felt a surge of uneasiness. "Why, what's happened? Anything wrong?" she said.

The expression had faded from Mrs. Taylor's countenance and she said, "Eh? What a nice young man. How stupid of me to forget my scarf. Yes, I'll have coffee, please—white."

No one really could remember afterward when it had begun, when it was first seen, or exactly what happened thereafter; many had their backs turned to the building or were engrossed in conversation, but the signal seemed to have been given by the sudden shock of a piercing scream emitted by Mrs. Wilson, followed by her cry of "Oh, my God! Look!" followed by a second scream, "Alexander!" and then there was the crash of an overturning table and the clatter of the service to the lawn.

For a moment there was utter confusion, with no one seemingly knowing where to look. People rose from their chairs at this new assault upon their nerves, and then saw that the blonde, slender woman, her face sheet-white, eyes distended with terror, was pointing at the conservatory, where Alexander Hero seemed to be in the grip of some scaly, monstrous horror risen from the Pit.

There was no question as to the apparition being imaginative or hallucinatory, for they all saw it—a monstrous head with two cold, goggling eyes, horrid corrugated proboscis like the trunk of an elephant, and long, glittering, dead-white body of a serpent.

The screams of another were added to those of Mrs. Wilson.

It was Meg crying, "Sandro! Sandro!" She was on her feet and straining toward him but, paralyzed by what she saw, unable to move. The foulness—demon, fiend, or whatever it was—had her stepbrother in its toils, the scaly body wound about one arm, the rank, venomous head and staring eyes a few inches from his own. To the cries and screams of the women were added the crashing of chinaware and silver as more tables were overturned, and the shouts of the men.

The paralyzing immobility was broken as Major Howard Wilson reached inside his jacket and produced a dark object which glittered momentarily as he raised his hand and pointed it toward the figures in the conservatory. At that instant Meg too came to life and her anguished cry of "Sandro! Sandro—look out!" topped all the others, but her dash across the lawn toward the Major came too late. There followed the stunning explosion of the heavy pistol in his hand. There was a "spang" and shattering of glass into a thousand pieces, and Alexander Hero was seen lying face downward on the floor.

Hero had had no difficulty locating Mrs. Taylor's scarf hung over the back of a chair in her room. It was a long white stola of Italian silk worked with heavy silver thread. He hung it over his arm, went out, and returned this time through the public rooms of the east wing, which led him once more through the conservatory. He had traversed no more than half the enclosure when he was brought up short by a woman's scream of terror, which penetrated the heavy glass of the tilted picture window and stopped him in his tracks to look out upon a weird and incredible tableau. It was as if all those sane, plain people he had left on the lawn chatting, smoking, or having their coffee had suddenly gone mad.

Hero had an equally lunatic impression that it was he who had set them off on the demented train of their actions, for they were all looking and pointing at him with mouths open and horror-stricken expressions of their faces.

Coffee tables and chairs had been overturned and they were standing rooted as though overcome and paralyzed by what they were seeing, and yet there was only himself passing through the conservatory with Mrs. Taylor's Italian stola over his arm.

Mrs. Wilson and her husband were on their feet, and the handsome blonde woman, with her hands to her cheeks, was emitting screech after screech. The three men—Paulson, Ellison, and Jellicot—were frozen in the strangest attitudes, like figures in a film stopped in mid-motion. Lady Paradine had thrown her arms about her husband's neck and buried her face in his breast, but Paradine's already prominent eyes, fixed upon him, looked as though they would drop from his head. His lips were moving, but Hero could hear no sound. Mark Paradine's arm was about Susan's shoulders, and on that calm, unshakable countenance Hero for the first time saw fear. Beth and Sir Richard were trying to reach one another and moving like figures trapped in one of those dreams where the limbs refused to move. Only Isobel remained seated, as though rendered powerless to rise.

For a moment the thought passed through Hero's brain: "*The coffee's been poisoned—they've all gone out of their minds,*" but he knew that this was not so, and wondered whether it was he who had somehow walked into some hideous nightmare and was bereft of his senses.

He then searched for and found Meg, who surely would not fall victim to whatever it was that held these people in such a thrall of terror. To his horror he saw that, of them all, she was in the direst straits of panic. Standing close to her, stocky Mrs. Taylor's face was a study in fear, she was trembling and pointing, but his sister's face was altered almost beyond recognition by the apprehension that seemed to grip her. He saw her lips moving, and she seemed to be straining and striving to reach him in some manner.

In an endeavor to break out of this nightmare or ascertain what it was about him that was so terrifying, Hero looked about him swiftly, and saw—nothing. There was no single solitary living or moving thing within the conservatory beyond the plants in their pots and the hanging ivy. Close to the wall the single lamp burned, illuminating him and his surroundings in the room, and revealing that there was nothing there besides the furniture. He was quite alone.

Now in this strangely static moment a new concept came to Hero. It was as though he was on a stage—a solitary actor in a glass-fronted stage. Out beyond were the footlights in the shape of the lanterns hung from the guardrail of the ditch—the ditch which was like an orchestra pit—and beyond that was the audience, but an audience driven to the point of insanity by some weird fantasy built around the scene they were witnessing—a solitary man crossing an empty room.

And then at last the paralysis lost its grip, there was movement among them. Hero caught the shine of something that had appeared suddenly in the hand of the Major—he was pointing something that glittered. Hero saw Meg burst her own bonds of immobility and heard the cry, "Sandro—look out!" that issued from her throat as she charged straight at the Major. Hero had only time to throw himself upon his face on the floor before the crash of the gun followed Meg's warning and the tinkling of glass as the bullet, striking the picture pane at its tilted angle, instead of passing cleanly through it, shattered it into fragments and buried itself with a fierce smack in the wall behind him.

He waited a few seconds, then got up and brushed glass dust off himself. There was broken glass over everything—a lake of it where the window had been, and there was nothing now between the spectators and himself. The picture had changed too, for while they were still staring the madness and the terror seemed to have gone out of their faces.

Hero came out through the shattered window and the mess of broken glass, almost like an actor approaching the footlights to take his bow. A woman leaped the ditch and now hurled herself upon his breast, clinging, holding, weeping hysterically, and crying, "Sandro, Sandro—you're alive!" It was Meg.

Now this was so strangely dramatic and histrionic for her that for a moment Hero was lost and did not know what to do. He was standing there center stage, so to speak, alive—oh, alive all right—after having been shot at with a Webley service pistol in the hands of an expert, with a weeping girl in his arms who was his stepsister. Her hands were at his face, his hair, his clothes, and she was crying, "Sandro, you're all right! It didn't harm you!"

He said, "There, there, pet—what is it? It's all right, old girl, I'm here. He didn't hit me."

Meg was still trembling as though with chill or ague, and she could barely speak. She said, "But the thing, Sandro—the monster. We all saw it. It had you by the throat——" She broke down and began to weep again hysterically, clutching Hero as though she would never let him go.

He bent down and whispered into her ear, "Pull yourself together, Hag," the pet name he had for her when they were both children together and growing up. It had the effect of calming and steadying her. She caught her breath and her weeping was stilled. Nevertheless, she clung hard to his arm as they crossed the ditch by the bridge and came to the others.

Sir Richard and Lord Paradine came running up. "My God, Hero, are you all right?" Sir Richard cried. "That monstrous specter—we all saw it!" Paradine added, "Yes, by God, Hero, we thought you were a goner." They were all about him in a crowd now, speaking in a jumble. But Hero went on through without seeming to listen, until he came to where Major Wilson was standing, the heavy service revolver hanging in his hand, pointing toward the ground, and Vivyan Wilson standing next to him, her knuckles pressed to her temples, staring at the gun and then at Hero as he advanced, and whispering, "Alexander—oh, Alexander!"

Hero, with Meg at his side, stood in front of the Major, looking at him and not saying a word. Major Wilson gave his shark smile and said, "Sorry, old man, if I gave you a scare. First time I'd ever seen a real ghost. Shook me, I guess. Horrible monster, staring eyes, long snout like an elephant. Have to admit it shook me."

Hero stood there looking and listening and did not reply.

The Major perforce had to go on. "Seemed to have you by the throat. Don't believe in that sort of stuff but, by Jove, there it was. Thought you were a goner, like the rest of us." He stopped.

Hero said, "I thought I told you not to hunt ghosts with a gun. I'll have that, please." He held out his hand.

Without another word the Major reversed the revolver and handed it to Hero butt end first. The investigator broke the gun and ejected the four live cartridges and the empty fired shell into his palm and examined them for a moment with an expression of distaste about his mouth. He asked, "Do you always load with soft-nosed ammo?" Now he knew why the pane of glass, in addition to the angle at which it stood, had been shattered into thousands of pieces. He also knew something of the size of the hole the bullet would have torn through his body had he not dropped when he did.

Major Wilson said, "Naturally," but his voice was not quite steady. "When you use a gun where I've come from in Africa, you want to stop whatever's coming at you."

Hero did not reply; he shrugged and dropped the cartridges into the side pocket of his dinner jacket and thrust the gun into the waistband of his trousers. He turned away from the Major and said, "Right. Now I want someone to tell me exactly what it was you thought you saw in the conservatory."

Paradine said, "No 'thought you saw' about it. 'Saw'—I'll take an oath on it."

"No question," Sir Richard corroborated.

"Well, one of you try," Hero said. "Susan, what about you—you've got a level head on you."

The American girl, still white-faced, pleaded, "I'm afraid I can't. I'm afraid I—I'm afraid for the first time in my life that I'm afraid." And then she finished in a half whisper, "And I didn't ever think I'd be."

Dr. Paulson said, "I think perhaps I kept my head as well as anyone, though I'll admit that I was badly upset. Still, by profession I'm trained to observe."

Hero said, "Very well, Dr. Paulson, I'd be obliged."

Dr. Paulson launched into a fair and reasonably accurate description of what they had seen from the moment his attention had been attracted by Mrs. Wilson's scream, his narrative drawing substantially corroborative remarks from the others, though Lord Paradine insisted that it had horns as well as a long snout.

Paulson said, "I didn't see horns, but the head was set upon a long body, white and shining, like that of a serpent."

"Was it moving?" Hero asked.

"The body undulated toward you, or seemed to have undulated, or to have you in its toils."

Meg said, "I shall never forget it as long as I live. Didn't you hear me cry out to you, Sandro?"

Hero said, "I heard you. I saw you all. What I am trying to determine is what it was you saw."

Sir Richard said, "It was as Dr. Paulson described it, except that I thought of it more as an octopus—or something horrid like an octopus—and that you were in the grip of its tentacles. You remained standing there as though you had been stung or paralyzed, the way a scorpion or a spider paralyzes its victim, and the strange thing was that none of us could seem to move either."

Hero nodded. "I know," he said. "Shock sometimes works that way. And then?"

Dr. Paulson resumed the narrative. "Well, then came the shot, and that seemed to release us all. I didn't see the Major draw his gun, but I heard it go off and the glass shatter."

"Yes—and thereafter?"

"Why, the monster disappeared as if"—he hesitated over the word for a moment—"as if by magic, as it had come. One moment it was there, and the next instant it was gone and you were lying on the floor. At first I thought you might have been hit, but when you arose a moment later we saw that the Major's shot had come in time and that you had been spared and were unharmed."

"Then you would say that the Major's quick thinking and timely intervention had saved my life?" Hero suggested.

"I have not the slightest doubt of this," assented Dr. Paulson, "and would so testify. I am sure everybody will agree that the disappearance of the monster coincided with the firing of the shot."

There was a murmur of assent. Major Wilson said with sudden affability, "Glad it turned out all right, old man. I fired at the thing, and I don't usually miss."

Meg opened her lips as though to speak, but Hero picked up her eyes swiftly with a glance and stopped her. He accomplished this with a suspicion of a wink. Meg looked at him in amazement but subsided. Hero said gravely, "Thank you, all of you, for your help and your concern. In an apparent supernatural apparition such as you all just seem to have witnessed, it is of the utmost importance to have written evidence set down at the earliest opportunity. I will therefore ask all of you to go to your rooms immediately and set down exactly—with all the detail you can supply—what you have seen and heard."

Startlingly, Isobel said, "Will you believe now there is a curse upon this house? It is not yet done."

Cousin Freddie said, "I say, look at that hole in the wall! Good thing you weren't standing there, eh, Hero?"

For the first time the engineer Dean Ellison became communicative. He said, "I should be interested in seeing *your* report, Mr. Hero. You were rather in the thick of it, weren't you?"

Dean Ellison was looking not at Mr. Hero but at the scarf that still hung over the investigator's arm. He looked at it then too himself and said, "Oh! Sorry," and handed it to Mrs. Taylor, who took it in a kind of daze, her eyes fixed on his.

She whispered, "I nearly got you killed, didn't I?"

"Nonsense," Hero said. "Will you all go up now and prepare your reports?"

Major Wilson said, "Look here, old chap, my report can wait. I'll just stay here, if you don't mind, and give you a hand. Never came up against anything like this in my life before. I'll help you get to the bottom of it."

Hero said, "You can help me most by preparing your account, Major Wilson, and I insist that you go and do so at once. Have I made myself clear?"

The Major tried to stare Hero down but in the end dropped his own eyes and said, "Come along then, Vivyan—perhaps he's right."

They filed away slowly and into the house until only Meg was left standing there alone and looking strangely pitiful. She said, "I don't want to leave you, Sandro."

He went to her, took her hand gently, and said, "It's all right, Hag dear, it's all over. Nothing's going to happen to me. Go to your room and get into bed. I'll come in and see you later, after I've had a bit of a snoop around."

She still lingered wistfully. "You're sure, Sandro?"

He said, "Oh, sure enough." He grinned at her. "And never mind about that report, you know, I just wanted to get rid of them. It's all just a good-natured little practical joke, a happy, boyish prank during which, but for the grace of God and your baying like the bitch of the Baskervilles, I could have had a hole the size of a grapefruit blown through my gizzard. They play rough here, but they won't any more." He took her by the shoulders and turned her toward the house and watched her go.

He went then and stood for a moment looking at the conservatory, the shattered window, and the ditch, in silent contemplation. He pulled his pipe from a side pocket, loaded it slowly, and got it going. Then he walked leisurely over to the ditch and looked in, and saw there exactly what he had expected to see. He gazed down upon the objects which were thus revealed and, to get a better look, sat on the edge of the cut and let his legs dangle over the side while he stared and pulled at his briar.

"Oh, my sacred aunt!" he said. "Old Dr. Pepper would have enjoyed this."

COURTESY OF
DR. JOHN HENRY PEPPER

Mr. Alexander Hero came into his sister's room an hour later carrying a paper parcel under his arm.

Meg arose from the couch where she had been sitting by the window and staring out into the darkness where but a short time ago the scene of horror had been enacted. She was pale and still shaken, but her expression was a curious mixture of both concern and contrition. Hero thought that she looked like nothing so much as a child who has been frightened. He experienced a feeling of tenderness toward this competent stepsister of his who, from a gay and even cynically sophisticated person, had turned into the unhappy and unstrung girl who stood before him.

Meg said in a still and almost little-girl voice, "Sandro, I'm sorry. Will you forgive me? I made an exhibition of myself and practically threw myself at your head before everyone, didn't I? You see"—and the merest hint of her old wry smile returned to the corners of her mouth—"you see, it was the first time—— I've never seen a ghost before." He noted that in spite of her efforts to control herself she was still trembling.

He went to her at this and simply took her in his arms and held her there and stroked her. He was pleased to see how it quieted her, how the trembling ceased as his comfort flowed from him to her, and surprised too at the curious kind of solace it brought to him as well. There had not been time for him to be frightened while it was all going on, but now that it was over and he realized how narrow his escape had been it was good suddenly not to be alone, to be close to someone so staunchly of his own side, of his own clan.

He released her and she looked up at him smiling gratefully. He then said, "All right, my old Hag, you can relax. It's over— and you still haven't seen a ghost." He went over to the parcel which he had dropped onto the table, unwrapped the paper, and revealed what was within. "There you are," he said, "that's your bogle, isn't it?"

For a moment recollection of the horror dilated Meg's eyes as she stared at the object, the goggling eyes of it, and the long corrugated snout, and then she burst into a sudden peal of laughter which concealed just a touch of hysteria. "Oh, Lord, Sandro," she cried, "to think that I never recognized it—it's a gas mask, of course—and all the hundreds that I saw during the war!"

Hero said briefly, "You weren't expecting to see one—under those conditions."

"But where did you find it?" Meg asked.

"In the ditch," Hero said, "where somebody put it but didn't have time to get it out—somebody who took me for a bigger fool than I am."

"In the ditch!" Meg cried. And then added with bewilderment, "But then—I don't understand—how did it get into the conservatory?"

"Stage illusion," Hero said. "One of the oldest. Discovery of a sixteenth-century Italian philospher by the name of Giovanni della Porta, and improved and adapted in 1863 by an ingenious bloke called John Henry Pepper, a professor of chemistry at the London Polytechnic Institute. It was known thereafter as 'Pepper's Ghost,' but it hasn't been seen for years—not since magic shows went out of style."

Meg was regarding him still with bewilderment.

"Did you ever walk into a darkened room carrying a candle and see your image projected as though coming toward you in the window but *behind* the glass? That's the illusion on which Pepper's Ghost is based. When it is done on stage a glass pane invisible to the audience is set up, tilted at an angle, close to the footlights. Down in the orchestra pit is the 'ghost'—usually a skeleton—manipulated by a couple of chaps muffled in black, who, aided by a strong light, work the trick. Since they are down in the orchestra pit the audience cannot see them. The skeleton is reflected by the tilted glass and appears in animation on stage behind the glass, and in depth, where, worked by the fellows in black who can't be seen, he can actually be made to appear to engage in a fight with a living actor. Someone recognized that the angle of the new pane of glass for the conservatory window and the ditch cut in front of it for the drains was almost the perfect setup to create the illusion. The gas mask had been put into the ditch with a lantern and covered with a tarpaulin with a rope attached. A twitch of the rope by someone sitting close to the ditch—off came the tarpaulin. The lantern illuminated the mask and threw the reflection via the tilted glass so that the apparition actually appeared to be inside the room. I walked into it carrying Mrs. Taylor's scarf, and obligingly furnished the thing with a handsome serpent's body which you all thought was coiled about my arm. Q.E.D."

Meg stared at the thing on the table before her. "But who?" she asked.

Hero replied, "The Major, I fancy. The rope which was attached to the tarpaulin had been thrown into the ditch opposite where he was sitting."

The horror returned to Meg's face. "He was trying to kill you," she said.

"I rather think so," Hero agreed, "but perhaps not. Perhaps his original idea was only to make a fool of me by creating a ghost which would take me in, and then exposing it. He had no way of knowing I was going to fetch Mrs. Taylor's scarf at that moment, and probably didn't even know that I had gone. He might have hoped that when I saw the apparition from the lawn I would rush into the conservatory, which would have given him the chance to unlimber his artillery, but he couldn't be certain. However, when unexpectedly I came walking onto his set, so to speak, and his wife started the hullabaloo, it must have seemed like a golden opportunity. There were a half a dozen witnesses there who would have testified that I was in the grip of some monster, and that he had fired to save my life—including, probably, my little sister. That would have been an irony, wouldn't it?"

Meg shuddered and said, "He'll try again."

Hero said, "I don't think so. The Major has a regard for his neck and won't want it stretched."

Meg did not reply but gave the thing on the table several tentative pokes with her forefinger. "To whom does it belong?" she asked.

"Isobel," said Mr. Hero.

"No!" Meg cried. "How do you know?"

"I showed it to her and asked her. She was air raid warden for the district during the war. She said she hadn't seen it for years and it had been probably lying around in a closet somewhere. I suppose the Major found it, and it gave him the idea."

Meg asked, "And did you tell her what you told me—as to how it was used?"

Hero looked thoughtful. "Yes, I wanted to see what her reaction would be. She is a remarkable woman. She looked me straight in the eye and said, 'It was clever of you to have seen through this, Mr. Hero. This in no way alters the curse that lies on Paradine Hall.' And then she simply turned and walked away from me."

Meg reflected a few moments, twisting strands of her hair. She said, "Then you're really no further along?"

Hero shrugged. "The case always does seem to fall apart just as I appear to be getting somewhere, doesn't it? You name it— the case of the Lethal Magician, the case of the Photogenic Nun, the case of the Non-existent Harpist, or just the case of the Too-damned-many-for-comfort Ghosts. We've just about run through the lot, you know. The only one we haven't had is the chap in the ruff carrying his head under his arm, and I wouldn't be surprised to see him turn up at any moment. And I still have to prove that Major Wilson had knowledge of how to work Pepper's Ghost." Then he added bitterly, "And so far Mrs. Taylor has been fifty per cent right. If she achieves a hundred per cent, the next strike will be at Susan Marshall."

"Sandro," Meg began in a tentative voice, "might I suggest something?"

"Ay, my pet. You don't think I only got you down here to take snapshots of a fat little man in his underwear pinching crested stationery for his memory book."

Meg smiled somewhat bleakly at the picture and said, "I've remembered something about tonight. It's about Mr. Ellison. It's the first time he's ever said anything, and he was looking most curiously at Mrs. Taylor's scarf over your arm."

Hero said, "Yes, I remember."

"Why don't you have a word with him, Sandro? He knows something. I thought he was almost issuing some kind of an invitation."

"Ellison," Hero repeated, "why ever?"

"I'm being contrary," Meg said, "and illogical. In other words —a woman. Just because he never says anything. He's never made any contribution. Paulson is an opinionated fool; Jellicot a poor, deluded little man; Horace Spendley-Carter an ass, and Mrs. Spendley-Carter the wife of one; the Major is a jealous husband; and we all know Cousin Freddie is an adder—but what about Mr. Ellison? Can anyone be *that* negative? He sits like a buddha while all hell breaks loose over the house, and says nothing. I just don't believe it. He's an engineer, isn't he? Sometime ago you said that to diddle the harp one would have to be some kind of acoustical engineer. Isn't Ellison at least half of what you're looking for—at least the engineer part?"

Hero went over to his stepsister, took her face in his hands, and kissed her gently on one eye. He said, "Thank God somebody in our family has some brains." He picked up the gas mask, rewrapped it, and went to the door. "I'll just go and show Mr. Engineer Ellison my little toy."

By then it was close to midnight. The house was dark and had quieted down, but there was a light shining from beneath Ellison's door. When Hero knocked it was opened by the engineer, in dressing gown and slippers. There was a bottle and two glasses on his table, and a black, japanned box. "Come in, come in," he said. "I've been rather expecting you. As a matter of fact I've been wondering for some time how long it would take you to get around to me." The stocky man closed the door, pointed to the bottle on the table, and said, "Pour." While Hero did so, he opened the tin box and disclosed a box of Havana cigars. "Smoke?" he suggested.

"Thank you," Hero said. He placed his package on the table, poured himself a drink, and accepted a cigar. Both men then performed the ritual of snipping off the ends, the slow, luxurious lighting, and the savoring of the first and best of all the puffs.

The paper wrapping around the gas mask had come undone and revealed what was there. Ellison motioned to it with his cigar and said, "I see you've found it."

So Ellison knew! It was something of a shock to Hero to discover his sister so right so quickly. He replied briefly, "Yes."

Ellison said, "I rather thought you would. Anyone belonging to the Magicians' Circle would be bound to recognize Pepper's Ghost."

Hero said sharply. "What do *you* know about Pepper's Ghost?"

Ellison laughed. "I used to belong to the Circle myself until I resigned many years ago. But I still get their literature. That's how I knew you were a member. Does that surprise you?"

Hero said, "Frankly, yes—in spite of the fact that I've had several hints that you were not always an engineer."

Ellison smiled and savored his drink. He said, "You've heard, of course, of the oriental magician Rajah Rham Singh?"

"Joe Bernard!" Hero cried in utter amazement. Rajah Rham Singh, the last of the great magicians, who in skill and showmanship had been on a par with magicians of the caliber of Maskelyne, Houdini, Goldin, Chung Ling Soo, and Will Goldsten, had been born a Cockney boy at Eastchapel; his real name had been Joe Bernard, and his oriental make-up and fake accent had helped to disguise his antecedents. Dean Ellison a former magician! Hero's mind, working at top speed to fit this into all facts and theories, suddenly ground to a halt. "But that's impossible," he said. "Joe Bernard died ten years ago, at the age of eighty-three. I read about his funeral."

"I was his mech," Ellison said quietly.

Hero's mind absorbed this startling revelation and leaped ahead. "Good Lord," he repeated, "you were his mechanic!" And then he remembered conditions that he had laid down for someone who could make a harp play without hands—acoustical engineer, magician's helper.

Ellison was speaking again. He said, "When I was a young lad, some forty-odd years ago, just starting out, I found myself with a degree, no money, and no job. I answered an advertisement for someone with a knowledge of engineering and a mechanical turn of mind. The advertiser was Joe Bernard. We got along fine. For the next five years I invented and adapted most of his routines."

Hero drew on the Havana filler and emitted a long streamer of gray smoke. Were things going to fall into place at last at Paradine Hall, and from this wholly unexpected quarter, and only because of Meg's extraordinary intuition? Hero said, "Joe Bernard was before my time. I regret that I never saw him perform. But I wonder if, having been so frank, you might care to go on and tell me why you have been haunting Paradine Hall and producing some of the late Rajah Rham Singh's illusions gratis?"

"I?" said Mr. Ellison in astonishment. "Are you serious, Mr. Hero? I assure you, the only thing I have been haunting is that confounded bunker in the fairway on the sixth at Eastward Ho."

It was Hero's turn to be astonished. "Do you mean to say you deny having had a hand in the manifestations that have been taking place here?"

"Of course I do," Ellison said. "Man, use your head—whatever would I be playing such silly tricks for?"

"But you knew about them, didn't you?"

"Certainly."

"Then would you mind telling me why, since you recognized the basis of what was going on here, you didn't speak up and say something."

Dean Ellison regarded Mr. Hero over that insuperable gulf that separates an older man who has lived his life from a younger one. Then, extracting a card from his case, he handed it to Hero. There was a string of letters after his name, including M.C., O.B.E., several other decorations, and membership in the Royal Society of Engineers.

"I like to mind my own business," Ellison said. "Besides, it just wouldn't do, you know, to have it noised about that this pillar of the hydroelectric industry of Great Britain once toured the country with a Cockney mountebank inventing tricks for him to mystify the boobs. In any case, it seemed to me that you were quite a capable young man and were doing very well by yourself, until you got yourself shot at by that Major fellow. I gather you'll be doing some checking up on our friend. I don't care for gunplay, so I thought we'd best have a talk. I was sure you were on to all that hocus-pocus and nonsense going on around here. The kid, of course, was working some of it. What is it that is puzzling you?"

Hero said gloomily, "That confounded harp." He was feeling like a fool now to have suspected Ellison. He was wondering whether his mental abilities and judgment were succumbing to the atmosphere of the house, or even whether he might have been taken in somehow by Mrs. Taylor and her performance. "I know how it could be done, except for one thing which is missing."

Ellison regarded him silently, pulling on his cigar.

"Look here," Hero said, "when you were with Bernard you had been already graduated as an engineer—would it be possible for someone untrained to work out an illusion independently and arrive at the same conclusion as a professional?"

The engineer snorted. "Certainly," he said, "you ought to know that yourself. All of the greatest illusions are based upon the simplest of principles. If they weren't written up or the secret handed down, they would be reinvented at least once every two or three generations. Anyone with a mechanical turn of mind could hit upon them. There's a gimmick in everything—what makes them illusions is the showmanship."

The thought startled Hero even as he realized that Ellison was right—he should have known it. His mind turned to the ugly child who had hit upon a way of moving a chair in a darkened room as though by unseen hands; by herself she had reinvented one of the oldest tricks used by fake mediums in their disgusting séances.

Ellison asked, "Have you checked whether there is anyone here more than usually handy with tools?"

Hero regarded the older man morosely: was it possible that he had arrived in one at what Hero was just beginning to consider after a long, tedious, and painful investigation? He said, "But it won't work, sir, that's the frustrating thing. I've hunted this damn place high and low—there's no second harp. It is almost impossible to hide a concert harp, or even chuck it into the river, without someone noticing—it takes two men to lift it."

Ellison asked, "What other harp?"

"The other one that would have to be used to make the first one play."

Ellison grinned. "Robert-Houdin performed the trick a hundred years ago with two harps; when the great Rajah Rham Singh did the illusion we had neither a harpist nor a second harp," he said. "It cost too much to lug a pair of them around. But one of our assistants who traveled with the show wasn't too bad with the violin—it works just as well, you know."

Hero was on his feet with an exclamation. "Oh, Lord!"

"Think of something?" Ellison asked.

Hero had. He remembered now what it was that had been missing from the music room; it was the cello that had stood in the corner the first time he had visited it.

The gray, stocky engineer was looking at the end of his cigar with great suspicion, sniffing at it. He drew in smoke until the end glowed, then sniffed again, shaking his head and saying, "I thought it couldn't be this Havana at ten bob apiece—but then what the devil is it?"

Hero too was sniffing. Some execrable stench seemed suddenly to have invaded the room—a sickening, miasmic odor. The investigator wrenched the door open and went out with Ellison at his heels. The stink filled the corridor—there was more of it and it was more noxious. From the west wing there came the distant sound of an agonized voice bawling, "Hero! Hero! Where are you?"

In spite of the change in pitch induced by some new agony of fear and tension, Hero recognized it as Sir Richard Lockerie's. He shouted, "Here, Sir Richard—coming," and ran. Halfway he encountered the baronet, sheet-white, disheveled, in slippers, trousers, and dressing gown, his eyes almost starting from his head.

"For God's sake, Hero," he cried, "come at once—something ghastly has happened!"

Hero felt his heart sink within him. "Susan!"

"No, no—Beth."

Other cries arose: the voice of Lord Paradine shouting, "What the devil is that stink?" and then the agonized scream of a woman. Doors were opening. Susan appeared in dressing gown—Meg— somehow Cousin Freddie was there too. They went pounding down the hall at the heels of Sir Richard until they came to Beth's room. They seemed to reach the door simultaneously and crowded inside.

Stretched out on the bed, still as death, lay a nun in black muslin habit, black hood with white starched lining. There was no mistaking the pale face and the figure within the cowl and the habit—it was Beth Paradine. She lay still as in sleep, unconsciousness, or death. On the night table by her bed was a glass with some milk still in the bottom. Beside it was a bottle of sleeping tablets.

Sir Richard was on his knees by the bed then in a frenzy of anguish, holding her, shaking her, calling to her, "Beth, Beth—oh, why did you do it? Is she dead, Hero? For God's sake, someone, get a doctor!"

Lady Paradine too was on her knees at her daughter's side, distraught and frightened, calling to her. "My baby! My baby!" she moaned, and then cried, "She was upset by what happened and said she was going to take a sleeping pill. Isobel brought her some hot milk—my child has killed herself—why, oh, why?" Mark stood anxiously too at his mother's side.

Cousin Freddie, his fat face flushed and perspiring, said, "My God—so it was Beth who was the nun all the time!"

The implication of his words reached everyone in the room and reduced them to stunned silence, except for one hoarse cry from Sir Richard, who looked as though he were about to be bereft of his reason. "Oh, Great God! My Beth the nun!"

There was the tableau then: the still figure on the bed who by her very stillness and the habit she wore seemed to admit to her guilt, and all the horrified people who had loved her—parent and friend, brother and lover—staring at her.

In the silence, his own thoughts and emotions in desperate turmoil because of things he now knew, Hero went to the bed. He picked up the glass, sniffed it, tasted the milk, knelt and put his ear to Beth's breast, where the heart was still faintly fluttering, sniffed at her lips and breath, opened the eyelids and looked into the unseeing eyes, and said sharply, "Mark—call Dr. Winters at once! Meg—get some hot coffee going!"

Sir Richard's head was shaking from side to side, and he was saying, "My Beth the nun? But how could she be when we were together that night?"

Hero went over to him, took him by the shoulders and shook him, and said, "Pull yourself together, man. What night? When? Where?"

"The last time the nun was seen and the harp played. I found her in the library alone—terrified. I took her in my arms—— She had tried to follow the nun. That was when—when we found one another. We were still together when the harp began to play."

As though the blackest of abysses had opened up at his feet, Hero saw his mistake then, and the consequences of it, and groaned aloud. "What a fool I've been! Why didn't I see? Why didn't I know?" For from the moment that Beth had found her way into Richard Lockerie's arms Susan Marshall had been as safe as though she had been in her own home. The hatred into which Mrs. Taylor had tuned had transferred itself to Beth Paradine.

The nun's habit lay empty in a crumpled heap upon the floor. Held upright in the grip of Dr. Winters and Mark Paradine, Beth, clad in slippers and dressing gown, was being walked up and down, up and down the length of the room. Her eyes were still glazed, her mouth vacuous, but locomotion had returned— she was moving her limbs of her own volition. Hero, with Meg, stood watching her narrowly.

Meg asked of her stepbrother, "Sandro, do you know who— what has happened?"

Hero nodded grimly. "I think I do." And then said, "She's had an overdose of barbiturate," and pointed in the direction of the night table on which the two-thirds empty glass and the bottle were still standing.

Sir Richard had regained some of his composure, though he was still a badly bewildered man. "Why did she do it?" he groaned. "We were happy. We had found one another. Had I not come to her room to see that she was all right she would be dead by now."

Hero said, "Have some faith, man. She didn't. Look at that bottle—it is almost full. She took *a* sleeping tablet, at the most two, then she drank her milk. The overdose had been dissolved in it. Afterwards, when she became unconscious, that thing was put on her."

They all looked with distaste at the empty habit on the floor, and Lord Paradine shouted, "You mean someone has tried to kill my daughter?" and Lady Paradine moaned, "But why—why? Why was this done to my baby?"

"I can give you two reasons, and one of them is probably symbolic," Hero asserted: "compulsory retirement from the world of love—and life. This case has been stiff with symbolism from the beginning, or have you forgotten the condition in which Susan's room was found, and the hand at her throat?"

Sir Richard cried, "Then you mean she wasn't the nun at all, Hero?"

"Certainly not!" the investigator snapped. "How could she be, man, when she was in your arms the night the harp played? If I had known that before—I might have prevented—— Harp and nun are inseparable, and always have been."

Cousin Freddie suddenly raised his head and large nose and sniffed. "I say," he said, "whatever's got into this house now? That frightful stink—it's worse!"

Now that Beth's crisis had passed and it was clear that she would recover, they were all again made aware of the horrid, mephitic stench through the house.

Susan Marshall's nerves gave way. She sat down upon a chair suddenly, white-faced, and asked, "Are we then really haunted, Alex?" and at her words horror seemed to return to the room.

"No," Hero replied, so sharply that it was almost like a slap designed to bring them all out of approaching hysteria, "don't be a fool! Haven't we had enough of this confounded fakery? That's the easiest trick of all. Why should a ghost smell?"

The odor had intruded itself upon Dr. Winters, now that his patient was out of danger, and he asked, "In God's name, what are you burning in your furnace here?"

"Dr. Winters," Hero asked, "have you prescribed tincture of valerian for anyone here recently?"

Dr. Winters looked at Hero frowning for a moment, and then replied, "Why, of course—several days ago I took a bottle of it up to Mrs. Spendley-Carter. I still use it as a sedative." His face suddenly lit up as he cried, "By Jove, that's what it is! I thought it was something familiar. What the devil does it mean spread all over the house?"

Lord Paradine said, "What? Mrs. Spendley-Carter? Do you mean to say she's at the bottom of this?"

It was Mr. Hero who was pale and sweating now, for he had remembered the last part of Mrs. Taylor's warning. He said, "If it means what I think it does——" At that moment, and for the last time, the handless harp of Paradine Hall once more tinkled forth the tune of "My Bonnie Dear."

"Dear God—let me be in time," Hero prayed, and ran from the room.

He went pelting along the corridor and down the narrow inside staircase that led to the floor below two at a time. He did not even pause as he ran past the door of the music room from behind which the ghostly strains of the harp were sounding; he knew that the door would be locked, that there would be no one in the room, and that the harp strings would be vibrating as though plucked by human fingers. His mind was trying to place how much of the song had already been played, and at the same time trying to count the bars that yet remained to the closing lines:

And now thou'rt cold and laid upon thy bier—
Good-by, my bonnie, good-by, my bonnie dear.

When that song would be ended for the last time, so too would Paradine Hall, and the Lord only knew how many of its inmates along with it.

Ought he to have remained first to warn those above of what was about to happen, and get them to a place of safety? It was too late now. He had gambled on one last desperate attempt to stem the disaster.

He crashed through the pantry door and made for the steps that led to the cellar, grateful that this time the lights had not been tampered with, and trying as he flung himself down the stairs to revisualize the layout and the labyrinth of corridors, passages, and dead ends that spread out in all directions underground at the Hall.

Whether it was his fear for the safety of those he had left above or the breathlessness engendered by the rapidity of his descent, at the moment of crisis Hero found himself momentarily confused. Then from down one of the darkened passages came drifting those final strains:

And now thou'rt cold and laid upon thy bier—
Good-by, my bonnie, good-by, my bonnie dear.

And thereafter silence.

"Lord God," he cried aloud, "I'm too late!" Nevertheless he hurled himself down the dark corridor, knowing he had not even had the wit to seize a fire extinguisher or so much as a bucket of sand on the way.

He did not try the handle of the door that led from the passage into the storeroom, for he knew it would be locked; he could only hope it would be flimsy. He crashed against it with his shoulder with all the power of his body behind it, cursing helplessly as it held, but on the second attempt it gave way inward, and he burst into the large, dimly lit enclosure where the almost overwhelmingly powerful fumes of petrol that had been poured over a huge piled-up mass of paper, old rags, and wood kindling assailed him.

A paraffin lantern was burning on the floor nearby. It was a miracle that the fumes had not yet ignited from its heat.

In a corner, a spot that Hero knew was directly beneath the golden concert harp in the music room on the floor above, sat the Hon. Isobel Paradine.

She held between her legs a cello with a curious contraption—a thin rod of fir wood—attached to the sounding board; the rod ascended to the ceiling and vanished there. The bow of the instrument lay on the floor at her feet. She sat motionless as a statue with the fingers of her left hand still upon the frets of the instrument, her right forefinger crooked upon a string close to the bridge.

As Hero hurled himself through the door she made an attempt to reach for and upset the hot, glowing lantern. But in that instant when time stood still Hero saw that her eyes were glazing and that her movements were slowed as if she had been drugged. If she succeeded, there was enough petrol soaked upon the pile on the floor to create one vast explosion that would send the flames roaring aloft and through the centuries-old building.

Barely conscious, Isobel's long fingers were still trying to reach the lantern when Hero seized it, ran from the room, and extinguished it. When he returned and switched on the single electric light bulb overhead Isobel, overcome by the fumes, had slid to the ground and was lying face to the floor, her head close to the pile of inflammables; the silver white of her hair seemed almost like a flame creeping close in one last desperate attempt to lick at the pyre and set off what was to have been the immolation of them all.

There were three departures from Paradine Hall the next day —one so early that nobody was about to witness it. Shortly after sunup a tall, silver-haired woman carrying a suitcase in each hand walked from the Hall to the garages, where she deposited the bags in the small car and got in herself. She started the engine, drove it down the long, broad avenue of trees and out through the gates leading to the estate with never so much as a single backward glance. Car and woman disappeared down the road in the direction of the yellow sun that was climbing into the sky. But the other two departures Alexander Hero attended, there being still some unfinished business. He had several parcels with him.

The Wilsons were leaving in their own car; the Spendley-Carters were to be driven to the station in the Country Club shooting brake and were awaiting its arrival. The Major was sitting in the driver's seat attending his wife, who was still making her farewells in the Hall. Hero opened the door of the car and climbed in beside the Major, who regarded him half with amazement, half with amusement, saying, "Well, I must say you have your nerve with you, old boy—paying a sort of return visit, eh? I saw you and my wife canoodling that day in the ruins, you know."

Hero said, "Yes. I'm sorry about that. Well, you know what's in this, of course." He handed one of the packages over to the Major. "It's your gun."

The Major nodded and said, "I wondered when you were going to return my property."

Hero said, "I thought you might like this too as a souvenir."

The paper was loose as he handed the parcel over, and the Major could see what was inside; it was the gas mask. The Major rather goggled at it for a moment and then broke into his shark smile and silent laughter. "So you got onto my little joke?"

Hero said, "You really didn't expect me to be taken in, did you, Major? I thought at first it was clever of you to have recognized the physical elements of Pepper's Ghost in the conservatory setup, until I telephoned London this morning and found that you'd served as a Captain under Major Maskelyne, the magician turned camouflage expert, in Egypt and Libya."

The Major was unabashed. "Oh, you checked that, did you?" he said. "I've learned a lot of tricks from old Maskelyne. Used to put them on for the troops, or to scare the Wogs. Just thought I'd find out how much you really knew about this ghost business—you seemed so cocksure of yourself, eh? No harm, what?"

Hero tapped the package containing the Major's gun and asked, "Was that a boyish prank too?"

The Major threw his head back, opened his shark's mouth, and indulged his soundless mirth until satisfied. He was a very tough customer. When he had finished he said, "You near as nothing had it, old boy, didn't you—if you hadn't managed that flop to the floor. I rarely miss, you know—and not at ten yards, with back illumination. That will teach you, I guess."

Hero nodded and said, "Lucky for both of us, since you were as near as nothing, too, had you hit, to swinging for it."

The Major turned and stared at Hero. "Huh," he scoffed, "don't you believe it. Do you take me for a fool? There were more than half a dozen witnesses there who saw the thing in the conservatory and who would have testified either that I lost my head or fired to save you. That one was 'on the house,' old boy, as the Americans say. I rather regret it didn't hit you."

Hero said, "Don't. One of your witnesses was an old hand with Dr. Pepper himself—Dean Ellison used to be mechanic and inventor to a stage illusionist. He of course recognized, as I did, all the elements that go to make up the illusion. I might have been dead, but Mr. Engineer Ellison would have been very much alive. It was he who suggested that I check your service."

The Major sat looking straight ahead of him. He had gone quite pale, and Hero noted with satisfaction sweat dampening his brow and temples, and did not doubt that it was equally hot under the moustache as well.

"You'd have swung, Major," he said cheerfully, "down the little black hole with a nasty jerk. Next time you decide to play practical jokes like that you'd better check your script. Well," Hero concluded, "I guess that's just about that, and perhaps that will teach *you* not to jump to conclusions—Mrs. Wilson was telling the truth that night." He opened the door of the car.

The Major looked at him and said, "Not much point in our shaking hands, is there, Hero?"

Hero said, "None whatsoever, Major," and got out.

Mrs. Wilson appeared from the house. She was tidied for travel, and looked as neat as a pin in a gray suit and small hat. Hero held the door of the car open for her and she came to him, gave him her hand, and said, "Good-by, Alexander," and then reached up quietly, put her hand on his shoulder, and kissed him. Then she got in beside the Major and Hero closed the door.

"Good-by," he said.

The Major's face was dark with rage. He clashed the car into gear and took it off the mark like a sprinter, with a grinding of tires and a volley of gravel spurting out from beneath the wheels.

Hero stepped back and aside, and as the Major twisted the wheel the rear end of the car missed him by inches.

"Dear old Major," he murmured to himself, "just a big, impulsive lad." He felt in the pocket of his jacket where the cartridges of the gun reposed. "Probably just as well I didn't give him back his firecrackers."

A voice behind him said, "Why was he angry, Mr. Hero?" Hero turned. It was Noreen. Then she added, "I saw her kiss you. Is she in love with you?"

Hero replied, "Everyone is in love with me."

Noreen said, "But most of all me. And don't forget you promised to marry me."

Hero suggested, "I thought you were going to be a nurse instead. How's that going, by the way?"

Noreen reflected, and finally the ugly little child said, "I'm going to be a real nurse. They're going to let me—Daddy and

Mummy said so. But you could be my friend on the side, couldn't you?"

Hero nodded gravely. "That's one way of putting it. We're engaged to be friends." He took her by both shoulders and hissed at her, "You be a good nurse, do you hear, or there'll be what-for. I'll be watching you."

The shooting brake drew up, filled with the Spendley-Carters' luggage. Noreen suddenly threw her arms round Hero's neck and clung, and when he bent down she whispered, "I'll be ever so good a nurse. Please don't forget me—I'll never forget you. You kept your promise. No one ever has before."

"And what about yours?" Hero whispered.

"My promise?"

"No more poltering."

"Oh, *that*," Noreen replied with a kind of scorn, "of course," and Hero realized that it was not so much that she had forgotten as that she had put the whole business out of her mind.

Her father and mother came up. Mrs. Spendley-Carter said, "She adores you. Thank you for being so kind."

Hero said, "Not at all."

Spendley-Carter brayed jovially, "Kids know who like 'em— like animals, what?"

Hero replied quietly, "Yes, kids know—and don't ever forget it."

Spendley-Carter's moist eye caught his own in a semisecretive glance. "Mum's the word, eh?" Spendley-Carter said.

Hero repressed a smile. "Mum's the word."

They piled into the car. The chauffeur tipped his cap, eased the vehicle into gear, and they drove off. From nowhere, seemingly, out of the sky perhaps, a round, smooth stone fell at Mr. Hero's feet. He picked up the apport, grinning to himself. Noreen was waving a frantic good-by. It was her farewell to him— and to the art of the poltergeist.

"Damn your impertinence, sir!" roared Lord Paradine. "How dared you take it upon yourself to let her get away?"

They were all collected that same forenoon in the library of the west wing at Mr. Hero's request. There were Lord and Lady Paradine, Mark and Susan Marshall, Sir Richard Lockerie and Beth, Cousin Freddie, and Meg. Meg was dressed for traveling. Hero, too, had relinquished his country clothes, but not his favorite briar. Meg saw that he looked as drawn and tired as the others, who had been sitting around uneasily like relatives gathered to hear the reading of the will, or anxious participants in a tragedy waiting to learn the end of the story. When Hero had quietly revealed what he had come upon in the cellar—the holocaust that he had been able to avert, and Isobel's subsequent departure—it had left them still more shaken. But Lord Paradine was stunned, humiliated, bewildered, and genuinely outraged as well. His round face crimson with choler, his already protuberant eyes seemingly half out of their sockets, he shouted, "Well, explain yourself."

Hero replied gently enough, "She was your sister, sir."

But Paradine's rage only grew more towering. "Damn and blast!" he raved. "The would-be murderess of my daughter, and an arsonist to boot—you'll have to answer to the authorities!"

"'Damn and blast' it is, then," cried Hero suddenly with equal thunder. "She was a woman and a tortured human being, and she was not like any other."

His outburst so startled them that a kind of shocked silence ensued, and it was then Hero was again aware of their subtle, almost imperceptible drawing together. Even Cousin Freddie seemed to have moved a fraction or two closer to his angry and indignant uncle.

But Meg did it somewhat more ostentatiously. She had been seated on the divan at the far end of the room watching Hero with her grave, intelligent eyes and that curiously wry expression at the corners of her mouth. Now she deliberately rose, walked across the room, and sat down on a chair quite close to her stepbrother.

Before they had a chance to recover, he continued, "I should like you to remember, Lord Paradine, that I am neither a police detective nor a magistrate. In my work I often come in contact with much that is worst in human beings, when in a sense I am searching for the best that is supposed to survive of the human spirit. If this stems from the fact that people are sometimes wicked, weak, or human, I did not invent this. You called me in because you were troubled by what seemed to be hauntings. I undertook to eliminate them. I have done so. There will be no more manifestations of any kind at Paradine Hall."

His sharpness and incisiveness had the effect of cooling Lord Paradine's anger. He was now ashamed of his temper but not ashamed to say so. He said, "Sorry, Hero. Perhaps you're right."

But it was Cousin Freddie who said, "Oh, is that so—what about the jolly old nun? I mean, the real ghost."

Hero had had enough of Cousin Freddie too.

"As far as the story of the nun is concerned, I never heard a set of grown-up people talk such a lot of unadulterated piffle. That legend is a hodgepodge of ingredients from Coeur-de-Lion and Héloise and Abélard right up through the sensational Sunday sheets. Do you really believe that an Englishman behaved that way just because the year was 1564? Don't you suppose that they had police courts, competent police, trials, and criminal justice in those days, and do you imagine that a nun could disappear from a convent without a thorough investigation resulting? For your information, there never was any nun from the very beginning."

Oddly enough, it was Lord Paradine who entered the most vigorous objection, he who at all times had been an outspoken skeptic and critic of the disturbances which had bedeviled his ancestral home. But now it seemed almost as though Mr. Hero in abnegating the nun was robbing him of a family heirloom.

"What's that?" he protested. "No nun? Why, it's written down in a book, sir. Can you substantiate your opinion?"

"Certainly I can," Hero replied. "It was the first thing I looked into even before I came down here, and thereafter. The old verger over in East Walsham has a volume full of research on it himself. Even the stones of your ruins over there deny the whole thing as nonsensical. Look here, the story of the nun is supposed to have taken place about 1564, during the reign of Elizabeth, when Lord Philip Paradine was approximately thirty years of age. Her name was supposed to have been Sister Rose, and that of her peasant lover from whom wicked Lord Paradine filched her, Thomas Drew. But the records show that the cloister of St. Relinda—which was part of Wytrim Priory—burned down in 1539 and was never rebuilt."

Susan Marshall was performing some mental arithmetic that was setting her eyes to dancing with amusement. "Why then—" she began.

"Exactly," concluded Mr. Hero solemnly, "give and take a few years, Lord Paradine accomplished her seduction at the ripe old age of five."

Cousin Freddie sniggered. "Trust the Paradines . . ."

Mark Paradine said, "But the story of the harp?"

"Equally pure piffle," Hero replied. "Nobody around here questioned that Sister Rose seemed to have no difficulty shifting from the sixteenth-century twelve-stringed Irish harp to the sixty-four-string, six-and-a-half-octave modern double-action instrument! But the real crux of the matter is that she wouldn't have been able to play any harp at all—farm girls weren't taught music in the sixteenth century." The investigator grinned suddenly. "History in retrospect grows wilder and looser; ancestors tend to deteriorate and become chillingly wicked. Nobody, you know, is really proud of virtuous or charitable forebears. In this instance it even managed to turn a respectable butler into a yokel lover snuffling about the walls of Paradine Hall for his lost Rose. His name was actually Thomas Drew, his wife's name was Rose. They married in 1569 and were servants of the Hall during the incumbency of Philip, and later on through half a lifetime of his son William, the fourth Lord Paradine."

Beth, still pale after her experience, less shy, and secure in her new-found love, exclaimed, "But if there was never any Sister Rose, then . . ."

"That is exactly the conclusion to which I was forced," Hero said. "Someone here at the Hall was up to some very unpleasant tricks. If one wanted to assume disguise, shape, or form—call it what you will—for haunting, there is none more practical than a nun's costume, easily enough acquired from any theatrical purveyor, or a monk's robe and cowl. Anyone could be inside it.

In a darkened corridor it very easily becomes a spectral and unidentifiable figure. A man, a woman, or even a child could operate it. In this case it was a woman. The woman was Miss Isobel."

Lord Paradine said, "But why in heaven's name—why would she do such a thing? Have you any idea as to the reason for this?"

Hero replied, "I have. Miss Paradine herself told me."

Startled, they were all gazing at Hero again.

"Yes," Hero continued quietly, "she was lying unconscious on the floor from having inhaled petrol fumes. Had she succeeded in overturning the lamp she would have died and the Hall gone up in flames. I managed to smash a small window light and get some air into the place. Then I placed her on a couch stored there, and brought her to. The first thing she asked was, 'Have I done it? Have I succeeded?' and when I told her what had happened, and that she had failed, she appeared to be neither glad nor sorry—only drained. She was changed, almost as though she had turned some kind of corner and would never go back. I would say that the madness that had driven her for so long had gone out of her. Medievalists would have said that she had been possessed and that the devils that had possessed her had fled. They might very well have been right, you know. We sat together and talked for a long time." His voice dropped and he paused.

Lord Paradine was irritable again, as he always became in the face of things he did not understand, such as medieval thought and the theory of possession. He said, "Well, get on with it then. What did she say?"

Mr. Hero got his black briar out of his jacket pocket. "Look here," he said, "may I suggest we drop it? The ghosts of Paradine Hall have been relegated to limbo—the case is closed."

The members of the family all exchanged glances, seeking to find in each other an answer to Hero's suggestion.

Lady Paradine suddenly said flatly, "But I want to know—I want to know what made Isobel do it."

Hero was still occupied with his briar and without raising his head said simply, "No matter whom it might hurt?"

Paradine said brusquely, "We are all one family here."

Hero looked up quickly and once more felt and saw the truth of this, and wondered if that drawing together was not tinged with just the slightest echo of Lord Paradine's hostility toward him. For all of her seeming bird brain, Lady Paradine was devoted to her husband, and he saw the pride and love with which Susan now looked at Mark, and the warmth that suffused her as she felt herself included in the family. It was Sir Richard and his new-found togetherness with Beth that worried him.

Yet it was Sir Richard likewise who urged him and put in his word slightly pompously. "We ought to know, Hero," he said. "I agree with Lady Paradine."

"Very well then," Hero said, addressing Sir Richard directly as he set a match to his briar. He was braced half standing, half sitting on the edge of the library table. "It is both simple and tragic. For all her life, ever since she was a little girl, Isobel Paradine has been in love with you. At one time she believed herself promised to you, and that when you came back from the war she would marry you."

"What?" Sir Richard cried indignantly. "Oh, I say now, Hero—look here—that's not true. Is there any point in raking up the past like that?"

Hero's silence was eloquent, but it was Meg who said inexorably, "Go on, Sandro—they wanted to know."

Hero said, "You're right—it wasn't true, but Miss Paradine *thought* it was. When you kissed her good-by before leaving at the beginning of the war, did you say to her, 'I'll come back'?"

Sir Richard's face had flushed. "Well yes, perhaps—something of that kind. One always says one will come back—or hopes one will—when one goes off to war, doesn't one? But I meant nothing by it—I was never in love with Isobel."

"I don't doubt it," Hero said gently, "but Isobel read it as 'I'll come back to you.' It was self-delusion. The first blow that fell upon her was when Sir Richard returned from France at the end of the war accompanied by his French wife."

There was a kind of gasp from Beth. "Oh, poor Aunt Isobel!" she said, which caused Lord Paradine to look at his daughter curiously and Sir Richard not to look at her at all.

Hero nodded. "Yes. But worse was to follow, for in more recent times Isobel suffered a triple catastrophe: the death of her adored father, who in a sense replaced Sir Richard; the transformation of his and her passionately cherished ancestral home into what I am afraid, for all its restrictions, amounts to a public hotel; and evidence that Sir Richard, now a widower with a nine-year-old son, far from turning toward her, had fallen in love with the American girl who had come to visit Paradine Hall."

Hero drew on his pipe for a moment to marshal thoughts. "What kind of woman," he mused, "would have been able to stand up under such hammer blows of fate? Miss Paradine was liked by all who came in contact with her; she was a great lady—kind, helpful, and yet, you know, the background for her violent reaction was always there. Of all the Paradines alive, she was the strongest and the truest in the dynastic sense. Whatever she seemed to be, underneath she was not as other women. She might have been a queen in her cold ruthlessness. It was this underlying coldness and hardness too which perhaps made her unable to accept and care for the child of another woman. Had she given love and warmth to young Julian, Sir Richard, the father, might have turned to her. But she was incapable of this. She had hated the Country Club ever since necessity had brought it into being, for it went against everything her father had stood for. The opportunity arrived for her to rid herself of the rivalry of Susan Marshall and at the same time destroy the

Susan's plate, and the nun in the minstrels' gallery. That wasn't Aunt Isobel, because she was at the table with us when we all saw it."

Hero replied, "You all saw it because you had been conditioned to see it. When nerves and minds have been properly prepared a ghost can be nothing more than an overcoat thrown over a chair, a shadow, or a blowing curtain. Isobel had arranged the drapes in the minstrels' gallery beforehand. It then needed darkness with but the light of only one or two candles to complete the illusion of the robe and cowl, that's why all the others had to go out."

"But how did they go out?" queried Sir Richard.

"Oh, that was no trick at all," said Hero, "anyone could hit upon it with a little thought. It wasn't the 'how' that interested me but the 'why.' Heat up a skewer and run it through a set of candles in the center halfway down, and you destroy the wick. When the flame reaches the break in the wick, out it goes. I found the skewer that Isobel used still with some of the wax on it."

"But what put you onto all of it, sir?" Mark asked.

Hero said, "If you like, I will take it from the very beginning."

Susan said, "Please do, Alex."

"You might as well," Lord Paradine grunted, "you've gone this far."

Hero settled himself more comfortably and relit his briar, which he had allowed to go out. He began, "It was apparent not only from what Sir Richard told me when he came to see me, but also upon my arrival here, that we were involved with not one type of occult manifestation but several. I told you at the beginning there were too many ghosts."

Sir Richard said, "I don't see why, Hero—isn't one ghost pretty much like another?"

"No. Study the literature on the subject and you will find not only varying species but subspecies. There is the aural ghost, who raps, taps, thumps, and bumps; he has his chain-clanking brother, his footstep-imitating relatives, and his vocal cousins, who sigh, sob, moan, wail, and sometimes render selections on musical instruments. There is the visual ghost, or apparition, which for some reason seems to prefer eighteenth- and nineteenth-century costume, and then there is the mischievous ghost—the poltergeist, or unincorporate, unseen haunt which nevertheless without fingers to grip or hands to hold, manages to throw weighty objects about, tip over furniture, and generally make a nuisance of itself. But the point is, these manifestations rarely overlap—the ghost that wails or bumps or shuffles isn't seen; the apparition of the distressed lady or the murdered lover glides about soundlessly, passing neatly through closed doors and windows; the poltergeist is *never* accompanied by a visual appearance. But we had the lot going at the Hall."

"Including the olfactory, sir," commented Mark Paradine.

"If you like," Hero said, "though with the exception of the veiled lady of fiction whose perfume is sometimes wafted as she floats down dark corridors, and the odor of brine and seaweed that is supposed to accompany the apparition of parties drowned, ghosts usually don't smell. And in this instance the purpose of what you took for still another manifestation was quite different. Isobel had pinched Mrs. Spendley-Carter's bottle of valerian and chucked it into the hot-water-heating system. By producing a bad odor she covered up another one—that of petrol."

While they waited in silence for him to go on, Hero too remained sunk in thought for a moment before he continued, "But these are fictional ghosts I have been enumerating. They exist only on the printed page or in the minds and imaginations of gullible or neurotic percipients. It is almost as though the ghost population read its own notices, or what it was supposed to do, and then did its best to fill the bill. In one sense the ghosts here were performing their proper fictional rites—knocking, thumping, dousing lights, playing a musical instrument, and appearing in apparition form—but underneath this nonsense lay something far more serious and pointing equally to the fact that more than one entity was involved."

Cousin Freddie sneered, "Oh, come off it, master—in one breath you say there weren't ghosts, and in the next you say there were."

Hero regarded Cousin Freddie quizzically for a moment and

then said, "Your question is more intelligent than one has come to expect from you. What I am actually saying is that when I came here I not only found a mixed-up multiplicity of manifestations, but there was also a diversity of character exhibited in them. I must return again to what I have said about ghosts and people: if there are ghosts, or spirits, or disembodied souls—hangovers from the living—they once were the animate part of people, and people have character—ergo, why should not ghosts have character?"

Cousin Freddie sniggered and said, "Q.E.D., Professor."

Lady Paradine asked, "What was that, Freddie? I don't understand."

Lord Paradine said, "Never mind, dear. Go on, Hero."

Hero did so. "For instance," he said, "there were three poltergeist characters, each one differing from the other. The first did blind, insensate damage apparently in Isobel's room; the second was mischievous, impish, naughty, willful, sometimes even spiteful, and yet from the nature of some of the objects produced or tricks played, naïve and almost amusingly childish—it hurt no one physically, its attentions appeared to be focused upon Mrs. Spendley-Carter, a highly neurotic woman; the third laid something nasty on Susan Marshall's plate. There was still another character loosed in the house, a fourth ghost, and through it ran the thread of evil and wickedness in a steady and recognizable pattern. This force for ungood was concentrated upon Susan Marshall and the Paradine Country Club. The fifth and last ghost, which I will come to presently, was a nasty trick and was directed at me. All of these forces were operating independently, and yet eventually they became interdependent and in the end almost inextricably entangled, as the lives and behavior of people are likely to become entangled and interdependent. Point one, then: ghosts don't congregate usually. Point two: they don't co-operate. It was as though all the known laws of the supernatural had been suddenly abolished or turned topsy-turvy. On the other hand, if you ascribed such behavior to people, you would find yourself in no difficulty understanding it."

Hero paused and glanced at his stepsister. He said, "At this point I sent for Margaret and her assortment of cameras, including infra-red film and flashes which will photograph in total darkness. On that night of infestation after her arrival, we were able to secure a photograph of the nun."

There was stir enough then. Hero produced an enlargement from his coat pocket and held it up. "You can see," he said, "that it is solid. It is probable that there never has been an honest spirit photograph taken. The subject in all likelihood would be transparent to the eye of the camera. In other words, in my opinion the lens would register nothing at all. Here then was the nun, whose ankle tripped the thread that set off the infra-red flash. Unfortunately it was not possible to tell who was inside the garment. Therefore at one time or another you were all under suspicion."

Lord Paradine looked sour at this. Mark Paradine asked, "But how could Aunt Isobel do this without one of us finding her out?"

"It seems difficult when you look at the affair with hindsight," Hero answered, "but Miss Paradine was the one person who could—she knew the house as did no one else, probably even including several secret passages which enabled her to appear and disappear. She was mechancially inclined, handy with tools, and effected all kinds of small repairs about the house—it was easy for her to diddle the lights, lock and unlock doors, create noises in the plumbing, or slip away and upset Susan's room before the exorcism. Since the manifestations started in Isobel's room originally and she was really the first victim, you would never suspect her of continuing them. What you do not look for you do not see."

Susan Marshall was thinking hard. She said, "But she was only *one* ghost—what about the chair that moved and the rabbit on my plate, and the other things?"

"Oh," Hero said, "that was little Noreen. I told you we had an assortment of ghosts here at the Hall."

There were cries of astonishment. "Noreen!"

"Yes," Hero said, "Noreen was the poltergeist in the east wing. It is usually a mischievous or vengeful child, a hysterical servant, or a neurotic woman. While Isobel was engaged in driving Susan Marshall and the guests from the Hall, Noreen was only interested in frightening the wits out of her mother. She is an adopted child, you know, and her parents are not very nice people. Noting how terrified her mother was when she heard of the original so-called haunting in Isobel's room, she decided to give her really something to worry about. When she thought she wasn't being watched one day she threw an object to make her mother jump. Mother jumped. Noreen became a poltergeist."

Sir Richard said incredulously, "But how can a child learn to fool . . ."

"They learn extraordinarily quickly, these poltergeist children," Hero said, "and people are astonishingly blind and gullible. Furthermore, once a poltergeist child is loose in a house, practically everything that happens in the normal way and which would create no comment ordinarily—the slamming of a door due to a draft, the creaking of joists cooling, the disturbing of an object through the blowing of a curtain, and particularly articles misplaced, such as scissors, spectacles, pens, books, et cetera—are all then ascribed to the machinations of the poltergeist. Not that little Noreen wasn't an adept and didn't very quickly become an expert. She moved the chair that night at dinner——"

"What?" interrupted Lord Paradine. "The one that wrestled with me and knocked me over? Impossible!"

Hero said, "I am afraid you're going to be disappointed, sir. Like the explanation of all magic tricks, it is the simplest thing in the world. So easy, in fact, that even a child could think of it, and did. You loop a length of stout string around the legs of the chair, lead the string along the floor under the rugs, beneath the table, and take the two ends in your hand. When you pull, the chair moves apparently by itself. Someone seizing it would find difficulty in stopping it, because the power is being applied at the strong part of the chair. Release one end of the string, and the power is removed. If you happen to be tugging at the back of the chair at that moment—over you go."

"A. over tip," murmured Freddie.

"The rabbit, of course," Hero concluded, "she had hidden in her skirts."

"But what had she against me?" Susan asked. "I had been kind to her and batted tennis balls for her to miss——"

"Nothing," Mr. Hero said flatly, "she admired you tremendously. She was very sorry about the rabbit and has asked me to tell you so. It was an accident. It was just that the two performances, hers and Isobel's, happened to coincide—in the dark little Noreen dropped it onto the wrong plate. She hadn't expected the candles to go out. Actually, she hadn't needed darkness for her little trick. The chair was in shadow at the side of the room. She had meant to deposit the rabbit on her mother's plate while everyone was watching it move—but Isobel, who happened to have her own haunt going and needed lights out for her nun illusion in the minstrels' gallery, couldn't have been more delighted."

"Do you mean that Isobel was hand in glove with that horrid child?" Lady Paradine asked.

"Not at all," Hero retorted. "They worked quite independently, but Isobel knew—she had watched Noreen and caught her at it, and simply let her go on, since it was grist to her mill. But what she did not realize was that hauntings fall into categories. There were four things happening at the dinner that night: the chair moved, the candles went out, the ghost appeared in the minstrels' gallery, and a dead rabbit materialized on Susan's plate—but any student of occult manifestations would see at once that the four must be paired—the candles and the nun belonged together, as did the chair and the rabbit. Hence two hauntings were involved and not one."

"I suppose," Cousin Freddie said, "the great detective can also explain the harp then—how it could play in a locked and empty room. Are you going to tell us you suspected it was Isobel all along?"

Hero reflected soberly for a moment before he replied. "No," he said, "I didn't. I was completely baffled by it, worried and, I might add, frightened. I thought for the first time that I was in the presence of something genuinely paranormal. There was actually something genuinely paranormal going at the Hall, but it was not that. You remember that my definition of paranormal was something I did not understand or could not reproduce myself. The playing of the harp seemed to fall into this category, even though the locking of the room made it suspect."

He turned his grave, intelligent gaze upon Cousin Freddie and there was no rancor in it. "You have paid me the doubtful compliment of calling me a detective—one of the assets that any investigator must have is luck. I was very lucky. At the peak of frustration in the music room I sat down at the piano and played to relieve my sense of inadequacy. The thunderous chord at the end of a Bach fugue provided the assist. When it died away I noticed that the harp strings were faintly vibrating. Then I knew that it could be done, but not yet how. I wasted an entire afternoon looking for the second harp, until Dean Ellison put me on the right track."

"Dean Ellison!"

"Yes, he was in his day a—ah—a student of stage magic——"

Hero saw the satisfied little smile develop at the corners of Meg's mouth. "I am a pretty fair adept at magic and stage illusions myself, but this was one with which I was not familiar. Mr. Ellison put me onto the fact that the trick could be worked with any stringed or fretted instrument other than a harp, and this, of course, explained the locked door as well."

Sir Richard said, "I don't see that. How can the locking of the door . . . ?"

"Because," Hero said, "if we had all come rushing into the room too soon we would have seen how the trick was worked. The thing is simplicity itself, and anyone musically inclined, plus a knowledge of carpentry, and the simple physics of sound waves, could have hit upon it. Miss Paradine probably thought that she had invented it herself, but it was performed over a hundred years ago by the magician Robert-Houdin. A harp was set up on the stage and another in a room exactly beneath it. The sounding boards of the two were then connected with a rod of fir wood that came up through the stage but was invisible to the audience. When the harp beneath was played the music was heard to come from the one above, and the strings vibrated as though played by ghostly hands. A very pretty illusion. I forgot that the strings of a cello can be plucked as well as bowed. In the cellar Miss Paradine thrummed the tune of 'My Bonnie Dear'—upstairs in the locked room the harp, connected by a thin rod to the cello, vibrated and you heard it play, and even saw the vibrations. When she had done she had only to give the fir rod a slight twist to disconnect it from the harp and pull it down through the floor. That is what we should have seen had not the door been locked. The thick nap of the carpet with only a slit for the fir rod to come through effectively concealed the hole—and there you were. But in the meantime I suspected every instrumentalist in the house with the exception of Isobel—Cousin Freddie, Beth, and, I am afraid, even Lady Paradine, who plays that harp in a box, the piano."

Lady Paradine looked at him reprovingly and said, "My dear Mr. Hero, how could you have?"

Meg said, "You must forgive him, Lady Paradine, he's always had a nasty, suspicious mind. Can you imagine how ridiculous—he thought you were dead set against Mark marrying Susan."

Lady Paradine managed a divine and ineffable smile. "How absurd," she said. "My children have made me very happy—both of them."

Hero tapped the dottle of ashes from his stone-cold pipe into his cupped hand and carefully deposited it in an ash tray. He said, "And that just about winds up the ghosts of Paradine Hall, with the exception of Major Wilson's bit of nastiness, the details of which I will not bore you with, except to say that it is one of the oldest and most widely known stage magic illusions, and that Wilson probably picked it up out East with the camouflage and dirty-tricks unit commanded by Major Maskelyne, himself a former stage magician."

Susan Marshall shook her head decisively so that her dark hair swung. She said, "You're not boring me. When I was a little girl my father taught me there were no such things as ghosts. Last night I thought that he was wrong. For the first time I was frightened. I want to know, Alex."

Hero replied, "You were conditioned by then. Your nerves had been shaken by a series of unpleasant shocks. All of ours had been. That was why Major Wilson counted on getting away with it. Very well then, I will tell you how it was done," and Hero launched into the description of Pepper's Ghost that he had previously given his stepsister.

When he had finished Sir Richard said with a gesture of impatience and disgust, "How utterly ridiculous for grown-up people to be taken in by such childish nonsense!"

Lady Paradine said softly, "That's all very well, but I cannot see why this dreadful man would do such a thing."

An unpleasant and slightly indecent smirk appeared upon the face of Cousin Freddie; Meg stirred in her chair near her stepbrother, and something hung in the air for a moment. Freddie opened his mouth as if to make the remark that had caused the expression on his face, but Mr. Hero caught his eye and there was a hard and almost audible clash of looks and wills. Something that Cousin Freddie saw in the investigator's face made him change his mind and subside. Hero said distinctly and succinctly, "He didn't like me."

The ghost of her smile touched Meg's mouth again. The dangerous moment had passed.

When Cousin Freddie finally spoke it was to remark, "Not much to the whole business when you know the answers, is there?"

Hero felt a sudden onset of immense weariness and distaste. He was aware of the subtle acquiescence in most of them with at least the spirit of what Freddie had said. It was somehow the same old story of contempt for the magician when he has revealed the simplicity of the trick he has just demonstrated. He had rooted the rotten apple out of the barrel for them, and they were now drawing together in their family solidarity. Every Jack had his Jill, and they were probably as tired of him as he was weary of them. He saw his wry stepsister Meg throw him the life line of her devoted glance and caught at it with a kind of grateful desperation.

Mark Paradine said, "A little while ago you said that there had been one thing at the Hall that had been genuinely—what did you call it—paranormal? Would you tell us what that was?"

Mr. Hero did not reply immediately, and wondered whether he should go into it, but he reflected that his bill would soon be going in to Lord Paradine; it was after all their story, and they were entitled to all the trimmings. He said, "Very well. A few days ago I had three warnings of events to come: that I was in some personal danger, that a great wickedness was to be perpetrated upon a member of the household—a young girl, and that an attempt was to be made to burn down Paradine Hall."

Sir Richard asked, "From whom did you receive these warnings?"

"From Mrs. Geraldine Taylor."

"What?" The cry that went up was almost a shout in unison.

Sir Richard said, "But how on earth would she know?" and Lady Paradine remarked, "I'm not at all surprised. I always thought she was an inquisitive woman, nosing and poking about."

Hero said, "One afternoon Mrs. Taylor laid out a game of Tarot for me. The Tarot is an ancient set of gypsy or Middle European fortunetelling cards. You will recall I found them when I first came here, and showed them to you. They belonged to her. The cards are laid out in a pattern. It is not like the ordinary pack of fifty-two, but contains additional suits of figures, symbols, and pictures, and is supposed to connect with the life pattern of the questioner and the communicant."

"What?" said Lord Paradine. "Are you serious, Hero?"

"Yes, I am afraid so. There isn't much more to it. In the midst of the usual rubbishy fortunetelling spiel about going off on trips and meeting dark strangers, something odd occurred and Mrs. Taylor began to talk about other things, almost as though she were listening to things being said—or thought—by people who were not there. It was during this time that I received the warnings. The mistake I made was in believing that the one whose life was threatened was Susan Marshall. It wasn't—it was Beth."

The young girl shuddered and moved closer to Sir Richard, who put his arm about her without self-consciousness, drawing a sunny smile from Susan. The others were uneasily silent, until Cousin Freddie sniggered and said, "I suppose you can explain that too."

"Ah, that's just it!" Alexander Hero said softly. "I can't. I just don't know."

Lord Paradine gave a snort of derision. "Well now, if you ask me," he said, "I consider that utter damn nonsense!" and he looked around him for corroboration, and found it. The ranks were closing again.

Hero sighed and said, "I didn't ask, sir, but if I did, it would be to inquire into the human perversity willing to swallow the most incredible chowder of fake spooks and spirits, and refusing to credit the one genuinely paranormal manifestation that took place here. The only field where if you ask me, 'How was it done?' I must reply to you, 'I don't know'—the field of transference of thought. It happens. God knows, there was enough wickedness adrift here. Mrs. Taylor tuned in on some of it."

Lord Paradine flushed momentarily. He was not certain whether or not he had been rebuked, and then decided, since he did not understand it, that he had not. "Ah-hm, Hero! Well!

Whatever, I think undoubtedly you've kept your end of the bargain. I will be sending you your check."

Sir Richard, who was looking embarrassed, said, "Damn fine job, Hero." He was sincere. Nevertheless it sounded faintly patronizing.

Lord Paradine continued, "Though, mind you, Hero, I'm not saying I approve of your somewhat highhanded action in permitting my sister to depart."

"Oh, as to that," Hero said, pulling out the words against the immense fatigue he felt, "I can give you your pound of flesh. She will not go unpunished—she has committed herself to life imprisonment in France, where she has gone to enter the strictest of closed orders. For the rest of her days she will wear the habit of the nun and never speak again except to pray."

They were on the road home, the Lady Margaret Callandar and Mr. Alexander Hero, driving in his Bentley down the broad highway of A.12 that led to London. After a long silence, disturbed by the bitterness about her stepbrother's mouth and the lines on his brow, Meg said, "Tired, Sandro?"

"Yes—very."

Meg said tentatively and delicately, "What's wrong, Sandro? You did a good job, but you're disappointed."

"People," he cried, unburdening himself, "the smugness and intolerance of them! How can a ghost—if we ever do encounter one—be anything but wicked, since it first had to be human?" Then suddenly and fiercely he said, "Lean your head against my shoulder will you, Meg—there's a girl."

Meg gave a little sigh, for it was where she much wanted her head to be. She leaned her temple against his shoulder. "Why?" she asked.

"I just want to feel it there," he said. "It is a good head—what's inside is clean and honest."

After a while Meg looked up at him, "Better?"

"Yes, thanks—much. You may have it back now if you wish."

"I'm quite comfortable." And then after a moment, "Sandro —were you hurt on this job?"

"One always is a little on this sort of case. You know how I feel about people who play at spooks."

"No—I mean you inside. Which one of those girls were you in love with a little?"

Hero said somewhat grimly, "Not Vivyan Wilson, I can promise you that."

Meg smiled her funny little smile and said, "Do you know, of all those there, she was almost the most normal. She was simple and direct. I came close to taking a fancy to her. But of course you're right. One doesn't cherish caviar—one eats it and has done with it. Well—and Isobel?"

Hero smiled and said, "Much as I admire ruthless women, I don't want to be the one that's eaten. By Jove, but she was artistic in her choice of retribution!" He fell silent for a moment and then concluded, "I suppose in a way it was Susan Marshall."

"And now she's to marry Mark and become Lady Paradine eventually. How do you feel about that?"

Hero slowed down through a thirty-mile zone and reflected. "Oh, I think they'll do well," he said. "They both have character. I suspect once she's married to him she will out-dynast even Isobel—Americans do when they marry into old families."

Meg said, "I rather meant in relation to you."

Hero turned his head for a moment to smile at her and say, "Oh, I'm all right," and Meg could see from the expression on his face that quite suddenly he really was. He turned his attention back to the road and said, "There's no doubt but that we were drawn to one another for a moment—at least, I was to her. Lord, but she was a handsome beast! I've never seen a virginal quality so attractively displayed or quite so shamelessly put up. I suppose that's American—they all have the muscle to defend it if necessary."

Meg asked diffidently, "Did Susan have to defend hers?"

"Not exactly," Hero replied. "At the moment when she might have the ghost—or rather, Auntie Isobel—opportunely had a go at the doorknob."

Meg inquired, "What happened afterward—I mean, what

spoiled it between you? She was a dear, you know—a fine and splendid girl."

"I think we got to dislike one another's minds," Hero said. "Can you see that? You know mine—nasty and suspicious, particularly during business hours. The reason I didn't open the door was that while I suspected it might be our friend the nun coming to call I also thought it might have been Sir Richard or perhaps Mark. I'm afraid she twigged."

"What a horrid man you are!" Meg said happily.

"It was my business not to trust her, wasn't it?"

Meg said, "Of course it was, Sandro—you did quite right," and at her tone he began to laugh.

Hero said, "She started to dislike me for not trusting her, and I was disillusioned with her for not understanding that I couldn't."

Meg sighed again and said sardonically, "You're going to make someone a wonderful husband one day, Sandro."

He said piously, "God forbid that I should ever." And then, "Lean your head a little harder, Meg—it feels so good."

His stepsister sighed again, snuggled a bit deeper in the seat, and leaned harder. She was a sensible, practical girl and not given to idle romancing or useless sighing and mooning. Someday, perhaps, the scales might fall from his too clever and preoccupied eyes and let him see how dearly she loved him. In the meantime, somehow she had managed again to bring him through another jungle filled with predatory females to emerge reasonably unscathed. She felt pleased with herself, and happier than she had been in a long time.